What people are saying about
A Very Innocent Man:

"*A Very Innocent Man* is a very good novel. Part parable, part parody with a dash of whodunit and tragedy set in the tony nabes of the Upper West Side of Manhattan and the dreary asbestos hovels of Long Island. We follow the Teflon rise of telemedicine rainmaker Dr. Robert Rosen as he morphs from a cynical crusader against pill pimps to a true oxy-moron. It's a jagged little pill we willingly swallow as author Ed Belfar weaves the tale of Rosen's downward spiral with a deft hand for dialog and a sharp ear for storytelling. Belfar fills the reader's prescription on every page."
—Jerry Mikorenda, author of *America's First Freedom Rider* and the novel *The Whaler's Daughter*

"New York City physician Dr. Robert Rosen is obsessed with fame and fortune and is prepared to do whatever necessary to achieve them. Rosen quickly falls victim to his own hubris and finds himself entangled with shady characters every bit as unethical as himself. A compelling and highly entertaining novel, *A Very Innocent Man* delves into the seedy worlds of illegal opioid sales, multilevel marketing schemes, and motivational life coach fakery. We can't look away from this repellent cast of characters even as we yearn for their comeuppance. Very well written and employing razor sharp humor that leans toward the satirical, Edward Belfar's twisted redemption story perfectly mirrors the well-earned cynicism of our times. Highly recommended."
—Kathy Fish, author of *Wild Life: Collected Works*

"When trouble comes knocking, Dr. Robert Rosen doesn't hesitate to open the door. He has no interest in doing the right thing, but does wrong things in entertaining, ever-escalating ways. The result is a darkly comic roller-coaster ride through a political, cultural, and legal landscape where nice guys may or may not finish last."

—Caitlin Horrocks, author of *This Is Not Your City*, *The Vexations*, and *Life Among the Terranauts*

"Most readers will probably not be surprised to learn that Dr. Robert Rosen, the main character in Edward Belfar's novel, *A Very Innocent Man*, is anything but an innocent man. Something about the title seems ironic, and the irony becomes clear in the first few pages, when the medical doctor and public speaker, who cannot resist the temptation of selling prescriptions for opioids and Adderall, poses this question to his audience during a televised motivational speech: 'Is your doctor turning you into a drug addict?' Lies and hypocrisy abound in this witty, farcical, hilarious story, so full of corruption that it feels, well, a bit like the world in which we live, complete with a president, admired by Robert and his friends, who bears a striking resemblance to former President Trump. Strategic writer that he is, Belfar presents the reader with a few characters who are caring and compassionate, thus creating foils for Robert and his associates—characters such as Robert's brother, who mourns the loss of his wife, and his mother, who loves Robert, even though she sees him for what he is—anything but an innocent man."

—Brian Duren, author of *Ivory Black* and the award-winning novel *Whiteout*

A Very Innocent Man

A VERY INNOCENT MAN

a novel by
Edward Belfar

Flexible Press
Minneapolis, Minnesota, 2023

Print ISBN: 979-8-9862459-6-6
eBook ISBN: 979-8-9862459-7-3

Flexible Press LLC
Editors William E Burleson
Vicki Adang, Mark My Words Editorial Services, LLC
Cover William E Burleson

For Rachel, Alexandra, and Nora

PART I:

FAME
AND
INFAMY

CHAPTER 1

"This is it! This is for real!" Dr. Rosen exulted. "Chicago. Third largest TV market in the United States. Barry says if it goes well, he'll have his agent pitch the station on a whole series. Coping with depression, coping with anxiety, coping with grief. After that, it's the *Today Show*. Can you imagine me on the *Today Show*? I'm telling you, babe, six months from now, I won't be flying economy anymore."

His young companion, Tamika Jones, who had never been on a plane before, replied, "I won't be flying at all if I can help it."

She sat with her torso pitched forward, her head down, her left forearm braced against the seat in front of her, and her right hand on her stomach. A slightly built woman with a caramel complexion, she had lustrous brown eyes, hair black at the sides and closely trimmed, with golden curls on top. Dressed in tight jeans and a blouse imprinted with roses and lilies set against a blue background, she wore a gold choker upon which hung a tiny cross.

"Trust me," said the doctor. "It's nothing to worry about. A little turbulence. You get used to it when you travel as much as I do."

"If this doesn't stop soon, I'm gonna be sick."

"Barry says the Dr. Sober-Up shtick that I did in Reno would be perfect for the *Today Show* around the holidays. Actually, Dr. Sober-Up's good for any holiday or anytime, really. Everybody needs a hangover cure sooner or later. Be nice if he could hook me up for a gig somewhere around the Fourth of July."

"Why'd you have to bring Barry along, anyway? He's bad news."

"I don't know what you have against him. If it weren't for Barry, we wouldn't be here at all. I would never have gotten on TV."

Though he generally attached little weight to anything Tamika said, the doctor had wondered on occasion whether the trust he had placed in his mentor, Dr. Barry "Bulldog" Bullard, was entirely warranted. Barry billed himself as a motivational speaker, life coach, financial guru, entrepreneur, and bestselling author of numerous self-help and leadership tomes, most famously the bulldog series, comprising *The Way of the Bulldog: How to Seize Control of Your life in Six Easy Steps*; *The Way of the Bulldog II: Hang on to What You've Got; The Way of the Bulldog III: The Tenacious Leader;* and the regrettably out-of-print *Doggie Style: How to Be a Bulldog in the Bedroom* (which promised to reveal to men lacking that bulldog confidence the "seven secrets that will leave her begging for more"). The books, however, were self-published and had never appeared on any bestseller list that the doctor had seen. The online, for-profit "university" that had bestowed upon Barry his doctorate had gone out of business amid a blizzard of lawsuits by former students alleging fraud. An inveterate name-dropper, he had plastered his office with pictures of himself standing beside, or shaking hands with, the likes of Dwayne Johnson, Warren Buffett, Shakira, and even President Dreck in his previous incarnation as the star of the hit reality show *Find It! Flip It!* As far as Dr. Rosen could tell, though, Barry's relationships with those luminaries existed entirely within the sixteen-by-twenty or twenty-by-thirty-inch frames that contained the photographs.

Still, unlike the motivational speakers/life coaches/financial gurus/entrepreneurs/bestselling authors previously employed by Dr. Rosen, Barry Bullard had delivered for him. He really did know people in the TV industry, and through those connections, the doctor had secured his first television bookings. Further, Barry's coaching had enabled Dr. Rosen both to craft a succinct and forceful message suitable for the medium and to master the tricks of voice modulation and gesture essential to driving that message home.

The morning after he and Tamika arrived in Chicago, however, Dr. Rosen had fresh cause to worry that their reservations about Barry might be well-founded after all. The three of them were in Barry's hotel suite, where the windows rattled whenever a plane passed overhead on its way to O'Hare. With but an hour or so to go before they would need to depart for the studio, Barry appeared nowhere near ready to show himself in public. Dressed only in a white terrycloth hotel bathrobe and a pair of boxer shorts, he sat alone at a small, round glass table upon which rested a bottle of vodka, another of Bloody Mary mix, and three cans of Diet Coke, one turned on its side, its contents snaking across the translucent surface and dripping onto the beige carpet. His hair looked like an untended lawn, his face a field of stubble. Flecks of white powder clung to his nascent moustache, for the Diet Coke was not the only coke on the table. Sometime in the hours before dawn, he must have stumbled or fallen, for the nasty red-and-purple welt at the center of his expansive forehead had not been there last night when Dr. Rosen had left him at the hotel bar.

"Do it, man. Do a line."

Dr. Rosen, looking uneasy in his easy chair, his back stiff and his hands clasped tightly on his lap, replied, "I don't like it. That stuff makes me paranoid."

Refraining did not make him any less so. He was convinced that at any moment, the police would break down the door and drag all three of them off to jail, leaving him disgraced and ruined.

Nerves and airplane noise had kept him awake for much of the night, and the puffiness around his eyes half-obscured their dark irises. Having reached the wrong side of fifty, he had noticed of late, for the first time in his life, the years beginning to show on him. His cheeks had grown fleshy, and his short, wavy hair, though still solid black, unsullied by even a strand of gray, had begun to thin slightly on his crown. He wore a pink dress shirt, open at the collar; the starched white lab coat that he donned for all his television appearances; black trousers, the snugness of which highlighted the substantial paunch he had developed over the last year-and-a-half or so; and around his wrist, an oystersteel and platinum Rolex Yacht-Master. A strong citrusy smell, like that of an air freshener, albeit with a faint undertone of perspiration, wafted in the air about him.

"It makes you a fucking bulldog, man," Barry said, pounding on his chest. "A fucking bulldog."

Suddenly, Barry was down on all fours on the carpet, his hands balled into fists, elbows bent, chest thrust out, nose and mouth scrunched in, cheeks bulging. He barked four times—deep, throaty bulldog barks, each louder than the last. Then, with short, jerky bulldog steps, he charged, panting, toward Dr. Rosen. Springing up onto his hind legs, Barry, an aggressive bulldog with opposable thumbs, grabbed the lapels of the doctor's lab coat. Placing his forehead flush against the doctor's, Barry bellowed, "Be a fucking bulldog!"

The bulldog's hot, moist breath smelled of last night's margaritas and this morning's Bloody Marys.

Dr. Rosen turned his face away.

"You really want me to film this?" asked Tamika, peeking out from behind her camcorder.

Her expression turned to one of revulsion when, as Barry stood up and whirled around to face her, his robe fell open, and a tuft of black pubic hair sprouted from the fly of his boxers. Dr. Rosen frowned as he patted his lapels, trying to restore them to their former smoothness.

"Yes, I want everything. Every goddamn minute in real time—here in the hotel, in the car, behind the scenes at the studio, the doc on camera, the debriefing."

"Why don't you try some briefing? There's too much debriefing going on here already if you ask me."

"This is something totally new we're doing here. Totally, totally new. It's a documentary and a master class in coaching all rolled into one. It'll go on YouTube first, maybe as a free download for a week or two. After that, it goes behind the paywall. Maybe I'll even adapt it into another book. *The Way of the Bulldog IV: Master Class.*"

"The way of bullshit," Tamika murmured under her breath.

The doctor was still smoothing his lab coat when again Barry grabbed hold of it.

"Bulldog! You hear me? You're gonna go out there and be a fucking bulldog."

After emitting several deep, throaty bulldog barks, Barry ordered the doctor to do likewise.

"Come on, Barry. I don't bark. I'm a doctor."

"Oh, excuse me. I'm no ordinary wuss. I'm Dr. Wuss."

"Arf. Arf. Arf," offered Dr. Rosen through gritted teeth. "Are you happy? Now will you please let go of me?"

Instead, Barry yanked the lapels with such force that he nearly pulled the doctor out of the easy chair.

"The big shot Dr. Wuss who's gonna go out there and put the whole city of Chicago into a friggin' coma. You might as well skip the whole thing and get your ass on the plane back to New York."

Another blast of Barry's hangover breath induced nausea first and then rage. If the fool wanted a bulldog, a bulldog he would get. An alpha bulldog. A bulldog who would bite his fucking head off. Dr. Rosen emitted a bark of such fury and volume that Barry and Tamika both drew back in fright. The doctor barked again, seven, eight, nine more times. When he paused for a breath, Barry barked back at him.

"It sounds like a damn kennel in here," said Tamika, but the two alpha dogs paid her no heed.

Dr. Rosen answered one of Barry's barks with his loudest yet, and the competition continued, with both men down on the carpet on all fours. At last, Barry faltered. Lying face down on the carpet, sweaty and flushed, sucking in air as if he'd just finished a sprint, he gasped, "Fuckin' aye! Now that's what I'm talking about. You're gonna crush it."

Dr. Rosen, ready to do just that, sprang to his feet and, pounding on his chest, emitted one final top-dog howl.

"You're both crazy," muttered Tamika.

Within an hour, Barry had undergone a miraculous transformation. Clean-shaven and neatly coifed, he looked almost dapper in his navy blue suit, white shirt, and red tie. A bit of concealer, picked up at a CVS during the drive to the studio, made quick work of the welt on his forehead. While the black Lincoln Navigator with Tamika behind the wheel inched its way along the Loop, Barry, seated beside his pupil in the back, offered some last-minute counsel and words of encouragement.

The doctor needed them. Nibbling at his thumbnail, his legs bouncing up and down, he appeared to have left his alpha dog confidence back in the hotel room.

"Relax, bro. You'll be fine. Just remember: MARS. Message. Amplify. Repeat. Stupid. You're better prepared than ninety percent of the jokers who go on these shows. You know your stuff, you got a great message, and the technique is really coming along. MARS works just as well in Chicago as in Columbus."

The makeup artist, a petite, cheery blond woman wearing a light blue smock, led Dr. Rosen into a narrow cubicle that smelled of hairspray and coconut-infused skin lotion, sat him down, and immediately set to work. Though she looked just slightly older than Tamika, the deftness with which she hid the doctor's blemishes beneath layers of moisturizer, foundation, and under-eye concealer was that of a seasoned professional.

"We don't do those ridiculous anchorman's eyebrows here," she said as she dexterously applied gel to Dr. Rosen's. "It's much more subtle. You can hardly see a difference, but the camera will pick it up. You'd be surprised at how much more authority that little bit of darkening and filling, that little extra contrast, can give you."

As the artist painted her human canvas, Tamika, directed by Barry, circled the cubicle with the camcorder, filming the doctor's transformation from front, back, high, and low.

"I'm going on today to talk about opioid addiction," said the doctor, unprompted. "All the celebrities you read about who keep going in and out of rehab. People don't realize that the ones who got them hooked were their doctors, not street dealers. Doctors are a big part of the problem. They overprescribe. Some of them have these pill mills where they sell prescriptions for cash."

"I see."

"But it's not only celebrities. There are about 200 opioid-related deaths every day in this country."

"Uh-huh."

"Then I'm going to talk about how you can tell if you're addicted and what you can do about it. It's a huge problem. That's why I need to get my message out there."

"That's wonderful. I'm sure you're doing great work."

The lack of inflection in her voice irked him. Was she even listening?

"You know, people don't realize how serious . . ."

"We just need to do a little something about the hair," she interrupted, her index finger hovering just above his crown.

She retrieved from the shelf in front of him a small cylindrical container that looked like a pepper shaker.

"Now, keep still," she said as she began to sprinkle the contents onto his scalp.

"What's that?"

"Instant hair. Hair fibers. Just a little filler for the thin spots."

"That's amazing," he said, marveling at the suddenly younger, invigorated Dr. Rosen staring back at him from the mirror.

"It's an amazing product."

"Do you have any I can take home with me?"

"I don't, but you can order it online."

"How long does it stay in?"

"Until your next shower. So stay dry."

Turning away from the mirror, he looked up at her and, with studied casualness, inquired, "Are you doing anything for lunch?"

"Going to the gym."

"How about dinner?"

Wagging her finger to show off her wedding ring, the makeup artist replied, "I'll have to ask my husband."

"We have a 4:05 flight back to New York," Tamika interjected.

"Oh, come on. Do you have to ask your husband's permission for everything?"

"No. That's just what I say to be polite when I want to get out of doing something I don't want to do. Husbands are useful for that." Unsnapping his apron from the rear and whisking it away, she added, "I think we're done here."

Tamika, too, was done here, having stopped shooting and stomped off. Dr. Rosen did not notice her absence.

As he left the makeup artist's cubicle, a silver-haired woman approached carrying a legal pad. Dressed in a gray jacket and skirt with a Scottish check pattern, she wore a locket featuring a gold *fleur de lis* pendant and exquisite cameo earrings—amber reliefs of a profile of a young woman with long, flowing hair. Even in heels, she stood barely over five feet, but her rigid posture and the hard, unyielding stare with which she appraised the poor specimens of humanity around her gave her a formidable presence. Introducing herself as the show's executive producer, she greeted Dr. Rosen with a perfunctory handshake—her hand felt icy—and then got down to business. After viewing the video of Dr. Rosen's Columbus appearance, the station's chief legal counsel had expressed to her the concern that certain claims made by the doctor in the course of that presentation, including but not limited to the naming of individual celebrities alleged to be opioid addicts, and the equating of said individual celebrities' doctors with common drug pushers, could expose both the station and Dr. Rosen himself to the risk of litigation by the celebrities, celebrities' doctors, and possibly other parties on various grounds, including but not limited to defamation.

"In other words, all that stuff about drug-pushing doctors has to come out."

"You've got to be kidding. That's my whole opening hook."

"I'm sorry about the short notice. The issue was just brought to my attention. I'm surprised no one has warned you about this before."

The host in Columbus had, in fact, confronted him, asking whether he had any actual evidence that pointed to wrongdoing by the doctors he denounced. Dr. Rosen had simply cranked up the volume and talked over her, while offstage Barry pumped his fist and cried, "Yeah!" In the executive producer, the doctor had a much more formidable adversary.

"How am I supposed to fill up that time?"

"If you have to cut it short, we can always go to a commercial early."

"Fucking unbelievable!"

Barry, who had vanished briefly, now reappeared, dragging a sullen-looking Tamika by the arm.

"Get the camera on me," he whispered to her. "This is gonna be good."

Stepping between the executive producer and Dr. Rosen, he asked the former, "Is there a problem here?"

"Who are you?"

"I'm Barry Bullard. His coach."

"His coach?"

"I'm a media-wealth-life coach. Among other things, I help people like Dr. Rosen get booked on shows like this one. I've done quite a bit of TV myself. I've been on *Good Morning Tallahassee*, *Today in LA*, *Pittsburgh Today Live*, and a whole bunch more. You must have seen me."

"I don't think so."

"I'm the author of the *Bulldog* series. Maybe you've read some of them? *The Way of the Bulldog: How to Seize Control of Your Life in Six Easy Steps*; *The Way of the Bulldog II* . . ."

"I'm afraid I haven't had a chance, but they're going right to the top of my Amazon wish list. Believe me. Anyway, the issue is that I can't have him on this show if he's going to go out there in front of the camera and make all kinds of wild, unsupported accusations that so-and-so is an addict and her doctor is a criminal."

"What fucking bullshit! What am I supposed to do without my hook?"

Placing a comforting hand upon the doctor's shoulder, Barry replied, "The first thing you need to do is relax. You'll be fine."

He assured the producer that she needed only to leave everything to him, and all would indeed be fine. All he required was a few minutes alone with his client in a vacant office.

In an instant, the executive producer procured one for him. Barry ushered the doctor and Tamika inside, the latter requiring a push. Then he shut the door.

"Fucking postmenopausal bitch," said Dr. Rosen. "Who the hell does she think she is?"

"OK, enough of that," Barry replied. "Shut up and listen to me. First, we're gonna do some jumping."

"Oh, come on, Barry."

"Either you're gonna jump, or I'm gonna take a hike. Now watch me fly."

Crouching low, he launched himself a foot off the ground.

"Think you can beat that? Let's see you try. Come on. You can do better than that. That's it. Now, higher still. Now faster. Like you're on a pogo stick. All right, let's stop. Feel better now? Feel the bulldog energy? Good. Now let's do the patting exercise."

Starting at the shoulders, the two men vigorously patted themselves all over, first working each arm, then onto the chest, the stomach, the lower back, the hips, the glutes, the thighs, the shins, and back up again.

"All right. Now we have to get the voice warmed up." Barry broke into a chant: "Blub-blub-blub-blub-blub-blub-blub-blub."

He pointed at Dr. Rosen, who responded in kind: "Blub-blub-blub-blub-blub-blub-blub-blub."

"Good. Now let's do it together. Louder. Really loud: BLUB-BLUB. BLUB-BLUB.

"Now, really soft, a whisper: Bluhhb-bluhhb. Bluhhb-bluhhb. Now, we go way up high: Blub-blub-blub-blub-blub-blub-blub-blub.

Now, way down low: BLUUBB-BLUUBB-BLUUBB-BLUUBB-BLUUBB-BLUUBB-BLUUBB-BLUUBB-BLUUBB."

"All right," said Barry, clapping. "Now you're ready. You are gonna take Chicago in your bare hands and crush it."

The two men exchanged fist bumps.

The set was cozy, designed to simulate a living room. In the center were two upholstered armchairs, one beige and the other apricot, angled toward each other at about forty-five degrees. The wall behind them had a fake fireplace at one end and wrought iron shelving that supported some potted plants at the other. The picture window in the middle provided a panoramic view of the city. In front of the chairs stood a round, low coffee table, upon which rested a silver vase filled with white and pink roses.

Bounding onto the set, Dr. Rosen greeted the host, a skeletal young blond woman wearing knee-high suede boots, with a nod, a smile, and a graciously extended hand. Waving at the audience and grinning, he settled himself in the beige chair.

"How many of you watch TV?" he began, drawing some puzzled looks from the studio audience. "Silly question, right? Well, what I'm going to talk about today is deadly serious. Anyone who has been watching TV has probably seen a lot of stories lately about celebrities who keep getting busted for drug possession, going into rehab, coming out, getting their lives and careers back on track, and then relapsing. I'm sure you've heard of them. An actress who's been in some big hit comedies, including one set in a high school here in Chicago. You know who I'm talking about. Another one: a child actor who was washed up by the time he was seventeen thanks to opioid addiction. A famous radio talk show host. Now I've been told that for legal reasons, I'm not allowed to say these people's names on this show."

The executive producer, he thought, must be giving him the stink eye. Well, too bad. He would not let her get the better of him.

"Lawyers. What's the difference between a lawyer and a leech? After you die, a leech stops sucking your blood. Am I right?"

The audience laughed and applauded.

"Now, now," said the host.

"I could tell you a thing or two about lawyers. Believe me. But that's another subject for another day. Today I'm here to talk about addiction. All of those celebrities you've heard about or read about were turned into oxycodone addicts by their pushers. And their pushers were their family doctors. So here's a question for you: Is your doctor turning you into a drug addict?"

Gasps from the audience.

"How do you know if you're becoming a drug addict?" asked the host.

"We'll get to that in a moment. First a little background."

Gravely, he recited the shocking statistics: an estimated 3.8 percent, or 10 million, American adults currently abusing opioids; a 28.5 percent increase in emergency room visits caused by opioid overdoses over the last two years; 200 deaths by overdoses per day.

"That's unbelievable," said the host. "I had no idea."

"Oxycodone is like . . ." Here he paused to let the tension build, and the audience held its collective breath. Doubling his volume, he amplified just as Barry had taught him to, concluding the sentence with a single word that echoed like a thunderclap: "*Heroin!*"

The shock that registered on every face in the studio had a cartoonish aspect. Eyes bulged, and mouths hung open. Nobody made a sound.

Dr. Rosen waited a good fifteen seconds before resuming.

"I know that sounds crazy, but oxycodone is the same class of drug. It's like prescription heroin."

The oxycodone pills themselves provided a simple but dramatic prop. Dr. Rosen would pour a dozen or so from a vial into the palm of his hand and hold them up to the camera—or so went the original plan. In his first television appearance, his hand had shaken so badly that he had dropped a couple of the pills. Since then, he had taken the precaution of having the host perform the demonstration.

"These are oxycodone pills. They're called blueberries on the street. And they sell for thirty bucks a pill."

"Thirty dollars a pill?" asked the host incredulously.

"That's right. So you see, this is big business. That's why so many people want to get in on it, including doctors, who should know better. It's a quick way to make money, but if you're a doctor, you have a lot to lose. Your practice, your license, your freedom." Staring directly into the camera and pointing, he added, "So don't do it.

"Now I'll get to the question you asked a little while ago because it's an important one: How do you know if you're addicted? There are two big warning signs," he said, ticking them off in turn with the index and middle fingers of his right hand. "One is tolerance. You find you need more and more pills to get the same high. You start out taking three pills a day. Then you need four, and then five, and so on. Number two is withdrawal. You decide you want to quit, and you try to go cold turkey. Big mistake. You get sick. You have nausea, vomiting, cramping, diarrhea, anxiety, depression, sweating, insomnia, goose bumps, and a whole bunch more. You can't handle it. So you give up and go back on the pills.

"So what should you do? There are three steps," he said, ticking those off with his fingers. "RRR we call it: Recognize. Rehabilitate. Recover. First, recognize you have a problem. Watch for those signs—tolerance and withdrawal. What's going on in your life? Is getting your high all you care about? Have your relationships suffered? What about your performance on the job? When you have recognized that you have a problem, you've taken a very big first step.

"Now comes the second: Rehabilitate. Very few people can kick the habit on their own. As I said, they can't cope with the withdrawal symptoms. That's why you need to be in a rehabilitation program. For some people, the only thing that works is intensive inpatient treatment. For others who may not in be in such an acute situation, there are day clinics like the one I run in New York. We use a unique, cutting-edge, multidisciplinary, holistic approach—what I call a whole-person approach because we treat you like a real person, not a patient—and we have a tremendous success rate. We'll taper you off the pills gradually and provide cognitive-behavioral individual therapy and group therapy. I'm board certified in psychiatry and pain management. A psychologist conducts the groups. I have a nutritionist working for me too. We stress the importance of diet and exercise.

"You can find out more about our program at www.drrobert.co. That's www.drrobert.co. And if you like what you see, then drop in. You might think it's a long way to travel from Chicago, but the return on your investment will make it all worthwhile. We get people coming in from all over the country and overseas too. Because our program works."

Applause filled the studio.

"So we've talked about the first two Rs: recognize and rehabilitate. The third R is recover. Get your life back. Get back to doing the things you enjoyed before the drugs began to rule your life. It sounds simple, right? Actually, it's hard work. And you'll be doing it for the rest of your life. Because the cravings will still be there. But now you'll have the tools to fight them. Eat right, exercise, spend your time with people you can trust and who will support you, and stay out of situations where you may be tempted to start using again."

When he had finished his talk, the host thanked him warmly, and the studio audience gave him a rapturous ovation. Backstage, Barry greeted him with a tight embrace.

"You did great, man. Great. You made me proud."

As the elevator descended to the parking garage, the two men beamed, their giddiness barely held in check. When the door opened, all restraint vanished.

"Feeling good now?"

"I feel great."

"You should, bro. You just fucking crushed it."

"I did, didn't I?"

"Duh. You have to ask? Damn right, you did. We are gonna celebrate tonight. Tamika, you getting all this?"

"Yeah," she replied, winding her way backwards through the parking garage with the camera.

"You're sure? You got enough light in here?"

"The light's fine."

In fact, the men's faces, bobbing in and out of the shadows, were at times visible only in their outlines. She knew the lie would catch up with her eventually, but she could not bear the thought of standing around in the heat and inhaling noxious exhaust fumes while Barry fiddled with the camera for the next half-hour.

"Perfect. This is all going into the video."

"I crushed it. I fucking crushed it. So suck on that, Ms. Executive Producer."

As if his adversary were standing before him, the doctor threw a wild right hook, his feet leaving the ground on the follow-through.

"I fucking crushed it, bitch!"

"*Crushing It in Chicago*. That's what I'll call the documentary. This is gonna be big, bro."

Clapping and stamping, the two men shouted in unison, "Crush, crush, crush, crush, crush!" Barry, dropping to his hands and knees, became once more the barking-mad bulldog of the hotel room. The doctor assumed the same position. A prolonged barking competition ensued, until the doctor suddenly metamorphosed from *Canis familiaris* to *Canis lupus*. His feral wolf howls reverberated through the cavernous garage.

The dominance display aroused only disgust in Tamika, who stopped filming and turned her back on Drs. Bullard and Rosen.

CHAPTER 2

When Tamika and the doctor returned to the latter's commodious Upper West Side co-op, they found his son, Nathan, asleep on the massive white leather Chesterfield sofa in the living room. Eyes shut, mouth wide open, left arm hanging down, head perched precariously on the front edge of a seat cushion, Nathan lay inert as a sack full of dirty laundry and exuded the same musty smell. He wore neither shoes nor shirt, and when he exhaled, the outline of his ribs became visible. His hair, just a shade lighter than his father's but straight and shoulder-length with an oily sheen, partially obscured a narrow, chalky face marred by acne.

In the middle of the coffee table stood two white cardboard Chinese takeout boxes and a grease-soaked paper plate. The lavender-and-orange blossom air freshener that the young man had sprayed liberally around the apartment did little to mask the pungent aroma of marijuana.

"Who does he think he's fooling, spraying that crap all over the place?"

Even more incriminating evidence stood at one end of the table, perhaps six inches from Nathan's head, in the form of a beaker-shaped lime green bong with embers still glowing in the bowl.

Scowling, Dr. Rosen dealt the sofa a powerful kick. Purchased in the delirious early days of his marriage, the Chesterfield was the one piece of communal furniture he had retained after the divorce. Liz had dragged him to countless furniture stores, haggled with salespeople until she wore them and herself down, agonized over her choice, and, after a brief spasm of buyer's remorse, grew to cherish the sofa. On the day of its delivery, Dr. and Mrs. Rosen christened it with multiple couplings. When they separated, though, she wanted it gone. To her new life, she told the doctor, she would take no reminders of their one-time intimacy. He took the sofa because he needed one. Only now, with his ungrateful son sprawled upon it, did he reflect on the price he had paid for it in cash, aggravation, and, perhaps most of all, labor, due to Liz's insistence on rearranging the living room every six months or so.

"Hey, idiot!" he shouted, kicking the sofa a second time.

Nathan did not stir.

Dr. Rosen stared for a moment at the enlarged black-and-white photograph hanging above the sofa—the only other piece of communal marital property he had kept. It showed a couple riding in a carriage in Central Park. The man, tall and slender with slicked-back hair and a pencil moustache, wore a topcoat and bowtie and casually held a lit cigarette between the middle and index fingers of his right hand. As he glanced at his companion out of the corner of his left eye, he showed the camera a wry, knowing smile. The woman, a young Sofia Loren lookalike, outfitted in mink and pearls, appeared to be laughing, her head tossed back with abandon. Liz, who had picked the picture up at a gallery in Soho, tossed it in the trash when Dr. Rosen moved out. Needing something to hang on his apartment walls, he rescued it. Though he had grown to like the photograph, he wondered sometimes whether he would have done better to leave it to the trash collectors. His marriage was something best forgotten.

"The hell with him. Let's go eat. Barry will be waiting for us."

Still seething over the doctor's flirtation with the makeup artist, just the latest in a series of such humiliations she had endured over the past month or so, Tamika would gladly have forgone the outing in favor of an early night. Only her unease about remaining alone in the apartment with the mercurial Nathan kept her from excusing herself.

Barry had chosen for their rendezvous a steakhouse, a brand-new restaurant designed to look old, with muted overhead lighting, dark brown paneled walls, a high-beamed ceiling, and a parquet floor. Upon those walls hung black-and-white photographs of such vanished New York landmarks as the old Penn Station, the Singer building, Ebbets Field, and the Biltmore Hotel, and such departed luminaries as Jackie Gleason, George Gershwin, and Joe DiMaggio. The shouting, laughing, stomping, and clapping of the youngish, predominantly male crowd filled the cavernous hall and shook the glasses on the tables.

Tamika ordered a side salad, of which she consumed little, and a glass of white wine. Barry and the doctor each enjoyed a slab of filet mignon and toasted their way through a magnum of Dom Pérignon.

"You watch," Barry told the doctor. "You're gonna get more gigs than you know what to do with. Next thing, you write a book. Monetize your expertise. Strike while the iron's hot."

"I wouldn't know where to start."

"It's easy, bro. You got the material already—the script for your TV talks. You don't need much more than that. You want something simple, something someone can read in an hour on an airplane. No medical jargon. We're talking seventh-grade level here, with lots of bullet points, illustrations, white space. You can crank it out in a couple of weeks. Getting it published will be a cinch. You already have the platform. You're a doctor, an expert. You got the diplomas from the fancy schools. More important, you've been on TV. And the best thing is, once you have it in print, you can plug it when you're on TV, which means more book sales and more TV. The sky's the limit, bro. Imagine going on the *Today Show* to plug your bestseller. Fuckin' aye, man!"

As they exited the restaurant, Dr. Rosen slipped Barry a prescription blank.

#

Back in the apartment, Dr. Rosen stripped off his clothes and got into bed. While he lay waiting, already hard, Tamika, in the bathroom, lingered over the task of removing her makeup.

"Hey, what are you doing in there? You're taking forever."

The voice that reached her through the door betrayed something beyond Dr. Rosen's usual impatience. It sounded aggrieved, belligerent.

"Be out in a minute."

She did not emerge, though, until she heard him snoring— a sound that, on this night, evoked both relief and revulsion.

CHAPTER 3

She awoke the next morning to the discordant sounds of a father-son battle.

"And there better not be any missing this time," she heard the doctor say.

"Or what?"

"Or you can go back to Scarsdale and live with your mother."

Tamika remembered, to her chagrin, that it was Wednesday—pain center day. In addition to her duties as a receptionist in Dr. Rosen's office, Tamika had of late taken on those of a part-time driver. Having determined that he could trust her much more with his Jaguar than he could Nathan, the doctor decided that he had better things to do than to drive out to Queens every Wednesday morning to deliver his quota of oxycodone scripts to the Peninsula Pain Center. He delegated the driving to Tamika and, despite his misgivings, the business transactions to Nathan.

The trip was a slog—an hour-plus on the best days, typically closer to two—through crosstown Manhattan traffic, then down FDR Drive to the Queens-Midtown Tunnel and across Queens southbound to a forlorn corner of the borough that had seen its best days a century ago. Nathan, whose body odor permeated the Jaguar, did not offer the sort of companionship that helped to pass the time. At best, he was sullen and silent, with his earbuds jammed far up his ear canals, and at worst, openly hostile. Tamika usually spent the drive listening to a gospel station, occasionally humming along. As her belief in the doctor had begun to waver, she had increasingly reverted to an earlier faith.

For the first few weeks, she clung to the hope that Dr. Rosen was telling the truth when he assured her that nothing untoward went on inside the Peninsula Pain Center. By now, though, she knew better.

The pain center stood between a Chinese takeout joint and an auto parts shop on McBride Avenue, a broad, litter-strewn street lined with discount stores, fast-food restaurants, check-cashing establishments, and a couple of bondsmen's offices. Tattered, soot-coated awnings fronted many of the shops. Directly across the street from the pain center was Torpedo's, a local Subway knockoff, where Tamika had been working when she had met Dr. Rosen. At the time, he was writing scripts in person at the center on Wednesdays and would drop into Torpedo's at lunchtime, wearing the lab coat that he would later don for his television appearances. The lab coat did not impress the often contentious pain center patients the way he had hoped it would, but for Tamika, it radiated authority. That, along with his confident bearing, set Dr. Rosen apart from the scruffy lot that frequented Torpedo's. He would chat Tamika up while she assembled his Chicken & Bacon Ranch Melt, and she found his attentions flattering. Somehow, she did not draw the connection between the handsome doctor and the disheveled types who would stumble in from across the street because the sub shop's restrooms afforded them the privacy they needed to crush and snort oxycodone pills or sell their newly acquired scripts to still less fortunate souls offering sex in lieu of cash. Nor did she have an inkling that Dr. Rosen was on the lookout for someone who would deliver the scripts for him from Manhattan, thereby sparing him the costs and aggravation associated with both the drive and his interactions with the pain center patients.

One day, as Tamika rang up his purchase, he asked for her mobile number. Within a month, she had become his receptionist and live-in girlfriend. After two or three more months, she had begun to suspect that he was not in the market for a second wife but rather an office gofer also willing to do some light housework and suck him off on demand. Then he had made her his drug runner. Each Wednesday when she set off from Manhattan, she vowed that that week's trip would be the last, that she would leave Dr. Rosen if he tried to force her to continue. Her resolve, though, would dissipate the moment she made the turn onto McBride Avenue, for there lay the life from which she had fled.

Torpedo's was her Scylla; the pain center, her Charybdis. Fearful of the prying eyes of her former coworkers on one side of the street and worried that the police might be watching the other, she tried to make herself as inconspicuous as she could behind the wheel of a silver Jaguar, donning a gray hoodie and a pair of oversized sunglasses, no matter the weather.

Nathan evinced no such concerns. Over the past few weeks, he had made a practice of opening the envelopes his father would give him, rummaging through the prescription sheets inside, pocketing one, and replacing the rest in a second envelope before leaving the car. Once, when Tamika asked just what he thought he was doing, he snarled, "That's my business. I don't answer to my father's bimbo of the month. You can take it up with him if you want. Maybe he'll call the cops on me. Oh, but then he'd go to prison. And so would you." The look on Nathan's face on that occasion could have curdled a gallon of milk. She had never raised an objection since, and even on this sodden morning, when Nathan helped himself to three prescriptions, she held her peace.

A parking space lay open directly in front of the clinic, but Tamika bypassed it deliberately, seeking out, as she always did, a spot farther up the street or even around the corner. Nathan, who possessed a talent for histrionics that he might better have employed on the stage had he had the motivation, assumed a martyr-like pose, palms upraised, face wracked with anguish.

"I don't believe it," he wailed to his phantom audience. "She's making me walk a half mile in the pouring rain. The bitch does this to me every damn time."

Often, in such situations, Tamika had maintained her equanimity by telling herself that God had placed Nathan on Earth to test her patience, her forbearance, her compassion, her faith. Today she failed that test: "If you don't like it, why don't you drive yourself here?"

"Why don't you find another sugar daddy? My father's getting tired of you already."

Squeezing the steering wheel as she would have liked to squeeze Nathan's neck, she inched the Jaguar up the street, passing up two more vacant parking spaces before settling on one she found suitable. She carefully backed the Jaguar toward the curb. With the car still in motion, Nathan jumped out and slammed the door. Stumbling over the curb, he fell forward onto the sidewalk. There he lay for half a minute before scraping himself off the pavement. On his knees, he screamed to the heavens, "Bitch!"

He returned ten minutes later. Finding the passenger door locked, he banged hard on the window. In a faint show of resistance that did not escape Nathan's notice, Tamika let her finger hover over the release button for several seconds before pushing it.

Once inside, Nathan pulled the door shut. His hair dripped rainwater, and his black leather jacket had a scuff on the left sleeve below the elbow. The raw skin on his right patella showed through a tear in his jeans. His face was white and rigid.

"Just keep me waiting out here on this lovely street like the passive-aggressive bitch you are. The fake doctor had a gun in his desk. The whole time he was talking to me, he was cleaning it. This is the situation my father puts me in."

Without replying, she steered the Jaguar away from the curb. A sustained horn blast, coming from behind and to her left, caused her to step hard on the brake. Nathan had yet to fasten his seatbelt, and his torso jerked forward with such force that his face nearly hit the dashboard. A rust-eaten, faded-green Chevy sped past, the passenger in the front seat holding his middle finger aloft.

"He isn't forcing you to do it," Tamika said. "You could tell him no."

"He's not forcing you to fuck him either. You could say no and sell your cunt on the street for a living."

He looked at her as he might have gazed upon a particularly repellant insect.

"I could be the skankiest street whore in New York City, and I still wouldn't take you as a customer."

"Cunt!"

Nathan shoved his earbuds back in his ears. Once the Jaguar reached the highway, he drew an overstuffed brown envelope from his inside jacket pocket. He picked at the flap, trying to slip his fingernail underneath it. His patience quickly exhausted, he tore the envelope open and removed three hundred-dollar bills.

Tamika mouthed the words of the psalm, "The Lord is my shepherd; I shall not want . . ."

Back on the Upper West Side, Tamika, after parking the Jaguar in the garage under Dr. Rosen's apartment building, did not go into the office. Instead, she wandered for a while in Central Park, then boarded the subway with no particular destination in mind. She came to the surface in Midtown, where she found herself caught up in a tide of pedestrians that bore her along Seventh Avenue. A work crew had cordoned off a portion of the avenue, and traffic had come to a halt. The wailing of sirens, the blaring of car horns, and the pounding of jackhammers filled the air. Heat and exhaust lay trapped in the caverns between the grime-covered buildings. For a few minutes, Tamika idly perused the Macy's window displays, but she did not enter the store. She had not come here for window-shopping, but for a purpose she had kept half-hidden from herself when boarding the subway: to make a break from the doctor and his son. She could not endure another Wednesday like this one. While descending into the maelstrom of Penn Station via the escalator from the street, she phoned her mother, who inquired of her belligerently, "What you want?"

"I'm in Penn Station. I'm coming home."

"You got a lot of nerve coming back here, child."

Descending another level, she stood on the platform, hesitating, while the herd of commuters racing to board a Long Island Railroad train bound for the McBride Avenue station shoved and elbowed her aside. The doors closed, and the train left with her still standing on the platform, weeping.

CHAPTER 4

The doctor had awakened that morning in a foul mood induced by a crushing hangover and the galling recollection of Tamika hiding in the bathroom and denying him the orgasmic culmination his day of triumph ought to have had. He also had a nagging worry that the endorphin high that came with winning an audience's love had led him to speak too freely on the set in Chicago. He had improvised that bit about the cutting-edge, holistic approach to substance abuse treatment. For a few months, he had run a substance abuse clinic out of his office. He never did get around to hiring a psychologist or a nutritionist, though, and he soon concluded that the return on his investment did not justify the time, effort, and aggravation that the enterprise entailed. Medicaid, which provided coverage for most of his clinic patients, did not compensate him adequately. The patients themselves proved irksome. Far too many of them came to him seeking opioids rather than treatment for addiction to them. Obliging them had brought him some tax-free income, but they had made nuisances of themselves, hanging around the office on days when the clinic was not in session and spooking his private patients. He had decided that rather than compromise his practice, he would do better to close the clinic and shunt the patients off to some venue that would give them their opioids while continuing to provide him with an income stream. Thus had his involvement with the Peninsula Pain Center and its Russian proprietors come about.

To that hellhole he could not send any viewers from Chicago who took literally his words about journeying to New

York for holistic, cutting-edge substance abuse treatment, lest he risk national exposure as a fraud or worse. Rather, he would have to reconstitute his clinic in a hurry, complete, this time, with a psychologist and nutritionist. He would also need to find someone who would make him a convincing facsimile to hang in his office of the credential that he had boasted of during the broadcast but did not have—that of a board-certified pain management specialist.

As was his wont, he took out his anxieties and resentments on Nathan, but the morning blowup provided no catharsis. No matter how loudly he shouted, he could not penetrate that maddening insouciance, that marijuana-tinged haze that cordoned Nathan off from his father and the rest of the world.

Brooding over his son's unaccountable failings, Dr. Rosen lost track of time and had to skip breakfast and his morning shower. He dressed with such haste that he stumbled out of the apartment wearing mismatched socks, an untucked shirt with the buttons and buttonholes misaligned, an open collar, and no tie. Worst of all, he had neglected to take an umbrella. The Uber he had ordered had parked across the street, and by the time he reached it, he was drenched. Dr. Sober-Up looked as if he had just emerged from a three-day bender.

In that abject condition, he headed out to Brooklyn, where, as the defendant in a $2.5-million malpractice suit, he was to be deposed. The suit was brought by the widow of one Salvatore Agnello, a patient at the St. Agnes Nursing Home in Flatbush, where Dr. Rosen did some occasional moonlighting. Mr. Agnello had died suddenly while under Dr. Rosen's care. The patient's demise, the widow and her lawyer contended, resulted from a fatal prescribing error committed by the grossly negligent Dr. Rosen.

In a stuffy, windowless conference room, its white walls bare save for an outsized monitor mounted on the rear one, the opposing parties gathered. On one side of the long, burnished conference table sat the widow and her attorney. Mrs.

Agnello, a tiny woman with stooped shoulders and patches of pink scalp visible beneath her white curls, wore a long black dress. Her attorney, D.L. Sheridan, III, was tall and silver-haired with a Kirk Douglas-like cleft in his chin and a maroon handkerchief in the breast pocket of his charcoal Armani suit jacket. Opposite them sat Dr. Rosen and his lawyer, one Patrick McKinley, a genial sort, ruddy complexioned and stout. At the far end of the table, seated perpendicularly to the principals, was the stenographer, a young, very attractive redhead whom Dr. Rosen hoped he might have a chance to get to know after the proceedings.

"Long night, Doctor?"

Sheridan had the eyes of a predator and a measured smile that radiated menace. The doctor, conscious that with his open collar, untucked, carelessly buttoned shirt, wet hair, and puffy eyes, he must have appeared a sorry specimen indeed, squirmed in his chair.

"I was on call."

"As Dr. Sober-Up? I looked at some of the videos of your TV appearances on your website. Can you really cure a hangover with a Bloody Mary?"

"Yes. There's nothing I say in that video that's contraindicated medically."

"Let's talk about what is contraindicated medically. On November 4 of last year, you prescribed Haldol, a 1-milligram dose, for Mr. Agnello. Is that correct?"

"Yes."

"Had you ever prescribed Haldol for him before?"

"No."

"Had you ever seen Mr. Agnello before that day?"

"No. He was a new patient."

"Actually, he'd been at St. Agnes for over a month. But you'd never seen him?"

"No. He must have been one of Dr. Harris's patients."

"What was Dr. Harris's diagnosis?"

"Severe dementia, among other things."

"You're sure about that?"

"I know dementia when I see it."

"Do you? Geriatric medicine is not your area of specialization, is it? Which makes me wonder why you were working at St. Agnes in the first place."

"Geriatric medicine is like other medicine. You just prescribe smaller doses. And I've seen lots of dementia patients in my practice."

"Had Dr. Harris ever prescribed Haldol for Mr. Agnello?"

"Not to my knowledge."

"What led you to prescribe Haldol, at a pretty high dosage, to a geriatric patient who was naïve to it and whom you had never seen before that day? That's not standard practice, is it?"

"The staff requested it. He was aggressive and violent. They couldn't control him."

"Liar," the widow hissed.

She drew a handkerchief from her purse and dabbed at her eyes. Between the dress and the tears, reflected Dr. Rosen, she was milking her widowhood for all $2.5 million worth.

"What made you think that Mr. Agnello was dangerous?"

"He was showing clear signs of delirium. He was disoriented. He didn't know where he was or why he was there or what day of the week it was. He was agitated. His speech was disorganized."

"But dangerous? What was he doing that was dangerous?"

"I've already explained that. He was agitated. He was . . . very agitated."

"That's very . . . illuminating. Now tell me, when you see your patients at St. Agnes, how much time do you spend with each of them?"

"Enough to gauge their mood, their level of orientation and overall cognitive functioning, their ability to interact socially. It varies from patient to patient, but I've been doing this a long time, so I can usually size them up pretty quickly."

"Is fifteen minutes enough time?"

"Usually."

"What about ten?"

"It could be ten."

"Five? Three? How much time did you spend with Mr. Agnello on November 4th of last year? Two minutes? One minute? Did you see him at all?"

"Of course I saw him. What kind of question is that?"

"One that you'll have to answer under oath if we go to trial. Now, you claimed earlier that Mr. Agnello had been diagnosed with severe dementia, and I take it that you attributed his alleged delirium to that. Isn't it true, though, that something other than dementia—an infection, say—may cause delirium in an elderly patient?"

"A lot of things can. My immediate concern with Mr. Agnello was for his safety and that of the staff."

"Were you aware that Mr. Agnello was being treated with Cipro for a UTI?"

"No."

"Why not?"

"Someone must have forgotten to note it in the chart."

"That's funny," said the lawyer, removing a printout from a manila folder and sliding it across the table to Dr. Rosen. "Those are your notes. Do you see the medication list? Is there, in fact, an entry for Cipro, 500 milligrams, twice a day?"

"Yes."

Feeling lightheaded, Dr. Rosen tugged at his collar. His shirt, saturated with rain and sweat, clung to his torso.

"How is it possible that you don't know what's in your own notes? Did you actually write those notes, or was it a copy-and-paste job?"

"I wrote them."

"Hmm. A bit of a puzzle there. You wrote the entry in his chart, but you didn't know he was taking Cipro? Can you explain that?"

"There must have been a mix-up of some kind."

"Is it sound clinical practice to prescribe Haldol for an elderly patient already taking Cipro?"

"No."

"Why not?"

"Both drugs can both prolong the QT interval, and when they're prescribed together . . . Well, they can cause the patient to go into ventricular fibrillation."

"That's a form of arrhythmia, isn't it?"

"Yes."

"That can be fatal?"

"You don't know that that's what caused his death. It could have been anything. He was a very sick, old man. Things like this happen all the time."

Flushed and trembling, the widow whispered in a most unforgiving tone, "May God forgive you. May God forgive you."

Pat McKinley grimaced as though someone had punched him in the stomach.

Afterwards, on the sidewalk, the lawyer laid his beefy hand on the doctor's shoulder.

"Look, I hate to sound discouraging, but I think it'd be in your best interest if I were to sound them out about settling."

The rain had stopped, leaving a suffocating humidity in its wake. Removing his suit jacket, the doctor wiped his forehead with his shirtsleeve.

"I don't settle. Settling is for losers."

"I find that it's the people who don't know when to settle who usually end up the losers."

"Whose side are you on anyway?"

"Yours, as long as you're paying me."

"For what I'm paying you, I expect you to fight for me. I need a killer, like her lawyer. You just rolled over in there."

"You're paying me to advise and represent you in such a way as to get you the best legal outcome I can. And based on what I heard in there today, I wouldn't be doing that if I were to encourage you to go to trial. It would be more profitable for me, but it would cost you a whole lot more, and not just money. You have a practice and a reputation to uphold. The stuff that came out today—especially that business with the chart—is bad. Really bad. I don't see how we get around that in court. Then there are your billing records, of which you have not produced anywhere near what Dan requested."

"You two are on a first-name basis? No wonder I'm screwed. The fix is in."

"I can't stall him forever. He could subpoena them. If there's anything funny going on there . . ."

"There isn't."

"Especially if it involves Medicare or Medicaid. The feds might start sniffing around. They take that stuff pretty seriously."

"Fuck the feds. I got nothing to hide."

"I certainly hope not. You haven't been very forthcoming with me either. I can do a much better job when I'm not flying blind. I don't like surprises."

In fact, the doctor had much to hide. The allure of increasing his cash flow by billing Medicare for consults with deceased nursing home patients had proved too tempting to resist. For the first time, the possibility occurred to him that perhaps he not given due consideration to the risks. The billing records that the plaintiff's attorney sought would reveal that Dr. Rosen had paid a second visit to Mr. Agnello some thirty-six hours after the first administration of Haldol. Though the patient had, by that time, been lying in the morgue for a full day, the doctor found him alert and fully oriented. He had continued to document the patient's miraculous progress through two subsequent visits. Dr. Rosen had experienced similar success with several other patients he had treated postmortem.

"Fine!" said the doctor, throwing up his hands in a gesture of surrender. "Do what you have to then. I'll even write them a check today, just as long as I don't ever have to be stuck in a room with that bloodsucker and her lawyer again. If she cared so much about the old bastard, why didn't she keep him at home instead of dumping him in a place like St. Anus?"

"I'll give Dan a call when I get back to the office and see what kind of offer he and Mrs. Agnello are willing to entertain."

"But you have to get them to come down. Like way down. My insurer isn't going to pay more than $1 million. I can't pay a million out of pocket. I'll be bankrupt."

"I'll see what I can do," replied Pat in a tone that did not inspire confidence.

Without saying goodbye, Dr. Rosen walked off toward the subway entrance at the corner.

"Hey, doc. One more thing."

The doctor turned around.

"What?"

"Did you ever actually see Mr. Agnello?"

"Fuck you, Pat."

"I'll take that as a no."

CHAPTER 5

Upon his return, Dr. Rosen found the apartment empty. Nathan could be anywhere; his comings and goings followed no discernable pattern, and he never answered his cellphone when his father called. Tamika was not answering hers either, nor had she responded to the two text messages he had sent her on his way back from Brooklyn. During business hours, she answered the phone at his practice, but this time, his call went to Kellyanne, the office manager.

"No," she told him, "your little, ahem, receptionist has not seen fit to grace us with her presence today. It's very hard to get my own work done when I have to do her job too."

Assuring Kellyanne that he would get to the bottom of things and discipline Tamika as appropriate, he hung up. At the moment, however, he felt less miffed at the latter than at the tart-tongued office manager, whose frequent, well-grounded insinuations about his and Tamika's relationship had become grating. Had Kellyanne not run the business end of the practice so capably and applied her knowledge of the intricacies of Medicare and Medicaid billing to such remunerative effect, the doctor, who had a decided preference for young, docile women, both as employees and bedmates, would have fired her long ago. She was roughly his age and preternaturally thin, the contours of her body marked by sharp angles rather than curves. Her permanently raised eyebrows and the tautness of the skin around her mouth suggested that she had had some facial work done. Her hair color changed almost as frequently as her shoes, ranging across the periodic table from copper to silver to gold to platinum. She accented her custom-fitted business suits with bright designer scarves.

Between her and Tamika there existed an ongoing cold war. Kellyanne's hostility, the doctor suspected, stemmed from her envy of her perceived rival's youth, beauty, and perhaps most of all, the place Tamika occupied in his life outside the office. For her part, Tamika, who had a facility with numbers that even the doctor could not help but recognize, would, on slow days, sometimes infuriate Kellyanne by poking around in the billing records. Tamika had become convinced that her rival was embezzling from the practice.

"One day Kellyanne's gonna steal your chair out from under you."

"You don't know what you're talking about."

"Don't I? Do you think she can afford those Hermes scarves and Louis Vuitton handbags and Ferragamo shoes on what you pay her? Do you know how much those things cost?"

"Do you?"

"Why would you think I don't? Because I'm black?"

"Why do you always have to bring race into everything?"

"I don't bring it. It's already there."

Unable to make heads or tails of the spreadsheets that Tamika showed him and disinclined to take her opinions on any subject seriously, Dr. Rosen chose to place his trust in Kellyanne. After all, she boasted an MBA from Wharton and had managed various doctors' practices for as long as Tamika, who had but a high school diploma to her credit, had been alive. On occasion, he did wonder how Kellyanne paid for the suits, scarves, handbags, Tuscan vacations, and the Mercedes she drove and why someone with a Wharton MBA would have made a career out of managing doctors' offices. Because she managed his so well, however, he had never felt the need to verify her academic credentials.

Though he rarely praised her, Dr. Rosen viewed Tamika as a very capable and conscientious employee. Her going AWOL thus caused him some consternation. Had a calamity, such as a police raid or a robbery, ensnared her and Nathan at the pain center? Better the latter, as long as no one got hurt, for Nathan would relish the chance to turn him in to the police.

Tossing his suit jacket onto the sofa, the doctor proceeded to the kitchen. He had not eaten all day. His stomach was rumbling, and a piercing pain extended across his forehead, just above the eyebrows. Finding nothing in the refrigerator of which to make a meal except the remnants of Nathan's Chinese takeout from last night, he angrily tossed the food cartons into the trash.

Leaving the kitchen, he spied a torn brown envelope on the dining room table. He counted the money inside the envelope and calculated the shortfall.

"Damn him!"

He kicked over two dining room chairs and flung a third across the room with such force that the back legs, which struck the wall first, left two large indentations.

What to do about Nathan? He had begun by stealing cash—a hundred here, a hundred there. Each time he discovered the theft, Dr. Rosen would rage at his son, often threatening to throw him out onto the street. The lack of follow-through, however, only encouraged Nathan to become more brazen in his thievery. Of late, not only money but, apparently, scripts as well had gone missing.

Leaving the apartment, Dr. Rosen headed east to McDonalds on Broadway for a Big Mac, fries, and a soda. He all but inhaled the food, ruminating on his son and the stolen prescriptions. The theft of the scripts was a bigger problem than that of the cash, potentially a dangerous one. For three weeks running, the center's medical director had complained about a shortfall and had reduced his payment to Dr. Rosen accordingly. At first, Dr. Rosen suspected the director, who called himself Dr. Sergei Zhukov, of cheating him. The sullen Russian, who had a plaque hanging from his office wall that read, "SPECIALIZE CHRONIC PAIN AND SUFFERING," kept a gun in his desk and, once or twice, had taken it out and cleaned it while transacting business with Dr. Rosen, just as he did with Nathan. Dr. Zhukov never wrote any prescriptions himself. Whether he had the requisite credentials, Dr. Rosen did not know. Printed in Cyrillic lettering, the putative diploma that hung on the office wall beside the plaque looked less like an actual one than a photocopy. During the deposition, when Dr. Rosen had had his phone switched off, Dr. Zhukov had sent him a text and left a voicemail, both containing cryptic references to unfortunate accidents that had befallen untrustworthy business partners in the past.

Dr. Rosen returned to his apartment to find a stranger sitting on the Chesterfield. Leaning back against the cushions, legs spread as he leafed through the doctor's copy of *The Way of the Bulldog II: Hang on to What You've Got*, the man appeared very much at home. In his early thirties, or so the doctor guessed, trim but muscular, he wore jeans, a white T-shirt, and knee-high engineer boots. He had a shaved head and a silver stud on the right side of his nose. His visible tattoos included a spider on his neck, a skull on his left forearm, the letters ОМУТ on the back of his right hand, and extending the entire length of his right forearm, a dagger with a red-tipped blade. The stranger smelled heavily of sweat and tobacco. A brown leather briefcase lay on the sofa beside him. On the coffee table stood a half-empty bottle of the doctor's Merlot and a full goblet. Making quick work of the wine, the man stubbed out his cigarette on the table and dropped the butt into the goblet. He put the book down, stood up, and extended his gnarly right hand. Unfazed by his host's failure to reciprocate, he reached out and squeezed the doctor's hand with a vice-like force and shook it with such vigor that Dr. Rosen feared his shoulder might become dislocated.

"Dr. Robert, I am Alexey Ivanovich Golovorez, CFO of Golovorez Solutions."

"CFO of what?"

The man looked like anything but a CFO.

"Golovorez Solutions. We do consulting. We use cutting-edge performance metrics to assess and optimize clients' business processes and provide solutions for companies of all sizes throughout tri-state area. We are retained by business partner of yours, Dr. Sergei Zhukov, CEO of Zhukov Pharmaceuticals and medical director of Peninsula Pain Clinic."

"Zhukov Pharmaceuticals?"

"Zhukov Pharmaceuticals is parent of Peninsula Pain Center."

"So what does any of this have to do with me? What are you doing in my apartment?"

"I am coming to that. So Dr. Zhukov, CEO of Zhukov Pharmaceuticals and medical director of Peninsula Pain Clinic, calls me, and he says, 'Alexey Ivanovich, we have supply issue. We want you to do business process analysis and find solution to this issue. Every Wednesday, for last four weeks, there are prescription shits missing from Dr. Robert's delivery. Before today, just one. Today, three shits are missing.'"

"I sent him the full order. There was nothing missing."

"This is not good, Dr. Robert. Some patients do not get their prescriptions. They are unhappy. Maybe they go somewhere else for treatment of chronic pain. Then clinic loses revenue, and investors do not get return they expect. This makes them unhappy. At Zhukov Pharmaceuticals headquarters, people are unhappy. Dr. Zhukov is most unhappy of all. He weeps so because he cannot relieve patients' pain and suffering. And also, he weeps for lost revenue.

"So we at Golovorez Solutions conduct business process analysis like he asks. We find solution is you pay $25,000."

His eyes full of menace, the man moved a step closer.

"So what you say, Dr. Robert?"

The doctor tried to stare the man down.

"I don't know what you're talking about. I've never shorted him. Maybe he's pocketing the scripts himself."

Golovorez retorted with a blow to the solar plexus, delivered with such swiftness and economy of motion that Dr. Rosen could not fathom how he came to be writhing on the floor, breathless, feeling as if he had been gutted. Never had he experienced such pain.

"That is not helpful, Dr. Robert. We at Golovorez Solutions pride ourselves in customer service. We like to find win-win solution for everybody. But if party is not agreeable, win-lose will do just as well."

He pressed the sole of his boot against the doctor's cheek.

"In there," the doctor groaned, pointing toward the dining room. "On the table, there's an envelope. It has cash."

"That's better. Now we are getting somewhere."

Golovorez went to fetch the envelope. Returning and settling himself on the sofa again, he took out the notes and began to count them.

"There is $11,200 in here. That is not even half. Dr. Zhukov will be very unhappy."

The doctor pushed himself up from the floor. He was dizzy, still short of breath. His legs felt gelatinous.

"That's all I have. The rest I can get tomorrow. The bank's closed now."

"Bank may be closed, but Dr. Zhukov doesn't like to wait. Still he is reasonable man sometimes, when he has just enough vodka in him but not too much. I will call Dr. Zhukov. If he says all right, I will take this as deposit and come back tomorrow morning after you get money from bank. If he says not all right, well . . . But let's not worry about that just yet."

He placed a call but got no response and left no message.

"Dr. Zhukov does not answer. Maybe is good for you. Maybe is not so good. If he is in good mood, is best not to upset him. I will come here at 10 o'clock tomorrow. You must give me rest of money then."

"I have appointments," the doctor began, but he stopped midsentence when Golovorez stood up and again advanced toward him. "Yes, 10 o'clock. I'll have it all."

"Oh, and I will take Rolex Yacht Master as collateral."

"What?"

"Is nice watch. I've wanted one for long time."

Dr. Rosen unclasped and meekly handed over his Yacht Master. Donning the watch, Golovorez stood for a moment admiring it.

"Is thing of beauty. Anyway, as I was saying, total amount due is $25,000. That is $14,800 for prescriptions, plus late fees, interest, and 10 percent commission for me. Minus $11,200 nonrefundable down payment today, that is $13,800 balance due by 10 o'clock tomorrow. I will present you with itemized receipt upon payment."

"Commission?"

"I must make living too. Plus, I am doing you big favor that I don't know Dr. Zhukov would approve. I am waiving interest charges that would accrue overnight."

Though stung by the injustice, Dr. Rosen felt disinclined to argue the eminently reasonable case that Dr. Zhukov, as Golovorez's alleged client, ought to pay the commission. The likelihood that the visitor would administer another of his win-lose solutions to the gut seemed far greater than that of his granting a fair hearing.

Placing the cash in his briefcase, his business apparently concluded, the interloper turned as if to leave. To the doctor's consternation, however, he lingered, admiring the photograph of the couple in the carriage.

"This is charming picture. I like very much. Very elegant couple. I take photographs too. I have some with me. Maybe you'd like to see?"

On his phone, he pulled up a shot of a man lying supine on a carpet, the face bloated and blood streaked, the nose flattened, the eyes ringed by swollen purple flesh, one fully shut, the other open just a slit. The doctor gagged.

"Is for marketing. To show potential customers that we at Golovorez Solutions are highly trained professionals who do quality work. Is true subjects don't always look so good in pictures, but customers don't care about that. I take pride in composition, but one must make compromises in name of commerce, no? I do videos too. I did one of US attorney in bed with woman not his wife. Was very useful.

"But I think I am made for better things. Maybe someday I get studio of my own and take only pictures I want, nice pictures like one of this elegant couple."

He had already removed the picture from the wall and tucked it under his arm when Dr. Rosen said plaintively, "You already have my watch."

"What does picture mean to you? How many times in day do you walk past without noticing? Do you even remember it's there?"

Dr. Rosen shrugged.

"Picture like this belongs with someone who can appreciate it. I will give it good home."

"Take the damn thing then. I'm tired of looking at it. It reminds me of my ex."

"I appreciate your generosity. Good afternoon, Dr. Robert. We will meet again tomorrow. It is pleasure doing business with you."

When Nathan came home, an hour or so later, Dr. Rosen, still feeling the aftereffects of the punch the visitor had dealt him, was lying on the sofa, his body curled up, his hands pressed against his solar plexus.

"Where have you been?" asked the doctor, regarding Nathan's backpack with suspicion, for he doubted that it contained books or documents or anything else a student or employed person would need to carry.

"Out."

Though his anger had returned, the doctor hardly felt up to doing battle. In a voice more weary than accusatory, he said, "You've been stealing from me. Money and prescriptions."

"I don't see it that way. I'm just taking what I earned. If my father drags me into his filthy drug-pushing business and I have to deal with lunatics who point guns at me, the least he can do is compensate me. Though it's kind of a moot point now because I'm never going back to that place again. You can deliver the scripts yourself from now on. Imagine what Mom would say if she knew what you got me mixed up in."

"What are you doing with the scripts? Are you dealing?"

Nathan's eyes zoomed in on the picture hook from which the portrait of the elegant Central Park couple had hung.

"Where's Mom's picture?"

"Don't change the subject. It's not your mother's picture. It hasn't been in years. I got tired of looking at it, so I gave it away."

"You had no right."

"I had every right. I also have the right to know what you're up to as long as you're living under my roof."

"Maybe I am dealing. Maybe I'm just a chip off the old block."

"I had a 3.9 GPA and was applying to medical schools when I was your age. Not much resemblance there."

"And get off my lawn, kid. I didn't say I was a dealer. I said maybe. Or maybe I'm a police informant. Wouldn't it be funny if the scripts I took turned up as evidence and helped put you away for the rest of your life?"

The doctor felt another spasm in his stomach.

"Hilarious." As Nathan turned his back on him and walked off, he added, "I was also getting laid at your age. A lot."

The 3.9 GPA might mean nothing to his son, but that jibe would sting. Nathan had never had a girlfriend, as far as the doctor knew, and likely had never slept with a woman.

Dr. Rosen heard Nathan's bedroom door slam. Moments later, the smell of marijuana began to seep into the living room. Was Nathan exchanging the scripts with his worthless stoner friends for dope? He must be. How else would someone without a source of income maintain an endless supply of the stuff? He could imagine Nathan trading $1,000 worth of scripts for an ounce of pot.

"Hey, idiot," he shouted, though he knew his son would already have his earbuds in and not hear a word. "You better not be dealing. Because you're the only person I know who could go broke doing it."

Soon afterwards Tamika entered. Grimy and sweaty, her eyes swollen from crying, she looked exhausted.

"Hey, where the hell have you been?" asked the doctor, who had not moved from the sofa.

"Out."

"Out where?"

"What do you care?"

"I care because I'm paying you to do a job, and you didn't even bother to show up at the office today. That's the kind of crap I expect from Nathan."

"You don't know half the crap you're getting from Nathan."

"What's that supposed to mean?"

She took a sniff.

"It stinks in here. Why do you let him smoke that stuff in the house anyway? What kind of father does that?"

"The kind that's so fed up he's about ready to kick both of your worthless asses out onto the street. Why didn't you go into the office today?"

"Where's the picture that was here?"

"I got rid of it."

"Why'd you go and do a dumbass thing like that for? It was a nice picture. One of the few nice things in this whole apartment."

She began to walk away.

"Wait a minute. I'm not finished with you yet. Look at me. One: You don't ever turn your back on me when I'm speaking to you. Ever. I don't know what's gotten into you today, but it better not happen again. Two: You blow off work again, you're out. Out of a job. Out of here. Three: I can't have Nathan making the deliveries to the pain center anymore. From now on, you're doing it."

"I ain't going there no more."

"As long as you're working for me, you'll go where I tell you to go."

"I know what goes on there. They selling oxycodone prescriptions for cash. I don't want no part of that."

"You're already part of it, just as much as Nathan and I am. You have been for as long as you've been driving him there."

"Well, I ain't gonna be no more."

"Your ghetto is showing."

"What?"

"Whenever you're upset, you start speaking ghetto. I find it charming."

"Racist asshole!" she cried, stamping her foot.

Tamika rushed off to the bedroom and slammed the door behind her.

Furious, the doctor tried to pursue her, but as soon as he stood up, the pain in his gut forced him back down onto the sofa. There he remained until morning, unable to sleep, brooding over all the wrongs inflicted upon him that day by the greedy Mrs. Agnello, her ruthless attorney, the ineffectual Pat McKinley, the crooked Dr. Zhukov and the thuggish Golovorez, the thieving Nathan, and the newly defiant Tamika. He would set things right though. He would make them all pay. With interest.

CHAPTER 6

First, however, he had to pay a debt of his own.

Dr. Rosen groaned when, upon his return from the bank the next morning, the reek of tobacco greeted him. Having somehow gained access to the apartment again, Alexey Ivanovich Golovorez, today sporting leather trousers, lay on the Chesterfield perusing the doctor's autographed copy of *The Way of the Bulldog III: The Tenacious Leader*. He held the book in his right hand and a cigarette in his left.

"Excuse me, Dr. Robert," said Golovorez, flicking ashes onto the carpet. "Sofa is so comfortable, I couldn't resist. How are you this morning? You make sound like something hurts."

"Here's your money," the doctor answered stiffly, tossing two envelopes stuffed with cash to his unwanted guest.

Golovorez sat up and stubbed his cigarette out on the coffee table, as he had the day before. He took his time counting the notes.

"It's all there," said the doctor.

"I trust you, Dr. Robert, but I must count anyway. Dr. Zhukov would be very unhappy if there are any more mistakes."

When he finished counting, he stuffed the money into the briefcase, which he snapped shut. Curiously, though, he remained seated.

"I think we're done here. Aren't we?"

"Almost, Dr. Robert, almost. Just one thing more. There is little cash flow issue at clinic that has come up. Dr. Zhukov says he cannot pay you anymore $500 a shit. Now it will have to be $200 a shit."

"Are you kidding me? I'm already giving him half off. People give me $1,000 for a 120 blueberry script. I could do a lot more business like that, but I don't want those lowlifes hanging around my private practice. That's why I send them to Zhukov. But I'm still taking a huge risk doing this. My name is the one on the scripts. If you get raided, the cops will come looking for me next. For $200, it's not worth it. Tell Zhukov to write his own damn prescriptions. Or find another sucker."

Rising from the sofa, Golovorez shook his head.

"I don't think you assess risks correctly, Dr. Robert. Police are least of your worries. Is problem when business partner of Dr. Zhukov tries to break agreement. Agreement is not all that gets broken. You understand?"

He cracked his knuckles, stretched his arms over his head, leaned to his right and then his left, and rotated his shoulders. Crouching like a boxer, bouncing on the balls of his feet, he dodged a blow from an imagined opponent and struck back with a swift right-left-right combination.

"I am peaceful man by nature, Dr. Robert. I find violence personally ab . . . ab . . . What is word I'm looking for?"

"Abhorrent?"

"Yes, abhorrent. But personal and business—they are two different things."

"Right. Of course. Two hundred a script will be fine."

The doctor opened the front door, but to his dismay, Golovorez made no move in that direction.

"You seem to be caught between rock and hard rock, Dr. Robert. I am truly sorry. But I will talk to Dr. Zhukov. Maybe today he is in good mood. Then I can mediate and find win-win solution, like your friend Mr. Barry Bullshit says in his book. You may be surprised to find out that I know Mr. Bullshit when he is doing honest work running chop shop in Brooklyn and is calling himself Barry Boucek."

"Boucek? Chop shop? What are you talking about?"

"Dr. Zhukov thinks chop shop is good investment opportunity, so we help Barry to ship parts to Russia. Unfortunately,

Barry is late with payments, so is necessary for Golovorez Solutions to intervene and find win-win solution. Well, maybe not win-win for Barry. We have to break a few ribs. Ah, well. It can't be helped.

"But in principle, win-win is good. Is core value at Golovorez Solutions. We have mission statement even: *Golovorez Solutions—we sort you out.* Well, really, is not our mission statement yet. I just make it up right now. But is good, no?"

"It's great. And $200 is fine too. Now I have to get to work. So if you don't mind . . ."

"No, no. You deserve much more than $200. Dr. Zhukov is lucky to have prominent anti-addiction TV doctor like you as partner in business selling opioids to addicts. I will negotiate with him for you. I insist."

A drawn-out and very animated telephone conversation ensued between Golovorez and another Russian speaker, presumably Dr. Zhukov. Though, to his knowledge, Dr. Rosen did not have any neighbors who spoke the language, he took the precaution of closing the door anyway. Sinking into an armchair, he leaned his head back, ruing the day he had gone into business with Dr. Zhukov.

The revelation that his life coach, the semi-famous Barry Bullard, was formerly Barry Boucek, chop shop owner, troubled Dr. Rosen almost as much as Golovorez's presence. He had expected the appearance in Chicago, after which Barry's agent had signed him on as a client, to launch him into stardom, but he had not had even a nibble from another station. Nor had his television pitch brought him any new patients, from Chicago or elsewhere, and the fact that he had not had to hire a psychologist or a nutritionist or acquire a bogus certificate had done little to assuage his disappointment. For Barry's services, he had already paid upward of $10,000. Had he given his money away to a con man?

Golovorez was beaming when he got off the phone. He had talked Dr. Zhukov up to $300 a prescription.

"That's wonderful."

"Is best I can do. I am sorry you do not appreciate my effort."

"No, I do. Believe me. It's a real win-win."

The doctor stood up. He opened the door again, but, as before, Golovorez did not take the hint.

"And since I help you, maybe you do little favor for me in return, yes, no?"

"What now?"

"Is nice sofa this. Very comfortable. Would look good in my living room."

"It looks fine where it is."

"I have truck around back of building. We at Golovorez Solutions have moving-and-storage business too. I will call men up now. They are very professional. Will take just few minutes."

Further protest, Dr. Rosen realized, would likely prove useless at best and hazardous at worst. Without another word, he dropped back into his armchair.

The three men Golovorez summoned might well have been his brothers. All had the same wiry build and shaven head. All were shirtless, their torsos covered with a dazzling array of tattoos: eagles, stars, suns, skulls, hooded executioners, and dragons. One wore the face of Stalin across his chest.

They worked quickly and with an enthusiasm for the task that alarmed the doctor, disconnecting the television and cable box and setting both on the sofa, along with two valuable antique pendulum wall clocks.

"Hey, come on," he pleaded. "Not the clocks. They belonged to my mother. She left them to me in her will."

Sheila Rosen, still very much alive and in a nursing home, had indeed promised to leave him the clocks upon her passing; however, Dr. Rosen, suspecting his estranged brother, Jeffrey, of having designs on them, had not waited for that eventuality. A brief visit with her in the hospital the morning after her disabling stroke sufficed to convince him that she would never return home. From the hospital, he drove directly to her house to claim that portion of his legacy, forcing the backdoor lock with a screwdriver.

Golovorez shrugged.

"Sometimes they get overenthusiastic. But you are right. Please, please, gentlemen. Is just sofa for which we came. Nothing else. Is not respectful to take family heirlooms. Is not in keeping with Golovorez Solutions' core values of honesty, integrity, and great customer service. Is bad for business too. We don't want Dr. Robert to give us bad review on Yelp."

The two men carrying the Chesterfield tipped it over, sending the appliances and the clocks crashing to the floor. Dr. Rosen winced. The men tried to force the sofa through the doorway, angling the Chesterfield in every conceivable way, but managed only to chip some paint off the doorframe. They backed away from the entrance and set the sofa down, while the third member of the crew removed the door from its hinges and flung it aside. It landed on the television with a report like that of a gunshot. That obstacle dispensed with, the two sofa bearers promptly exited with their cargo, their colleague in tow.

The commotion had disturbed Nathan's sleep. Wearing briefs and a gray T-shirt that bore the logo of the school where he had spent a single semester—the letters NYU printed in purple beneath a graphic of a lit torch—he yawned as he entered the living room. Stunned, he surveyed the carnage.

"What happened?"

"You happened," said the doctor. "This is all your doing." Turning to Golovorez, he added, "You want my first born too? You can have him. This is my genius son, Nathan. The one who's been stealing the prescriptions."

"Is true, Nathan?" asked the Russian, looking the part of a disappointed suburban father whose son had totaled the family minivan.

"I have no idea what he's talking about."

"I see you are—what is expression?—chip off old block."

Golovorez held out his hand, squeezed Nathan's tightly, and twisted. Nathan dropped to his knees and then cork-screwed onto his back. Only when he began to wail did the Russian release him.

"Stealing is not good, Nathan. Nor lying. Business is based on developing relationships and building trust. Is like best-selling author Barry Bullshit says: Trust is like skeleton of business. When trust is broken, bones are broken too. Well, he didn't say that part. But it follows, no?

"But you are young still, Nathan. For you, maybe is still hope. Maybe you get away from bad influence of father who turns you into criminal and then rats you out. Maybe you go live with mother instead."

"It's his mother who made him what he is today."

"Is not mother. Is shit father who drags son into shit business. Into shit world of shit people. What is difference between you and me? Only one is I am not hypocrite. I never take oath not to harm."

As Golovorez tried to light another cigarette, his hands trembled so violently that he could not hit his target with the lighter flame. Tossing the unlit cigarette away, he stamped several times on the clock that lay near his feet, shattering the glass and wood exterior, dislodging and bending the pendulum, crushing not only the works but any hope of repair.

"Maybe you never live in shit place before, Dr. Robert. Now you know what is like."

Earth's gravitational force felt as if it had increased tenfold, rendering Dr. Rosen powerless to move from his armchair. What he saw all around him—a living room strewn with jagged bits of glass, plastic, wood, and clock innards, and a gap where the front door belonged—he could not process. Even his ability to speak had deserted him. He listened in silence to Nathan's accusations and lamentations:

"I can't believe you got me mixed up with Russian mobsters," cried the young man, still on his knees and rubbing his smarting wrist. "You were a terrible role model for me. You cheated on Mom and broke up the family. You made me grow up in an unstable environment where I was always caught in the middle. You did nothing to provide for my emotional needs. It's pretty pathetic when even a hired goon can see how deficient your parenting skills are. I'm going to live with Mom. At least there I won't get killed."

"Oh, I don't know about that. One of you will probably kill the other. But go ahead. You deserve each other. And this time, don't come running back here when she flushes your dope down the toilet. I can use some quiet here."

Dr. Rosen did not answer either his cellphone or landline when Tamika called to tell him that he had patients waiting in the office. Eventually, he bestirred himself to reply to the text she sent him: "accident. not hurt. cancel all appts." He set the cellphone facedown on the lamp table beside him. The device buzzed again, and he turned it off.

When Tamika came home that afternoon, the doctor was still in his armchair, and the door still lay atop the broken television screen. Her eyes, as she entered through the void lately filled by the front door, looked like those of a cartoon character, poised to pop out of their sockets.

"What happened here?"

"What happened is that my son is a thief, and he stole from the wrong people, and you were with him when he did it and did nothing to stop him."

"I ain't his fucking parent. I ain't nothing to him but his daddy's bimbo of the month."

She had endured a long, wearisome day of attempting, and mostly failing, to mollify all the patients whose appointments the doctor had instructed her to cancel. A male patient had threatened her over the telephone with bodily harm; a woman who had shown up early for her appointment had hinted, upon being turned away, that she might harm herself; another woman had sat down on the waiting room floor and cried for over an hour. Tamika, wanting nothing in the world at that moment as much as a long nap, shambled toward the bedroom.

On any other day, Dr. Rosen would have shouted back at her, but on this one, he had no stomach for a fight. What he needed was to restore some measure of order, some calm, to his life. Following her into the bedroom, he found her lying facedown on the bed, sobbing. He lay down beside her.

"Bimbo of the month? Who called you that? Nathan?"

She nodded.

"He says these things out of spite. I don't have a bimbo of the month. That's not the kind of person I am. Oh, maybe I was before I met you, but not anymore."

His life, he told her, had been spiraling out of control until she had entered it and given him the stability that he had lacked for so long. Maybe, he added, if he had found her sooner, he would never have made the foolish decision to get entangled with the Russians. He would terminate his partnership with them, he promised, at the first opportunity, and then the trips to the Peninsula Pain Center would end. He just needed a little more time. Making a clean break from people like them was hard.

Huddling against her, he began to grope her breasts and kiss her neck, and though she was weeping still, when he slipped his hand inside her panties, he found her ready. Frantically, they shed their clothes. He got on top and entered her with a sudden, violent thrust. Heaving and grunting, he came quickly—too quickly. While he lay upon her, panting, his dead weight pressing her into the mattress, she held on, her arms and legs locked around him. After a few minutes, he rolled off her and onto his back, stroked her cheek, and soon fell to snoring. She wondered: Did that fleeting post-coital touch on the cheek signify affection on his part, or was it just a reflex action? Did he need her as he said he did, or was she merely his bimbo of the month?

CHAPTER 7

The next day Tamika swept and vacuumed up the glass in the living room, piled the other debris in a corner, and arranged with a hauler to take it away. When the following Wednesday came around, she drove out to Queens to make the doctor's weekly delivery.

Three times Tamika drove around the block before parking the Jaguar, as she usually did, well down the street from the pain center. She sat for a few minutes, steeling herself, then hurried off toward the building.

The yellow paint on the walls of the waiting room was peeling. The room's furnishings consisted of a couple of end tables, a scuffed coffee table, and orange hard-plastic chairs arrayed in no discernable pattern. Most of the room lay in shadows, a buzzing, crackling LED fixture, recessed into the ceiling, providing the only illumination in the room. Adjacent to the fixture was a brown water stain shaped like Spain. Somewhere an air conditioning unit strained mightily, but the room felt like a sauna and smelled of mildew, cigarettes, and sweat.

A motley crowd occupied the plastic chairs. Many were age mates of Tamika, a few even younger. Some looked as though they had not slept indoors for a week, their faces emaciated, eyes rheumy, hair greasy, and clothes rumpled. At least a quarter of the people smoked, notwithstanding the no smoking sign. Several dozed, while others fidgeted, rocking in their chairs, their legs twitching. A young woman scratched at her forearms so furiously that she drew blood, while nearby a man hugged himself to keep his arms still. A middle-aged white man in a camo jacket banged on the locked bathroom door with his fists and shouted at the deserted reception desk, "Where the fuck is the goddamn key?"

Tamika stood in the center of the room clutching a manila envelope. A woman seated in a far corner, who occupied two chairs and whose rolls of exposed flesh were covered with red and pink blotches, gave her a hostile once-over. Others did likewise, and soon everyone's eyes, except those of the man banging on the bathroom door, were on Tamika.

"Who's she?" someone asked in a voice laden with suspicion.

"Bet she's a cop," another replied. "I'm getting out of here."

A door beside the reception desk swung open. From behind it emerged a heavily tattooed man with a shaved head. He wore a T-shirt emblazoned with an image of the Statue of Liberty.

"Mr. Tillman, please," said the newcomer to the man banging on the door. "You must stop this at once. Bathroom is out of order."

"It's been out of order for a goddamn month."

"I will remind Dr. Zhukov again. But now," he added, grabbing the other man's wrist, "you must take seat."

Grimacing, Mr. Tillman meekly obeyed. The tattooed man turned to Tamika.

"And how can I help you, young lady?"

"Dr. Rosen sent me. I have something for Dr. Zhukov."

"Ah, good. This is pleasant surprise. Come with me, please."

He guided her through the door from whence he had come. They continued down a narrow hallway to a dingy supply closet where columns of manila folders, piled crookedly on the floor, left little space for two people to stand. The door slammed shut behind them.

"Sorry we must meet in such place like this, but customers get nervous when they see stranger in waiting room. They are afraid of police, even though police have no reason to come here since Dr. Zhukov's business is completely honest and above-the-board."

"I'm not with the police."

"I believe you. You seem like honest person. Too honest to be police. I am Alexey Ivanovich Golovorez. It is great pleasure to meet you."

He shook her hand and held on for too long before releasing her. The way his gaze lingered on her breasts discomfited her even more. She was sweating, for she had worn her customary hoodie, not having anticipated that she would find herself stuck in a superheated closet.

"And you are?"

"Tamika."

"Tamika. Tamika is pretty name. Pretty name for pretty girl. Maybe Dr. Robert he sends you to me as present? Yes? No?"

His guttural laughter revolted her.

"He just sent me to deliver the scripts," she said, thrusting the envelope at Golovorez. "Then I have to go to work. Dr. Rosen's expecting me in the office."

"Of course, of course. I will not keep you. But is no need to be afraid of me. I am perfect gentleman."

While he counted the prescription blanks, she backed toward the door.

"Good. All is correct. It looks like Dr. Robert has learned his lesson."

He handed her an envelope. With her free hand, she reached behind her and groped for the doorknob. It would not turn in either direction.

In Golovorez's crooked grin, she saw a threat.

"You need key to open. To get inside and out, you need key. What is hurry anyway?"

"Dr. Rosen is . . ."

"I know. He is expecting you. He can wait. Don't you want to count money?"

"I'm sure it's all there."

"You are very trusting. I like that in woman. I think you and I will get along well. Between us there is already trust, no?"

"No."

"No? That makes me sad. But maybe you change your mind someday. Anyway, is no reason to be afraid. I will let you go back to Dr. Robert, even though he is big *mudak* and does not deserve you."

He reached into all four of his trouser pockets in turn, but each time his hand came out empty.

"Now where is key?"

As if contemplating the mystery, he cupped his chin in his hand. When he opened his hand to find the key lying flat on his palm, he feigned surprise.

"Strange, no? Like magic."

"Will you please let me out now?"

"Such impatience."

Golovorez saw her out through a side door that opened on an alley.

"It has been great pleasure to meet you, Tamika. I hope we will become good friends."

When he offered his hand once again, she did not reciprocate. He looked disappointed.

"Where are your manners, Tamika? Little things like smile, handshake, friendly greeting—they make life so much more pleasant. Don't you think?"

"Locking me in a closet ain't good manners."

"I mean no harm. Is for security. You have to be careful in this business. But, as I tell Dr. Robert, business and personal are two different things. In business, anything goes. Off duty, I am different person. I am true gentleman. You will see as you get to know me better. Maybe I take you to dinner sometime. I know nice Russian place on West Fifty-Seventh. Is almost like home. Such *blinchik* as to make you weep with joy."

He kissed his fingertips.

Tamika hurried up the street to the Jaguar. As she started the car, she felt a surge of nausea. She let the engine idle for a couple of minutes, the air conditioner on full blast. Prying the Jaguar out of its tight parking space required so much maneuvering—inching forward and back, cutting the wheel left and right—that she began to feel ill again. She tapped the rear bumper against the Ford pickup in the space behind her and the front one against the rust-eaten Chevy ahead. Reversing again, she backed a wheel up onto the curb. The scraping noise she heard as she steered the Jaguar back into traffic told her that the side of the car had clipped the Chevy. Cursing Dr. Rosen, Tamika pounded her fists against the steering wheel.

CHAPTER 8

Dr. Rosen's private office occupied the second floor of a brownstone that dated from the 1890s. Though the cost of decorating pained him, he had deferred in almost every particular to the recommendations of the professional he hired, as she had a much clearer sense than he of the expectations that the clientele of an Upper West Side psychiatrist would bring to the office. The waiting room was accoutered with potted aloe, spider, and **Dieffenbachia plants;** plush beige armchairs; and hardwood tables, upon which rested stacks of New Yorkers. Reproductions of Degas's dancers and Renoir's water lilies adorned the walls. The classical offerings of WQXR streamed in from four discrete wall speakers. Scents of essential oils—lavender, eucalyptus, or cinnamon bark, depending on the day—permeated the room. Against the far wall, Tamika sat behind a curved cherry wood reception desk. The inner office boasted a mahogany desk with a green blotter and a rosewood-and-silver pen and pen holder set. The doctor sat behind the desk in a black leather swivel chair, opposite two leather wingback chairs. A massive bookshelf supported row upon row of medical reference books, along with other weighty tomes that the doctor would never read but that suggested erudition and well-roundedness: leather-bound volumes of Freud, studies of medical history, a biography of Pasteur, an edition of Shakespeare's tragedies, Gibbon's *Decline and Fall*.

Dr. Rosen classified his patients as an airline does its passengers. While all enjoyed the first-class accommodations of his office, the service varied greatly. He had mostly abandoned talk therapy for med checks years earlier, having come to regard the former as excessively labor-intensive, inefficient, and demoralizing. The sorrows, griefs, fears, hatreds, and obsessions of which his patients unburdened themselves had become too heavy for him to bear. To his economy-class patients—mainly commuters from the outer boroughs, as well as the odd Egyptian or two from Jersey City—he gave fifteen minutes each, at most, and, inevitably, refills of the same antidepressants they were already taking. He had Tamika double- and sometimes triple-book them. For every one of those losers he saw, he had one or two others in the waiting room on standby. To his Upper West Side peers, whom he sometimes encountered at Zabar's and usually prescribed benzodiazepines for anxiety, he allowed twenty minutes. He would on occasion allot a little extra time to the stay-at-home moms, particularly the young, attractive ones, who so desperately craved some adult conversation in the middle of a weekday. He lavished his time much more freely upon his dozen or so first-class clients (he viewed them as such, rather than as patients): corporate lawyers, CEOs, investment bankers, hedge fund managers, developers, and a cable news producer. These clients, mostly male, flaunted the accouterments—Ferraris, yachts, trophy wives, penthouses overlooking Central Park, and mansions in the Hamptons—that Dr. Rosen desired and, in his view, deserved. Paradoxically, the strenuous efforts the doctor exerted for these men yielded less in the way of results than his desultory sessions with the lower orders. The sociopathy and narcissism that predominated in his prized cohort made most of the individuals therein impossible to treat.

From time to time, Tamika would remind him his business model had some flaws.

"You lost six patients in just the last month, and you're not getting new ones to replace them. You should see what they're saying about you on Yelp. 'Worst. Doctor. Ever.' 'I'd give him

zero stars if I could.' 'Doesn't pay attention when I talk.'
'Doesn't care.' 'Forgets what medications I'm on.'"

"Well, those are the patients I don't care about. I'm better
off without them wasting my time."

Besides, Kellyanne, the office manager, assured him that
all was well.

While Alexey Golovorez had Tamika detained in a closet at
the pain center, three economy-class patients, all booked for
10:30, sat in Dr. Rosen's waiting room: a sobbing Rite Aid
store manager from Hoboken bearing the burden of caring for
two children and a father with Alzheimer's, a hulking teenaged boy who had assaulted a teacher at his prep school and
grudgingly chosen treatment as an alternative to expulsion,
and a spectral-looking man dying of prostate cancer at fifty-
two. Kellyanne, meanwhile, bantered with a drug rep who,
while also waiting to see Dr. Rosen, was trying to entice her to
join him for a nice dinner at his employer's expense.

Inside his office, the doctor sat alone, caught up in a frustrating telephone conversation with Pat McKinley. The offer
of $1.25 million that Pat had conveyed to Mrs. Agnello on the
doctor's behalf had evoked laughter from D.L. Sheridan III,
who countered by raising the ante to $3 million.

"All right if I counter with $2 million?"

"Where am I gonna get a million from to pay them out of
pocket? One-and-a-half tops, and I can't even afford that. And
the settlement has to be sealed. That old hag really wants my
blood, doesn't she? How the hell does she afford someone like
Sheridan anyway? He must charge three times what you do."

Pat sighed.

"A little more cooperation on your end with the billing records might generate some good will. Dan thinks you're not
turning them over because you're hiding something. He's
threatening to subpoena them. If we can get that issue out of
the way, we might just be able to sit down and work something
out. Assuming there's nothing hinky in the billing, of course."

"I have nothing to hide."

"Good. So you tell me. How do you want to proceed?"

"Tell him one-and-a-half. Or else we go to trial."

"Have you listened to a word I've said? We're not negotiating from a position of strength here."

"One-and-a-half. And if you can't get it done, I'll find someone who can."

"Fair enough. Oh, and in case you need it, I know someone who specializes in defending Medicare fraud."

"Fuck you, Pat."

"Love you too."

The crying store manager proved difficult to move along. She kept Dr. Rosen for twenty-five minutes, by which time, the 10:45s and two of the 11:00s had arrived.

He recovered some of the lost time with the surly boy, who mainly communicated by snorts and eye rolls and never took his full fifteen minutes. As he did every week, the doctor obliged the boy by writing him a prescription for Ritalin.

"Same time next week?"

The patient shrugged.

The dying man, a long-time Upper West Side resident, had dropped from middle to economy class in the doctor's reckoning as his condition worsened. Withdrawn, morose, apathetic, he demanded less time and attention with each passing week.

"Good morning, Mr. uh . . ."

"Wasserman. Herb Wasserman. I should be easy to remember. I'm the dying one."

Having plucked the wrong folder from his filing cabinet, Dr. Rosen had before him the case notes he had written up on an anorexic female patient in her early thirties. To fumble around now in search of the correct folder would make him look unprofessional. He would press on instead. A little self-deprecating humor might help.

"Of course. I was just having a senior moment there."

"Not the first time. Even though you're not a senior."

"How are you feeling this morning, Mr. Wasserman?"

"Like I'm about to die."

"Have you been having suicidal thoughts?"

"That's funny."

"I'm sorry?"

"I doubt that. I'll tell you what, Doctor. I think maybe I should just be on my way. I'm a little short on time."

Mr. Wasserman stood up. His legs wobbled, and he braced himself against his chair.

"I don't understand. Is there something that's upsetting you today?"

"For a shrink, there seems to be an awful lot about people that you don't understand."

The patient turned around and shuffled toward the door.

"What about your prescription?"

"I don't need it."

"You said it was helping you."

"It can't help now."

"You can't stop it all at once. You have to taper off. Look, before you make a decision like this, you really need to think it over. Why don't we talk about it next week?"

Mr. Wasserman did not look back.

Unmoved, the doctor watched him leave. Having long ago grown weary, after more than two decades of practice, of the vocation that he had chosen, Dr. Rosen had little sympathy to spare anymore for even those patients who, like Mr. Wasserman, came to him in genuine distress. For the rest—the ones who spent their time with him whining, ranting, bemoaning, rationalizing, excusing themselves everything and their spouses, parents, children, and lovers nothing—he had even less. They filled the office with a noxious cloud of misery. Enduring even fifteen minutes with many of them had become intolerable. Worse, because they brought with them the expectation that he would somehow fix their disordered lives, when he failed, as any mortal would have, they lashed out at him. They vented their rage in one-star Yelp reviews laced with slander and vitriol. Sometimes, he thought he would have done better to have gone into a field such as radiology in which he would have pored over ghostly images of body parts all day long, but no flesh-and-blood patient would ever have crossed his threshold.

He decided to give his agent a call. Maybe by now she would have turned up another gig for him.

CHAPTER 9

She had found him a booking.

"It's another morning show."

"Where?"

"Salisbury, Maryland."

"Where the hell is that?"

"It's on the Eastern Shore."

"I can't believe this. After I've been on in Chicago, third largest market in the country, you give me freaking Salisbury, Maryland."

"It's a CBS affiliate. It's the biggest station out there. It's Delmarva's leading source for news, sports, and weather."

"Big whoop."

"And while you're out there in Salisbury, you can see the cathedral."

"What cathedral?"

"That's a joke. Ha ha."

"Ha, ha. I don't know. I'll have to think about it."

"Well, don't think too long. They want an answer by tomorrow."

He called Barry to voice his displeasure. His coach urged him to take the gig.

"It's a tough business, bro. Things don't always move in a straight line. The important thing is you keep getting your name out there. Even a small market's better than no market. If you like, I'll ride down there with you. We'll make it a bachelors' road trip, bro. It'll be fun."

#

Over the course of the five-hour drive, only Barry had fun, swigging Jack Daniels in the car and snorting cocaine in rest stop men's rooms. With Dr. Rosen driving, Barry took charge of the stereo. Mostly he played hip-hop at a deafening volume, drumming on the dashboard to a rhythm of his own. In Delaware, however, he switched to a talk radio program hosted by a right-wing screecher. The monologue oscillated between screeds against deviants who used gender-neutral personal pronouns and did not respect the sanctity of girls' bathrooms and prayer-like paeans to President Dreck. Dr. Rosen, who had no more than a passing interest in politics, found the pundit's rapid-fire falsetto delivery even more irritating than Barry's drumming.

"Why do you listen to this stuff?"

"It's research, bro. I'm thinking about doing something a little different for my next book. I already have a title in mind: *Dreck! How to Lead Like a President*. Or something along those lines. I have to work in the word *secrets* and a number. There have already been a bunch of books written about him. There are gonna be a whole lot more. Best to get mine in before the market's totally saturated. This could be a blockbuster. Really big. And I got a leg up. I know someone who's close to him. Like really close."

"Who's that?" asked Dr. Rosen skeptically.

"I wish I could tell you, but it's all very hush-hush. I don't want to get in trouble with the Secret Service."

"Right."

"You know I almost got on *Find It! Flip It!* back in the day as one of his apprentice flippers. Dreck liked me, but I ended up on the cutting room floor thanks to that idiot of a producer. You ever watch the show?"

Dr. Rosen yawned. Barry had a lot of *almost* stories. He had told the doctor this one too many times.

"I may have caught an episode or two. I don't have time to watch a lot of TV."

"You can still find the show on YouTube. You should watch some episodes. It's amazing what you'll discover. Learning about the Motivated Seller Principle turned my whole life around."

"The what principle?"

"Motivated Seller. To make a profit flipping houses, you need to buy low. The best way to do that is to find a motivated seller—some schmuck who's behind on his mortgage, who just lost a job, who's going through a divorce. By the time Dreck would finish squeezing them, they were practically begging him to take their dump of a house off their hands at half the asking price. Like he was doing them a favor. Sometimes he'd have sellers from previous episodes come back on the show to give testimonials. He'd rob them blind, and they would thank him for it on TV. It was unbelievable. I've never seen anything like it."

"I have," replied the doctor. "I see it all the time in my practice. There are abusers, and there are victims. The abusers are really hard to treat. A guy like Dreck—he's never going to change. He likes things just as they are."

"Exactly, bro. Why should he change? It's like he said to me on the set of *Find It! Flip It!*—I'll never forget it—he said: 'Barry, I'll let you in on a little secret. In this life, you're either predator or prey. There's no middle ground.' Dreck is the ultimate predator. King of the jungle. He's strong and fierce. That's what people want in a leader. I bet you were surprised when he got elected. I wasn't because I had been watching the show."

"Right. Whatever. You mind if I change the station? There's something about the pitch of this guy's voice. I just can't stand it."

"What's eating you, bro?"

"If you want to know the truth, Salisbury is what's eating me. It's not exactly *The Today Show*."

"You want to be on *The Today Show*? You got to work your way up to it. Here's a homework assignment for you: Watch *Find it! Flip it!* Watch every episode you can find. You just might learn something."

While the Jaguar jerked its way through clogged traffic, Barry rhapsodized about his book idea. Dr. Rosen brooded behind the wheel, troubled by a growing suspicion that Golo-vorez's soubriquet—Barry Bullshit—fit the man. By the time they reached Salisbury, the doctor had a pounding headache.

Owing to the meagerness of the appearance fee offered by the station, Dr. Rosen, who while en route to Chicago had boasted that he would never fly economy class again, decided to economize on his Salisbury accommodations. He booked rooms at a place called the USA Motor Lodge, on Route 13, just outside town. The motel had seen better days—in the 1970s. Dr. Rosen's room smelled strongly of insect spray. The screen in the front window had several holes in it. The air conditioning unit sounded like a taxiing airliner. Either the maid had done a poor job of cleaning the tub, or the grime had become too deeply embedded in the acrylic to remove. In places, the grout between the bathroom tiles had begun to crumble.

Owing to fatigue from the long drive and the paucity of dining options in the area, Dr. Rosen and Barry had dinner at an Olive Garden in a shopping center near the motel. Afterward, Barry wanted to go in search of a "tittie bar."

"Barry, I'm wiped out. And besides, I want to go over my presentation again tonight."

"Come on, bro. It'll do you good. You're too tense. Best thing you can do for yourself tonight is relax, have some fun. Believe me. Have I steered you wrong yet? What would you have done in Chicago without me to calm you down when you were having that meltdown with the executive producer?"

"I'd have done fine, just like I did with that obnoxious host in Columbus. I know how to handle myself on camera."

Still, Dr. Rosen relented.

The dancers at The Tender Trap were all of a type, and not one that the doctor favored: skinny, small-breasted, pale, and heavily tattooed. They looked bored. Only two other patrons were present when Barry and the doctor entered. Stocky, bearded men, similar enough in appearance that they might have been brothers, one wore a red cap bearing the slogan DRECK FOR AMERICA!©, while the other sported one that bore the John Deere logo. Within fifteen minutes or so, the men had left, and Dr. Rosen wanted to do the same. Barry, however, had become engrossed in a conversation with a dancer who had just finished her turn on the platform to the right of the bar and had bought her a drink. As she perched herself on Barry's lap, Dr. Rosen sat beside them, nursing his beer and his anger. When the dancer took her next turn on the platform, he said, "Come on, Barry. Let's get out of here."

"She gets off in another hour, bro. I'm thinking that maybe she'll get me off after that."

"I left my prescription pad at home, so if you catch something, I can't give you oxy to ease the pain."

Reluctantly, Barry, after a final wave at the dancer, went along.

A beer- and fatigue-induced drowsiness nearly caused Dr. Rosen to drive off the road on the way back to the motel. He pulled over to the shoulder, handed Barry the keys to the Jaguar, and promptly fell asleep in the passenger seat. In the parking lot of the USA Motor Lodge, Barry shook him awake. Reentering his room proved a challenge for the doctor. He needed several tries to unlock the door, jiggling his key card in the slot until at last he hit the sweet spot, and the tiny light on the doorplate flashed green. Still the door refused to yield, until he bulled it open with his shoulder. He stumbled to the bed. Just before dropping off to sleep, he remembered that Barry still had his car keys, but he could not rouse himself to go ask for them back. During the night, he woke briefly and heard, or thought he heard, the sounds of sex in the next room—Barry's room.

On the way back to his room the next morning after a breakfast of stale bagels and watery coffee in a tiny dining nook off the reception area, Dr. Rosen saw that the Jaguar's right taillight had been shattered sometime during the night, and the bumper was scuffed. Having just had the gouge on the door left by Tamika's scrape in Queens with the Chevy repaired, the doctor was furious.

"Barry, what the hell?"

"I don't know, bro. Someone must have backed into it or something."

"Did you go out again after you dropped me and bring that dancer back here?"

"Not me, bro. I went right to bed."

As he had no proof to the contrary, Dr. Rosen let the matter drop. Adding to his pique though, when he tried to get back into his room, his key card did not work, no matter how much he manipulated it. He went back to the reception area and, finding no one there, brought his hand down hard upon the bell atop the desk. For ten minutes, the increasingly agitated doctor pounded on that bell until the proprietor, an elderly Indian man, came shuffling up to the desk. Back to Dr. Rosen's room the two men went, the older one falling farther behind the impatient doctor with each step. The proprietor inserted the key card, turned the handle, and pushed, and the door swung open.

"See? No problem," he said, handing the card back to Dr. Rosen.

Owing to the delay caused by the recalcitrant lock, Dr. Rosen had to skip the jumping-patting-blub-blub-blubbing warm-up ritual he had run through with Barry in Chicago. He had just enough time to give his host the briefest overview of his presentation before the two of them went before the cameras. The studio set, a much smaller, more austere one than in

Chicago, consisted of two plush chairs with a round table be-tween them. There was no audience.

Dr. Rosen gamely began his talk, but he felt unmoored in the mostly vacant space; lines that had elicited powerful reactions from the studio audience in Chicago sounded flat to him with nobody laughing or expressing shock. The host, who looked like the twin sister of the one in Chicago, proved far less capable. She seemed to have difficulty following his presentation. At one point, she spoke about her own bad experience with oxycodone.

"My doctor gave it to me after I hurt my knee skiing. All day long, I was itching myself."

"Itching yourself?"

She scratched at one arm and then the other.

"Scratching, you mean? Well, that's not the same thing. What you had was a bad reaction. I'm talking about addiction."

"It was terrible. I'm not surprised that some people die from it."

"Yes, well, people do die from opioid overdoses. A lot of people. But I haven't heard of any cases where they scratched themselves to death."

He had not had time to coordinate with her the presentation of his prop—the blueberries—and as he poured them into his hand, he lost his grip on the container. It fell, scattering the pills all over the floor. He raced through the remainder of his talk.

"Well, that was a freaking disaster," he said to Barry in the Jaguar afterward.

"You didn't have that Chicago energy this time, bro. It's like your heart wasn't in it."

"It's Salisbury. What do you expect?"

"Wrong attitude, bro. You gotta give it your best shot no matter where you are. You never know who's watching. One time, I had this gig in Bemidji, Minnesota. Talk about the middle of nowhere. It was January. Well, who wants to go trekking out to Bemidji, Minnesota, in January, right? But I thought, ah, what the hell? Might as well give it a shot. Turned out to be one of the best decisions I ever made. There was a CBS producer watching the show . . ."

"Will you please shut up?" Dr. Rosen thought—but never said aloud—over and over for the next five hours.

That night he released his pent-up anger on Tamika. Reviewing his schedule for the following day, he found that she had neglected to cancel an appointment with a troublesome patient of whom he wanted to rid himself. True, what he had communicated to Tamika was not so much an instruction as an aspiration, but she should have recognized his intent.

CHAPTER 10

His treatment of his economy-class patients notwithstanding, Dr. Rosen mostly conducted his private practice in a manner that would not attract undue scrutiny from health authorities or law enforcement. In the past, he had had affairs with patients, but a bad breakup with one who had threatened to file a complaint against him with the Department of Health had prompted him to change his ways. Ever since, he had maintained, for the most part, a proper clinical distance in his interactions with even the most attractive and overtly sexual female patients. In shutting down his drug-rehabilitation clinic, he had rid himself of the squirrely types who came to him to feed their oxy habits and lurked about the office, scaring off the private patients.

One of those squirrely types, however, had refused to go away. She called herself Boadecia Wilde, though her driver's license gave her name as Anne Smith. Sporting a thick shock of neon purple hair that she haphazardly brushed from right to left, she had a long, thin face with a milky complexion and lips that desperately needed some balm. She had an exotropia of her right eye so pronounced as to leave part of her pupil obscured. Though she eschewed makeup, she wore a stud on the side of her left nostril and another in the cleft beneath her nose, and she had numerous rings of varying sizes attached to the cartilage and lobes of both ears. Tattoos ran up and down her spindly arms and legs: roses, tulips, vines, and a crescent moon. The halter tops that she often wore allowed her to show off the enormous zipper tattoo on her belly.

Before he became her oxy supplier, Dr. Rosen had treated her with Adderall for ADHD. He also diagnosed her with borderline personality disorder, as he did most of his female patients and, for that matter, most women of his acquaintance. He suspected that she might have anorexia or bulimia as well, though she insisted that she ate as much as she felt like eating, and if people thought she had a disorder, well, that was their problem. By her third visit, she had begun to hint that she wanted something more than Adderall. She complained of chronic pain in her neck, a consequence of a fall she had suffered while performing gymnastics in high school. He doubted her story, as he did most everything she told him, for when he asked about the type, severity, and location of the pain, she answered evasively or sought to change the subject. Nevertheless, he prescribed the oxy, and she paid him in cash. Where the money for the sessions and the prescriptions came from, he had no idea. She had no job, and though her father managed a hedge fund, she insisted that he had cut her off—another claim that Dr. Rosen had difficulty believing.

When he first broached the subject of her going to the Peninsula Pain Center for her oxycodone, she became enraged. Why, she demanded to know, should she schlep all the way out to some den of muggers and rapists in Queens when she lived just a few blocks from the doctor's office? Besides, how would she get there? Her eye condition, she claimed, prevented her from driving. Take the subway? Was he kidding? The subway freaked her out. She couldn't stand being pressed upon in the middle of a crowded car, and besides, the stations all smelled like pee.

Then, one day, he tried another tack: an offer of employment.

"I have this guy in Baltimore I work with named Eric Kleinzach. He used to be a pharmacist up here. I'd send him my oxy patients. I still do some business with him from time to time."

He proposed that if Boadecia would serve as his courier, taking scripts down to Baltimore and bringing back cash, he would give her a free 120-pill script for each trip and pay her train fare and other expenses. The arrangement, he said, was a win-win: He could do more business with his partner there, and she would at last have gainful employment.

The plan, he knew, had some flaws—chiefly that its success would hinge upon Boadecia's reliability, honesty, and discretion. Whether it succeeded, though, mattered less to Dr. Rosen than the hope of having her out of his hair once and for all. With luck, she would soon grow tired of the arrangement, and he would be quit of her.

She showed him what she thought of his offer by whipping off her top to reveal the zipper tattoo in its full glory. It snaked up between her breasts, which looked to the doctor like anthills topped with pencil erasers, and then opened outward.

"I open my heart to you, and you want to send me to fucking Baltimore."

He had not seen such hatred in a person's eyes since his last encounter with Liz.

Unfazed, he swiveled his chair sideways and began scrolling through the messages on his phone.

"When you're ready to put your top back on and act like an adult, let me know, and we'll resume. By the way, I've seen better."

A wad of spit caught him on the cheek. Still uncovered, clutching her top in her right hand, she bolted from the office and sprinted through the waiting room, startling Kellyanne, Tamika, and three economy-class patients, all booked for the same time, and all of whom had shown up early in the hope of grabbing an extra minute or two of the doctor's time. The sight of the topless Boadecia running wild quickly disabused them of such fantasies. One by one, they followed her out the door.

The episode would have much more far-reaching consequences for the doctor than the loss of the three patients, which, at the time, he thought a fair price to pay for ridding himself of Boadecia. As heedless of her legal exposure as that of her breasts, she proceeded directly from the scene of her humiliation, crying all the way, to the headquarters of the Twentieth Precinct. There she handed over three prescriptions she had purchased from Dr. Rosen, one for oxycodone, one for Subutex, and one for Adderall. Among many other things, she told the officer who interviewed her of the doctor's job offer. The interstate trafficking between New York and Baltimore made the case a federal one, and she rode downtown to the FBI's New York office in a police cruiser.

Over several hours, four different agents interviewed her. Weary of answering the same questions over and over again, Boadecia amused herself by adding some color to her story. In its final iteration that day, Dr. Rosen's practice had become a virtual dispensary, where drooling addicts gathered early in the morning outside the Amsterdam Avenue brownstone, menacing bystanders and pushing and elbowing one another to get a better place in line to buy scripts.

The task of sifting through Boadecia's tales to glean from them a close enough approximation to the truth to provide evidentiary value ultimately fell to Special Agent W.E. Hardin, a tall, rangy Ohioan with a high forehead, a pate shaded as if with a pencil by a fine layer of salt-and-pepper fuzz, and a phlegmatic manner. In the mercurial and attention-challenged Boadecia, he did not initially see very promising informant material. Having no concept of either evidence or narrative and little regard for the law, she could hardly be counted on to elicit from the doctor anything useful. Over time, though, Agent Hardin's assessment improved somewhat. She did have a facility with gadgetry and quickly grasped the art of deploying a hidden camera. Moreover, her disorganized speech and seeming inability to modulate its volume might, paradoxically, prove an asset. If just fifteen minutes of listening to her and staring into her wall eye could leave Agent Hardin feeling vertiginous, surely she could get the doctor to lower his guard. Also counting in her favor was her enthusiasm for the task, though at times it became excessive. Yes, Agent Hardin patiently explained, if she did her job well, she would likely get to see the bastard in an orange jumpsuit, but no, she could not slap the handcuffs on him herself. The FBI had trained professionals to do that. Yes, she should be proud of the role she would play in shutting down Dr. Rosen's illicit business and keeping him from hurting anyone else, but no, she could not tell her friends that she was a confidential informant for the FBI. The work of a confidential informant had to remain confidential.

After happily handing her off to a couple of undercover agents for training, he began familiarizing himself with his target by scouring Dr. Rosen's website, devoting particular attention to the videos of the doctor's television appearances. The glint the doctor had in his eyes when he spoke into the camera and his barely suppressed smirk suggested to the FBI man that thrill seeking, as much as money, lay at the bottom of the business. Dr. Rosen seemed to revel in publicly denouncing his peers as criminals while secretly committing the crimes of which he accused them. Agent Hardin had busted many of his type before. Their hubris often made the task easy.

CHAPTER 11

In fact, the doctor did need the income his illicit side enterprise brought him. He would soon find out just how much.

With Kellyanne away enjoying life in a rented villa in Tuscany for three weeks, Dr. Rosen, wanting to avoid the expense of hiring a temp, reluctantly allowed Tamika to fill in for her. Away from the prying eyes of her enemy, Tamika took upon herself the task of scouring the books. She began at 8 o'clock on a Monday morning. A little over two hours later, she told the doctor, "Kellyanne is robbing you blind."

"You don't know what you're talking about."

Only when Tamika began to lay before him the evidence of Kellyanne's malfeasance did he change his view. *The New Yorker* no longer came because Kellyanne had marked the subscription renewal bill as paid without ever having sent in the payment. Payments allegedly made to vendors exceeded the invoice amounts by two or three times. Countless copays had been received but never deposited in the bank. Various insurers and the US taxpayers had provided reimbursements for sessions that the doctor had with patients whom he ought to have remembered, if only because of their unusual names: Ben Resor Tor, Ben Roter Ros, Ben Torre Ros, Ben Rose Torr, Ben Oster Orr, Ben Orest Orr, Ben Terr Roos, Eben Torr Ros.

"I see what she did," said Tamika. "What you call that when you take a word and scramble the letters around?"

"I don't know. An ana . . . An ana something."

A quick search on her phone provided the answer.

"An anagram. It's all anagrams of your name. You see? Eben Torr Ros. You got your *r-o-s* in Ros, your *e* and *n* in

Eben. That's Rosen. Two other *r*'s, an *s*, and a *t* in Torr. Then you got your *b* in Eben. That's Robert."

"It's coincidence. Kellyanne isn't smart enough to think of something like that."

"She's smart enough to steal a million dollars from you."

"Don't you have something to do other than annoy the hell out of me?"

When Tamika left the room, Dr. Rosen sat down at his desk and pored over the printouts. Down the list he went, unscrambling every name, and all of them came up Robert Rosen. Kellyanne had not merely stolen a fortune from him but had reveled in her betrayal. He felt no gratitude toward Tamika, however, who in exposing the office manager's misdeeds had inadvertently rubbed another shaker full of salt into his wounds. That a twenty-year-old receptionist with a high school diploma could prove so much more perspicacious than he would have been unthinkable twenty-four hours before.

The auditor he brought in two days later found that in estimating the scale of Kellyanne's thievery, Tamika had likely erred on the conservative side. Kellyanne had stolen $663,000 over the last three years and likely at least that much during her first five years in Dr. Rosen's employ. Many of the records from that period, however, had vanished. For one of those years, there were none at all.

"Wow," the auditor repeated over and over again, as if in awe. "She's a smart one, all right. She knew what she was doing. And the anagrams. Wow! And all this time, you had no idea?"

Later that day, Dr. Rosen called Kellyanne in Tuscany.

"You . . . You thieving bitch!" he spluttered. "You've stolen over a million dollars from me."

"I have no idea what you're talking about," she replied with a maddening insouciance.

"I have proof. I have the numbers. It's all there in black and white."

"I have numbers too. Yours are wrong."

"No, you're wrong. I had an audit done. It confirmed what I suspected all along. You've been embezzling from me since the day I hired you."

"Anyone can pay an auditor to give them the result they want. Even if what they want is to have their paranoid delusion confirmed."

"Now you're gaslighting me."

"Gaslighting? I don't even know what that is."

"Yes, you do. You know exactly what you're doing."

"You're just raving now. You're being irrational. I can't talk to you when you're like this. Goodbye."

When he called her the following day, she dropped her pretense of innocence and took a more aggressive tack. Did he think she did not know that he sold oxycodone scripts in the office for cash? For that matter, she knew all about his phony pain center business too, and as for the nursing home patients he treated posthumously, he had had her handle that billing too. The feds took Medicare, Medicaid, and insurance fraud pretty seriously, to say nothing of drug trafficking. If he tried to turn her in, he might just spend the rest of his own life in prison. Of course, he had a choice. He could make this a win-win. Silence would benefit both parties, and a suitable severance package could buy hers. A one-time payment of $250,000, say, in the form of an international wire transfer would do nicely. She loved Tuscany and could happily stay there a very long time. With $250,000, she might even think about settling there, and he would never have to hear from her again.

"I won't give in to blackmail."

"Blackmail? After all the illegal things you forced me to do, you accuse me of blackmail? How dare you?"

"Forced you? I forced you? How in the world do you . . . ?"

"When you're ready to talk to me like a civilized person, we'll discuss terms. For now, goodbye."

Many more phone calls followed over the next couple of days. Chastened, the doctor tried a more conciliatory approach, pleading poverty. Kellyanne, however, held firm in her demands for the first forty-eight hours, motivated, Dr. Rosen suspected, at least as much by the pleasure she derived from toying with him as by any realistic hope of extorting $250,000 that she well knew he did not have. In the end, she settled for a promise of $10,000 and a glowing letter of recommendation that, upon her return, would enable her to find another employer from whom to embezzle. Dr. Rosen vowed to himself that he would never pay her a penny, though he would happily provide the most flowery of testimonials in order to rid himself of her.

He had a more immediate concern: keeping the lights on in his office. In one of Kellyanne's desk drawers, Tamika found a stack of past-due bills and collection notices. One of the latter, from Con Edison, threatened to cut off the electricity if the bill, two months in arrears, were not paid five days hence. The amount exceeded the available funds in the dedicated account by $247.53. Dr. Rosen would have to make up the difference from his own savings.

Clearly, he needed to cut his office expenses. Could he still afford Tamika?

CHAPTER 12

A phone message from his agent offered a flicker of hope, until Dr. Rosen called her back and learned that the gig she had turned up for him was in Bismarck, North Dakota.

"Bismarck? You give me Bismarck? How did I go from Chicago, the third largest media market in the country, to Salisbury and Bismarck?"

"It's a tough business. And to be honest, that brouhaha in the studio with the executive producer didn't do you any good. That woman knows a lot of people in the industry. Word gets around."

"Well, I'm not interested. For what they're offering, it's not worth the time and effort. I have a practice to run. With the appointments I'll have to cancel, I'll end up losing money."

"Suit yourself, but you'll regret this. These opportunities don't come around every day. If I hear of something else, I'll give you a call."

"Don't bother. I'll be my own agent. I can do the job better than you."

"Knock yourself out."

Dr. Rosen attributed his dry spell not only to the agent's indolence, but also to the slapdash video that Barry had produced, with the shaky-handed Tamika as cinematographer. Without any training or experience in matters having to do with camera positioning, lighting, or tracking, Tamika had filled the screen with random arms, legs, and backs of heads. In close-ups, faces took on strange dimensions, with ballooning foreheads, gaping mouths, elongated noses and chins. Barry did minimal editing, aside from clumsily inserting some overlong close-ups, probably recorded later, in which he plugged his coaching and mentoring programs. To his credit, he had not included any scenes from the hotel room and just a few seconds of the atavistic celebration in the parking garage, the insufficient light and consequent obscuring of faces rendering most of that footage useless. Barry had not seen fit, though, to edit out the argument with the executive producer, which the doctor thought unfairly showed him in a bad light, both literally and metaphorically, or the application of the fake hair, which he now found embarrassing. The video had stayed up on Barry's website for just over a week, garnering but twenty-seven views, eight of them by Dr. Rosen himself.

"Look, bro," Barry told him. "It's not my fault. You said the girl knew how to use a camera. What she gave me was a hot mess. You think Michelangelo could have painted the Sistine Chapel with Sherwin-Williams?"

"It would have been better not to put it up at all. It made me look like an amateur."

Late that night, still seething, Dr. Rosen turned on his computer and Googled Barry's name. The suspicion had grown in his mind that his erstwhile mentor might be grabbing all the prime gigs for himself. What he saw made him wish that he had a Golovorez he could call upon to exact a sanguinary revenge. Appearing on a morning show in St. Louis, Barry, dubbing himself Mr. Sober, had appropriated the doctor's hangover-cure talk almost to the letter, even using the same Bloody Mary recipe.

After leaving a message on Barry's voicemail filled with obscenities and threats to sue, Dr. Rosen began to pace up and down his living room. He felt a sudden burning in his gullet, far more intense than any heartburn he had ever experienced. Barely chewing four chewable antacid tablets, he sat down in his easy chair. The burning intensified. A second dose of antacids proved as ineffective as the first. The pain spread up and down his chest. The effort required just to rise from his chair left him feeling as if he had run a sprint. The room began to whirl around him, and to steady himself, he grabbed the back of the chair. Staggering out the door, he took the elevator down to the lobby and hailed a cab.

He spent much of the night on a gurney in the emergency room, rendered immobile by the electrodes fastened to his chest and the IV line stuck into his forearm. Doctors, nurses, and technicians hovered about him, drawing his blood and asking the same questions over and over. Then a new, more urgent case would come in, and they would rush off and leave him abandoned. In the quiet intervals between critical cases, the doctors and nurses chatted about the stock market and home renovations.

Often during the course of his medical training, Dr. Rosen had seen death up close, but until this night, it had remained, somehow, an abstraction for him, a thing that happened to other people, to strangers. The possibility that it might come this very night to claim him so prematurely, in a triage room, unaccompanied by family, friends, or anyone who might experience his passing as a loss, shook him to his core, made him weep copious tears. He remembered his last aborted session with the dying Herb Wasserman. If he survived this night, he vowed, he would reach out to his former patient, apologize for his callousness, and, if still possible, make amends. He would change his life: get out of the oxy business, give even his economy patients first-class treatment, stop taking Tamika for granted, repair his frayed relationship with Nathan and, perhaps, his even more vexed ones with his brother, Jeffrey, and his mother, Sheila.

Dr. Rosen did survive. His pain gradually subsided. The EKG, blood tests, and sonogram revealed only that the most likely culprit behind the episode was the Sichuan chicken he had eaten for dinner.

The sun had risen by the time he left the hospital, and he decided to walk home. The morning was brisk, the sky a soaring blue dome, almost too bright for his heightened senses to accommodate. Beneath it, the city and all its inhabitants, whether walking on two legs or four, in throngs, in twos, or alone, whether traveling in cars or buses, whether laughing, shouting, barking, or whistling, seemed, somehow, more vibrant than ever before. He felt light, free, hopeful, buoyant. No matter his current circumstances, life, he felt certain, would soon get much better. Long afterward, he would remember that walk back from the hospital with a certain wistfulness.

Arriving at home, he found Tamika, clad only in a white bath towel, just emerging from her morning shower. Exuberant and lustful, he kissed and embraced her, then worked his hands inside the towel, which fell away. Steering her to the bed, he kissed her mouth, her neck, her breasts. Sliding his tongue down her abdomen and then between her legs, he immersed himself in her. She began to thrust against him. Her body convulsed, relaxed, convulsed again, and then, after she let out a prolonged, throaty moan, went slack. As he rested his cheek upon her pubic mound, she reached down and ran her hand through his hair.

"It's been so long," she murmured.

Then he mounted her, and after they had spent themselves, she clung to him, kissing his forehead, his eyes, his nose, for even with her sexual desire sated, a terrible need remained.

He was remembering a time when he, too, had felt such need. A week or so after his separation from Liz, he had returned to the house in Scarsdale to pick up some clothes. They had sex that afternoon for the last time—after having slept in separate bedrooms for the better part of a year. Afterward, as she lay beneath him, panting, her sable hair in disarray, a faint flush on her cheeks, a smile of contentment on her lips, he felt a longing such as he had never experienced before. If only he could erase the years of discord that had preceded that moment and hold in abeyance what would follow, if only he could

remain there with her, entwined in that bed and that moment
. . .

"It'd be a shame to give this up," he said.

Even to his own ears, his words sounded flimsy, inadequate.

Her mouth constricted, as if she had tasted something bitter.

"What?" he asked as he rolled off of her.

She rotated her body the opposite way, turning her back toward him.

"This is great, but then there's everything else," she said, covering herself up to her shoulders with the comforter. "Outside of the bedroom, you're irredeemable."

All these years later, the memory still rankled. As was his wont, he turned his anger on the nearest available target— Tamika— prying himself loose from her embrace with a roughness that stunned her.

"You need to get to the office, like, this minute," he said in a gruff voice as he rose from the bed. "Before all hell breaks loose there. It's been chaos since Kellyanne . . ."

"Why don't you ask Kellyanne to come back?" answered Tamika. "Oh, but she wouldn't. There's nothing left for her to steal."

Just as the doctor came out of the shower, Pat McKinley called. Mrs. Agnello had told her lawyer that she might consider an offer of $2.1 million. Did the doctor want to settle or make a counteroffer?

"Settle," replied Dr. Rosen without hesitation.

"You're sure now?" Pat sounded surprised. "You're not going to change your mind?"

"I'm sure. I just want the whole ordeal over and done with. I need to get on with my life."

As he considered the price of getting on with his life—over $1 million out of pocket—he felt his heartburn returning. The high he had felt upon leaving the hospital—the joy, the hope, the sense of renewal—had dissipated within an hour after his return to the apartment.

"But I have another ask."

He told the lawyer about Barry's perfidy.

"Interesting. I'm not sure that you could convince a jury that demonstrating how to make a Bloody Mary on TV counts as practicing medicine, with or without a license. As for theft of intellectual property, if the court's definition of intellectual property is broad enough to encompass your Dr. Sober-Up script, then maybe. In any case, that sort of thing is outside my bailiwick."

"You're useless."

"No, I have my legitimate uses. They're just not the ones you would put me to."

Pat hung up.

The following day, while eating lunch in his office, Dr. Rosen happened upon a death notice for Mr. Wasserman in the *Times*. Though he did feel a twinge of regret, he did not put his sandwich down while he read through the notice. He had three patients scheduled for 1 p.m.

CHAPTER 13

When Boadecia made her surprising and unwelcome return to Dr. Rosen's office after a short but intensive period of undercover training, she proudly bore the most exalted title anyone had ever bestowed upon her, that of FBI confidential informant. She longed for the day when she could show her friends Dr. Rosen's indictment and say, "Look, you see here where it talks about CI-1 making the secret video recording? That's me. Confidential Informant-1."

Since her reappearance, the doctor had made sure to schedule her as his first, or preferably last, appointment of the day. In the former case, he even built in a time cushion to ensure that the office would still be empty when she left, for the boob-flashing episode had already cost him three patients.

On this sticky summer morning, her tattoos covered more of her skin than did her clothes. She wore a tank top that matched her purple hair, along with low-cut, skin-tight, bleached denim shorts, the pockets of which appeared to serve only as design features, for she walked into the office with keys, phone, and purse in her hands. The latter two she set down on the doctor's desk. She held onto the keys though. Curiously, since she claimed not to drive, she had a car key fob, which she pointed at the doctor. Sprawling sideways across the wing-backed chair, her legs draped over one of its arms, she ordered the usual and, to her dismay, found the service not up to par.

"Look, I really can't keep this up. The Adderall I can give you, but if you want the oxy, you'll have to go to the pain center. I'm not a pain specialist. When I do the oxy here, it raises red flags."

"But I'm in payyy-enn," she whined, though she seemed quite comfortable in the chair.

The pitch of her voice caused Dr. Rosen to grind his teeth.

"Besides, you don't even pay me. You only gave me $600 last time. You still owe me $400."

"I'm in such payyy-enn. I can't sleep at night."

"I can do the Subutex, but not the oxy."

"But the oxy is worth so much more."

"Great. So you are dealing. At least now I know how you pay me for the scripts."

"I am not dealing."

"Then what difference does it make to you what the pills are worth?"

"Well, the Subutex doesn't work as good."

"You mean the profit margin is smaller? How much do you get for the Subutex anyway?"

"Fifteen each. I could get thirty for the oxy. If I was dealing. Which I'm not."

"You told me the Subutex was twenty."

"I said fifteen."

"But I can give you more of it than the oxy, so, theoretically, if you were dealing, you could make up the difference in volume. You could even do better with the Subutex."

"I am not dealing. I swear to God. I need the oxy. I'm in payyy-enn. All day long and all night too. I can't sleep. I can't eat. I can't do anything. It's killing me."

"And you're killing me."

"Besides, if you give me the oxy, I can bring you more business. I know a lot of people."

"The people you know are the same assholes I told to get lost because I didn't want them hanging around here. Dealers, informants, people who'll shoot you for a handful of pills. I don't want to end up in jail or dead because of the business you bring me."

"I'll do it slow and careful."

"Right. Because slow and careful is how you roll."

Dr. Rosen sighed wearily. As fervently as he wished never to see her again, given the state of his finances, he could not dismiss her offer out of hand.

"All right. I'll give you your damn oxy. As long as you have the money. But this is the last time. From now on, you go . . ."

His voice trailed off. Beginning in his solar plexus, where Golovorez had hit him, a sudden burning pain flared up through his chest to his esophagus. What did he have to gain by sending her to the pain center? Why should he risk his license to profit the thieving Russians?

From her purse, Boadecia pulled out a wad of hundred-dollar bills and slid them across the desk. He scooped up the money, counted it, and then scrawled upon the top sheet of his prescription pad those cryptic numbers and directives that only pharmacists can decipher. He tore off the sheet and held it in front of him. When she reached for it, he pulled it back.

"You still owe me the $400 from last time. When am I going to get that from you?"

"Next time."

"I don't know why I keep falling for your bullshit. You tell me you want the oxy because it's worth more than the Subutex, and then you insist you're not dealing. What am I supposed to think? For all I know, you could be working for the police. Is this the Twentieth Precinct's money you're paying me with?"

"No, the FBI's."

The knowledge that the tiny camera concealed in her key fob was recording the look of shock and horror on the doctor's face made her gleeful.

Agent Hardin, watching on his laptop in his downtown office—a much more modest one in size and furnishings than the doctor's—slapped his forehead and murmured, "Why, God?"

"I'm kidding. I'm not working for the police. You can't sell drugs and be with the police."

"You have a point there," said Dr. Rosen. "Or maybe not. How do I know you're not informing on me while doing a little side business on your own?"

"Because I'm not."

"Why should I believe you?"

"Because I'm telling you I'm not, and I always tell the truth."

He laughed.

"The scary thing is you probably think you do."

"Besides, I've never been a snitch. I hate snitches. And I've been coming here for over two years. Don't you think I would have informed on you by now if I was an informant?"

"Good point. You probably flunked out of informant school before they got a chance to teach you that you're not supposed to deal the evidence on the street. The one thing I do know about you for sure is that you are a great big pain in my ass. Here's your damn prescription. You want the Adderall too?"

"Nope. Don't need it."

"You don't need the oxy either. Now get out, and don't ever come back here again, except to drop off the $400 you owe me."

Snatching the prescription sheet from his hand, she chortled, "See you next week, doc."

CHAPTER 14

For a man already in thrall to Russian mobsters, the prospect of entering into a business partnership with the erratic Boadecia Wilde offered little appeal. Dr. Rosen mulled over other possibilities. Might he heed Barry's advice and write a book about curing addiction, thereby monetizing his expertise and enhancing his media profile? One evening, he sat down at his computer to begin the task, but after fifteen minutes or so of staring at a blank screen, he despaired. He needed cash now, not months or years down the road. The following day he made several calls to television stations in midsize markets in an attempt to arrange a booking for himself, but those efforts yielded no fruit.

One day Barry called him with a peace offering and dangled before him a hope of financial salvation. Yes, he conceded, he really ought to have asked Dr. Rosen's permission before appropriating his hangover cure routine, but the doctor should view that borrowing as a tribute rather than a theft, imitation being the sincerest form of flattery. And there was plenty of market share to go around for people offering hangover cures.

"Barry, you're so full of shit."

"No, I mean it, bro. I got mad respect for what you're doing. As I keep telling you, you're a natural-born killer. You're gonna make it big on TV.

"Anyway, there's no point in holding a grudge. Life's too short for that. And I just may have something hot for you. Something that pays a whole lot better than the Dr. Sober-Up shtick. Remember the guy I told you about who's close to the president? Well, it turns out he also deals in nutritional supplements. He wants to grow his company, and he's looking for a doctor to do some promotion work, be a sort of front man, the face of the business. I don't think you'd have to do much at all. Some promotion on the internet and late-night TV maybe. You can make money hand over fist in that business."

"What's in it for you?"

"Nothing, bro. Just thought I could help out a friend."

Though he doubted that altruism lay behind Barry's offer, Dr. Rosen reasoned that he had nothing to lose by hearing out whatever business proposition an associate of the president might have. He told Barry to arrange a meeting.

"Oh, and bring your prescription pad. He likes his oxy."

"Barry, I have to be careful. I can't go giving the scripts out like candy to everyone I meet."

In weighing out the relative risks and rewards, however, he saw that plying Barry's enigmatic contact with a single oxy prescription made a lot more business sense than did supplying batches of them to the pain center, where Zhukov and Co. did, in fact, dispense them like candy. In this instance, at least, he stood the chance of realizing a significant return on investment. His earnings from the pain center barely justified the bother of filling out the scripts. Fear alone kept him from severing his ties to that business.

"Fine. I'll bring it."

The three men met at a place called Maxwell's Gentlemen's Club, a couple of blocks from Madison Square Garden. Full of sharp angles, polished metal surfaces, neon signs, and mirrors, the interior looked just a tad smaller than the nearby arena. On platforms behind the main bar and in various corners, pole dancers in stiletto heels and G-strings whirled and strutted to '80s pop hits, which much have first aired on the radio, Dr. Rosen surmised, before many of the dancers and patrons had entered the world. Among the latter, slicked back hair and suits abounded. Everyone was shouting, but rarely could Dr. Rosen make out a word. He had to use his elbows to defend his space at the bar. Barry, he surmised, must have chosen the venue.

The third member of the party, the enigmatic figure whom Barry introduced as Michael Stonecypher, looked to be in his mid-thirties and bore an uncanny resemblance to the president of the United States. He had darker hair than President Dreck, but his cheeks and his midsection had the same bovine thickness; when displeased, his lips formed the same truculent pout; and his voice had the same abrasive timbre. When standing still, he had the same gravity-defying forward lean, and when in motion, the same lumbering gait.

The doctor arrived first. Stonecypher and Barry, both already visibly drunk when they entered, began to banter with the dancers and the bar girls, whose job it was to entice the clientele to run up tabs and spring for lap dances. Holding aloft a $20 bill, Stonecypher beckoned to one of the nearby dancers. The tall redhead with the emerald eyes stepped down from her riser, clambered up onto the bar, and shimmied her way toward Stonecypher. As she knelt before him, her hands behind her head, her pelvis gyrating, he stuffed the twenty into her G-string, perhaps a touch farther down than strictly necessary to keep it lodged there. When she tried to wriggle away, he pulled at the G-string.

"Creep!" she hissed as she tore herself from his grasp.

She jumped off the bar. Within half a minute, she returned, accompanied by a bouncer, a tall, olive-skinned man with a weightlifter's build. The bouncer grabbed Stonecypher by the shirt and yanked him off his chair.

"No touching the girls, buddy. You touch, you're gone. Zero tolerance."

"I never even touched her. She's a lying bitch!"

The bouncer turned Stonecypher around, took hold of his shirt collar with one hand and his belt with the other, and marched him toward the door.

"You're gonna regret this. Do you have any idea who I am?"

The bouncer laughed.

"I bet you say that to all the bouncers."

"Well, you'll find out when the Secret Service come busting down your door for assaulting the president's son."

"The president's son? Now there's one I haven't heard before. I am deeply honored, sir. Someday I'll be able to tell my grandkids I threw the president's son's ass out onto the street."

So saying, the bouncer did just that, and Stonecypher fell face-first onto the sidewalk. Barry, who had followed him out, helped him to his feet. Despite Barry's yeoman efforts to keep him upright, Stonecypher, owing to his drunkenness and his forward tilt, fell again. Barry tried a second time, but Stonecypher got his feet tangled and dropped to his knees. The doctor, watching from far enough away that he could deny any association with the men should someone ask, saw that Stonecypher was weeping.

"That's right!" Stonecypher roared. "Toss the bastard out onto the sidewalk. If it were my father . . . But, of course, he's the president. Nobody throws him out of the club. When you're the president, they let you do it. Or the legitimate sons, the two morons who fly all over the world on the government's dime shaking people down. Nobody would think of throwing them out of the club. But the bastard? When Dreck has the whole family up on stage at the end of the convention, who's missing? Michael Stonecypher, of course. Can't have the bastard in that lovely picture. People will ask questions. Election night reception—same thing. No bastards here. Inauguration? They don't even send him an invitation. Bastards not wanted. Damn it! I'm going back in there. Somebody has to stand up for bastards. If not the first bastard, who will?"

Stonecypher rose again, this time without Barry's assistance.

"Let's hear it for bastards!" he shouted, waving his fist in the air. Then he charged toward the door.

After three steps, however, he fell yet again, his jaw smacking against the pavement with a sickening thud. Blood from his nose and mouth began to pool on the sidewalk.

On the street outside Maxwell's, the pedestrians showed no inclination to stand up for bastards who could not stand up for themselves. Some of them steered so far clear of him as to leave the sidewalk altogether.

Dr. Rosen, of similar mind, hailed a passing taxi. Whatever business proposal Stonecypher may have had to offer—of which he had said not a word—no longer interested the doctor. He doubted that Stonecypher could stick a shipping label onto a box straight. And what of Barry? Was he, like all the other life and business coaches to whom the doctor had attached himself, just one more dead end?

CHAPTER 15

After a good night's sleep, his first in a while, Dr. Rosen felt more sanguine. Barry Bullard the person may have disappointed him, but the central message of the *Bulldog* books—that persistence and resilience counted for far more than talent in achieving success—was one worth heeding, especially in hard times. No, Dr. Rosen would not let himself fall prey to despair—not while he still had other options available to get himself out of his fix.

That night he called his mother, Sheila, with whom he had not spoken in several months. His last visit with her, almost the whole of which he had spent trying in vain to persuade her to switch her power of attorney from his older brother, Jeffrey, to him, had ended in acrimony.

Where her Robbie was concerned, though, her capacity for forgiveness had no limits. Moreover, he called at an auspicious time. Before he even broached the subject of a visit, she asked him when he planned to come see her. This Saturday, she suggested, would be perfect, as she was expecting Jeffrey too. In whatever time she had left, she said, she wanted more than anything else to see her two sons reconciled. Also, she was worried about Jeffrey.

"He's lost everything. His wife, his job with the government. He's in such pain. He needs you. He needs his brother."

The call gave Dr. Rosen renewed hope. A vulnerable Jeffrey might well prove more malleable than the obstinate Sheila, might willingly yield up that power of attorney that she refused to grant him. Still, Dr. Rosen would assume nothing. This time he would prepare. He would heed Barry's advice and catch some episodes of *Find It! Flip It!* While he set great store by his own persuasive powers, maybe he could pick up a few tips from the man who had flipped his way into the White House.

Though his wife, Lori, had died some five months before, Jeffrey Rosen still spoke with her regularly. In hospice, during the last weeks of her life, he would sit by her bed while she slept and speak to her aloud, for he felt certain that she could hear him. The closer she came to the end, the more she slept, and the more voluble he became. Less confident after her death that she still heard him, he kept up the conversation anyway, silently in public, sometimes still audibly when alone in the modest, gray-shingled Cape Cod house that they had shared for more than thirty years in a verdant Maryland suburb of DC. He talked to her most often at night and when drunk, and because his sleep had grown fitful when it came at all, and he drank more than ever, those talks had become quite frequent of late.

On a Thursday at 3 a.m., he sat on his living room sofa, a squared-off, dark-blue, midcentury-modern piece that he and Lori had purchased early in their marriage. On the stereo, a recording of Bel Canto arias played softly. A near-empty bottle of Chianti and a half-full wine glass stood on the coffee table in front of him. From the wall opposite the sofa hung a reproduction of Goya's *The Drowning Dog* that Lori had bought from the gift shop at The Prado. He and Lori had quarreled over the print of the little black dog, depicted in profile, sinking—already neck-deep—into a vast ochre void. The dog's expression, one of fear, bewilderment, and hopelessness—"Why this? Why now? Why does no one hear me?"—unnerved him.

"The more I drink, the harder it is for me to get drunk," he said out loud, his eyes fixed on the doomed dog as if he were addressing it. "So I have to keep drinking more. It's like Rob says when he goes on TV: 'Tolerance! Withdrawal!'"

"I hate to see you this way," he imagined Lori answering.

"I hate to see myself this way, to be honest. But it's not as if I have to go to work in the morning. Besides, I need to fortify myself. I'm driving up to visit Mom again this weekend. She hasn't been doing well."

The image came to him unbidden, as it had countless times before, of his mother alone in the den of a house that, in the two months since she had become a widow, must have come to seem as vast and empty as an airport hangar. Feeling light-headed, she would have set her knitting down on the table. Maybe she would have lost that second or two during which she fell and then have wondered how she came to be lying prone on the carpet. Unable to rise, the entire right side of her body inert, she would, like the drowning dog, have sensed that something catastrophic that she did not yet understand was happening to her.

"Again? What about Rob? He's in Manhattan, an hour away from her."

"He's still doing his part. He visits her once a year, whether he needs to or not. Maybe twice, to give him his due."

"It's so unfair."

"If life were fair, you would still be here."

He finished his glass and then poured himself another, emptying the bottle.

"And that poor little dog wouldn't be drowning. God, I've always hated that painting. One of these days I'm going to take it down and put it in the basement."

"You can do as you like. You don't have to please me any-more."

"Madrid was nice though. We had a good time."

He took another sip of wine.

"Anyway, it's just as well that Rob visits her so rarely. The less he does, the less likely I am to run into him. And his visits only upset her anyway."

"Why?"

"Same old thing. The power of attorney business. Every time he goes to see her, he badgers her about it until she tells him to get lost. And then he calls here to say hello and, oh, by the way, threaten to sue me for every penny I have and will ever have. On what grounds, I don't know."

"I just find this all very sad. In a way, I pity him. He's driven everyone away. He has nobody left, really."

"You're more forgiving than I am. How can you pity a person who has no pity? It is sad though. Very sad. Because there were times when we were close. I don't recognize him anymore. Or maybe I overlooked a lot."

Finishing the Chianti, Jeffrey put the glass down on the table. He lay back on the sofa and began to count the concentric circles within one of the swirls on the textured ceiling. As with all his previous attempts, however, the circles refused to cooperate. Their boundaries crossed here, overlapped there. Many were not circles at all but mere fragments, truncated arcs. The whole was an impossible muddle. He soon abandoned the endeavor.

"Do you ever have any regrets?" he asked.

"Regrets? About what?"

"I don't know. Not having kids? It would have been nice, maybe. When I picture growing old now, it all seems so desolate."

"I would have liked very much to have a family."

"True. You wanted one much more than I did. I'm sorry."

"There's no reason to be sorry."

"Maybe it's just as well. I doubt that I would have made much of a family man. Too self-absorbed."

"Nonsense."

"Too unstable."

"Wrong again. You're great with kids. You would have made a wonderful father."

"Well, it's water under the bridge now. I don't have too many regrets, really. I hope you don't. I know I wasn't the easiest person to live with. It was good though, mostly, wasn't it? OK, at least?"

"If you have to ask now, I wonder whether you ever knew me at all. Was I the sort of person who would have stayed married for thirty-one years to a man I didn't respect and love dearly?"

How would she have posed that question? Irritably? Tearfully? The uncertainty made him fearful, and he realized then that he was weeping. He turned his face toward the back of the sofa, as though wishing to conceal his tears from her, and brushed them away with his hand. *Una furtive lagrima.* Would there soon come a day when he would no longer hear her at all? He saw her fading, pulling away. Mistrusting his memory, he relied more and more on photographs to summon her.

Rolling over onto his stomach, he reached for the one on the adjacent end table. The picture, 8-by-10, enclosed in a silver frame, showed Lori in a sleeveless white summer dress outside the Coliseum. Beside her, a grinning fake gladiator brandished a plastic sword. She wore the weary smile of a woman trying to humor a hyperactive child. Her hair, long at the time, straight, and in uncharacteristic disarray, appeared fairer than Jeffrey ever remembered it in life, almost a honey brown. The observation troubled him. Had the Roman sun bleached her hair a touch or caused the camera to render an unfaithful image, or was the reproduction more accurate than his memory?

"Ten euros for that lousy picture," he could hear her saying, as she had many times.

"The photographer was a crook, but I've always liked the picture. Anyway, it was a good day, all in all. We went to that little gelato shop afterward, the one on the Via Nazionale by our hotel. That fig-and-walnut gelato was amazing. I've never had anything like it since."

"The pistachio too. That was a good day. Most of our days were good ones."

"I'd like to think so."

"So now that you have your answer, you can let me go. I'm dead. I have no existence outside your imaginings. Stop wasting your breath talking to a shadow you've conjured up to keep you company at night. You have responsibilities. There are people—living people—who need you. Your mother, for one. Without you, where would she be? Would you leave her to Rob's tender mercies?"

"No. Of course not."

"All right, then. Goodbye."

"Good night. I love you."

"Goodbye. I'm dead. The dead can't love you back."

"They speak very bluntly, the dead. As ever."

Returning the photograph to the table, he glanced over again at the dog, still mutely despairing as it sank into oblivion. Yes, he resolved as he closed his eyes, he would consign the dog to the basement. Tomorrow. He felt much too tired to bother now—so tired that he dared hope he might get some sleep. In the morning, if he needed to, he might just give Dr. Sober-Up's Bloody Mary hangover cure a try.

CHAPTER 16

On Saturday morning, Dr. Rosen and Tamika drove out to Long Island, stopping first at the beach for a couple of hours. They arrived at North Shore Meadows Nursing and Rehabilitation with wet hair and feet coated with sand. Dr. Rosen wore flip-flops, white shorts over his bathing suit, and a colorful T-shirt that he had acquired on a trip to the Bahamas. It featured silhouettes of flamingos and palm trees set against a circular yellow, orange, and turquoise backdrop that evoked a sunset over the water. Tamika wore low-cut blue denim cutoffs and a black tank top that left her belly exposed.

Jeffrey was seated on the bed when they entered, with Sheila facing him in her wheelchair. Since the brothers had last met, he had undergone a transformation that Dr. Rosen might have found disturbing if the two had had a stronger fraternal bond. Jeffrey looked emaciated. His white hair wanted brushing; his tired eyes, some sleep; his face, a shave; his jeans and black T-shirt, a good going-over with an iron; and his running shoes, a dumpster. Dr. Rosen acknowledged his presence with a barely perceptible nod that went unreciprocated.

The doctor bent low to kiss his mother on the cheek and, at the same time, deftly rotated her wheelchair a full 180 degrees, leaving her with her back to Jeffrey.

The smile—if a smile it was—on Jeffrey's face looked acidic enough to eat through steel.

From the far corner, the doctor fetched an armchair with a yellow vinyl covering and pinewood arms and sat down in it facing his mother. There being no other chairs in the room,

Tamika, who had entered a couple of steps behind the doctor, stood by the dresser, fidgeting with her keys.

"Would you like to sit down?" asked Jeffrey, rising from the bed.

"No, I'm good," she replied.

"You're sure?"

Sheila shot a glance at her and then turned a questioning eye toward the doctor. Dr. Rosen, failing to pick up on the cue, did not introduce Tamika.

Like Jeffrey, Sheila looked much the worse for wear since the doctor had last seen her. As she and Dr. Rosen exchanged small talk, her torso, which appeared to have shrunk in the interim, slowly sank in her wheelchair and listed rightward. From time to time, Jeffrey would arise from his perch on the bed, slip his forearms under her armpits, and pull her back up. Her head, too, tilted toward starboard. Her complexion had a grayish cast, and her lips a slight blue tint. She was receiving oxygen through a nasal cannula connected by several feet of tubing to a black generator, as massive as a guitar amplifier and just as noisy, which sat beside her bed. Heart failure? She drooled continuously, an effect, Dr. Rosen surmised, of the paucity of upper teeth, a progressive loss of facial muscle control, a second minor stroke that had escaped the notice of the nursing home staff, or all three. Every so often, she would move her left arm—the functional one—across her body and furtively dab at the corner of her mouth with a tissue. When she spoke, she sounded again the way she did the day after her stroke—as if she had a mouth full of peanut butter. Dr. Rosen, sizing her up with a clinical eye, gave her three months to live, six tops. The power of attorney could not wait.

He played for her the video of his Chicago appearance on his phone, pausing every so often to provide color commentary. ("The lawyer joke was a spur-of-the-moment thing. It worked great. Beginning with a joke is a good way to get them hooked. Now look at what I did here. You've heard of the rule of three, right? People remember things in threes: the Three

Little Pigs, Goldilocks and the Three Bears, the Three Musketeers. We're hardwired that way. That's why I have three *Rs*: recognize, rehabilitate, recover.")

When the video concluded, she squeezed his hand. She was beaming.

"My son, the celebrity. Who knew? It's wonderful. I'm so proud."

Neither Tamika, who had seen the presentation up close, nor Jeffrey, who either lacked interest in the doctor's doings or wanted to appear as if he did, watched the video, both fiddling with their own phones throughout. Both were sweating, for in deference to the many patients on blood thinners, the management at North Shore Meadows kept the heat in the building at greenhouse level.

In the corridor outside, chaos reigned. Harried-looking nurses and aides, summoned by high-pitched bed alarms and cryptic directions from overhead speakers—"two alert west 236"—scurried up and down the hallway. Directly across the hall, two aides were attempting to calm and restrain a panicked resident who was trying to squirm out of her wheelchair, while alternately pleading with and screaming at them to let her go. She had to get to her job in her mother's flower shop, and she was late. Would they pul-e-a-s-e let her go? From the agitated woman's room, the reek of human feces wafted its way into Sheila's.

Dr. Rosen got up to shut the door and then returned to his seat. He played for Sheila the video of his Reno appearance as Dr. Sober-Up. All the while, the room grew hotter still, so hot that she too, though herself on a blood-thinner regimen, began to perspire.

He had had a lot of fun as Dr. Sober-Up, he told her. Also, because he made sure to throw in a plug for the brand of vodka he used when performing his Bloody Mary-making demonstration, he hoped that if he got to do the routine a few more times on TV, the company might take notice and offer him some kind of marketing deal.

"What is this nonsense?" asked Sheila. "You're a doctor. What kind of doctor goes on TV to sell vodka?"

"It's called multiplatform marketing. I'm building a brand. The TV appearances are like free advertising for my practice. To get the vodka tie-in would be the cherry on top. It's all about generating passive income. That's how you make real money. Not putting it in a savings account the way Dad did."

"Your father did all right by us. You have nothing to complain about. And I don't see how this kind of advertising helps your practice. It demeans you. It makes you look crass. What do you need it for?"

He clenched his jaw and folded his arms across his chest.

"My practice is doing great. Better than ever. I have money rolling in faster than I can spend it."

Tamika stared at him in disbelief. Jeffrey, eying the door, stood up.

"Mom," he said, "I, uh, think I'll go get some lunch. I'll be back later."

"Great minds think alike," said Dr. Rosen, brightening suddenly. "There's a little Vietnamese place in a strip mall about a mile from here. Why don't we all go? Mom, when was the last time you went out for lunch? I bet you get sick of nursing home food."

"I only eat pureed food now," replied Sheila. "It's awful. But Jeffrey can go with you."

Jeffrey looked alarmed. With a sudden and surprising vigor, Sheila squeezed his hand and pulled him close. "You go with him."

"Come on, Jeff," said the doctor with an ersatz heartiness. "It's been such a long time. We have a lot of catching up to do."

"Do we?"

"Stop it already," said Sheila. "Stop the nonsense. You listen to me for once. I don't have much time left. Before I go, I want the two of you to be close again, the way you were. Is that too much for a mother to ask?"

She looked imploringly at Tamika.

The phone dropped from Tamika's hand and hit the floor with a thwack.

"No, no, not at all," Tamika answered, stooping to pick up her phone. "Not at all."

Sheila's gaze turned toward her wedding picture, which hung on the pale green wall to the right of the television inside a gold filigree frame. Holding a bouquet of roses, the bride wore a luminous smile. The groom, stiff and unsmiling, looked as though he had buttoned his collar just a bit too tightly.

"Sheldon could never understand why you two couldn't get along. It made him so sad."

The look she gave Jeffrey would have broken the resistance of the most hardened of sociopaths.

"You go with him."

"I'll go, Mom."

"Good."

She smiled and released his hand.

CHAPTER 17

They drove to the restaurant separately. The doctor and Tamika rode in his Jaguar, which was gleaming again after a post-Salisbury repair job and detailing. Jeffrey drove his pale blue Prius. In the presence of his brother, the appearance of the Prius, to which Jeffrey usually paid little heed, embarrassed him. Besides the ordinary dings, dents, and scrapes acquired over a decade or so of use, the car had accumulated a thick coating of grime in the months since its last washing. The droppings of numerous birds lay spattered over the roof, and a line of paw prints traversed the hood.

Outside, a light rain had begun to fall. Inside the restaurant, there was clamor and confusion, and the heat rivaled that of the nursing home. The condensation on the windows in front, which faced the parking lot, rendered them opaque. The doctor, Tamika, and Jeffrey stood in the vestibule, just inside the front door, for twenty minutes, jostled by other patrons continuing to crowd inside. Then an elderly waiter guided the three of them in silence to a booth so confining that the paunchy Dr. Rosen had difficulty wedging into it. The glare from the overhead light made reading the laminated menus a challenge. The doctor gave his a cursory glance and then set it down. After a while, a waitress appeared, deposited three glasses of water on the table, and asked, "Are you ready to order?"

Her voice had an unnatural flatness, as if she were reading from a script. Without waiting for an answer, she turned to leave.

The doctor called her back—loudly: "Yes, we are. I'll have the spring rolls, the pho soup—the first one on the list here—and a Vietnamese coffee."

Tamika and Jeffrey ordered the same.

Waiters and waitresses came and went, leaving dishes on the table in no discernable order, delivering the spring rolls and the soup simultaneously to the doctor; the soup, sans spring rolls, to Tamika; and, initially, just a bowl of bean sprouts, cilantro, and lime quarters to Jeffrey, who was perspiring as copiously as he had at North Shore. By the time his soup came, he had little appetite for it. Dr. Rosen slurped his greedily, while Tamika, after abandoning a brief struggle with her chopsticks in favor of a spoon and fork, also ate with gusto.

"You like the pho?" asked Dr. Rosen, sitting back and draping his arm over her shoulders.

"It's delicious," she answered.

"Before you met me, you never ate Vietnamese food, did you?"

"No."

"You can't say I don't show you new things."

She replied with a smile that, to Jeffrey, appeared forced.

Pushing his soup bowl aside, Jeffrey took several sips of water.

"By the way, I'm Jeffrey," he said, wiping the sweat from his face with a handkerchief. "I don't think we've been properly introduced."

"Tamika is my receptionist."

"Nice to meet you, Tamika."

"Nice to meet you. I've heard so much about you."

In fact, until this day, she had not known that Dr. Rosen had a brother or that his mother was still among the living.

"Some of it may even be true."

Again, she labored to produce a smile.

"Your mother . . . she's sweet."

"Her heart's in the right place."

Having emptied his bowl, Dr. Rosen set it aside and whispered something to Tamika. Looking surprised, her spoon in midair, she excused herself. Dr. Rosen stood to let her pass, and she slid out of the booth and headed for the ladies room at the rear of the restaurant.

Outside, a thunderstorm had commenced.

Sitting down again, the doctor leaned over the table and said softly, "Mom told me about Lori. I'm so sorry."

"Are you?"

"What kind of question is that?"

"A serious one. Not rhetorical."

"Well, Lori and I . . . We never did really hit it off. She was always cold to me."

"Curious, isn't it?" said Jeffrey. "Everyone used to tell me what a warm person she was."

"Not to me. And I tried."

"Oh, you're always trying in your fashion. Did Mom tell you I would be driving up here this weekend? It seems an unlikely coincidence that you'd drop in on her just when I happened to be here."

"It wasn't. She told me you were coming. She's dying, and she knows it. You can tell just by looking at her. She has the terminal O sign. It could happen today, tomorrow, any time. She wants to see us reconciled before she goes. You heard her."

"And you? What do you want, Rob?"

"I want that too. I'm your little brother."

Jeffrey snickered.

"No, really," he said. "What do you want?"

"Why do you always think I have some ulterior motive?"

"Because you always do. How old is the girl?"

"Tamika? She's twenty. Why?"

"Nathan's twenty, isn't he?"

"He's cool with it."

"Pretty sweet deal you got there. You probably pay her next to nothing and work her like a dog. Does she keep house for you too? I suppose you do have to take her out someplace nice every once in a while so your aura doesn't fade, but you probably write that off as a business expense."

Dr. Rosen's eyes glinted like two chips of graphite.

"You don't hear her complaining, do you? You're trying to provoke me, but I'm not going to let you. Look, it's been God knows how long since we last saw each other. The last thing I want to do is to spend this time sniping at each other."

"Then let's not. Let's get the stuff that matters to you out of the way. I know you don't believe me, but I'm not hiding any of Mom's assets from you. There are none left. That's why she's on Medicaid. The proceeds from the sale of the house are long gone. Her Social Security all goes to the nursing home every month, except for the pittance they allow her to keep for haircuts and the like, which also goes to them ultimately. It's less than what I paid the locksmith to replace the back door lock that you forced when you took the clocks."

"I don't know what you're talking about."

"And yet the lock was forced, and you have the clocks."

"She promised me those clocks."

The memory of what Golovorez and company had done to the clocks pained the doctor far more than admitting to the break-in.

"True. But you could have asked her. I wasn't going to take them. You assume everyone is like you."

The doctor put on his clinical face, one that conveyed both compassion and an appropriate professional detachment. Modulating his tone accordingly, he said, "Your mood seems low today. Do you think about hurting yourself?"

"At the moment, my thoughts are running more toward homicide than suicide."

The clinical mask fell away; in its place there appeared on the doctor's face an expression that to Jeffrey's cold eye looked like a poor counterfeit of sorrow.

"I don't know what you imagine I've ever done to you to make you feel so much rage toward me, but you can't live this way. I know you're going through a very difficult time. Between Lori's death and losing your job—"

"I did not lose my job," Jeffrey interrupted. "I'm on paid administrative leave."

"Great use of my tax dollars. Mom told me you got fired."

"Mom gets things wrong sometimes."

"Well, she wasn't very clear on the details. She said you were insubordinate or something."

"Not insubordinate. I refused to sign a so-called nondisclosure/non-disparagement agreement—essentially, a loyalty oath to President Dreck. Supposedly optional but not really."

"Why not? It's a piece of paper. It means nothing. Hardly a hill worth dying on."

"I'm a civil servant, not an employee of President Dreck. And unless or until the Supreme Court says otherwise, it's blatantly illegal. Not that that matters a whole lot these days. Hey, the market's up, so who cares if the president and his goons rip up the US Code, trample all over the Constitution, and make the Treasury their personal piggy bank?"

"As a matter of fact, the market is way up, and I did get a nice tax cut. Am I supposed to be sorry about that? Look, I didn't even vote for Dreck. I don't know a lot of people who did. He's not too popular on the Upper West Side. Tamika turns off the TV every time he comes on. But there are a lot of people who like the way he talks. He's blunt. He projects strength, decisiveness. People want a strong leader."

Jeffrey laughed.

"You know, you would fit right in with this administration. My boss is stepping down as secretary of HHS. Why don't you apply? You could make the Medicaid regs even more onerous than they already are and see to it that Mom gets kicked to the curb. That's one way of getting back at her for giving me power of attorney."

"We do need to have a talk about Mom," answered the doctor.

"No, we don't. I really have to go anyway."

Spying their waiter, who was collecting orders at a nearby table, Jeffrey waved to him. The waiter, never looking his way, scurried off toward the kitchen.

"Do you honestly think that you should be the one making decisions for Mom now?" asked Dr. Rosen. "I don't see that you're doing a great job. The place you put her in is a shithole. I could find a much better place for her."

"It's not a shithole, and she doesn't want you handling her affairs. She doesn't trust you."

"That's really unfair. Unfair and hurtful. But I'm not going to get angry. I know this isn't you talking. It's your illness."

"No, it's me. Really."

"You're not thinking clearly now. Your judgment is impaired. You look like you haven't slept or shaved or showered or changed your clothes in a week. You need to recognize that you're not well. Then we need to get you some help, get you back on your feet. After that, there'll be time to talk about Mom."

Behind his closed eyelids, Jeffrey saw again the image of the hopeless sinking black dog. He felt an insupportable weight in his head and his limbs.

"Stop!" he cried. "Just stop it already. Please."

From a well-worn brown wallet bursting with cards and receipts, Jeffrey drew out a twenty-dollar bill, which he tossed onto the table. He slid out of the booth, stood up, and narrowly avoided a head-on collision with Tamika who had been hovering near the booth for some time.

"Sorry," he murmured as he sidled past her.

Exiting the restaurant, he gave the front door a violent push. The door failing to close behind him, Tamika watched for a moment as he plodded toward his car through sheets of rain and swirling ankle-deep puddles.

A thunderclap—alarmingly close—startled her. Rain blew inside as if through a fire hose, soaking the people waiting by the door. The proprietor yelled something in Vietnamese, and two waiters rushed to the front. They wrestled with the door, one pulling on the handle from inside, the other outside, pushing. By the time they got the door closed, both men were drenched.

Returning to the booth, Tamika sat down in Jeffrey's place, opposite the doctor. Hunched over the table, his hands clasped over his mouth, he appeared pensive.

"Are you OK?" she asked him.

"Yeah, fine. Everything's great. Ah . . . I just handled it all wrong."

Dr. Rosen had gleaned enough from his viewing of *Find It! Flip It!* to grasp that the star would have arranged such a lunch with much greater care than he had. Dreck would have chosen a quiet restaurant and would not have brought a third person along. He always sought to isolate his targets before turning up the pressure.

Reaching across the table, she squeezed his hand.

"I don't know anymore. He's a mess, but he's still my brother. I want to have a relationship with him. I try my best, but there's no getting through to him."

Feeling a tenderness toward him that had been absent for months, Tamika crossed over to his side of the booth. He let his head drop onto her shoulder.

"At least I'm going to get some tonight," said Dr. Rosen to himself.

CHAPTER 18

The next day, Dr. Rosen returned to North Shore without Tamika and without stopping at the beach. He wore dress trousers and a white shirt and carried a briefcase.

He timed his visit for early afternoon to avoid Jeffrey, who, when in town on a Sunday, typically dropped in on Sheila in the morning before driving back home to Maryland.

When Dr. Rosen arrived at North Shore, during the somnolent hour between lunch and the regular Sunday entertainment program, a stillness pervaded the building. Patients dozed in wheelchairs, while at the nurses station, staff caught up on their paperwork. Here and there as he walked through the corridors, Dr. Rosen caught bits of Mets and Yankees play-by-play, snatches of dialogue from afternoon movies, and fragments of family conversations, some redolent with forced cheer, others muted and grave.

He found his mother sleeping in her wheelchair with the television tuned to a CNN news/talk show. Between the TV and Sheila stood a small mobile utility table, upon which lay a tray that held the remnants of her lunch: an empty cup; an empty container of Thick & Easy Vitamin Enhanced Dairy Drink, toppled over onto its side; a plate of pink, purple, and yellow puree, barely touched; a half-consumed cup of tapioca pudding; an unopened juice container; and several crumpled napkins. The room had a faint sour milk smell.

"Mom."

Dr. Rosen tapped her on the shoulder. She did not stir.

"Mom."

He shook her gently. She straightened up, blinked several times, and gave him a quizzical look, which soon brightened into a smile.

"I wasn't expecting you again today, but I'm glad you came."

He kissed her on the cheek.

"Turn the TV off, please," she said. "I've had all the Dreck I can stand for one day. It's nonstop Dreck. Are you ever going to bring Nathan with you? I can't remember when I saw him last."

"Next time. He's visiting his mother this weekend."

"They're getting along now? How is he? Is he working? Back in school?"

"He's doing great. Since he's been with me, he's been fine. He was a mess when he was living with Liz."

"Are you still fighting with her? I wish you'd stop. It's not good for Nathan. He's been caught in the middle for half his life."

"Mom, let's not talk about that. Look, I have something else I want to play for you. I didn't get around to it yesterday. Would it be all right if I turned off the oxygen for a little while? The machine is really loud."

"Go ahead. I don't really need it. I don't know why they have me on it all the time."

Sitting opposite her in the yellow armchair, he played a recording of a podcast in which the host, a psychologist who specialized in working with geriatric patients, had interviewed him on the topic of successful aging.

As the podcast played, a man in the adjacent room began screaming: "I wanna die! I wanna die! I wanna die!"

"That's my neighbor," said Sheila. "He's not aging successfully. None of us here are."

"I didn't hear him yesterday."

"His daughters were here. When they're here, he's quiet. The rest of the time . . ."

Dr. Rosen turned up the volume on his phone.

"Would you switch that off, please?"

The doctor frowned.

"It's almost at the end. Don't you want to hear the rest?"

"Another time. I have a headache."

"Has he been screaming like that all day?"

"Pretty much."

"How can you stand it?"

"It's hard. I try to be understanding. He's demented and wheelchair-bound. He's also the only man on this corridor. He's probably mad because now that he can have his pick of the ladies, it's too late."

"I see you haven't lost your sense of humor."

Dr. Rosen took hold of her right hand—the one she could not move at will. It was cold.

"Do you ever think about moving someplace better?"

Her back stiffened.

"No."

"Why not?"

"I don't want to move."

"Why wouldn't you, if I could find someplace better for you?"

"Because I don't want to."

"That's no answer."

"I don't want to talk about it now."

From the nursing station, there came an announcement that the entertainment program would begin in fifteen minutes. All who wished to attend should gather in the dining room.

Dr. Rosen got up to close the door.

"I'd like to go to the dining room and hear the music," she said, though she did not much care for any of the several Sinatra knockoffs who rotated through North Shore on Sunday afternoons. "Would you take me there, please?"

"Look, we need to talk."

"Later."

Grudgingly, he wheeled her out.

The singer, a beefy, black-haired man with thick whiskers, wore white shoes, dark trousers, a pink shirt open at the neck, and a pale blue blazer. Accompanied by only by a laptop and speakers through which played the backing tracks, he began his set with a medley: "Volare" segued into "That's Amore," then into "O Sole Mio," and then back to "Volare." Undiscouraged by his audience's tepid reaction, he redoubled his efforts, for what he lacked in ability, he made up in enthusiasm.

"All right. Now we'll do one that'll get you moving your feet."

Swiveling his hips like Tom Jones, he performed a rousing "It's Not Unusual." Few in the mostly nonambulatory crowd moved their feet, but some of the women in the audience enjoyed his hip action. He got a more generous round of applause than he had for the medley. Wiping the sweat from his forehead with his sleeve, he followed with "Mack the Knife."

"Now let's all snap our fingers to the beat."

Those patients not too afflicted by debilitating arthritis or Parkinson's or some other condition that prevented them from doing so snapped their fingers in time with rhythms that only they could hear, no two listeners keeping the same beat.

A Sinatra medley followed. Weaving his way among the wheelchairs as he crooned "You Make Me Feel So Young," the singer stopped and knelt in front of Sheila.

"Come on and sing with me."

She gave him the iciest stare in her repertoire and made not a sound. Rising, he executed a brisk retreat.

Afterward, as Dr. Rosen wheeled Sheila back to her room, she grumbled, "Until I came here, I never thought anyone could ruin Sinatra for me."

"Now can we talk, Mom?"

"Leave me. I want to rest now. You can come back later."

"How can you ever rest in here with that racket?" he replied, for the screaming in the next room had started up again.

He did not leave. Closing the door, he turned Sheila's wheelchair around and again slid the yellow armchair up close. He sat down and leaned forward, intruding upon her space as if he were the star and she one of the motivated guest sellers on *Find It! Flip It!*

"If you'll let me, I can help you. I can move you someplace better where you won't have to listen to that screaming all day."

"Wherever I am, I'll have to listen to somebody screaming. It's the same everywhere. At least here I have my own room."

"I can get you your own room there too."

"Where? Where is 'there'?"

"I know a lot of good places. There's one I work in. It's called St. Agnes. It's in Brooklyn."

He had not worked in that facility since the unfortunate incident involving Mr. Agnello, but among the many other expedients he considered to ease his financial straits, he did, from time to time, entertain the possibility that sometime in the future, when memories of the case had faded a bit, he might seek reinstatement there.

"What? You're going to put me in a Catholic nursing home? With nuns? With Jesus hanging on every wall? No thanks."

"It's not like that. Not everyone there is Catholic. They're not going to try to convert you. But they will take better care of you. It's a much better facility than this one. One of the best. Believe me."

"I don't care if it . . . All right, all right. I'll think about it. But I'm tired now. I want to rest. We'll talk about it another time."

"I don't see what there is to think about. I'd be around all the time, looking in on you. I'd see to it that you're treated like a queen. In this dump, you have to wait a half-hour for someone to take you to the bathroom. Did they give you your medications on time today? Did they give them to you at all? You're being abused here. This is what happens when you leave things up to Jeffrey. He dumps you in a shithole like this and lets you rot while he's robbing you blind."

"Stop making up stories."

"I'm telling you the truth. I always tell the truth. You just don't want to hear it."

"I've heard enough of your truth for one day. Leave me alone."

"No, I can't leave you alone. What kind of son would I be if I did that?"

"The same kind you've always been."

"What's that supposed to mean?"

"Do I have to draw you a picture?"

"Sometimes I don't know why I bother. If you weren't my mother, and I didn't love you so much . . ."

Again he reached for his mother's hand—the one that she could not move. His lips trembled, and his eyes pleaded with her for forgiveness—a look that he could usually count on to melt her resistance. This time, however, her demeanor did not change.

"I'll let you rest, Mom."

He kissed her again, stood up, took a couple of steps toward the door, and then turned back around.

"Oh, ah, just one little thing."

Moving the armchair out of the way, he rolled the utility table up close to the wheelchair. From his briefcase, he took two documents and set them down side by side on the table.

"What are these?"

"One's a power of attorney, and the other's a health care proxy form. I need you to sign them."

"What?"

Drawing a pen from his trouser pocket, he placed it on the table between the documents.

"What is this? You give me a bunch of papers, and you tell me to sign them without knowing what's in them?"

"They're for your own protection. I would never do anything to harm you."

"I already have a power of attorney and a health care proxy."

"Jeffrey made you sign them over to him?"

"He didn't make me do anything."

"But he brought you documents, and you signed them?"

"He was here after I had my stroke. You weren't."

"What are you talking about? I came to see you in the hospital the next morning. Or have you forgotten?"

"For fifteen minutes, and then nothing for a month or more."

"It was more like a week, if that. I'm a doctor. It's not easy for me to get away. But after that first week, I was here almost every day. Maybe you've forgotten."

"That's not something I would forget."

"I'm not saying you're wrong, but it's easy to get confused. It was a very traumatic time for you, and you were pumped full of medications, which have all kinds of side effects."

"Sometimes I look at you . . ."

She began to cough.

"Please let me handle this stuff instead of Jeffrey. You'll be much better off. I promise you. I only want to do what's best for you."

"I look at you, and I say to myself, 'Who is this person? He can't be my son.'"

"That's not fair. That's very hurtful."

"I think you should leave now. I'm tired. How many times do I have to . . ."

The coughing started again.

"I'm not leaving until you sign these."

"Get out, and take your papers with you!"

She pressed the call button.

A roaring flame rose in Dr. Rosen's gullet. He snatched the documents and the pen off the table.

"Fine, then! Let your good son handle everything. Your good son, who's just waiting for you to die, so he can grab whatever he couldn't when you were still alive. He told me so. He laughs at you behind your back. Yes, I'll get out, all right. I'll get out, and I won't come back. And you'll never see Nathan again."

Dr. Rosen closed the door behind him with a bang that rattled the furniture.

Sheila dabbed at her eyes with a tissue so the nurse who would soon bring her afternoon pills would not see her tears. A leaden fatigue set in, rendering even her serviceable limbs inert. Her body tilted far to the right, the armrest pressing hard against her ribs. Feeling light-headed, she pressed the call button. She waited for several minutes, then pressed it again.

CHAPTER 19

The heartburn that afflicted Dr. Rosen the remainder of that Sunday rivaled in intensity that which had driven him to the emergency room. In the days afterward, as June gave way to July, it continued to plague him. No amount of antacids could tamp down the flames.

Dr. Rosen experienced another painful flare-up on July 4, which happened to fall on a Wednesday. At the Peninsula Pain Center, the holiday went unobserved by Dr. Zhukov, to whom it meant nothing, and by his customers, whose cravings never took a day off. Tamika had stuffed an oversized canvas beach bag with towels, sunscreen, sandwiches, and drinks in anticipation of a day at Jones Beach, followed by an evening of fireworks. When the doctor told her that she would have to make her usual delivery to the pain center instead, she said, "You can shove those scripts up your fat white ass. I ain't going back to the pain center today or ever again. You can do your own dealing, like any other lowlife street dealer. You wouldn't even make a good street dealer. You're too much of a pussy. You make your girlfriend and your son do it for you."

"I'm in no mood for this now, OK? The scripts have to be delivered. It can't be helped."

"A drug dealer. A doctor who kills his patients because he don't care enough about them to read their charts. A businessman who gets robbed blind by his office manager because he can't read a spreadsheet. This is who I'm living with?"

"Nobody's forcing you to stay here."

"A son who tries to rip off his mother. No wonder she hate you."

The previous Sunday, in a moment of weakness that he now regretted, Dr. Rosen had given Tamika a partial—in both senses of the word—account of what had transpired between him and Sheila.

"That's bullshit! I'm doing what's best for her. And she doesn't hate me. She's been alienated from me by my brother."

"She hate you. Your own mother hate you. You always calling other people losers. You the biggest loser I ever met."

"Sorry, but you'll have to translate. I don't speak ghetto."

She flung the tote at his head—he ducked just in time—and ran off to the bedroom, where she stuffed as many clothes as she could into the battered suitcase that she had brought with her when she had moved into the apartment. On her way out, she slammed the front door with such force that the mounting plate of the top hinge, already loosened as a result of the depredations of the Golovorez Solutions crew, broke free from the frame.

After gobbling down a handful of antacid tablets, Dr. Rosen drove out to Queens himself. Unlike Tamika, he counted the money Golovorez gave him and found that, contrary to the agreement he thought he had with Dr. Zhukov, his fee amounted to only $200 per prescription.

When he protested, Golovorez shrugged.

"What can you do? That is Dr. Zhukov. As they say, his word is your bond."

"Nobody says that."

"Dr. Zhukov does."

With Tamika absent on Thursday and Friday, chaos reigned in the office. Unable to log into the scheduling program because he had forgotten his password, Dr. Rosen had no idea who was coming and at what time. Mixing up files and forgetting names, as he had with Mr. Wasserman, he drove three patients to tears. Before he hustled one woman out the door, she spent the few minutes he allotted her talking somberly of how she saw no relief from her troubles except through suicide. Another threatened to report him to the Department of Health.

He did not despair, though, for he expected that Tamika, who had gone back to Queens to stay with her mother, Janise Hawkins, would return before the weekend was out and restore order on Monday. Ms. Hawkins was a three-hundred-pound terror who, though shy of forty, relied upon a quad cane for locomotion when she could not avoid it altogether and lived on the proceeds of her oxy dealing, her SSI disability benefits, and whatever she could cadge from Tamika, her other children, and anybody else who came within her orbit. Never would she let a day pass without reminding Tamika of how she had suffered through sixteen hours of labor to bring her into the world. She expected Tamika to atone for that original sin by supporting her financially; shopping, cooking, and cleaning for her; and making sure her supply of oxycodone never ran short. Tamika's flight to the Upper West Side had enraged Janise. Her daughter's return, the doctor imagined, would, like the pricking of an abscess, cause the foulness within Janise to come gushing forth. Life with her would quickly become insupportable for Tamika.

He called Tamika on Friday night. Even though she insisted that she would never, never, never, never, never go back to him, he heard the wavering resolve in her voice. By then, she had endured two days' worth of harangues from her mother—the mother whose joints ached, so she could hardly take two steps without wanting to cry out in pain; whose enlarged heart and exhausted lungs left her gasping for breath all day long; who had suffered the torments of Job while her ungrateful daughter had run off to live with a rich white doctor in Manhattan. Tamika had endured, as well, two nights of fragmented sleep on a tattered living room sofa in Janise's sauna-like apartment, one flight up from a noisy dive bar.

By Sunday morning she could take no more. Before sunrise, while Janise slept, Tamika again packed her suitcase, which was older than she and had a broken wheel that made it impossible to roll. In the darkness, she dragged the bag six blocks to the nearest Long Island Railroad Station. At Penn Station, she had to haul it down the stairs to the subway platform and then, when she reached her stop, back upstairs to the street. From there, she had but three blocks to cover to reach the high rise to which she had vowed just a few days earlier never, never, never, never, never to return. For a slight young woman, however, dragging along the sidewalk, on an already stifling July morning, an overstuffed suitcase that kept threatening to topple over onto its side, three blocks may as well have been three miles. When she saw the doorman attired in his green livery, standing just outside the building's entrance, she just managed to gasp out a "hello." As usual, he did not return the greeting. When she had first moved in, he must have asked her at least a dozen times, "Excuse me, miss, do you have any business here?" Even after a year, he appraised her as though still unconvinced that she had any legitimate business inside.

As she started down the hall to the elevator, the spiteful suitcase rolled onto its right side and brought Tamika down with it. She cried out in pain, but the doorman did not budge from his post. Picking herself up, she pushed the suitcase, still lying flat on its side, into the elevator and, upon arriving at her floor, pushed it out the same way. It fell over twice more as she dragged it up the long corridor to the apartment. She unlocked the still unrepaired door and, anticipating the usual resistance, pushed against it with her shoulder. It opened but an inch or so—all that the heretofore never-used chain lock allowed. Through the slit between the door and the frame, she could hear a manic voice on the television offering stock tips. She rapped on the door and, after a moment, heard the doctor's approaching footsteps. As she waited, though, the sound of those steps grew fainter. He was now walking away from, rather than toward, the door. Hearing the refrigerator open and close, she knocked again, more loudly. Again she listened for his footsteps. She heard the sound of a chair being moved.

"Will you please open the damn door?"

No reply came from the doctor. The suitcase fell over yet again. She had not the strength to pick it up this time, so she sat down on it, pressed her back against the wall, and closed her eyes. The hallway felt as hot as the day outdoors but without even a leavening breeze. Somewhere on the floor a woman began to scream. The sound seemed to come from both directions at once. Belatedly, Tamika realized that it came from her. Rising again, she pounded her fist against the door, as if it were the source of her torment.

An eye appeared between the door and the frame.

"What's all this screaming about? You'll wake up the whole floor."

"What you think I'm screaming about? How long you gonna make me stay out here?"

The door closed. She heard the chain slide from its groove, but again the door opened just enough for her to see the doctor's eye.

"I don't know if I should let you back in. After the things you said to me."

The door closed again and then, after a moment, swung open. Dr. Rosen stood in the doorway wearing a white terry-cloth robe and a triumphant smile.

Tamika spit in his face, the wad of saliva catching him between the eyebrows and dribbling down his nose. Without another word, she turned and walked off, leaving the suitcase in the hall.

"You bitch!" he shouted.

Tamika did not turn around.

He dragged the suitcase into the apartment, emptied its contents onto the living room floor, and stuffed the whole pile into a couple of Hefty bags. Rifling through closets, dresser drawers, and bathroom cabinets, he did the same with the clothes, shoes, and toiletries that Tamika had left behind when departing for Queens the previous week. He then carried the Hefty bags, which contained the bulk of her worldly possessions, to the trash room. That act of vengeance did not provide the catharsis he sought, however. The touch of her saliva upon his skin had triggered an inscrutable chemical reaction, setting off a conflagration in his chest that would torment him for the rest of the day and much of the night.

CHAPTER 20

On Monday, at the end of his session with Boadecia, the doctor, leaning back in his chair, inquired with an affected nonchalance, "So, you can bring me some business?"

Boadecia, grinning, sprang from her chair, jumped six inches off the floor, and clapped her hands three times.

"I can bring you more business than you'll know what to do with."

"You seem pretty excited about it. What's in it for you?"

He stared into her wall eye, as though expecting to find the answer there.

"Nothing. I just like to help my friends."

"I'm sure you do. I can imagine what those friends are like. Don't bring them around here all at once, OK? We'll start with one of them, or maybe two, and go from there."

"I'll bring my friend Carol next week."

"Carol. I don't think you've ever mentioned a Carol before. How long have you known this Carol?"

"Just a few weeks, but she's become a real good friend. I've made a lot of new friends recently."

"Not in law enforcement, I hope."

"You'll like Carol. She'll buy a lot from you. Oxy is like Pez to her."

"Great."

Watching the livestream in his downtown office, Agent Hardin groaned.

As Boadecia pranced through the empty waiting room on her way out, Dr. Rosen lingered in the hallway, watching her mistrustfully. He had never seen her so buoyant. Who were these new friends of hers whom she wanted so much to help? She did not even try to cajole from him a free script or two as a finder's fee for bringing him a new customer. That was most unlike her. Might she be working for the police?

He quickly dismissed the idea. No police force would ever hire Boadecia. Besides, his recent misfortunes had left him in such straits that he could not afford to turn away any Carol that she might drag in. He needed her to bring him twenty Carols, and he needed them right away, rather than a week hence.

The lights would stay on for at least another month, but Dr. Rosen had to dispense with the office cleaning crew. He could do the job just as well himself, he decided, and he did for the first two days. Then the intervals between cleanings grew longer. He saw that the desk and shelves needed dusting; the carpet, vacuuming; and the wastebasket, overflowing with sandwich wrappers and crushed soda cans, emptying. Every day he swore that he would get to those tasks, but even when he found the time, lassitude would overcome him and sap his resolve, or yet another attack of heartburn would cause him to forget his good intentions altogether.

In Tamika's absence, folders, papers, envelopes, and professional journals accumulated atop his office desk until they covered the surface several layers deep. He hired a temp to take Tamika's place at the reception desk but dismissed her within a week for fear that she might find something compromising in his records.

Boadecia, who seemed to have a particular knack for detecting his vulnerabilities and poking at them, remarked one day, "What happened, doc? Did the maid die or something?"

"Very funny."

*

The X-ray film he held in his hands showed the neck vertebrae of the putative friend who had accompanied Boadecia to the office, a woman known to the doctor as Carol Burnett but designated as undercover officer 1 (UC-1) in the complaint Agent Hardin had already begun to draft. Pale, slender, and freckle-faced, the woman wore torn jeans and a black Metallica T-shirt with purple lettering. Her short, wavy hair was an anemic shade of red. She had the look and manner of a user: gray-green eyes that never quite met his; a vague smile, if a smile it was; a voice devoid of inflection. She might have been twenty-five or twice that age.

The first time Boadecia had brought her to the office, Dr. Rosen had prescribed 30 oxycodone pills, along with a muscle relaxant, rather than the requested 120.

"I can't give you that many right off," he told the new patient. "It raises a red flag. Bring me an X-ray next time, and I'll be able to give you more."

"OK."

Her too ready acquiescence made him uneasy. In a typical user, even one as lacking in affect as she, the doctor's demurral would have evoked anger or pleading or whining—anything but "OK."

His inability to spot any abnormality on the X-ray film she had brought with her on this, her second visit, made him warier still.

"So where does it hurt exactly?"

"In my neck."

Dr. Rosen turned his eyes to the ceiling and took a breath. This one's obtuseness tried his patience nearly as much as Boadecia's whining. For the sake of efficiency, he had again slotted the two women into one opening in his schedule; he resolved not to do so again.

"Yes, I know that. Did the doctor tell you which disc it was?"

"I don't know. Maybe he did and I forgot, or maybe he didn't."

"It would help me to know. Because I really can't tell a whole lot from this X-ray. Let me have a look."

He put the X-ray down and came around from behind the desk.

"Does this hurt?" he asked, pressing a thumb against the back of the patient's neck.

The first two probes elicited nothing; the third, a piercing scream the instant he made contact with her skin. Did she and Boadecia exchange conspiratorial glances, or did he imagine they did?

"On a one-to-ten scale, how much did that hurt?"

"A lot."

"Can you give me a number? If one is just a little tenderness, and ten . . . Oh, never mind."

Returning to his chair, he wrote out a prescription.

"I'll give you 90 this time. If you bring me an MRI next time, I'll be able to give you more. That's $1,350."

She counted out several $100 bills, laying them on the desk. Looking confused, she paused, started over, and soon lost her way again.

"Look, I'll give you a break this time. Just give me $1,000, OK? That's ten bills. You can count to ten, right?"

The exchange finally executed, he began typing on his laptop.

Watching from downtown, Agent Hardin pumped his fist and cried, "Woo hoo!"

"Carol Burnett. Is that your real name?"

Boadecia giggled.

"What's so damn funny?"

"Everything."

The doctor shook his head.

"I have two comedians in here. Everyone's a comedian. Occupation? I should have asked you last time, but I forgot."

"I'm a secretary."

"Not at the Twentieth Precinct, I hope."

"What's that?"

"I mean, you're not a cop, are you? Because I don't want to be in a segment on pill-pushing docs on *60 Minutes*."

"You'd be famous if you got on *60 Minutes*."

While Boadecia squealed with delight and kicked her feet up, UC-1, with her drifting eyes and spectral smile, remained a blank to the doctor.

Two days later, Dr. Rosen found himself poring over an even more enigmatic spinal X-ray. Taken from above, the image revealed some early disc calcification, but other aspects of it—the tapering of the ribs toward the bottom of the spine, the narrowness of the pelvis—puzzled him. The X-ray looked more like that of a child, he thought, than of an adult.

It was neither, as Special Agent Hardin would later attest in United States of America v. Robert D. Rosen: "UC-2 told Rosen that UC-2's X-ray was taken by the doctor who took UC-1's X-ray. Based on my conversations with UC-2, I learned that the patient whose X-ray was presented to Rosen was in fact a black Labrador retriever named Elmore. The X-ray was obtained from Elmore's veterinarian."

The man who had brought the doctor Elmore's X-ray gave his name as Chester Burnett and said he was Carol's brother. He did not resemble his sister, with whom he had come, any more than she did her famous namesake. Dressed in a gray tank top, denim shorts, and a pair of Birkenstocks, he had a round face covered by several days' growth of salt-and-pepper whiskers and silver-streaked brown hair pulled back into a ponytail. A pair of blue-tinted glasses with circular lenses concealed his irises.

To enliven the proceedings, he had brought with him an imaginary blues ensemble. Playing and vocalizing air guitar, air blues harp, and air bass, and drumming on edge of the desk, he jammed away while Dr. Rosen studied the film. The heretofore near-catatonic UC-1 startled Dr. Rosen by joining in with some blistering boogie-woogie air piano riffs.

"Hey, I'm trying to concentrate here, all right? Time for the band to take a break."

UC-2 capped a final short drum solo with a vocal representation of clashing cymbals followed by a sustained lupine howl.

The hijinks did not please Agent Hardin any more than they did the doctor. Over the course of his career, the strait-laced FBI man had learned to bend when necessary. Having worked undercover himself, he well understood the challenges and stresses his agents faced and tried to allow them as much leeway as possible, so long as they caught their prey. Still, a dog's X-ray was a bit much, to say nothing of the aliases Carol and Chester Burnett. He would have to have a chat with these two later and remind them that they were FBI agents, not a comedy act.

"Look, I'll be honest here," the doctor said. "I can't make heads or tails of this film."

UC-1 stifled a laugh, while UC-2 made no such effort.

"Heads or tails. That's a good one, doc."

Even Agent Hardin chuckled.

"I don't know what you find so funny. For the amount you want, I need MRIs from both of you. I have to cover my ass. I don't want to end up at Riker's Island."

"Nah, you won't end up at Riker's, doc," replied UC-2. "That's not the way the world works. Some of the street dealers you're supplying might though."

"How do you know that?"

"I just know. Everybody knows. Rich white doctors don't end up there."

"For now, I'll give you ninety and you forty-five," said Dr. Rosen, pointing at UC-1 and UC-2, respectively. "That's $900 for you and $450 for you. I'm giving you both a break this time because I think we can do business together. You bring me more customers, and I'll treat you right. People like Boadecia

I charge twice as much. I keep hoping she won't come back, but she always does. What a nut case. I know she's an addict, and I'm almost sure she's dealing. I used to worry that she might be some kind of informant, but can you imagine that airhead as an informant?"

"Boadecia as an informant?" said UC-2. "That's too funny."

"Too funny," echoed UC-1.

CHAPTER 21

To the surprise and dismay of Agent Hardin and his UCs, Boadecia, aka CI-1, soon discovered that she could monetize her position by becoming a not-quite-so-confidential inform-ant. Through her, knowledge of Dr. Rosen's prescribing habits spread widely, and from every new customer she reeled in, she took a finder's fee in cash or pills. All this she told Agent Hardin unbidden, so pleased was she by her own cleverness.

"This is not how it's supposed to work," he told her. "But thanks for your service. I think we can take it from here."

Her unexpected dismissal brought an outpouring of plead-ing and tears sufficient to empty the box of Kleenex on Agent Hardin's desk.

"It's not that you've done anything wrong," he assured her. "This Rosen is a dangerous character, and we have to get you out now for your own protection. That's the problem with un-dercover work. You stay in one place too long, and people start to notice. That's how your cover gets blown. But you've done a great job for us. You've given us all we need and more to take the bastard down. You're a natural at this. I'll tell you what. I'm going to put you on speed dial right now. The next time we need a top-notch informant, you're the first person I'll call."

Even after her termination, the effects of Boadecia's entre-preneurial efforts manifested themselves in the doctor's of-fice. A new type of clientele streamed in, a shabby-looking but also enterprising bunch. The waiting room became a market where customers carried on a brisk business exchanging money, scripts, and drugs. The newcomers discomfited and drove away the doctor's regular patients, even the economy-class ones.

The waiting room soon took on the grim aspect of the Peninsula Pain Center. Untended, the plants withered and died. The essential oil diffusers went missing, their soothing scents replaced by the smells of alcohol, tobacco, sweat, and sometimes urine that clung to the new class of customer. The wall speakers also disappeared. Once a patient waiting on Dr. Rosen might have collected his or her thoughts while on a vicarious cruise along Smetana's tranquil *Moldau*. Now fractious voices filled the room, haggling, cursing, muttering, threatening. An acrid cloud of smoke hung in the air. The doctor, sneezing and coughing all day long, purchased a large "Please Do Not Smoke" sign for the reception desk, but the customers ignored both the sign and the city ordinance that it represented. Adapting to his new circumstances, Dr. Rosen distributed ashtrays around the room, but all of them were gone within a week of their purchase, as was the sign. The customers continued to stub out their butts against the tabletops and walls or grind them into the carpeting with their shoes.

On the positive side, owing to the new business Boadecia brought his way, the doctor regained a measure of solvency. At the beginning of August, he made his mortgage, office rent, car loan, and utilities payments on time. In September, he did likewise and paid his quarterly malpractice insurance premium only a few days late. Pat, he decided, would have to wait for his fees, as would Mrs. Agnello for the first out-of-pocket installment he owed her. He could have met those obligations by drawing on the proceeds of his oxy business, from which he had accumulated a cash reserve of nearly $25,000 that he kept in a safe deposit box. That money, however, he vowed only to use *in extremis*. Even under better circumstances, he would have tarried as long as possible before paying Mrs. Agnello, for he wanted to make the process of collecting as costly as possible for her in both legal fees and aggravation.

He feared, though, and with good reason, that his new-found solvency would prove ephemeral. The brownstone's other tenant, an ophthalmologist, complained to the landlord about the noise emanating from the office above, the disagreeable and sometimes aggressive characters he and his patients encountered on the stairs outside and in the vestibule, and the litter that accumulated in both places. His practice, he claimed, had begun to suffer as a result of Dr. Rosen's negligence. When confronted by the landlord, Dr. Rosen denied all, suggesting that the complaints stemmed from the ophthalmologist's envy of his larger office space. Some neighbors must have complained as well, however. Late one afternoon, Dr. Rosen got a visit from the police. Fortunately, all the patients had gone by then, though traces of them lingered: the smells, the discarded cigarette butts, a torn gray hoodie draped over the back of one of the waiting room chairs, and, most alarmingly, an empty oxycodone vial lying on the carpet beneath the coffee table. Dr. Rosen took the same tack with the police as he had with the landlord, again successfully. One of the officers did remark, however, "You really ought to get this place fixed up. I've seen crack houses that look better than this."

Increasingly, he fell prey to fatalism and inertia. He wished he had never written an oxycodone prescription, had never gotten mixed up with the likes of Boadecia and, especially, the Russians. The oxy business, which now provided him with almost all his income, would surely prove his undoing. He could not keep fooling the landlord or the police. The former would evict him, or the latter would come back with a warrant next time. Even the return of customers he had previously banished to the Peninsula Pain Center, while economically advantageous for him, brought peril. Their sudden disappearance from the pain center had aroused Dr. Zhukov's suspicions—or so Golovorez informed the doctor via a voicemail delivered at 2:36 a.m. An arrest would result in disgrace, prison, and the loss of his medical license; from Golovorez and Zhukov, he could expect worse.

Every morning, though, he would return to the office and write more scripts.

Then one day in mid-September, the ever-watchful Agent Hardin decided he had seen enough, and he said to his supervisor, "OK. We're good to go."

CHAPTER 22

The arrest was as banal as it was terrifying—a scene Dr. Rosen had watched play out ten thousand times on television and in the movies without ever having imagined himself at the center of it. At 6 a.m., there came a thunderous banging on the door. The hinge plate that he had recently reset with plastic wood and new screws became dislodged again. When he opened the door, half-a-dozen FBI agents in blue jackets and khaki tactical pants, with holstered pistols at their hips, swarmed inside. One of them pinned him against the wall and handcuffed him, while the others fanned out into the living room, dining room, and bedrooms. Overturning tables and chairs, tossing aside seat cushions, and rummaging through drawers and cabinets, they left as much chaos in their wake as Golovorez's crew had.

Only one neighbor watched the agents hustle Dr. Rosen through the hallway to the elevator. A tiny octogenarian, she stood in her doorway with her hand over her heart, wearing a pink bathrobe and a shocked expression. She was one of the few neighbors with whom the doctor conversed with any regularity. He would, from time to time, change a light bulb for her, take a heavy box down from a shelf, or move a small piece of furniture. In return, she would bake him cookies. Dr. Rosen, who sometimes joked about his imperviousness to shame, could not look her in the eye.

#

The holding cells at the federal courthouse being filled beyond capacity, the agents deposited Dr. Rosen in a city jail. Devoid of any furnishings or fixtures save for benches that ran along the walls, a filthy toilet, sans seat, that afforded no privacy, and a small metal sink, the cell had a gray concrete floor and three cinderblock walls of the same dismal hue. The bars fronting the cell were also gray. On and under the benches, men in tattered clothes or underwear lay curled up, some snoring and others rolling and thrashing about. Still others sat or stood in tight circles and kept up a steady chatter in English and Spanish. One wild-eyed, bearded man, clad only in a pair of yellowing boxer shorts, was having a very animated argument with himself in a language he must have invented. All the conversations but his broke off when Dr. Rosen entered the cell. The men turned to stare at him. He smiled nervously. The stench, a noisome compound of sweat, vomit, alcohol, urine, feces, ammonia, poverty, loneliness, and despair, made him retch. The heat was insupportable, and his heartburn unremitting. Turning his back on his cellmates, he grabbed hold of the bars and squeezed them until his fingers turned white.

He maintained that pose until Pat McKinley came to bail him out some five hours later. Pat had required some persuading.

"I don't know why in God's name I should do this. One: You still owe me $4,500 for representing you at the deposition and negotiating the settlement for you, and I'm sure you have absolutely no intention of ever paying me. Two: Knowing you as I do, I have no doubt that you're guilty as hell and deserve to be locked away for a good long time."

The doctor's pleading and blubbering—"it was a setup"—eventually wore him down though. He agreed to appear on the doctor's behalf, with the stipulation that after the bail hearing, Dr. Rosen would find other representation and never bother him again.

In the courtroom, Pat put on a masterful performance, getting the doctor's bail reduced from the $250,000 requested by the prosecution to one-tenth that amount. Dr. Rosen, Pat argued, was a kind-hearted, selfless, devoted practitioner of medicine who had used his gifts to provide comfort and renewed health and life to thousands of patients, from nine-year-olds to nonagenarians. Surely the court had to recognize that one mistake could not blot out a lifetime of accomplishment and service. Further, as a pillar of the community, Dr. Rosen presented no flight risk whatsoever.

Standing with Pat on the portico of the federal courthouse building, in the shade of a pediment that bore at its base the motto "THE TRUE ADMINISTRATION OF JUSTICE IS THE FIRMEST PILLAR OF GOOD GOVERNMENT," Dr. Rosen massaged each of his sore wrists in turn. The cuffs had left angry red blemishes on both.

"I'm happy about one thing anyway. Mrs. Agnello will never get a dime from me now."

"Yeah, you really showed her. Now if you'll excuse me, I need to go home and take a shower. There's just one thing I don't understand. Why?"

"Why what?"

"Why did you do it?"

The doctor scowled.

"I told you I didn't do anything. This is bullshit. I was set up."

"You had everything going for you. A practice on the Upper West Side. Media exposure. Why would you throw it all away for a few extra bucks that you didn't even need?"

"Go to hell, Pat."

"I should for what I did in that courtroom today."

At the bottom of the steps, an attractive, young red-haired reporter, accompanied by a camera crew, stood in wait. The microphone that the reporter thrust in Dr. Rosen's face bore the red, white, and blue logo of the local Fox affiliate, Fox 5.

"Dr. Rosen, you've gone on TV to criticize other doctors for prescribing opiates. You've called them drug dealers. How does it feel to be arrested by the FBI and charged in federal court with illegally distributing a controlled substance?"

Dr. Rosen gave a start and threw up his hands to shield his face from the camera. His appearance at that moment embarrassed him as much as his fall in status from doctor and TV personality to accused felon. Could the camera crew not have allowed him even a moment to make himself presentable? He had no makeup artist to hide the bulges under his eyes or to give him a thicker head of hair, as he had in the Chicago studio. He wore the same rumpled trousers and white shirt, now with yellow stains under the armpits, as he had the day before; the FBI raiding crew had allowed him precisely two minutes to throw them on before dragging him off to jail.

Pat, who would normally have placed his bulky body between client and reporter in such a situation, instead sidestepped his way out of camera range, showing surprising agility for a big man.

"What about the charges? Is it true what they're saying about you?"

Dr. Rosen, letting his arms drop to his sides, glared into the camera.

"Of course not. It's all made up. Lies and slander. It's a total setup. A witch hunt. I'm innocent. I'm very innocent."

"Hey, doc," Pat chortled, "You're famous. Congratulations!"

CHAPTER 23

At North Shore Meadows Nursing and Rehabilitation, Sheila, suffering from a cold, ate dinner in her room that evening, watched over, intermittently, by a harried aide assigned both to her and the dining hall. On her plate lay two puddles of puree, one pink and the other green. After giving each a stir, Sheila slowly raised a spoonful of the green, which smelled vaguely of peas, to her mouth. She grimaced as she swallowed, then threw down the spoon, and pushed the tray away.

"Miss Sheila, you have to eat," the aide gently scolded her. "You've been losing too much weight."

"Why don't you try some, and see how you like it? Would you pour me some of my Thick & Easy? I'll have that. And turn on the news, please. Channel 4."

"You can't just live on Thick & Easy, Miss Sheila. You got to eat something from your tray."

Reluctantly she reached for her spoon again.

"All right. It's disgusting, but I may as well get it over with."

She began shoveling the pink puree, which she guessed was meat of some kind, into her mouth.

On the television, a commercial advertising leak-proof underwear for women with bladder issues melded into another for mobility scooters. Two "ask your doctor" commercials followed, the first for an erectile dysfunction pill and the second for a psoriasis medication with a vaguely Hungarian-sounding name. Then the newscast resumed.

Sheila put her spoon down.

"Wait. This is Fox. I never watch Fox. Would you change the channel, please?"

"I'll be back in a minute, Miss Sheila. I just have to take a peek at the dining room."

After a short preamble from the anchorman about the arrest of a prominent Manhattan doctor on charges of selling opioid prescriptions for cash, the broadcast cut away from the studio to the courthouse. Viewers got a glimpse of the façade of the building, and then, there on the screen was Dr. Robert Rosen, indignantly proclaiming his innocence of all charges and accusing the government of staging a "witch hunt" against him.

Sheila Rosen gagged and clutched at her throat. The aide, who had just returned from the dining room, smacked her between the shoulder blades, causing her to cough up a lump of puree. Still Sheila could not breathe or stop coughing. Her body jerked forward and back, pink puree spraying from her mouth in every direction. The aide ran out to the corridor and shouted for help. A nurse appeared but could do nothing except wait for Sheila to cough herself out, at which point she cleared the spittle, puree, and phlegm from Sheila's chin and neck with a wet wipe. The nurse then reinserted the cannula, which Sheila's aide had removed before dinner, and restarted the generator.

Just before bedtime, Sheila called Jeffrey.

"Could you please come up here?"

"Is there something wrong?"

"I don't feel well."

"What is it? Are you sick?"

"I just don't feel well."

"But what's . . . ? All right. I'll drive up tomorrow."

"Could you come tonight?"

"Tonight?"

Hours of solitary drinking had rendered him unfit to get behind the wheel.

"Mom, I don't . . . It would be the middle of the night when I got there. You'd be asleep."

"I won't be."

"I'll be there tomorrow. I'll start out first thing in the morning. I promise."

"Fine."

She hung up. When, after a few minutes, Jeffrey called again, she did not answer.

Wheezing like a kettle nearing a boil, Sheila lay awake well past midnight. She fell asleep briefly and then woke up gagging. Another coughing spell overtook her, and she could not catch her breath. Panicked, she groped for the call button, but the new aide who had helped transfer her to bed had not fastened it to the sheet in its customary place. She could not reach it.

When his phone rang in the middle of the night, Jeffrey assumed that the caller was one of the many scammers who plagued him day and night, and he did not get out of bed. After sleeping late, he awoke with a hangover of sufficient magnitude to make him vow never again to speak ill of Dr. Sober-Up. More painful still was the recognition that in having refused Sheila last night and already broken his promise to her to start out for New York early in the morning, he had treated her as shabbily as his brother did. When he checked his phone, he saw that someone from North Shore had left a voice message for him. The message—consisting in its entirety of a terse request that he call back—divulged nothing, leaving him to imagine the worst. He first tried to reach Sheila in her room, waiting more than a dozen rings. Her failure to pick up was not unusual, for she often had difficulty maneuvering her wheelchair to get to the phone, but on this morning, it worried him. He called the nurses station, but no one answered there either. On his second attempt, an aide passed him to a nurse.

"Whom do you wish to speak to?"

"Mrs. Rosen. Sheila Rosen."

"Mrs. Rosen? Who is this?"

"I'm her son."

"Wait, nobody called you?"

"There was a message. All it said was that I should call back. Is something wrong?"

"She was discharged last night."

"Discharged? What do you mean discharged? Discharged to where?"

"To the hospital."

"What happened?"

"Wait. I'll get the head nurse."

In the twenty excruciating minutes he held on before being disconnected, his hangover abated without the aid of Dr. Sober-Up's cure. Following a quick shower and three cups of coffee, he dressed, packed an overnight bag, tossed it into the trunk of his Prius, and headed north on I-95.

CHAPTER 24

After leaving the courthouse, Dr. Rosen retreated to his apartment, and for three days, he hid himself away. He had neither phone nor computer to distract him, the FBI having confiscated both. The television he had bought to replace the one destroyed by Golovorez's crew had never worked properly; he now unplugged it and turned it to the wall. Eating little, he nourished himself instead on lurid revenge fantasies against those he deemed guilty of having wronged him: Barry and Barry's agent, Tamika, Pat McKinley, Mrs. Agnello and her lawyer, Nathan, the FBI, Sheila, Jeffrey, and many, many more, for he had grudges stretching back decades. Mostly he drank and slept. Even while he slumbered, however, his notoriety grew.

Boadecia, informed of the arrest by Agent Hardin several hours after the fact, rejoiced. She took to Facebook, Twitter, and TikTok to trumpet, and exaggerate, her contribution to bringing the miscreant doctor to justice.

At about the same time, a complaint titled "United States of America v. Robert Rosen" appeared on the Department of Justice's website, accompanied by a triumphal press release lauding the arrest as a significant achievement in the ongoing effort of the DOJ to stem the epidemic of prescription drug abuse and addiction by protecting the public against unscrupulous medical professionals who exploited their positions for profit.

As Sheila was eating her ill-fated dinner at North Shore, Nathan, idly channel surfing in a living room in Scarsdale, happened upon the broadcast that had so discombobulated her. Delighted to find that Fox 5 had also posted the video and an accompanying article on its website, he did his best to make the clip go viral, uploading it to his Facebook page and including the link in a tweet. His mother shared the link on her Facebook timeline, under the caption, "My famous ex!" She prevailed on her two siblings to share the link as well, and for good measure, she texted and emailed it to several cousins and friends who did not have social media accounts.

Though only Fox 5 had the doctor on video, other local TV stations posted brief articles about his arrest on their websites. The New York tabloids, however, picked up the story with much greater enthusiasm, particularly the *Post*. Pat McKinley, while doing a little idle research on sentencing guidelines for violations of 21 U.S.C. § 841(b)(1)(c), the statute under which the government had charged Dr. Rosen, enjoyed a hearty laugh when he happened upon a headline on the *Post's* website: "HIPPOCRATIC OAF! Feds Nab Double-Dealing Doc." Over dinner, he showed the article to his wife.

"You're enjoying this too much," she said. "It's pure schadenfreude."

"Some days, honey, schadenfreude is all that keeps me going."

She had to concede that she did like the headline.

Schadenfreude abounded at a blues bar in the West Village, where vintage guitars and pictures of old bluesmen lined the brick walls, and massive exposed beams traversed the high ceiling. There, Agent Hardin, UCs-1 and -2, and the raiding crew celebrated the arrest until the early hours of the following day. Agent Hardin bought the first round of drinks, while UC-2, aka Chester Burnett, who fronted the house band, dedicated a medley of prison songs to Dr. Rosen: "Midnight Special," "Chain Gang," "Folsom Prison Blues," and "Jailhouse Rock."

"Now here's one," said UC-2, "in honor of a special person we call CI-1 who helped make this all possible."

Stepping up to the microphone, UC-1, aka Carol Burnett, showed off her vocal chops, leading the band in a rousing "Born to Be Wild."

When Barry Bullard saw the article in the *Post*, inspiration seized him. That very day he began work on what would become *Bulldog IV: The Bulldog is Back*, a self-help/memoir hybrid depicting his struggle to overcome the opioid addiction from which he had suffered after falling under the spell of a drug-dealing quack to whom he gave the name of Dr. Rupert Rosebud. To rid himself of an association that could only do him harm now, he also took down from his website the video testimonial that Dr. Rosen had recorded for him and the blurb touting the media success that the doctor had attained through the aid of Barry's coaching.

Janise Hawkins, another *Post* reader, saw the article and promptly fired off a cryptic but barbed text to her daughter: "ur white doc n trubl hahahaha." The news saddened Tamika, for she was not the sort to wish misfortune even on those who well deserved it. At the same time, the experience of having lived with Dr. Rosen and known him intimately tempered her sympathy. Most of all, she felt uneasy. Toiling again behind the counter at Torpedo's, but now trying to save as much of her meager earnings as possible in order to enroll at the local community college, Tamika had hoped to consign Dr. Rosen to the past. His arrest imperiled that hope. She had no doubt that in exchange for an offer of leniency, he would happily inform on her, thereby keeping her life on the same luckless course as ever. The justice system, she surmised, would likely deal more harshly with her than with him, due not only to her skin color and station in life but also to the huge stash of oxy pills and cash that Janise kept in her dresser drawer. That Tamika had no involvement with her mother's illicit enterprise would not matter to the FBI in the event of a raid on the apartment the two women shared.

Kellyanne, who also came across the article on the *Post*'s website, received the news with some ambivalence, her schadenfreude offset by her worry that the arrest could upend the mutual assured destruction pact she had made with the doctor. Might desperation lead him to offer her up to the authorities as part of a plea deal? Though he had never come across with the $10,000 he had promised her, she had upheld her end of their agreement, for she had much to lose if implicated in his crimes. Upon her return to the States, Kellyanne had moved across the country to Los Angeles, bearing with her a recommendation from Dr. Rosen laden with compliments as rich as the cheesecake at Eileen's that she so loved. There she had found a new employer and mark: a plastic surgeon with a significant Hollywood clientele. She called Dr. Rosen the day after his arrest to offer her sympathy while dropping a few pointed hints about the consequences he could face for crimes as yet undiscovered should he be so foolish as to point the FBI in her direction. Satisfied that he had taken her warning to heart, she celebrated with an excursion to Rodeo Drive, where she bought herself two more Louis Vuitton handbags.

At the Peninsula Pain Center, Alexey Ivanovich Golovorez, after hearing from one of the customers of Dr. Rosen's arrest, did a Google search on his phone and found the *Post* article, along with similar stories in the *Daily News* and *Newsday*, albeit with less inventive headlines, and the Fox video.

"*Pisdets*!" he roared, picking up a chair and flinging it against the wall. "*Derrmo*! *Blyad*! *Mudak*! *Khui*!"

His outburst so frightened the addled assemblage in the waiting room that they ran for the doors. He had the same thought as Tamika: Dr. Rosen would break quickly in custody and would bring the FBI his way. Golovorez immediately placed two calls, the first to Dr. Zhukov and the second to the moving-and-storage professionals of Golovorez Solutions, who, in addition to their routine practices of theft and mayhem, made something of a specialty of evidence removal.

Within three hours, the crew had shredded or burned whatever incriminating documents they could lay hands on at the center, cleared out all moveable furnishings of any value, and taken sledgehammers to the lights and the plumbing fixtures—water heater, toilets, and sinks—leaving the building to flood. They did the same in the ensuing days at three other pain centers, two in Brighton Beach and one in the Bronx, and as soon as they had finished, they and their bosses took flight for the Old Country.

High over the Atlantic, comfortably ensconced in the first-class compartment of a Moscow-bound 747, Golovorez and Zhukov clinked their Champagne glasses together.

"*Na Zdorovie*," said the unusually relaxed and buoyant Zhukov.

"*Na Zdorovie*," replied the other. "To America. Was good while it lasted, no? Now is *pisdets*."

PART II:

INNOCENCE
REGAINED

CHAPTER 25

Because Pat wanted nothing more to do with him and had referred his account to a collection agency, Dr. Rosen sought other representation. After a desultory search, he settled on a young lawyer named Andrew Le Bâtard ("Circumflex over the first *a*. Yeah, I know what Le Bâtard means, and that's what I am."). Andrew Le Bâtard was cheap as Manhattan lawyers went.

Had his finances not weighed so heavily in his deliberations, Dr. Rosen would likely have turned to someone else. Still several months shy of thirty, Le Bâtard had worked for a couple of years as a New York City public defender before striking out on his own. He had the physique of someone who spent a great deal of time in the gym. His closely cropped black hair accentuated the squareness of his head. With his five o'clock shadow and heavy-lidded eyes, he seemed always on the verge of sleep, making the sudden outbursts to which he was prone all the more shocking. While capable, for the most part, of maintaining a level of decorum suitable for a courtroom or judge's chamber, in less formal settings, the young attorney often showed little ability to modulate either the volume or the content of his speech.

At their first meeting, Andrew, after discussing some similar cases he had had, sounded Dr. Rosen out about a plea bargain. Dr. Rosen bristled.

"Well, my case is different. I'm not pleading guilty to a crime I didn't commit. I'm innocent."

"Very innocent. I heard you say so on the news."

"If you don't believe me, I'll find someone who does. I thought you were a fighter. I'm sick of lawyers who just roll over on me."

"Who said I wasn't a fighter? And what makes you think I don't believe you? When I saw you on Fox, standing in front of the federal courthouse, trying to hide your face from the TV camera, I said to myself, 'Fuckin' aye, man. There's a guy who's as innocent as a babe in arms.'"

"I am innocent, goddamn it."

"Cool. So we'll enter a plea of not guilty, and then we'll see what happens. Does ten years in a federal prison work for you? Because that's what you're gonna get."

The condescension infuriated Dr. Rosen, who was far more accustomed to giving than to receiving such treatment. In the course of his previous legal wrangles, of which the doctor had had many, he had changed lawyers with far less cause, never hesitating to write off his sunk costs if he thought that by so doing he could attain a better result. His current straits, however, allowed him no such flexibility. In reviewing the complaint and supplementary documents submitted by the prosecution, arguing with the doctor in person and over the phone, and beginning the research needed to draft a response, the attorney, even with his relatively reasonable fees, ate through several hundred dollars' worth of retainer within the first week. The buyer's remorse on which the doctor felt powerless to act manifested itself as a near-constant fire in his esophagus.

Money became an all-consuming obsession for Dr. Rosen during the weeks of filings and counter-filings that preceded his scheduled arraignment. Each day he saw his savings diminish.

His worries led him to contemplate the heretofore unthinkable: selling the Jaguar. Most of what he needed he could find within walking distance, and with the termination of his business at the Peninsula Pain Center, he rarely had use for the car anymore. The prosecutor, however, pointed out to the judge that Dr. Rosen had used the Jaguar in committing his alleged offenses. On the very day that the doctor put the car up for sale, the FBI seized it.

The doctor made a game—and for him, unprecedented—effort to economize, keeping the lights off until the evening had so advanced that he could no longer see his way around the apartment, sweating through the afternoons with the air conditioner set at 78 degrees, and unplugging appliances when not using them. After purchasing a pay-as-you go cellphone to replace the one the FBI had seized, he cut off his landline, thereby saving money and excising from his life the telemarketers, scammers, and, more recently, bill collectors who hounded him at all hours of the day and well into the night.

Even while he labored to cut expenses elsewhere, his grocery and takeout bills spiked. Lacking any appetite for days after his arrest, he fell prey to compulsive eating in the ensuing weeks. His Zabar's cravings, in particular, proved irresistible. He would walk there almost every day to pick up lunch—a routine that came to an end only after a mortifying encounter in the store one afternoon with a former patient and her toddler. The little girl pointed at him and said, "Look, Mom. There's the bad doctor who went to jail." He then began having his lunches delivered, though he fretted over the tips.

He did not skimp on broadband either. Finding comfort in the familiar, he would stay up late streaming action movies and watching reruns of sitcoms from the 1960s, '70s, and '80s. The liberal amounts of porn he also watched left him more frustrated than aroused, and over time, his consumption of it began to diminish.

He attempted to fill his empty daytime hours with legal research, but the hopelessness engendered by poring over case histories relevant to his own predicament caused his efforts to flag. As his mood sank and his concentration wavered, reading became ever more difficult. A paragraph longer than a couple of sentences would defeat him; by the time he reached the end, he would have forgotten the beginning. At most, he would skim the documents that Andrew submitted on his behalf.

The days and hours became indistinguishable from one another. He would sometimes sleep until noon or beyond and then awaken to begin a new round of eating, drinking, and indiscriminate television and movie watching. At other times, he would wake up before dawn, sleep from midday through evening, and then gorge himself. His already ample belly expanded, his wavy hair grew upward and outward, and his face became slack and doughy.

The FBI having seized his phone, Dr. Rosen never heard the voicemails about Sheila's hospitalization that Jeffrey had left for him in the days after the arrest. If he had, he might not have responded anyway, for he blamed the two of them as much as anyone else for his travails. If they had dealt with him fairly, had not kept from him the share of the family assets that, in his view, was rightfully his, he need never have resorted to selling oxycodone. Someday, he thought, he might forgive Sheila for her partiality toward his brother and Jeffrey for his theft and his betrayal, but they would have to beg him for that dispensation.

He passed his fifty-first birthday alone. Nathan did not return his phone call. Jeffrey did, after the doctor left him two voicemails, but not until a day later.

"You called?"

"Yes."

"So?"

"I guess you heard what happened to me."

"Yeah, you got caught."

"Very funny. I bet you're happy."

"No, I'm not, actually. Mom isn't either. She was in the hospital for nine days with pneumonia. She wanted to see you. I tried calling you several times."

"I didn't get any messages."

"I left at least two or three. Anyway, she's back at North Shore now, and she'd really like to see you. She's not doing well."

"I'll get there. With everything going on, I haven't had a chance."

"At least give her a call. She keeps asking me if you're all right. Are you?"

"What do you think? Of course I'm not all right. And we need to have a talk about Mom."

"About what, specifically?" A note of suspicion crept into Jeffrey's voice.

"About her money. It's not doing her any good, and I'm in a desperate spot. I have no income. My legal expenses are through the roof."

"Must it always come back to this? I'm sure she would help you if she could, but there's nothing left. How many times and in how many ways do I have to say this?"

"Bullshit! If she has nothing left, it's because you stole it all. After I get acquitted and I get my license back, I'm going to sue you for every penny you have and ever will have. I hope you have receipts for every dime of hers you've spent. I can't wait for discovery."

"Well, until then . . . Oh, I almost forgot. Happy birthday."

Briefly, Dr. Rosen considered making the trip out to North Shore, but getting there without a car entailed expenses and logistical challenges that he did not feel up to undertaking. Then, too, he could do without the guilt she would inevitably pile on him for his failure to visit her in the hospital.

Where others might have observed the changes in the doctor with alarm, Andrew Le Bâtard saw opportunity. The judge assigned to the case, a cranky septuagenarian named Everett Pound, had a reputation for showing leniency toward those offenders he thought deserving of it, believing that the loss of status, reputation, and income suffered by the likes of Dr. Rosen constituted punishment enough to obviate the need for custodial sentences. Attorneys representing clients of lower socioeconomic status and darker skin tones, however, joked mordantly of getting "Pounded" in his courtroom.

Andrew wanted Dr. Rosen to appear moderately disheveled for the arraignment, with suit a bit rumpled, tie slightly askew, cheeks covered by a day or two worth of stubble.

"With each hearing, we make you look a little worse so Pound can see the toll this is taking on you. I drew Pound with this other client I had last year—an investment banker who got nailed for fraud and tax evasion. A real slimebag. You kind of remind me of him. I would bring him into court looking like a homeless person. Pound ordered him to get treatment for his cocaine habit. No prison for him. That's only for poor defendants. So, anyway, after he started treatment, I began having him dress better for his court appearances. I wanted Pound to see how much the treatment was helping. I hated myself for it, but it worked. Pound was convinced that he was rehabilitated and gave him probation. It also helped that Pound has a soft spot for rich, white tax evaders. Miserable old fuck. This is how your justice system works."

CHAPTER 26

A continuance pushed the arraignment back to a raw, gray afternoon in late October. Beneath a steady, needlelike drizzle, judges, prosecutors, defense attorneys, witnesses, bailiffs, jurors, and defendants alike gingerly ascended and descended the slick courthouse steps. Andrew Le Bâtard, however, bounded to the top, leaving Dr. Rosen, upon whom the steps exerted an unearthly gravitational pull, far behind. Upon reaching the top, the doctor bent over, put his hands on his knees, and struggled to catch his breath.

Near the courthouse entrance stood a heavy-set man, arms folded across his chest, glowering at Dr. Rosen. The man had dark hair, dark eyes, a swarthy complexion, and a heavy five o'clock shadow. His green suit jacket, bunched up at the shoulders, its sleeves ending well above his shirt cuffs, would have fit a man half his size. Dr. Rosen hurried past him. Alarmingly, the man followed him inside and down the corridor to the courtroom. As Dr. Rosen and Andrew Le Bâtard settled themselves at the defense table, the doctor's case being first on the docket, the stranger in the green suit took a seat at the front of the gallery, directly behind them. Dr. Rosen felt the man's eyes burrowing into his back.

All rose as Judge Pound entered the room through a door located behind and to the left of the bench. Some courthouse wags called him "the Vulture" due to the physical resemblance. A bald, stooped little man, he had a long, wrinkled neck, hooded eyes, and a beaklike nose dotted by raised red lesions. Assuming his perch behind the bench, he banged his gavel and, in a voice as raspy as a file on rusty metal, ordered the assemblage to sit.

Andrew Le Bâtard presented Dr. Rosen to the court as a broken man, formerly prosperous and highly respected in the community, a man of sterling character who had led a blameless life up until a tragic error in judgment caused him to make a single, very unfortunate mistake. Further, it needed saying, though with no disrespect intended toward the FBI, Dr. Rosen would as likely as not have continued leading that blameless life had not a couple of overzealous and perhaps less-than-scrupulous undercover agents enticed him to stray.

The judge cut him short. "Get on with it."

"Yes, Your Honor," Andrew replied with a meekness that Dr. Rosen had never heard from him before.

Racing through his own part in the proceedings as though he had more urgent matters to attend to somewhere else, the judge advised Dr. Rosen of the charges and their potential ramifications and of the constitutional rights due a criminal defendant. Again and again, he asked, "Do you understand?"

For the first time since his arrest, the doctor truly did grasp the potential ramifications. The mere possibility, however slim, of spending up to forty years in federal prison made him feel faint.

In accordance with Andrew's instructions, the doctor kept his eyes downcast and limited most of his replies to a humble, at times abject, "Yes, Your Honor."

"How do you plead?"

"Not guilty, Your Honor."

"It went fine," Andrew reassured his worried client as the two men exited the courtroom. "He's bitten my head off in court before. It doesn't mean anything. You're the kind of defendant Pound likes. You are not going to spend one day in prison, let alone forty years."

In the hallway, the man in the green suit stood waiting, blocking the path to the exit door. Around him wafted the smell of Old Spice. He directed his ire not at the doctor but at Andrew: "A blameless life? A blameless life? This freaking murderer?"

"Look, man," said the attorney, "I don't know who the fuck you are, but you need to get out of the way now or you're going to find yourself face down on the ground with a team of US Marshals sitting on your back."

"I'm Nick Agnello. Salvatore Agnello's son. That's who the fuck I am. This creep killed my father."

Andrew shot a questioning glance at Dr. Rosen, who looked away. Traffic in the hallway came to a halt with all eyes, including those of a US Marshal, fixed on the three men.

"Your blameless asshole client killed my father with his negligence. He owes my mother a $2.1 million settlement. He's already two installments behind. Don't expect to weasel out of that, doc. My mother won't let it go."

"No, of course she won't. She wants her money," snarled Dr. Rosen. "That's the only thing she ever cared about. Maybe I ought to countersue her for defaming me."

Agnello took a step toward the doctor, who, in turn, retreated. Andrew interposed himself between the two antagonists.

"Defaming you? Like that's even possible? Karma's a bitch, ain't it, doc? My father wasn't good enough for you. His life wasn't worth ten minutes of your precious time. Well, I'll say this much for him. He wasn't a murderer or a deadbeat or a drug dealer."

"That's enough, man," said Andrew. "You've made your point. Now back off."

"You haven't seen the last of me, doc. Every time you go to court, I'll be here, watching and enjoying every minute of it."

"Is that a threat? Are you threatening my client? You better watch yourself, buddy, or I'll slap your ass with a restraining order so quick it'll make your head spin. Consider yourself warned."

"I'm not threatening anyone. I have a right to be here."

The marshal approached.

"Gentlemen, what seems to be the problem?" he asked.

"No problem. We're cool," Andrew replied.

Agnello, echoing that sentiment, began to back away.

Still the marshal stood watching as Andrew shepherded Dr. Rosen toward the exit. Just before they reached the door, a wounded cry resounded through the hallway: "Murderer!"

Dr. Rosen stood frozen, his right hand pressing against the door handle. Andrew, pushing the door open, shoved him outside. By the time the two men reached the bottom of the courthouse steps, however, the doctor had recovered from his fright.

"Old Spice," said Dr. Rosen. "Classy. He must pour on a gallon of it every day."

CHAPTER 27

The hearing had a sobering effect on the erstwhile Dr. So-ber-Up. In the face of the evidence against him, most of which, in the form of video recordings and prescription blanks, Dr. Rosen had unwittingly provided the FBI himself, maintaining his position of legal innocence became impossible. Gradually, he accommodated himself to the idea of a plea deal. Still, he held himself morally blameless; in his version of the story of his downfall, which he repeated ad nauseam, a couple of ma-nipulative rogue agents in search of a crime had entrapped and victimized him.

Andrew Le Bâtard would nod and give his client sympa-thetic looks, but his sympathy had its cost. Every one of the doctor's diatribes equated to a billable quarter-hour at a min-imum.

Negotiations over a potential plea deal commenced in the office of an assistant US attorney named Janel Moore. A thin, light-skinned African-American woman in her mid- to late-fifties, she had bony, angular features, weary-looking eyes, and loosely curled hair that fell to just above her shoulders. She wore black pumps with low heels, a charcoal business suit with a knee-length skirt, and unobtrusive silver stud earrings. On the wall behind her desk hung diplomas from Columbia University and Yale Law School. Amid the manila folders that covered most of her desk, a single personal item stood out: a 4-by-6-inch photograph of her smiling proudly, standing alongside a beaming young woman who wore a graduate's mortarboard and gown. The possibility that he would ever see

Nathan so accoutered seemed vanishingly remote to Dr. Rosen.

Apologizing for the Styrofoam cups, the prosecutor offered coffee all around. Dr. Rosen, already fidgety and suffering from heartburn, declined. The two lawyers chatted briefly about mutual legal acquaintances, and then all took their seats. Dr. Rosen and his attorney faced the prosecutor across the desk, while Agent Hardin, entering later than the others, settled into a corner armchair with his briefcase across his lap and his laptop open atop the briefcase.

Andrew made an aggressive opening move: In return for a guilty plea and no prison time, Dr. Rosen would agree to gather evidence against Eric Kleinzach, a big-time dealer in Baltimore.

Agent Hardin and the prosecutor exchanged glances. The FBI man had interviewed Kleinzach in Baltimore. Once Dr. Rosen's designated oxy pharmacist, Kleinzach had served time for opioid trafficking and then drifted back to his native city, where he established himself as a middleman, buying oxy scripts from doctors and selling them at a markup to street dealers and users. Dr. Rosen would throw small volumes of scripts his way now and then at a discount, likely as a manner of pacifying him. Kleinzach was a volatile sort, who, according to Boadecia's secondhand account, had once threatened Dr. Rosen's life. Agent Hardin decided that unless the case went to trial—which he did not expect—and he needed Kleinzach's testimony, he could leave the small-time dealer to the not-so-tender mercies of the Baltimore police.

The prosecutor fixed a cold stare upon her younger counterpart.

"Maybe you're new to this, Mr. Le Bâtard, so I'll explain to you how this process works. Each side has something the other wants, and each brings something of value to the table. You want no prison time for your client. We want his help in catching some bigger fish. You're offering us a minnow. We don't see enough value to make your offer worth discussing."

"Hey, I spent two years as a New York City public defender, so I don't need any lectures on how this bullshit system works, when it works at all. You're used to railroading people who have nothing. Well, my client's a medical doctor, and we're not going to stand for it."

"A felon is a felon, no matter his occupation. And your client could be spending a long time in prison."

Beset by visions of himself in shackles and an orange jumpsuit, Dr. Rosen grimaced. Perhaps he had underestimated the cautious, accommodating Pat McKinley.

"And anyway, this Baltimore guy is no minnow. He's not only a drug trafficker; he's a homicidal maniac who needs to be off the street yesterday. He once threatened my client with a gun."

"Maybe he had his reasons," the prosecutor replied dryly.

"That's a very prejudicial statement. I could move to have you dismissed from the case."

"Knock yourself out."

"This is so fucking wrong."

Rising, the prosecutor stepped out from behind her desk.

"I think we're done here, Mr. Le Bâtard. When you have a serious offer to put on the table, we can talk again."

"We just made a serious offer. This is so fucking wrong. You can't treat my client this way."

"Actually, we can," she said, holding her office door open. "Goodbye, Mr. Le Bâtard."

At the next session, a week later, Dr. Rosen, on his own initiative, offered up Tamika.

"She was a drug dealer. She was dealing in my waiting room. When I found out, I tried to fire her. She threatened to go to the police and tell them that I was running a pill mill. She blackmailed me into writing oxy prescriptions for her friends. She said she would go to the police if I interfered with her business."

The prosecutor gave Dr. Rosen a withering look. Agent Hardin laughed.

Tamika Jones, the putative drug dealer and blackmailer, was a terrified twenty-year-old who, when called upon, had gone to FBI headquarters voluntarily, without a lawyer, and readily admitted to her role in the ex-doctor's sordid business affairs with the Russians. Agent Hardin had decided to let her alone for the time being, as she had suffered enough at the hands of Dr. Rosen, though he would use her as leverage against him if necessary.

"It's true. I swear. Every word."

Andrew, uncharacteristically silent, gaped at his client in shock and horror.

"Get out of my office," said the prosecutor. "Both of you. Now."

Outside the courthouse, a furious Andrew confronted his client.

"So you were being blackmailed, huh? What orifice did you pull that story from? You may have just blown your best chance to stay out of prison."

"Are you calling me a liar?"

"I hope that's what you are. The other possibility—that you actually believe the bullshit that comes out of your mouth—is even worse. It means you're insane. Either way, the more you speak, the more harm you do yourself. If you ever spring anything like that on me again, you can get yourself a new lawyer."

"No!" said the doctor the next day, when Andrew broached the idea of offering up Golovorez and Zhukov. "Absolutely not."

"Fine. Rot in prison the rest of your life."

"At least if I'm in prison, I'm still alive."

Over the next week, Andrew argued, cajoled, shouted, threatened to quit, and even drafted a request to the court for permission to withdraw from the case, which he showed Dr. Rosen but ultimately did not file. A screaming match in Andrew's office escalated until each man had his hands around the other's throat. The next day, the doctor relented.

Lawyer and client returned to the prosecutor's office with the new proposal.

"That's more like what we're looking for," said Janel Moore, flashing a rare smile. "Too bad you held out so long. Now that they're both back in Russia, this information is of no use to us. Or to you either."

Again, she ushered the two supplicants out of her office as briskly as Dr. Rosen used to dispatch his economy-class patients.

She called Andrew the following day, however, with a counteroffer. If Dr. Rosen would provide useful evidence against another Russian opioid operation, this one in Brighton Beach, maybe the two sides could negotiate an agreement along the lines Andrew proposed.

"Meaning no prison time," Andrew told the doctor.

"She said that?"

"She implied it."

"I want something firmer than that if I'm going to take that kind of risk."

"I think we'll get there. I'll keep pushing her. But this is as much as we can hope for right now."

"Sure, I'll do it. Why wouldn't I? My life is over anyway."

After his talk with Andrew, the doctor completed the long-postponed task of drafting a living will and priced cemetery plots on eternalsolutions.com. Then he waited for the FBI's call. Two weeks passed, and still it did not come.

"You could be waiting a long time," said Andrew.

"Why is that?"

"I hear they've been told to lay off the Russians right now. Orders from the White House. It's good for you."

"I don't see how. What happens to me if the operation never comes off? There's no deal, and I spend the next twenty, thirty, forty years in prison?"

"You won't, man. You're ready, willing, and able to cooperate. That's what counts as far as the judge is concerned. It's not your fault if the FBI can't get its act together. The only bad thing is you could be in limbo like this for years."

"Years? I'm supposed to live like this for years? What kind of life is that? How am I supposed to earn a living?"

"It's tough, I know. But it's better than prison."

"I am in prison."

"I have some former clients who would beg to differ."

"How is this different from being in prison?"

"I hope you never have to find out."

CHAPTER 28

Weeks passed, replete with filings and counter-filings, conference calls and meetings. Then would come a continuance, and all activity would cease. Nothing that did or did not happen during that time moved the doctor's case any closer to resolution, but either way, the bills mounted.

Having surrendered his medical license, the now ex-Dr. Rosen had lost both his legal and illegal means of making a living. After some deliberation, he concluded that letting the co-op go into foreclosure and finding himself some cheaper lodgings would prove less damaging financially than would draining his savings by continuing to pay his mortgage. His missed November payment earned him a "friendly reminder" from the bank. When he fell forty-five days in arrears, a much less friendly second reminder threatened him with eviction. Thereafter, he fed the envelopes into the shredder without opening them. Though not a superstitious sort, he half-convinced himself that as long as he could not see an eviction date written down in black and white, it would never come.

Agent Hardin, with his ever-more frequent "invitations" to "come down to the office for a little chat," plagued Dr. Rosen almost as much as his unrelenting heartburn. Hardin's office was perhaps a third the size of the one in which Dr. Rosen had conducted his practice. It had beige walls and a well-trod bluish-gray carpet. A bitter smell, like that of coffee left in a carafe for three days, suffused the air. Merit plaques lined the walls on either side of the room, and when Agent Hardin sat down in his desk chair, a portrait of President Dreck loomed above and behind him. Atop a bookshelf to Agent Hardin's left stood several family pictures of which the FBI man himself appeared in only one, flanked by his two pretty teenaged daughters. Two other photographs featured, respectively, his wife and the girls lying on a beach and hiking up a hill, accompanied, in the latter instance, by two chocolate labs. Yet another picture captured the older daughter celebrating with her teammates during a soccer match.

"I couldn't stand being in a closet like that all day," Dr. Rosen confided to his attorney. "What do they pay those guys, anyway? Probably not much."

"Nope. Not much."

"I'll bet he thinks he has a perfect little life with the wife and the kids and the dogs and the house in the suburbs that costs more than he can afford and the minivan that keeps breaking down when they're ferrying the girls to soccer practice. What a life. It's like being buried alive."

During the sessions in Agent Hardin's office, Dr. Rosen's eyes would often turn toward those photographs. Sometimes, Andrew noticed, his client looked angry, and at other times, wistful. Did Dr. Rosen perhaps secretly envy Agent Hardin's well-ordered suburban life? The FBI man also observed Dr. Rosen's attraction to the photographs but drew a different inference: that the doctor might harbor some sinister designs toward his family. One day after a contentious interview, Agent Hardin took the pictures home with him.

Though he suspected that he had little more to learn from his talks with Dr. Rosen, Agent Hardin continued, week after week, to invite him in for their "little chat." One question haunted the FBI man: Why? Why had Dr. Rosen risked so much for so little?

The ex-doctor had prepared an answer, to which he stuck, no matter how many times and in how many ways Agent Hardin would pose the question: "I come from a very dysfunctional family. There was alcoholism, abuse, depression.

Education, achievement—they counted for nothing. Less than nothing. My parents and my brother mocked me for wanting an education. I was determined to lift myself out of that environment, and I did. And I was proud of myself for that. But when Nathan was born, I realized it wasn't enough just to lift myself up. I wanted to give him everything I didn't have growing up. I wanted to be the perfect father."

By the third time he heard the tale, the usually unflappable Agent Hardin had lost patience.

"You couldn't have provided for him without selling oxycodone? You were a doctor, after all."

"His mom came from a wealthy family. I couldn't compete."

"So you were trying to buy his love."

"I resent that. All I wanted was to be the best father I could be."

Agent Hardin looked like a man who had just bitten into a wormy apple.

"I'm trying to understand this. Are you actually telling me that you sold oxycodone out of love for your son? Come on, now. I may be from Ohio, but that doesn't make me a fool."

When the agent asked Dr. Rosen what had possessed him to go on television and accuse his professional colleagues of the very crimes that he was committing, the answer he got was no more satisfying: "The message is a good one, and people need to hear it." Sometimes Dr. Rosen would go on to boast about his success in Chicago.

From time to time, the exasperated FBI man would resort to veiled threats: "Your Medicare billing records look very interesting. At least that's what the fraud division people scouring them have told me."

The agent would then lean back in his chair with his hands clasped behind his bony head. From time to time, an expression would appear on his face that Dr. Rosen took for a self-satisfied grin, but that was actually a grimace brought on by the onset of a cluster headache.

Dr. Rosen grew to enjoy telling the story of how he had risen in the world, and he began to embroider it. With every retelling, the family's poverty became more dire, the father's abuse more violent, the mother's despair more crushing, the brother's drug addiction more debilitating, and the ex-doctor's own alienation more profound.

One day the FBI man, feeling another cluster headache coming on, cried out, "Oh, shut up. Just shut up already. I can't listen to this anymore."

"Are you calling my client a liar?"

"Your client grew up in a four-bedroom colonial on Long Island. His father was a school principal, his mother was a teacher, and his brother is an economist with a PhD who works for the federal government in the Department of Health and Human Services. Now, you tell me. Is he a liar, or is he delusional?"

Andrew Le Bâtard jumped to his feet.

"This is fucking bullshit! This is harassment!"

Agent Hardin stood up too, and leaned his 6-foot, 3-inch frame over his desk.

"You think this is harassment? Just wait until . . ."

Until what? Agent Hardin found himself at a loss in midsentence. He felt a sudden tightness in his shoulders and neck, along with an uncanny sense that someone was watching him from behind. Le Bâtard's face was segmented by undulating black horizontal lines, as if viewed through the screen of the living room television set of Agent Hardin's boyhood, a black-and-white relic framed by a plastic, faux-wood cabinet atop which had stood a rabbit-ears antenna set. Some malevolent being was slowly driving an ice pick into the FBI man's forehead, just above the right eye. Dropping back into his chair, he massaged the painful spot.

"I'd like to see some of this cooperation you're talking about. So far he's given us nothing but false leads and made-up stories."

"He's been waiting for your call. He's willing to do whatever you ask. It's not his fault that the FBI can't get its shit together."

"Didn't your mother ever tell you to use your inside voice? Or don't you have one?"

The lawyer, whose volume control moved in only one direction, cranked it even higher. "This is my fucking inside voice. Fuck this shit. Come on, doc. We're outta here."

"Shut the door behind you, please."

That the attorney did, as loudly as he could, evoking a groan from the FBI man.

Swiveling his chair around, Agent Hardin stared up at the portrait of President Dreck. A copy of the official White House portrait, the picture now hung in every office in every FBI headquarters building, as mandated by the new acting director, Tom Hagen. It did not flatter its subject. The president's flabby cheeks had the sickly hue of a greasy meat product of dubious provenance that had lain for too long beneath a heat lamp in a convenience store display case. His yellow hair extended like a visor far over his brow. His veneered teeth dazzled the eyes; his grin was a burnished threat.

Thrusting two upraised middle fingers at the portrait, Agent Hardin, whose repertoire of profanity under ordinary circumstances spanned the narrow range from "darn" to "shoot," shouted, "Fuck you, Dreck!" Then he turned off the light, lay his head down on the desk, and closed his eyes.

CHAPTER 29

"Here's what you do," Andrew Le Bâtard told the doctor a week or so in advance of the change-of-plea hearing. "Four days before, you stop shaving. You pick out the rattiest suit you have in your closet, and you sleep in it for two or three nights. Two days before the hearing, you stop showering. In court, when the judge is talking, you keep your head down. I mean that literally. Except when he's asking you a question. Then you look up, but you don't make eye contact. You wait a few seconds before you answer, as if you're having trouble understanding the question. Then you say, 'Yes, Your Honor,' or 'No, Your Honor.' You say it slowly and softly. If he tells you a couple of times to speak up, that's fine. That's what we want. Just not too many times. We don't want him to get cranky."

The client could have played the part his lawyer had crafted for him without much coaching. Still living the most sedentary of lives, pasty-faced from a lack of sunlight, he had ballooned to over 250 pounds.

"You look," needled Andrew Le Bâtard, he of the gym-rat physique, "like the Michelin Man."

Piles of sooty snow, three days old, lined the curb on the morning of the doctor's hearing. Slush covered the sidewalk and the courthouse steps. Dr. Rosen and his attorney reached the top of those steps with waterlogged shoes. Again, Nick Agnello followed them inside the courthouse—too closely for the Dr. Rosen's liking. Inside, no decorations heralded the approaching holidays; the building looked as somber as it did during every other season of the year.

Unshaven, with tie askew and shoelaces dragging on the floor, Dr. Rosen wore the same light blue suit that he had donned for his medical school graduation. The trousers dug into his waist, the frayed sleeves left his tatty shirtsleeve cuffs exposed, and he could not button the jacket. Per Andrew's instructions, he had slept in the suit for the past three nights. After shedding it each morning, he had thrown it in the hamper with the dirty laundry.

"We want it to marinate," Andrew had told him.

In the men's room just outside the courtroom, the lawyer, head cocked slightly to the right, appraised his client.

"Almost perfect," he said before unbuttoning the doctor's collar and loosening his tie further. "There. Have to get all the details right. God, I should be disbarred for this."

Hewing to Andrew's script, the defrocked doctor played his part well. Judge Pound ran through a list of very simple questions: Did the defendant understand the charges against him? Did he understand the individual counts? Did he understand the federal sentencing guidelines as they applied to each count? Did he understand the constitutional rights he stood to waive by agreeing to bypass a grand jury and change his plea from not guilty to guilty? Had he discussed all of these matters with his counsel?

Dr. Rosen answered all those questions in the affirmative. Those responses came haltingly, and he looked confused whenever called upon to deliver anything more than a simple "Yes, Your Honor" or "No, Your Honor." He would repeat the judge's questions, or parts of them, and then fall silent, as though something had distracted him. On occasion he would respond too softly for Judge Pound to hear him. Once, when prompted to speak up, he shouted, startling the onlookers and evoking a dyspeptic look from Judge Pound.

Judge Pound had a few additional questions for him: Had he ever been or was he currently under the care of a psychiatrist? Had he ever been treated for a narcotics addiction? For alcoholism? Had he consumed any prescription or illicit drugs or alcohol in the last twenty-four hours?

Dr. Rosen answered negatively each time.

"Well, based on what I've seen today, a mental health assessment and appropriate treatment are in order. I can see all this has taken quite a toll on you."

"Yes. Yes, it has, Your Honor. I realize now that I have an illness and that it impaired my judgment and led me to make bad decisions that don't reflect who I am. It took me a long time to see that. As a professional who is used to treating people who are struggling, it was hard for me to accept that I was the one who needed help."

Judge Pound nodded approvingly.

At the conclusion of the hearing, a stooped Dr. Rosen shuffled out of the courtroom with Andrew's arm draped over his shoulders. In the hallway, however, the two exchanged fist bumps.

"Couldn't have gone better," said Andrew.

They strode buoyantly out the courthouse door—and almost collided with Nick Agnello on the portico.

"Still very innocent, doctor?"

"Hey, motherfucker!" shouted Andrew. "I warned you to leave my client alone."

"I bet you've been bullshitting your way out of trouble all your life. But not this time. Now there's going to be some justice. I hope you rot away the rest of your life in prison."

Agnello spit on the ground, missing Dr. Rosen's shoe by inches, then turned around and stomped off, kicking up slush as he went.

CHAPTER 30

The clinic to which the court referred Dr. Rosen was run by a pixyish, relentlessly cheery psychologist named Catherine Connolly. A woman of around fifty-five, she favored flowery dresses, which she complemented with turquoise or mixed-stone necklaces, and wore her blond hair in a bob that curved inward at the bottom to hug her chin. Her unfocussed gaze made her appear myopic, an impression reinforced by the bangs that crept below her eyebrows.

To the doctor, who had conducted his practice in much more luxurious surroundings, her office looked like one suited for shared use by paraprofessionals in a public health clinic. Small, spare, and generically furnished, the room had little to recommend it, save for a pleasantly soft leather chair and a reproduction of a couple of young dancers captured by Degas stretching at the bar in feathery white tutus. Though he held Catherine Connolly in low regard, Dr. Rosen soon grew to think of his time with her as an amusing diversion. The leather chair offered comfort, and she was even more yielding. When he told her of his childhood suffering, her face mirrored back to him the pathos of his story. She did not mock him, as Agent Hardin had, when he insisted that his mistakes in judgment arose out of his love for his son. His fulminations against the FBI for entrapping him and—in his telling—breaking down his door drew no rebuke from her.

"That must have been very traumatic for you. It's too bad they don't take a more measured approach with someone like you, who presents no threat."

She accepted without question his account of Jeffrey's perfidy and the peril in which it placed Sheila.

"Her situation must weigh on your mind a lot."

"It keeps me up at night. Some days it's all I think about."

On occasion, he would let actual confidences slip. He spoke of his frustrations with Nathan and even, once or twice, wondered whether some failing of his had contributed to his son's fecklessness. Once, after telling her of how his harrowing night in the emergency room had led him to promise himself to change his life, he lamented his inability to follow through on his resolution. Invariably, though, after letting slip such a confession, he would upbraid himself for his weakness and seek to restore the therapeutic relationship to what he regarded as its proper equilibrium by telling Catherine Connolly some outrageous lie and convincing her of its veracity.

In addition to the individual therapy, she held group sessions for clients undergoing court-ordered mental health treatment. She was just starting a new group, she told him, and she thought it could benefit him greatly.

"It'll be the usual bunch of losers," he told Andrew. "Moaning about how life is treating them so badly and always finding some excuse not to do anything about it. God knows, I've led enough of those groups."

"So what did you tell her?"

"That I'd think about it."

"Don't think. I do your thinking for you. *Capisce?* You want to stay out of prison? Then you grit your fucking teeth, and you do it. You're a lot luckier than most of the clients I used to have. You have a get-out-of-jail-free card, at least for now. Don't tear it up."

The group sessions took place in still less accommodating environs than the office Catherine Connolly used for individual therapy: a nondescript meeting room just large enough to accommodate four people. The walls were white and the furnishings spare: a rectangular table with mismatched office chairs arrayed on each side and a filing cabinet in one corner. No matter how they contorted themselves, neither Dr. Rosen nor the others in the group could find any comfort in those chairs. Often during a session, people would stand and stretch, clutching their backs and grimacing. A caustic glare radiated from the recessed ceiling lights.

At the first session, the group members mostly kept their guards up, despite Catherine Connolly's gentle urgings toward more disclosure. Dr. Rosen learned that Ralph Chamberlin, a short, rotund, rumpled-looking man of around fifty, with drooping shoulders, a large head, and thinning grayish-blond hair, belonged to an amateur theatre troupe; that Linda Parsons, a Missouri transplant with a stick-figure build and a perpetually pained look on her face, had three sons; and that the thick-necked, greasy-haired Jerry Karpinski, he of the booming voice and the raised pinkish scar that angled downward from his left eyebrow to his cheekbone, had grown up in rural western Pennsylvania and attended his first Steelers game at the age of four. The doctor did not discover what unfortunate set of circumstances had brought any of them to that conference room, nor did he say a word about the crooked path that had led him there.

At the end of the session, Catherine Connolly stood up and said, in the voice of a primary school teacher delivering the mildest of rebukes to a misbehaving class, "You know what you reminded me of today? Turtles. All hiding in your little shells."

Dr. Rosen glanced to his right. Jerry, he saw, was smirking.

"Next week we're going to really start working on getting out of our shells, out of our comfort zones. It's going to be hard work, and it will take a lot of courage. But that's how we learn and grow. A month from now, I expect that all you turtles will have turned into lions."

Dr. Rosen, once more feeling the peptic acid rising toward his throat, ground his teeth. Ralph hung his head, and Linda stared out the window into the adjacent parking garage.

Suddenly Jerry emitted a tremendous leonine roar. There followed a short but weighty silence. Then Jerry began to cackle, and the others, beginning with Dr. Rosen, followed his cue until laughter filled the room. No one looked more relieved than Catherine Connolly.

The following week's session began with a "feeling words" exercise. Most people's repertoire of feeling words, Catherine patiently explained, consisted of little more than "good," "bad," "happy," and "sad." Having such a limited emotional vocabulary inhibited change and growth.

The exercise did not penetrate the turtles' shells. Ralph and Linda, respectively, each produced one anodyne descriptor: curious and interested.

"I'm also curious," added Dr. Rosen, echoing Ralph.

A hint of a frown darkened Catherine Connolly's sunny visage. Then Jerry took his turn. "I'm ready to rock and roll! I'm ready to kick some ass!"

If Catherine suspected mockery, she gave no such indication.

"Now that's the spirit," she said. "That's what I like to hear."

Next came the "lifelines" exercise. Each group member was to step up to the whiteboard on the wall opposite Catherine and draw a line illustrating the trajectory of his or her life, from birth to the present, before extending the line into the imagined future.

Ralph went first. His lifeline had numerous peaks and valleys. He had grown up in a very conservative household in South Carolina, and his struggles with his sexual identity had caused him much anguish. His decision to come out as a gay man in his early thirties had led his family to shun him. Arriving in New York shorn of the twin supports of that family and of the church that had both nurtured and tormented him, and already too old—he thought—for an aspiring actor to launch a career in theatre, he fell into a series of abusive relationships.

He tried to drink, smoke, and snort away his pain, leading to his troubles with the law. Twice he had tried to kill himself.

"I guess you could say I've been seeking a new family for a long time. And maybe that's part of the reason I'm here."

His lifeline was already rising now that he had reestablished himself professionally doing marketing for a small theatre company and, more recently, celebrated three years of sobriety. It spiked sharply as he extended it into the future. Just yesterday evening he had learned that he had passed his audition for the part of Doc in a production of *West Side Story* put on by the theatre troupe that employed him. He returned to his seat humming the Jets' theme song.

Catherine clapped and shouted, "Bravo!" The others applauded as well, though not as demonstratively.

Jerry went next. His lifeline ascended steadily, through college, medical school, residency, fellowship, and his becoming a part owner of a very lucrative orthopedic practice. Then, with his guilty plea on a tax evasion charge and the suspension of his medical license, the line took a nosedive. Over the last several months, however, it had begun to rise again. With the lifting of the suspension, he had resumed practicing, though with a less prestigious group and not as remuneratively as before, and had also launched a telemedicine enterprise.

"That's the wave of the future," he said. "There's a lot of money to be made."

Still he remained bitter over the income he had lost and the stigma attached to him due to his felony conviction.

"The way I look at it, I was just trying to lock the safe before the government stole everything inside. I worked my ass off to get where I was. Four years of medical school, a five-year residency, another year of fellowship. All that time, the government didn't give me squat. Then when I finally started making some real money, in my thirties, they had their hands in my pocket."

"Well," said Ralph hesitantly, "if you took out federally insured student loans, then you can't say . . ."

Jerry shouted over him: "Fuck that shit, man. It's not like they gave me anything for free. I've been paying that back with interest for years. Paying and paying. It's like a second mortgage."

Ralph slumped in his chair.

"One of the things I think it's important to work on in a group like this," said Catherine, "maybe the most important thing of all, is taking responsibility. Taking responsibility for what we do, recognizing when we've wronged those who are dear to us and making amends. Only then can we move on with our lives."

"I did nothing wrong."

"Ever?" needled Ralph.

"I worked hard. I studied hard. I played by the rules. I took responsibility. I've always taken responsibility. For myself and my family. I did everything you're supposed to do, and the government still came down on me. Why? Because I tried to prevent them from taking money out of my pocket to give to drama majors with no work ethic who take no responsibility for their lives."

"Why don't we move along," said Catherine. "Linda?"

Stepping up to the whiteboard, Linda Parsons drew what looked like a sine wave, as undulant as her voice was flat.

"In high school I had my first real dip. I had an eating disorder, and I wasn't very popular, and I didn't have a date for the prom."

In her freshman year at the University of Missouri, however, her fortunes changed for the better. She met a strikingly handsome and ambitious prelaw student named Matthew Parsons. They married just after graduation. Her job as a tax preparer paid the rent while he worked his way through law school.

Their first child, Matthew Jr., was conceived during his father's final year in law school and born a week after the graduation ceremony.

"And that was a real high point," she said, pointing with her marker to one of the crests she had drawn.

The sharp dip that followed represented her subsequent discovery that during her pregnancy, her husband had been carrying on an affair with a fellow law student. The husband vowed to mend his ways and moved the family to Philadelphia, where he took a position in a prestigious firm, and then to New York, where, in an even more celebrated practice, he made partner. The lifeline climbed still higher as a second child was born; plunged again as her husband's cheating resumed, leading to a brief estrangement; and leveled off when husband and wife reconciled and attempted marriage counseling. Then came more infidelity, more separations and reconciliations. At sixteen, the older boy died of a fentanyl overdose. The husband, who had once enjoyed a glass of wine or two at dinner, began to get blind drunk every night and strike out at her and the surviving son. He broke her jaw and raped her, kicked the son down the stairs.

"It went on and on that way," she said, her voice still devoid of expression, "until the night I stabbed him."

Catherine and Ralph gasped. Jerry sat rigidly in his chair, his face red and his neck bulging. Dr. Rosen, who had heard hundreds, perhaps a thousand stories like Linda's during his years of practicing, had drifted during its telling, but the ending startled even him.

Holding out a tissue, which the dry-eyed Linda declined, Catherine called for a ten-minute break. She hugged Linda and stroked her hair.

When the group returned, Dr. Rosen had his turn at the whiteboard. Like Jerry's lifeline, his had a sharp ascent followed by a precipitous drop, reaching its low point with the loss of his license. Unlike Jerry's, it did not rise again, due, Dr. Rosen explained, to the uncertainty over his legal status and the chances of ever practicing again. He spoke as he had to Agent Hardin and to Catherine Connolly in the individual sessions of childhood deprivation, his struggle to rise in the world, and his love for his son. He admitted that in selling opioid prescriptions for cash, he had not exercised the same sound judgment that he had in all his other endeavors, but he insisted that he had already learned much from his experience and felt confident that he would come out of it a better person.

Catherine applauded, Ralph hugged him, and Jerry gave him a manly clap on the back.

The heretofore affectless Linda, however, looked at him with horror and disgust.

"How could you?" she cried. "I lost a son because of someone like you. You sicken me."

"I said I was sorry about what I did. I've accepted responsibility and moved on. Anyway, you can't blame me for your son. I didn't give him the fentanyl."

"Oh, God! You are sick!"

Linda bolted from the room.

CHAPTER 31

Linda disappeared for good after that wrenching second session. Dr. Rosen, who viewed the shaming Linda had given him as unfair on its merits and offensive coming from someone who had committed a much graver crime than his, returned only after much urging by Andrew Le Bâtard.

"Abandoning the group after two sessions is a bad look. Pound will think you're thumbing your nose at him."

The next week there was less introspection, the hour concluding with another anti-government diatribe from Jerry and a feeble counter from Ralph. The fourth session again degenerated into a political argument, with Jerry vociferously defending President Dreck against Ralph's aspersions.

"Keep it up, Ralph, and one day you'll be sorry. Just wait until all the Deep State holdovers from the last administration are gone and the president has his own people in there. You're gonna get yourself locked up."

Catherine, in general sympathy with Ralph, tried her utmost to steer the conversation back to the therapeutic realm. In the end, Jerry subdued his opponent by means of his superior lung capacity. When cornered in an argument, he would raise his voice to a wall-shaking volume. As the Pennsylvanian ranted, Ralph, struggling to make himself heard, deflated like a balloon. He and Catherine both fell silent. The latter, sneaking peeks at her watch every couple of minutes, looked defeated. Dr. Rosen, remaining aloof from the debate, perused his cellphone messages in defiance of Catherine's strict prohibition on such activity.

Viewing all politicians as opportunists and sociopaths, Dr. Rosen was of two minds about the president, whom most everyone else he knew either loathed or revered. His upbringing, training, and the Upper West Side milieu in which he lived and, until recently, practiced his trade—no western Pennsylvanian bone carpenter was he—urged him toward Ralph and Catherine's camp. A walking, talking DSM-V personality disorder cluster, President Dreck wore his psychopathology like a many-colored cloak. Scores of the former doctor's patients had seen in the president the faces of the tormentors who had warped their lives: the groping uncle, the philandering first husband, the con man who guaranteed a 15 percent annual return if entrusted with the money set aside for the kids' college tuition. Assuming his most empathic listening pose, Dr. Rosen would lean forward in his chair, his head cocked slightly to one side, his eyes meeting the patient's full on. "Yes, yes, I see," he would murmur. "It's like you're reliving it all." Then he would send the patient on his or her way with a lorazepam prescription and an admonition to "turn off the news." Secretly, though, Dr. Rosen felt contempt for those patients, viewing them as weaklings who lacked the capacity or even the insight required to adapt to the world as it was. For him, the very qualities that they found so unnerving in President Dreck and that the DSM held as pathological—the president's lack of scruple, inhibition, empathy, or capacity for shame—held a certain guilty attraction, one which his viewing of *Find It! Flip It!* videos on YouTube had reinforced. Unfettered by law or convention, President Dreck did as he pleased, made adversaries crumble, allies grovel, and followers worship him. Who else could look into a camera, deny having spoken the words he had uttered in front of that very same camera the day before, and have tens of millions of the faithful accept that denial over the evidence of their senses? Better predator than prey, as Barry liked to say, and President Dreck was indeed the ultimate predator.

#

As unproductive as Dr. Rosen found the group sessions, he soon realized a material benefit from his attendance. Jerry needed people to help him get his telemedicine enterprise off the ground, and Dr. Rosen needed income. He went to work for Jerry, trekking out to Long Island twice a week, first via the Long Island Railroad and Uber, and then by car after he bought a ten-year-old Honda CRV. From a cramped, noisy boiler room in a subterranean office suite in a strip mall, he would call Medicare patients and pitch them orthopedic devices, using a script created by Jerry:

Dear Mr./Mrs./Ms.____. My name is (he often used Barry Bullard), and I work for Medicare. You may be eligible for a knee/ankle/back/wrist/neck   brace/walker/pair   of crutches/wheelchair at absolutely no cost to you. Medicare will pay 100 percent. And it comes right to your door. You don't have to do a thing. But you need to act now because supplies are limited.

Dr. Rosen took to his new trade at once. On his first day, he learned how to calibrate his pitch and when to cut his losses and hang up. He discovered that women, though more easily persuadable than men, would keep him on the phone longer because he seemed like a nice young man and they enjoyed talking to him. He tried to cut the chatting short, however, because lost time meant lost money. The mildly impaired made the best customers. Those with hearing loss were easily confused; a brief pitch delivered at a rapid pace and high volume often sufficed to move them to buy. Those with slight cognitive deficits also made easy marks, for while they could not think quickly enough to question why an employee of a government agency was giving them a hard sell, they still had enough of their wits about them to provide their Medicare numbers when pushed. He learned that if a patient's adult child answered the phone, he would do well to hang up as quickly as possible and try again later so as to avoid a lengthy tirade: "You are sick! You're a predator! How do you sleep at night? I'm going to report you to the authorities!"

If he reached the same customer directly the next day, however, then that same adult child who had rebuffed him so rudely might have to spend countless hours navigating a maze of recorded messages in a vain effort to halt the unwanted daily delivery to her father of ComfyCare semi-rigid lumbar braces.

As much as he welcomed easy conquests, maneuvering or bullying a recalcitrant customer into yielding up his or her Medicare number gave Dr. Rosen far greater pleasure, and the secret thrill of taking his revenge on the government that had persecuted him became positively addicting. During sessions with Catherine Connolly, he sometimes had to fight the urge to boast of his exploits.

On days when he went to Long Island, he would often visit Sheila. To his disappointment, his mother showed much greater wariness toward him than did the hapless customers whom he bullied over the phone.

"I'm making good money again," he boasted on one visit. "I'm working in telemedicine now."

"I hope what you're doing is legal," she replied. "You're in enough trouble as it is."

He stormed out but returned the next day bearing a dozen roses and even offered an apology of sorts: "I'm sorry if you were upset yesterday."

She had grown weaker since her hospitalization, spending a good bit of her time sleeping in her wheelchair, and he suspected her of using that frailty as a weapon. When he tried to steer their conversation toward the disposition of her assets, she would promptly close her eyes and begin snoring.

Whether she was actually sleeping or only pretending, he could not tell, but either way, he could not move her. He would have to find a subtler stratagem.

CHAPTER 32

Father and son had not spoken since the day Golovorez and crew had laid waste to the apartment and Nathan had departed. In that time, Dr. Rosen had left a single voice message, saying, "You and I need to talk." Nathan, in turn, left one for him: "I want nothing to do with you. You're a sociopath."

Changing circumstances, however, spurred Dr. Rosen to make a more strenuous effort toward a rapprochement with his son. Nathan, he had concluded, was the one weapon he had left in his arsenal with which to overcome Sheila's resistance. The time seemed fortuitous because Liz, of all people, had called recently to say, of all things, "I think you should make some time for Nathan. He needs his father in his life."

"You've had enough of him already? I figured it wouldn't take long."

"Go to hell."

The next day, however, Dr. Rosen called her again and took a much more conciliatory approach. She confided in him that, yes, she had reached her wits end with Nathan. He did nothing around the house but play video games, leaving her to gather up the laundry he dropped on his bedroom floor, clean the dirty dishes that he let pile up in the sink, and dispose of the fast-food containers and half-eaten meals that he left in his room and on the dining room table. He would disappear almost every night, return well after midnight red-eyed and reeking of marijuana, and sleep away half the day. Though he claimed to be looking for work, he gave her no reason to believe him.

In her lamentations, Dr. Rosen heard an unspoken plea: "Take him back." That hardly seemed possible. Facing imminent eviction, Dr. Rosen, rousing himself at last, had arranged to move into a furnished one-bedroom basement apartment on Long Island, a short drive to where he now worked for Jerry. The landlords-to-be were not expecting a second tenant, and he doubted that he could live long with Nathan in such a confined space without yielding to the temptation to throttle him. Still, the idea of offering his son a temporary harbor held some appeal, if only as a means of getting back at Liz. Not only had she posted the Fox 5 courthouse video on her Facebook page; for good measure, she subsequently provided a link to the *New York Post*'s "Hippocratic Oaf" story, appending a caption of her own creation: "Requiem for a reprobate ex." She may have had her fill of Nathan now, but as soon as he arrived on Dr. Rosen's doorstep, she would change her mind. If Nathan would stay for a while, so much the better. To have her son forsake her and cast his lot with her reprobate ex would goad her beyond endurance.

The first voice message Dr. Rosen left for Nathan said simply, "This is your father. Give me a call back."

After waiting twenty-four hours, he tried again, this time providing an inducement. "Hey, why don't you come down for New Year's Eve. We'll go to Times Square like we did a few years ago. It'll be fun."

Nathan called back within fifteen minutes, and the next evening he traveled down from Scarsdale. The condition of the apartment—filled with boxes and almost emptied of furniture—shocked him.

"Where are all the chairs?"

"I sold them."

"And the dining room table?"

"I sold that too."

"What are we supposed to eat on?"

"We'll manage."

Nathan found the state of his old room even more discon-
certing.

"You sold my bed and dresser too?"

Dr. Rosen stood in the doorway, grinning.

"It's not like you were using them."

"What am I supposed to sleep on?"

Dr. Rosen disappeared for a moment and returned holding
something that looked like a yoga mat with two bungee cords
wound around it.

"This."

He tossed the mat at Nathan, who made no attempt to
catch it. It struck his chest, knocking him back a step, and then
fell to the floor.

"I can't believe it."

"You blow it up like a balloon. It'll be fine. You may be a
little sore in the morning, but what the hell? You've given me
enough bad nights. You want to sleep in a bed? Get a job and
buy one."

"I'll remember this on Father's Day."

"When have you ever remembered Father's Day?"

"When have you ever remembered to be a father?"

Dr. Rosen left the room again and this time returned with
a pillow, which he flung at Nathan's head. The young man
ducked just in time.

For all his complaining, Nathan enjoyed a more restful
night than did his father, whose legal and financial worries
kept him awake, as they so often did. Dr. Rosen awoke before
6. Unable to fall asleep again, he went out for bagels and coffee. At 7, he tried to rouse his son. Nathan moaned, rolled
over, and hid his head beneath the pillow. At 7:15, the doctor
jostled him again.

"Come on. I got bagels. We need to be on our way. It may
snow later."

"On our way where?"

"To visit your grandma. She's not doing well. For some reason, she wants to see you before she dies."

"You didn't tell me that."

"I didn't want to upset you."

"That's a first."

His glibness notwithstanding, Nathan looked pained. Whether his discomposure stemmed from the news about his grandmother or merely from being awakened before noon, the doctor could not tell.

In the parking garage, the presence in the doctor's reserved spot of a gray CRV with a scuffed exterior confused Nathan. He looked around for the Jaguar.

"Over here, idiot. These are my new wheels."

"What happened to the Jaguar?"

"I sold it. Just like everything else."

"Why?"

"Why do you think, dumbass?"

"I'm not the dumbass who got arrested for dealing drugs to the FBI."

"No, you're the dumbass son of that dumbass."

Though neither of them had ever shown much of an ability to laugh at themselves, they both found the joke hilarious. Dr. Rosen searched his memory: When had the two of them last enjoyed one another's company? He recalled a frigid New Year's Eve in Times Square, three years before, he and Nathan standing in the midst of a pulsing crowd. A young woman in a group just behind them had offered Nathan a sip from her bottle of Scotch. Dr. Rosen had partaken as well.

"You remember that girl we met that time in Times Square? What was her name? Carrie something?"

"I don't remember."

"Yeah, it was Carrie. I think she liked you. Why didn't you ask her for her number? That's what I would have done. You know, good things don't just drop into your lap. You have to make them happen. You have to take a chance sometimes. You're attracted to someone, you ask her out. What do you have to lose? The worst that can happen is she'll say no. If she does, you're no worse off than you were before."

Nathan, gazing out the windshield at the lowering clouds, hurriedly inserted his earbuds.

"Why do I bother?" Dr. Rosen muttered.

Why did his every attempt to reach Nathan fail? Why did they both fail so miserably in their respective roles as father and son?

Sheila was sleeping when Dr. Rosen and Nathan entered her room. The doctor tapped her on the shoulder.

"Mom, I brought someone with me."

Raising her head, her eyelids twitching, Sheila looked left and then right, as if lost. When her eyes lit upon Nathan, however, she brightened at once.

"Nathan! I'm so glad you came. Come here. Give me a hug."

He stooped to embrace her. She kissed him on the cheek, and as he straightened up again, she took hold of his hands.

"Let me look at you. Have you put on a little weight?"

He shrugged.

"Mom's a good cook."

"Well, you needed it. You look much better this way."

"He doesn't starve when he's with me," said Dr. Rosen.

"Why don't you come see me more often?"

"Well, I would, but it's hard for me to get here without a car. I'm living up in Westchester County now."

"What? You're not living with Robbie anymore?"

"No."

"Since when?"

"Six, maybe seven months."

Her gaze shifted from the son to the father and then back again. Nathan, shying away from eye contact, looked at once uneasy and defiant. Dr. Rosen's face, with its pouting lips and squinty eyes, she found much easier to read. She could see that he was furious with Nathan for speaking out of turn.

"You never told me about this," she said to her son.

"It never came up."

"What happened? Did you two have a fight or something?"

"Why do you always assume that? We get along fine when his mother isn't interfering. She's very good at manipulating him, and he can't see it. She has him convinced I'm a terrible person."

"Enough of that already. How long have you been divorced now, and you and Liz are still fighting?"

"At least living with Mom, I don't have to worry about getting killed by Russian mobsters."

"Russian mobsters?"

"He made me deliver oxycodone prescriptions to some sleazy pain clinic run by Russian mobsters. One of them pointed a gun at me. And then they came to the apartment and smashed everything up and almost broke my wrist. That's when I left."

Sheila's jaw quivered. She opened her mouth to speak, but her voice deserted her.

"He's lying," said Dr. Rosen. "He makes up stories. Just like his mother."

The look she gave him was one of incomprehension mingled with disgust.

"Are you insane? You do that to your own son?"

"Even the Russian mobster who twisted my arm said he's a terrible father."

"Are you my son? Did you come from my womb? Who are you?"

Dr. Rosen lowered his head.

"That's a very hurtful thing for a mother to say to her son."

"Having a son like you hurts me. Go away. Get out of my sight."

Nathan preempted the dressing down that he knew awaited him by inserting his earbuds even before he and his father left the room. All the way back to Manhattan, Dr. Rosen drove wildly, reaching 90 miles per hour, zigzagging through traffic without signaling, tailgating, and blasting his horn at any driver with the temerity not to get out of his way.

Arriving in the apartment, Nathan promptly shut himself in his old room. Dr. Rosen, beset again by heartburn, gobbled several antacid tablets and lay down for a nap, but sleep, that capricious and cruel object of his desire, refused him, as it so often had in recent months. A rage-fueled restlessness drove him back outside.

Though he had sworn off such places after his ill-fated night out with Barry and Michael Stonecypher, he found his way back to Maxwell's Gentlemen's Club. Standing amid the crowd at the bar, he had just put in his order when a woman brushed against him. A wisp of a girl, she had blond hair that fell to her shoulders and clouded gray-green eyes. She wore only a red bikini and heels. Her name, she said, was Candy, and she asked him to buy her a drink.

He bought her a piña colada, which she finished by the time he had taken two sips of his beer. When she asked him to buy her another, he demurred, pleading poverty, until she ran her hand over his crotch and whispered in his ear, "I can show you a real good time."

Not having slept with a woman since Tamika's departure, he needed no further persuading.

Polishing off her second cocktail—he still had not finished his beer—she took him by the hand and led him away from the bar, toward the rear of the building and down a dim corridor lined with cubicle-sized rooms hidden behind scarlet curtains. The room into which she led him had pink walls and an enormous rectangular mirror with a beaded frame. He sat down on the black leather settee against the wall to his right, and she closed the curtain.

Candy undid and tossed aside her bikini top, revealing her cupcake-sized breasts. With her arms extended over her head and her eyes closed, she began to sway, the rhythm of her body much slower than that of the music—an aural assault of guitar feedback, percussion, and screaming vocals. She looked uncomfortable in her heels. At one point she stumbled and almost fell.

Kicking off her shoes, she approached him, wearing only her bikini bottom and an uneasy smile. She straddled his legs, settled herself in his lap, and wrapped her arms around his neck, drawing him close. Her breath reeked of rum. Her eyes were watery now and unfocussed, and a jagged line of black mascara crept down below her left cheekbone. In the dim light, her face had taken on a yellowish tinge. She looked weary, beaten down, older than she had appeared to him at the bar, when the mirrors and lights had rendered him half-blind. Tallying up the cost of the drinks and the dance, he calculated that he had already spent $90 on her. What a waste.

Suddenly her body lurched to the left, and she grabbed his shoulder to steady herself. He felt her nails digging into him.

"I'm sorry. I'm not . . . not feeling well."

"I wish you had told me that before we came back here."

"I think I need to . . ."

She stood up, staggered backwards a step, dropped to her knees, and began to retch, spewing vomit all over the carpet and his shoes.

"Perfect. Just perfect. What a perfect fucking day."

Stepping over her, he flung the curtain open and made a beeline for the men's room, where he rinsed his shoes in the sink and tossed his socks in the wastebasket. Never, he vowed, as he had before, would he again cross the threshold of such a place as Maxwell's.

With his wallet emptied of cash, he resolved to walk home. After a few blocks, however, when he could no longer feel his toes, he called an Uber.

Even before he entered the apartment, he smelled marijuana. Without pausing to remove his coat, he rushed to Nathan's bedroom. Finding the door locked, he dealt it a kick and several blows.

"Open this damn door! Now!"

Whether out of sloth, malice, or both, Nathan took an inordinately long time to accomplish that sample task.

"I smell puke," said Nathan, punctuating his words with a theatrical sniff.

"Shut up! I've had enough of you for one day. I've had enough of you for one lifetime. I want you out of here now."

Nathan looked shocked.

"But what about Times Square?"

"We're not going to Times Square."

"Great. So we're just going to sit around here on New Year's Eve?"

"We are not going to sit around here on New Year's Eve. I may sit around here, but you are leaving. Get your things together and get out."

"Where am I going to go?"

"I don't give a damn. Just go."

"It's freezing out, and the trains aren't running on their normal schedule."

"Fine. I'll drive you back to your mother's. And then I never want to see your face again."

The sun had set, and gray-black clouds hovered low in the sky. Snow whirled about the CRV in windborne eddies and blew like smoke over the pitted surface of the Cross Bronx Expressway.

Nathan, with his earbuds stuffed in his ears and his eyes shut as he mouthed the words to a song, did not notice when his father veered off the highway. For a half-mile or so, the CRV bounced over potholed roads flanked by dilapidated high rises, some of which appeared abandoned. The snow had begun to stick to the road, and there was little traffic about. Dr.

Rosen inched the vehicle along the narrow side streets with his bright lights on, for many of the streetlights were out. Battered cars and vans, some missing wheels or headlights, were parked haphazardly on both sides, leaving barely enough space for the CRV to slip through.

Nathan, who had opened his eyes long enough to notice his surroundings, asked, "Where are we?"

His father did not reply. When an unoccupied stretch of curb appeared, he pulled the CRV over. To his left, behind a chain-link fence, lay a stony lot littered with tires, strollers, tricycles, and trash. On the right stood a six-story apartment building that must not have seen a tenant in twenty years. Its missing windows gave it a skeletal look, and it cast a jagged shadow over the street and the lot.

"This is where you get out."

"Yeah, right."

Dr. Rosen banged his fists on the steering wheel.

"Get out! Before I wring your fucking neck!"

Nathan leapt from the car. Never had Dr. Rosen seen such terror on his son's face. Paternal instinct led him to roll down the passenger-side window. Fear of showing weakness robbed him of his voice, kept him from calling out as Nathan began to trudge up the snowy street toward the corner. Shifting the car back into drive, Dr. Rosen pulled the CRV alongside his son.

"Wait. Come back here. Get back in the car."

Nathan, looking straight ahead as though he did not hear, kept going.

"Are you insane? Get back in this car now. You can't be out here by yourself. Where are you going to go?"

Nathan picked up his pace.

"At least get your overnight bag from the back."

Sneering, Nathan flipped him the bird.

"All right, don't. The hell with you."

Dr. Rosen pulled away from the curb, drove a couple of blocks, and then circled back, only to find himself driving the wrong way on a one-way street that he did not recognize.

When he found his way back to the derelict building, he saw no sign of Nathan. For half an hour, he searched in vain for his son, driving at walking speed, bright lights on, wipers flailing at the thickly falling snow.

By the time he reached the Cross Bronx again, he could barely see through the curtain of snow. Still, he sped back toward Manhattan, swerving to avoid a collision with an SUV that stopped in front of him in the middle lane of the highway for no discernible reason. The CRV went into a skid. He cut the wheel sharply to the right, and though he felt a jolt when the left taillight smacked against the highway divider, he kept the car moving. Counting himself lucky, he exhaled and let up on the accelerator.

Back in the apartment, he shed his clothes and crawled into bed, some three hours before the dropping of the ball in Times Square. Soon he fell into a twitchy, nightmare-haunted sleep. He had taken Liz and Nathan with him to a conference in San Francisco and, after delivering a very well-received presentation on the first morning, was enjoying a sunny afternoon's stroll with them by the water at Fisherman's Wharf. He had three-year-old Nathan perched on his shoulders, while Liz walked beside them, smiling up at the child.

"Dad, look!" cried Nathan, pointing at the sea lions languidly sunning themselves on a floating pier.

With his own attention drawn toward the sea lions, Dr. Rosen took a wrong step, the front of his shoe striking the edge of a misaligned plank, causing him to stagger forward. Within seconds, he recovered his balance, but he sensed that something had gone awry. What he felt, he realized, was an absence—that of the boy's weight on his shoulders.

"Help him!" he heard Liz scream. "Do something!"

He turned to see Nathan in the water, just his head, shoulders, and thrashing arms visible above the surface. Dr. Rosen jumped in and swam toward him. As he reached for the boy's hand though, Nathan vanished as if drawn into a vortex.

Down through the cold, murky water Dr. Rosen dove, his arms and legs churning, his lungs on the verge of bursting, but Nathan kept sinking. Again and again, he reached for the boy's hand, but it always remained just beyond his grasp.

When he awoke, Dr. Rosen was still holding his breath.

CHAPTER 33

When he saw Nathan's number on his caller ID the next morning, Dr. Rosen didn't answer. He had a hunch—which turned out to be correct—that the caller was Liz. Rather than alarming him, her high-decibel voice message came as a relief. Whatever actual hardships Nathan may have endured on his journey back to Scarsdale, and whatever imagined ones he may have added in telling the tale, he had returned there safely. Still, Dr. Rosen could not forget the look of terror on Nathan's face.

That faint sense of guilt—like a prickling in an atrophied limb—ceased altogether when Dr. Rosen discovered that Nathan had taken several selfies the previous night and posted them on Facebook in an album titled "Father of the Year kicks me out of the car in the South Bronx in the snow on New Year's Eve." Each picture had a barbed caption: "Burned-out building." "A syringe on the sidewalk." "Used condoms."

Later that day, in the hallway outside his apartment, a *New York Post* reporter accosted Dr. Rosen, seeking comment about the incident.

"What the . . .? Who put you up to this, my ex?"

He fled back inside and slammed the door in the reporter's face. Checking the paper's website a few hours later, he saw a headline that made his heart sink: "GROSS MALPARENTING! Drug-Dealing Ex-Doc Deep-Sixes Son."

The comments beneath the article denounced Dr. Rosen in yet more colorful terms, holding him up as the personification of the selfishness and irresponsibility that had brought down upon the heads of the citizenry all the plagues of modern life—the shattered family, teenaged pregnancy, violent crime, gay marriage, gender and pronoun confusion, flag burning—and cracked open the very foundations of American society. An unlikely reader of the *Post*, a professor of folklore and comparative religion, saw the episode as a debased Abrahamic sacrifice, the difference being that where the faith and obedience to God had driven the anguished patriarch to the brink of slaughtering his son, Dr. Robert Rosen had acted out of a perverse whim. Such was the age in which we now lived. A pastor opined that with a name like Rosen, the miscreant father likely adhered to the Old Testament code of an eye for an eye. The story provided a stark illustration of the anarchy that resulted when a society forsook the teachings of Jesus Christ, the Lamb of God. An even more atypical *Post* reader than the folklorist, a professor of African-American studies, archly noted that the new poster boy for absentee fatherhood (and a drug dealer, to boot) was a white man. The hard-working, God-fearing, salt-of-the-earth readers of the *Post* would have none of that. One reader responded, "Why do YOU PEOPLE have to bring race into everything?" Accusations of racism and elitism and all manner of ugly but inventive epithets flew back and forth until one commenter wrote, "Can't we all just agree that it makes no difference whether Robert Rosen is pink or blue or all the colors of the rainbow? All that matters is that he's a piece of s**t." Everyone could and did agree with that proposition, and the commenters once more turned their ire on the doctor rather than each other.

Dr. Rosen attributed the pile-on to the biased tone of the article. Angered that not a single commenter rose to his defense, he wrote in on his own behalf: "It's all lies. Fake news. Probably all made up by my ex-wife. The reporter never even spoke to me to get the truth."

His reply only brought more vituperation upon his head. A commenter with the soubriquet NAgNell076 wrote to say, "He's a murderer. He killed my father." Another wrote,

"Shooting's too good for him. He should be strung up with piano wire by the balls in the South Bronx and left there overnight." A third, calling herself WildeWoman93, signaled her agreement with an emoji— *100* —and added, "Ex-doc Rosen. Proving he doesn't need a license to kill." A fourth, who employed a moniker that aroused his suspicions— Xmrsrosen— wrote, "Totally on brand for him. Believe me."

Andrew Le Bâtard called that evening.

"Question," he said. "Are you out of your fucking mind? What the fuck is wrong with you? Do you want to spend the rest of your fucking life in prison? Do you want Judge Pound to laugh at me when I go into court at your sentencing hearing and tell him what an upstanding citizen you are?"

"It's all lies. It didn't happen the way they describe it."

"Bullshit! Stop bullshitting me or find yourself another lawyer. I spent two years representing violent sociopaths. They didn't bullshit me the way you do."

"Well, maybe the judge doesn't read the *Post*."

"He'll hear about it from the prosecutor."

When Dr. Rosen saw Catherine Connolly the following Wednesday, he spoke neither of the *Post* article nor of the incident that had given rise to it. He lamented the ingratitude of a son who had shunned him since his arrest, but he denied harboring any anger toward Nathan.

"The arrest must have been a shock for him too," suggested Catherine. "It can take some time to process. I'm sure he'll come around though."

"I hope so," said Dr. Rosen in a voice that suggested a lack of such hope.

In the group the next day, he spoke of the opprobrium he had to endure because society had labeled him a felon, branded him with a scarlet F.

"The other day I'm walking to the elevator, and a reporter from the *New York Post* started harassing me."

He checked himself too late. Catherine's no-phone rule notwithstanding, Jerry immediately whipped out his iPhone and began scrolling.

"This is not cool, man," he said.

Ignoring her own rule, Catherine reached into her handbag for her phone and quickly found the article. She looked stunned at first and then disgusted. Ralph, who had also found the story, shook his head and made clucking sounds with his tongue as he read.

"This is sickening," said Ralph. "How could you?"

"It's all lies," Dr. Rosen said heatedly. "It's all made up. It's fake news."

"Fake news. Where have I heard that dreck before? Why, of course. From Dreck. You're a sociopath, just like your hero."

"He's not my hero. I didn't vote for him."

"You're still a sociopath."

"Let's not resort to name calling, please," interjected Catherine. "There are some serious issues here that are worth exploring. But name calling only generates heat, not light."

"I'm sick of coming here every week and having to listen to this loser ragging on my president," said Jerry.

"What is it you cultists like to say?" Ralph replied. "Oh, I remember. 'Fuck your feelings.'"

"Communist!"

"Fascist!"

"Please stop this. Both of you. This is not at all productive."

"Libtard!"

"Gun humper!"

"Because I support the Second Amendment, that makes me a gun humper?"

"You're a sociopath too."

"Stop. Please stop this. Both of you."

Dr. Rosen slipped out of the room.

CHAPTER 34

Although he did not return to the felons therapy group, to keep Judge Pound mollified, Dr. Rosen scheduled one last individual session with Catherine Connolly. First, he apologized for walking out of the last group session, lamenting how everything today—even group therapy—had become so politicized.

"Sometimes," he said with a melancholy shake of his head, "it all becomes too much for me."

"Yes, Dreck is making everyone sick."

"Very true. I saw it all the time in my practice. Watching him on TV made people relive their traumas."

He regretted that he would have to terminate individual therapy too, he told Catherine, but he had no choice. He would soon be moving out to Long Island. With his mother in declining health, he needed to be closer to her.

"Of course. I understand perfectly. You will continue your therapy there though?"

"Absolutely. I've benefited a great deal. These sessions have really helped me process what happened to me. I think I'm a better person now for having gone through this ordeal. I've learned so much."

"How do you feel about the move?"

"Well, it's sad because New York City is my home. It always will be. But I've learned to accept things, and I'm eager to see what God has in store for me."

She looked surprised.

"You never mentioned your faith before. I had no idea it was so important to you."

"Well, to be honest, I had drifted away from it over the years. But lately I've gone back to reading the Bible a lot. The Psalms mostly." He then recited for her all that he had gleaned of the Psalms from overhearing Tamika and twenty minutes of Google searching: "'Yea, though I walk through the valley of the shadow of death, I will fear no evil: for thou art with me; thy rod and thy staff they comfort me.'"

What had suddenly possessed him to talk of religion, he did not know, but he was enjoying himself.

"Where do you worship?"

"Well, I, uh . . . I'm not a big believer in organized religion. But I'm a very spiritual person. My faith is a very personal thing."

At the conclusion of the session, she gave him a hug. He promised to keep in touch.

He had benefited from his quasi-compulsory therapy, he realized, more than Catherine Connolly knew, though not for the reasons she imagined. The skills in persuasion that he had honed on her would surely serve him well in court and in his future business endeavors.

He bid an unsentimental goodbye to his home of eleven years. After Golovorez's thefts and Nathan and Tamika's departures, the apartment had come to feel barren. The sale of most of his furniture left him inhabiting a space as impersonal as a hotel room. Before he left—mere hours ahead of the sheriff—he took a small measure of revenge on the bank that had dispossessed him, turning the heat up to 90 degrees and leaving the shower running in the master bath. As he walked out for the last time, he yanked on the doorknob until the hinge came loose again.

The move marked a return to one of his old haunts—a neighborhood of modest-sized single-family dwellings of mid-twentieth-century vintage with a heavy concentration of bars, pizza shops and taquerias, and convenience stores along its main drag. He had spent a good chunk of his adolescent years getting drunk in the basements of a few of those houses with friends of whom his parents disapproved.

To the basement he now returned, his landlords having adapted theirs into a subterranean studio apartment with its own entrance from outside. The apartment, he surmised, must have once served as a family rec room. It retained two amenities from that earlier incarnation: a wall-mounted television and a ping-pong table. Otherwise, the place had little to recommend it.

At some point during the remodeling, the money must have run out. The half-wall separating the tiny kitchenette from the rest of the apartment was unpainted. The bathroom, barely large enough to fit a toilet, shower stall, and sink, also had unpainted walls, as well as a gray concrete floor. Dark peel-and-stick wood paneling covered the walls. Only after Dr. Rosen moved in did he notice the warping and the white deposits at ankle level, as well as the chipped paint and yellowish spots along the baseboard. Somehow the ever-present odor of mildew had also escaped his notice when he viewed the apartment before the move. When the temperature dipped below freezing, the linoleum tiles felt like a sheet of ice, and he had to wear his shoes indoors. One end of the towel rack beside the bathroom sink had come unmoored from the wall. A wooden stairway had once led to the den on the first floor, but the owners had removed the door at the top. The outline of the door frame still showed on the bare drywall.

The telltale sounds of defective plumbing—the whoosh and gurgle of water coursing through the pipes and a constant drip—exacerbated his nocturnal restlessness. So too, at times, did the footfalls from above and the horn blasts and rumbling wheels of the trains that passed by at all hours of the day and night along the tracks that lay just a couple of blocks away.

Still worse were the voices. Dr. Rosen had a private entrance a few steps down from the backyard, and although the
owners, Paul and Pam Tucci—pronounced "Toosey"—did not
invade his space, the clamor of their marital spats did. They
argued frequently about politics. The husband, a car sales-
man, supported President Dreck; the wife, a substitute
teacher, loathed him. Although such tiresome epithets as
Jerry and Ralph had spat at each other in the felons therapy
group—"socialist," "fascist," "libtard"—did sometimes figure
in their battles, the Tuccis' barbs cut more deeply. Pam, in
Paul's telling, was a wooly-headed dreamer who had no clue
about the harshness of life in the real world and the toughness
one needed to succeed. She saw Paul as cold, hard, unimagi-
native, and lacking in empathy, a bigot, just like the president
he idolized. As vituperative and loud as those skirmishes became, they were but proxy fights. Every so often the couple's
real grievances boiled up to the surface. Paul Tucci had a lit-
any of them, all of which Dr. Rosen had heard a thousand
times or more in his practice: She spent too much and was a
lousy cook and an indifferent housekeeper. While she lay
around all day with her nose in a book, he would come home
after busting his balls for twelve hours at the dealership to find
dishes piled up in the sink, the dining room table covered with
junk, and a cold takeout pizza for dinner. Why should he
bother? Worse, she had let herself grow fat and unattractive,
wearing sweat suits around the house and no makeup. Paradoxically, he also sometimes accused her of flirting with other
men. Unlike Linda Parsons and so many of Dr. Rosen's former
patients, Pam Tucci hit back. Why did he have to stink up the
house with his two-pack-a-day cigarette habit? And that after
bypass surgery. He was going to smoke himself into an early
grave. Not that she cared. When he was gone, she would find
herself a man who wasn't a physical and emotional cripple—
one with balls, who could perform in the bedroom.

The fights provided fresh kindling for Dr. Rosen's heartburn—along with unsettling echoes of marital wars that he

had endured as a captive witness during his boyhood. Sheldon and Sheila Rosen had fought endlessly over money and the upbringing of their sons, Sheldon faulting her for coddling them and Sheila accusing him of ignoring them. To their credit, if they had ever had any bedroom issues, they had kept them to themselves, at least when Jeffrey and Dr. Rosen were within shouting distance.

But for the television and the ping-pong table, Dr. Rosen would not have lasted more than a week in the apartment. Most weekday evenings he would put on the television and crank up the volume to artillery-barrage level to drown out the voices upstairs. When feeling more energetic, or angry, he took advantage of the fortunate discovery he made that he could play solo ping-pong by folding one side of the table up and whacking the ball against it. The pastime so absorbed him that he sometimes played for hours, even after the Tuccis had spent all their verbal ammunition and declared a truce. The beatings he inflicted on the balls caused them to crack often, and every few days he had to go in search of new ones.

Pam Tucci, a stocky, slightly cross-eyed woman of about Dr. Rosen's age, with a smattering of freckles on each cheek and wisps of gray in her dark hair, began to drop by every so often, always when her husband was out. Such opportunities came frequently for her, for Paul often worked evenings. Sometimes she would ask Dr. Rosen to help her unload grocery bags from her car, move a table or chairs, or even hang a curtain rod. Then, as a reward, she would bake brownies or cookies for him, giving her a pretext for a longer visit. She did put on makeup when she came to see Dr. Rosen, and while still favoring baggy sweatshirts, she sometimes wore form-fitting jeans.

She volunteered much, and he, very little. He told her that he sold medical equipment for a startup, but he never revealed the name of the company, the nature of the equipment or customers, or how he had found his way to that occupation. His calculated taciturnity did not put her off, as he had hoped. Rather, it intrigued her. She would keep probing, and she seemed not to notice—or if she did, not to mind—the one-sided nature of their conversations. Sometimes, mid-visit, he would remember that he had to run out to do some errands. When she began to speak of her unhappiness in her marriage, he would talk of the cold, draftiness, noises, and musty smells of the apartment and hint that he might soon have to find lodging elsewhere.

She seemed attuned to his comings and goings, though he tried to vary them. Often she would knock on his door mere minutes after he arrived in the apartment. One afternoon, when he had left work early for a conference call with Andrew, the judge, and the prosecutor, she came to him in tears. She could not endure life with Paul for one more day, she told him. The next time he started yelling about her credit card bills, she would . . . What she would do she did not yet know. But she would do something that Paul would regret. He was so unfair. How often did she buy any new things?

"You see how I dress, what I look like. It makes me ashamed. And then he criticizes me for that too."

When she leaned against his chest, he offered her a half-hearted hug, his arms encircling her torso so loosely as to barely touch her at all. She looked up, into his eyes, and then, somehow, they were kissing. Prudence urged him to pull back, but he had not had sex since Tamika left, and he immediately became aroused. He lay her down on his single bed. Unlike Paul Tucci, he could and did perform. Only afterward did his gaze linger on the blemishes on her body, visible even in the anemic light that filtered into the basement apartment through the recessed windows: the sagging flesh on her arms and neck, the stretch marks on her abdomen, and the jagged keloid scars that crisscrossed it, mapping the cuts from an appendectomy, a C-section, and a hysterectomy. He would not sleep with her again, he told himself. When she dropped by two days later, though, they shed their clothes with barely a hello and again tumbled into bed.

Both of them reveled in the thrill of deceiving Paul Tucci. Oddly, the cuckold, who had accused Pam of flirting with male friends and acquaintances, never suspected anything. Perhaps, she confided to Dr. Rosen, Paul held her in such low regard that he could not imagine another man genuinely wanting to sleep with her.

For Pam, the deception provided an ancillary pleasure, while for Dr. Rosen, the only rewards of the liaison lay in the trickery and the physical gratification. Before long, she began to profess her love—an unwelcome development. He began to mull over how he might extricate himself cleanly from both the affair and the apartment.

Never the most attentive of lovers, as time passed, Dr. Rosen devoted less and less thought to her pleasure. When she would hint at what she wanted, speak of what she and Paul used to do in bed in their early, happy days together, Dr. Rosen would pretend not to understand. He would not bring her to orgasm unless she asked directly, and she seldom did. Never, though, did she complain, and always she would return.

One day, as they lay in post-coital languor, while Dr. Rosen brooded over his legal fees and whether the FBI might have Jerry's boiler room operation on its radar, she began to speak of the future.

"I'd love to go somewhere warm, somewhere tropical," she said, tracing with her finger the line of hair that ran down his front, from chest to groin. "Like the Bahamas. Someplace where I could just lay on the beach every day and do nothing, nothing at all. Wouldn't you like to live in a place like that?"

"It's a nice thought."

"I mean live there together."

"The three of us?"

She punched him lightly on the shoulder.

"No, silly. Not with Paul."

"What about him then?"

"I can't go on this way. I can't anymore."

"What would we live on?"

"We'll live on love."

She began stroking him again, but he was not yet ready for another round.

"That can run out pretty quickly."

She withdrew her hand. Her eyes filled with tears.

"Sometimes you sound just like Paul."

CHAPTER 35

"I must be insane," he said to himself one afternoon.

Dr. Rosen would have said as much to any patient of his who, while awaiting sentencing on four felony counts, made his living by defrauding frail, elderly people and Medicare, and had become embroiled in an affair with the married woman of the house in which he lived. Still, he went to work every day in Jerry's boiler room, and he continued to sleep with Pam Tucci.

At that moment, he lay naked in his bed with a dozing Pam beside him. With her head resting on his chest and her left leg draped over both of his, she had halfway wrapped herself around him.

He had begun to feel a revulsion toward her. Her clinginess, her vulnerability, and her sentimentality repelled him. He looked upon her scars and stretch marks with increasing disgust. At times he treated her cruelly. In bed he would finish, roll off her, and when she snuggled against him, turn toward the wall. Sometimes he would feign jealousy to put her on the defensive: "Are you going back to Paul now for round two?" He stopped answering the door when she knocked, even when the CRV was parked in the street and she knew he was inside. Once she lingered at the door for twenty minutes, sometimes knocking and sometimes climbing back up the stairs outside and trying to peer through one of the recessed windows.

He attempted, finally, to break off the affair. One afternoon, when the temperature had dropped into the twenties and the wind pierced to the bone, he again left her to stand outside and knock. Just as she turned toward the stairs, he opened the door. When she looked back at him, he saw that she was weeping.

"Look, I can't do this anymore," he told her, still standing in the doorway so she couldn't enter. "It's wrong on so many levels. It's morally wrong. And it's dangerous. Your husband is capable of anything."

The last he added for effect, as he thought Paul Tucci capable of very little. The effect, however, was not what he had hoped.

"Then let's go away somewhere."

"Where?"

"Anywhere. Let's just go. The kids are grown. I have nothing to keep me here anymore."

"Well, I do. I couldn't just pick up and go even if I could afford to. We need to talk."

At last, he invited her in.

"The truth is," he told her, "I'm a felon awaiting sentencing. I can't go outside the metro area without the court's permission, which it's unlikely to grant."

She looked stricken.

He continued, confessing more than he had to that point to anyone not associated with the FBI or the court, less for the purpose of unburdening himself of guilt, which, aside from its legal consequences, did not weigh heavily on him, than in the hope of scaring her away.

She dashed that hope at once.

"I don't care about any of that. I know you're a good, kind person. That's all that matters. You had a lapse in judgment. You learned from it. You've taken responsibility. There's no reason you should keep punishing yourself for what you did."

She kissed him on the forehead, the nose, and the mouth, and they soon found their way back to his lumpy mattress.

#

Meanwhile, as the court filings flew back and forth and his legal status remained in limbo, his financial woes continued to mount. One day he received in the mail a document titled "COMPLAINT TO DENY DISCHARGE OF DEBTOR'S DEBT TO MRS. PATRICIA AGNELLO." The document stated that counsel for Mrs. Agnello had initiated an adversarial proceeding "to prevent debtor, Dr. Robert Rosen, from using the Bankruptcy Code and this Court as a shield to avoid having to face the consequences of his malpractice, which resulted in the death of Mr. Salvatore Agnello." The plaintiff requested full payment of the debt and a granting of such other and further relief as deemed proper, including the payment of the plaintiff's court costs by Dr. Rosen.

"I'll be paying for the rest of my life," Dr. Rosen wailed into the phone. "I'll never be able to start over. I'll be out on the street."

"Not to worry," Andrew Le Bâtard replied. "They would have to prove that your actions were willful and that you purposefully harmed Mr. Agnello. Killing him with negligence? No problem."

"Fuck you, Andrew!"

Less than fully reassured—at a minimum, the filing meant more paperwork for Andrew and, therefore, more bills for him—Dr. Rosen began working the weekend shifts that he had previously spurned, spending sixty, seventy, eighty hours per week in Jerry's boiler room. The overtime provided two benefits: more pay and a ready excuse to avoid Pam. An unanticipated expense occasioned by the cracking of the CRV's engine mount, however, more than canceled out the extra income.

Living within ten minutes of North Shore, he began to visit Sheila regularly, but whenever he touched on the subject of her assets, she would shut down. So pitiable did he find his own plight that one day he dissolved into tears in front of her. Sheila hugged and comforted him, but later, when he again steered the conversation back to her finances, she stiffened.

"You and your brother can fight over the will when I'm gone, if there's anything to fight over. Don't worry. You won't have to wait long."

"Fine. See you at the funeral."

He stomped out of the room.

One morning he arrived at work to find a fire truck in the parking lot and the building blocked off. As he stood on the sidewalk watching in apprehension, a coworker named Kenny van Cott approached him. A man of uncertain age, about five-and-a-half feet tall, and slender, Kenny had a feathery moustache, salt-and-pepper stubble on his cheeks, brown and yellow teeth, and hair of no definitive color that hung in tangles down the back of his neck. The whites of his eyes had a faint yellow tinge, as though he suffered from a mild case of jaundice. He wore a bomber jacket, camouflage trousers, and a sweat-stained red cap printed with the slogan that President Dreck had employed to such great effect during his election campaign: DRECK FOR AMERICA!© Between the calloused index and middle fingers of his right hand, Kenny held a burning cigarette.

"The water's a foot deep in there. They're not letting anyone in." Leaning in closely, he added in a conspiratorial whisper, "You ask me, this was no accident. I've been hearing things. I think Jerry was worried that the feds were on to him."

His breath stank so powerfully of nicotine that Dr. Rosen took a step back.

Because Kenny saw hidden hands and nefarious plots everywhere, Dr. Rosen tended to discount most of what he said; however, these mutterings worried the ex-doctor. He could ill afford to have a Medicare fraud charge added to the four felony counts for which he already faced sentencing.

"Has Jerry said anything to you about it?"

"I'm not gonna reveal my sources. Let's just say I've been hearing things."

"I see."

Those sources, Dr. Rosen suspected, existed entirely inside Kenny's head. A call from Jerry a short time later, however, led him to wonder if, perhaps, his oddball coworker had, like the proverbial blind squirrel, found his acorn for once.

"The bad news is we're done," said Jerry, not at all sounding like the deliverer of bad news. "What are you gonna do? The funny thing is it may have been for the best. Just between you and me, I got a tip from a guy I know at FBI headquarters that we were gonna be raided. Well, they won't find anything now. Everything is destroyed. All the records, not to mention the computers, fax machines, and copiers."

"Well, that's lucky, I guess."

Dr. Rosen felt his breath leave him, just as he had when Golovorez punched him in the gut.

"Damn right!"

Jerry sounded jubilant.

"I mean it's too bad, people being out of work and all. But what are you gonna do, right?"

"That's the question, all right," Dr. Rosen murmured.

The temperature having climbed past 40 for the first time in weeks, Dr. Rosen drove out to the beach at Sunken Meadow State Park, the site of many a family outing during his childhood and adolescence. A view of the water, he thought, might help him clear his head.

At the shore, however, winter still held sway. A cutting wind swept unimpeded across the boardwalk and the beach, roiling the typically placid waters of Long Island Sound. Foam-crested waves broke upon the wet sand, sending forth tendrils of sea water. On the boardwalk, pigeons outnumbered people. Besides Dr. Rosen, there were but a handful of joggers and a power-walking senior couple dressed in matching pale blue track suits, their arms working like pistons. The beach, equal parts stone and sand, littered with all manner of natural and manmade detritus that the waves had washed ashore—

clumps of seaweed, bits of reed, seashell fragments, and pop-sicle sticks—lay entirely deserted.

Cutting across the strand, Dr. Rosen clambered up onto the rock formation that rose from the sand and jutted into the sound. He scrambled out to the farthest point from shore. Above him stretched a high azure sky spattered with cirrus clouds. Several gulls circled above the rocks, their shrieks piercing the air. Below him lay the brackish water of the sound, the agitated waves slapping against the moss-covered rocks at the bottom of the pile.

Though the wind pierced him to the bone, he lingered on those rocks for the better part of the morning. He had no de-sire to return home, for he knew that Pam, who had no teach-ing assignment that day, would inevitably appear at his door, and he had no other place to go. When, he wondered, had his life gone so far off the tracks? When he had involved himself with the Russians? Or before then, when he had first yielded to the temptation of easy money and begun selling oxy to his own rehab clinic and private practice patients? Or earlier still, when rather than accepting an unjust divorce settlement offer, he had opted to fight what would become a years-long battle of attrition with Liz for custody of an ungrateful son? Or did all his woes originate on his wedding day, when he had bound himself to a woman who in a hundred different ways each day, through her words, deeds, gestures, and facial expressions, let him know that she regarded him and his family as her social inferiors.

A weariness such as he had never experienced before stole over him. He looked down again at the water. An adult, he had read once, may take ten to twelve minutes to drown. He won-dered though: Would the terror last forever?

CHAPTER 36

That night, still feeling bereft and in need of consoling, he made a rare attempt to mend a couple of fences. When he called Tamika Jones, he said to her, as he had to Jeffrey the first time he had spoken to him after the arrest, "I guess you heard what happened to me."

She was back at the same Torpedo's, across from the vacant building that had housed the Peninsula Pain Center, toiling fifty or sixty hours per week to pay the rent on her nearby studio apartment and put a bit aside so she could enroll in community college next year.

"I heard what happened to you. You got busted like the lowlife drug dealer you are. And then you ratted me out, and I got questioned by the FBI."

Their last encounter notwithstanding, the anger she still evidently harbored toward him took him by surprise.

"What did you tell them?"

"I told them the truth, which I bet is more than you did. I told them everything. About the pain center. About the Russians. About how you dragged your own son into the business. Everything."

He launched into a tirade, during which he somehow found cause to blame her for Kellyanne's embezzlement, his troubles with the Russians, and his arrest.

"You're crazy," she said and hung up.

He called Jeffrey next, and after a couple of minutes of stilted conversation, he confided, "I'm desperate. I need help."

"What kind of help?" Jeffrey asked warily.

"I need money. The legal expenses are killing me. I'm going to be out on the street."

Jeffrey hesitated.

"How much do you need?"

"I need my share of what you got from selling Mom's house."

"There's nothing left. How many times do I have to say it?"

"I need what you stole from me."

"Go to hell."

Somehow containing his rage, Dr. Rosen decided to take a different tack. In a softer voice, he said, "I've been having these thoughts . . . bad thoughts . . . thoughts about hurting myself."

"Then you should check yourself into a hospital."

"I tell you I'm thinking about hurting myself, and that's all you have to say?"

"Isn't that what you would have told your patients?"

Dr. Rosen punctuated the call with an obscenity. Seated at his table, his head buried in his hands, he vowed to exact a fierce revenge against both Tamika and Jeffrey. He would sue—sue them both into oblivion, humiliate and crush them. Or do something even worse, something he could not yet envision that would cause them even more pain than that which now clawed at his innards.

Rising, he flung his cellphone across the room. When the phone struck the wall, the battery cover flew off, and phone and battery rebounded in opposite directions. A sizeable divot was left in the wall for the Tuccis to repair. His anger, though, remained unassuaged, and the kick that followed the throw had even more force behind it, enough to blast through the drywall, creating a hole of sufficient size to contain his entire foot up to the ankle.

He surveyed the damage, and what had until then amounted to no more than idle musings inspired by Jerry's fortuitous flood crystalized into a plan. The Tuccis, he guessed, had not given the basement an airing in years; he

227

would give it a nice watering. One day, during an afternoon deluge, he opened all the windows of his apartment, a task that necessitated his standing on a chair and pushing against the bottom of each window sash with all the force he could muster. One particularly stubborn window required the use of a crowbar lifted from Paul Tucci's backyard shed. The rainwater came streaming into the apartment, but not, alas, in the volume needed to flood the place. To help things along, Dr. Rosen turned on the shower, pushed the curtain aside, and directed the showerhead outward. He closed the drain in the bathroom sink and turned on the water and did the same with the kitchen sink. His and nature's efforts bore fruit in the form of a flood that the insurer of the house, if no one else, would regard as one of biblical proportions when the time came for the Tuccis to renew their policy. The unnatural disaster not only provided Dr. Rosen with a pretext to leave his lodgings but allowed him to do so with a show of indignation, putting both Tuccis on the defensive and heading off a potentially combustible parting.

Pam did call him a few times after he moved out. He told her that they would do well to break off all contact.

"I have to be able to live with myself. It's wrong what we were doing."

"It's not wrong if two people are in love."

"It is if one of them is married. I have made so many mistakes, and I've paid such a price for them. I need to start over again and get things right. I need to be a better person."

"You're a good person. You don't need to be better than you are."

In the end, she said she understood his need for a new start, and she found his resolve admirable. However painful she would find life without him, she would respect his wishes. Even after that declaration, however, she called several more times. He never answered, and she left no messages.

He moved in with Kenny van Cott, who occupied a cramped one-bedroom apartment on the second floor of one of four identical low-rise buildings adjacent to an industrial park. Owing to the substandard wiring in the building, the overhead light fixtures and the few lamps Kenny had scattered around the apartment sometimes flickered in the evenings when most of the residents of the complex were at home, and a perpetual twilight pervaded the space. Peeling paint and drywall nicks abounded, and perhaps worse lay behind the many posters, flags, and pennants with which Kenny had adorned the place. Many of those items bore the likeness of President Dreck and his campaign slogan DRECK FOR AMERICA!© Others depicted heavy metal bands with names such as Death Grip, Avenging Devils, Sword and Mace, and Dark Lords. Kenny chain-smoked, and the apartment reeked of stale cigarettes. Dr. Rosen slept in the living room on an antediluvian sofa bed. The top layer of the rollout mattress provided minimal cushioning between him and its springs.

Even on nights when the mattress did not keep him awake, the neighbors often did. Many in the building appeared to have neither work nor school nor family obligations. Stereos blared pop music and hip-hop at all hours of the day and night. Worse, the couple in the two-bedroom apartment up-stairs, the configuration of which must have placed its master bedroom directly above Kenny's living room, had volcanic sex several times a night. Within the first week, sleep deprivation had begun to cloud Dr. Rosen's thoughts, while muscle cramps wracked his body.

Kenny's paranoid ramblings about the perfidious Deep State pedophiles plotting to bring the president down, the miles-long convoys of illegal aliens invading the country from the south and hijacking America's jobs and culture, and the randy interracial couple upstairs became another source of torment. Fluent in the lingo of firearms, Kenny spoke long-ingly of weapons he wished he possessed and the liberal poli-ticians and Hollywood stars he would gun down if so equipped. He fulminated often about his inability to acquire a gun legally due to a "bullshit" domestic abuse charge leveled by a one-time girlfriend. Dr. Rosen could only nod, make vaguely affirmative noises, and wait for Kenny to talk himself out.

At times the roles would reverse, with Kenny serving as an audience while Dr. Rosen vented his rage. He would rail against Boadecia Wilde, the vengeful informant, who had run to the FBI with her tall tales because he had rejected her advances; Tamika Jones, the drug dealer, who by blackmailing him had first gotten him caught in a web of illegality; the unscrupulous FBI agents who had entrapped him; and Janel Moore, less a prosecutor than a persecutor. When he wound down, he would regret that he had confided so much to a man so lacking in discretion.

Kenny imagined himself a musician as well as an independent thinker. He had played in a couple of bands, one while in high school and another after graduation, and he kept a cheap off-brand electric guitar and compact amp in the apartment. Creative differences with his bandmates, he said, had led to his expulsion from both groups, after which he had put his music aside for many years. Recently, though, he had taken it up again. Naturally, the lapse had proved detrimental to his musicianship, but he had regained much of his technical proficiency—"it's like riding a bicycle; you don't forget"—and claimed to have attained new heights of creativity as a songwriter. He hoped to resume performing in the not-too-distant future, this time as a solo artist. No more compromising for him. He played some of his original compositions for Dr. Rosen, the music consisting more of feedback than melody, the lyrics replete with violent revenge fantasies against faithless women.

"You're very talented," Dr. Rosen would tell him, though the noise aggravated his heartburn and sometimes induced headaches.

The praise made Kenny beam, and he increasingly sought it out, even enlisting Dr. Rosen's help in composing lyrics. "What rhymes with *bitch*?" he would often ask.

The exercise had one salutary effect for Dr. Rosen; repeating to himself, like an incantation, the words *witch, switch, hitch, twitch, glitch* during Kenny's musical performances and political rants allowed him some psychic distance, thereby dulling the pain of serving as a captive audience.

He longed, however, for physical distance. In his penurious state, though, he had nowhere else to go but the street. Desperate for any income, he joined Kenny in signing on with another telemarketing outfit, one at least as legally and morally dubious as Jerry's. On a typical Monday, Dr. Rosen might cloak himself in the authority of Officer Charlie Johnson, computer security specialist for Microsoft, calling to warn that the resident's Microsoft Windows license agreement faced imminent cancellation. On a Tuesday, he might represent the IRS and deliver a final notice of an impending lawsuit over a tax delinquency. On a Wednesday, as an Amazon Fraud Department representative, he would provide an 800 number for the target to call regarding a credit card charge of $750. A random Thursday might find him impersonating a police officer and threatening someone with arrest over an unpaid traffic violation. Far less remunerative than the orthopedic equipment sales, these scams also proved a much harder sell, as he had no actual product to offer his marks. All too often, those who answered his calls represented themselves as attorneys or law enforcement officers and threatened him with prison. Lunchtime and the morning and afternoon break periods, when the snack truck pulled into the parking lot in front of the building, offered him no respite. Crackpot conspiracists like Kenny abounded in the new workplace, and he found conversing with them painful.

#

Hoping to escape his dismal lot as a minimum-wage employee, Dr. Rosen set his sights on reinventing himself as a life coach/financial advisor/corporate health, wellness, and productivity consultant.

Help came from an unexpected quarter. On rare occasions, Kenny exhibited a modicum of imagination on topics unrelated to nefarious Deep State conspiracies. He also boasted some rudimentary web design skills, having created a site for himself on which he posted his music videos. Because Dr. Rosen himself had no such knowhow, he acquiesced, albeit with much trepidation, when Kenny, in a moment of inspiration, offered to help him revamp the drrobert.co website to suit its owner's current needs and circumstances. To keep Dr. Rosen from running afoul of his medical license surrender agreement, Kenny scrubbed the site of references to his roommate's former clinical practice. The videos of the doctor's television appearances as Dr. Robert and Dr. Sober-Up—a gray area legally—remained up, and Kenny uploaded new ones that he and Robert recorded in the apartment. Those covered such topics as creativity, resilience, and time management. The substandard lighting, Kenny's herky-jerky camerawork—reminiscent of Tamika's—and the lack of makeup or hair filler to flatter Dr. Rosen's looks, sound equipment to modulate his voice, or a coach to monitor his pace or hand gestures resulted in videos so deficient in quality that Dr. Rosen, after picking up some coding basics from Kenny, would take them down from the site after a day or two.

In search of more content and design ideas, he perused hundreds of sites belonging to men and women working in the profitable fields of life coaching, financial advising, and corporate consulting. Inevitably, he found his way back to Barry Bullard's site. There he saw that his prolific coach had two new "bestsellers" for sale. The first was titled *The Power of Dreck: How to Lead Like a President*. Dr. Rosen recalled Barry speaking of that project during the drive to Salisbury. The second had a more enigmatic title: *Bulldog IV: The Bulldog is Back*. Dr. Rosen clicked over to Amazon for a preview, and as he read, a spear of flame shot up through his chest and scorched his throat.

Though the day was Wednesday and the time 11:30 p.m., he called Barry, who, unexpectedly, answered.

"You bastard! It wasn't enough you stole my intellectual property. Now you go and defame me. I'm gonna sue your ass. I'm gonna take you for every penny you have and will ever have."

"Chill out, bro," said Barry, his unusual calm suggesting to Dr. Rosen that he may have chosen on this night to indulge himself with a recreational substance other than his favorite stimulant. "You're talking a mile a minute, and you're not making any sense."

"I'm talking about your damn book. You blame me for getting you hooked on oxy? That's textbook defamation. First of all, you were never my patient. Second, I never prescribed anything for you."

"You did give me scripts, bro."

"Not as your doctor."

"As what? My pusher? You know you're not gonna sue me, and I know you're not gonna sue me. In the first place, how could I have defamed you? Is your name Rupert Rosebud?"

"You think it's funny? You think a ridiculous fake name will fool anyone?"

"You got to admit that Dr. Rupert Rosebud is pretty good."

"I have a professional reputation. Something like this can destroy it, to say nothing of the emotional distress, which is worth a few million in itself."

"Professional reputation? Give me a break. That was gone the day you got busted, bro."

"Yeah, well how would you like it if word got around that Master Life Coach Barry Bullard is really Barry Boucek, former chop shop man, trafficker in stolen auto parts, associate of Alexey Golovorez and Sergei Zhukov? I heard that they gave you quite a beating, even broke a few ribs. Couldn't happen to a nicer guy."

"I don't know what you're talking about," Barry replied frostily. "But I'll tell you something. Unlike you, I do have a professional reputation. If you go spreading false rumors about me with the intent of damaging it, you'll be hearing from my lawyer."

"So you don't find it so funny when the shoe's on the other foot. Well, you can tell your lawyer that this story is all true. Which is the best defense against defamation."

The line went dead.

Surprisingly, however, Barry called back the following day.

"Look, bro, I was thinking," he said in a wheedling tone. "You could sue me, and I could sue you, but where's that gonna get either of us? No need to sweat the Rupert Rosebud thing. Nobody's gonna read that friggin' book anyway. The books are strictly branding materials, like mugs or pens. They aren't meant to be read. I just crank them out and forget about them. If I make a few bucks off one, that's great. If I don't, no biggie.

"But that's not what I called to talk about. Listen, I know you're going through a tough time now, and you could use a hand up. I'm involved with a new venture that I think would be right up your alley, and I could use a little help getting it off the ground. I think we just might be able to work together and make this a win-win. I'll be on Long Island Saturday morning. I'm doing a talk at the state university. Why don't you come on out?"

"I don't know, Barry. The last time you called me about a business proposition, it was with that Stonebreaker clown who you had to scrape off the sidewalk outside Maxwell's."

"Stonecypher. Yeah, that wasn't a good night. Believe it or not, though, he might just get that thing going yet. He told me there were a couple of Russians who showed some interest in backing him. You still may hear from him. He asked me for your contact info."

"And you gave it to him?"

"I didn't think you'd mind, bro."

"I do mind. Especially if Russians are involved. Jesus, Barry. How many different times and in how many different ways are you gonna fuck me over?"

"Well, I wouldn't worry too much about that. It was a while ago. If you haven't heard from him by now, you probably won't. Anyway, so what about Saturday?"

"I don't know, Barry. How much will it cost me?"

"Not a thing. This one's on the house. What have you got to lose?"

Pondering the question, Dr. Rosen drew a blank.

CHAPTER 37

The first quarter-hour or so of Barry's talk only reinforced Dr. Rosen's doubts about further involvement with his erstwhile mentor. By Dr. Rosen's count, the audience in the vast university lecture hall totaled seventeen people, two of whom he thought he recognized but could not place. To create the illusion of a crowd, Barry and his videographer had bunched all the attendees together at the front of the hall. A few appeared to be in their twenties or early thirties, with the majority middle-aged and tending toward plumpness. Most sported business-casual attire, the women in knee-length dresses and ballet flats, and the men wearing chinos, walking shoes, and polos or sweaters.

Up at the lectern, Barry wore black dress slacks and a scarlet blazer with gold buttons on the sleeves and a golden triangle stitched onto the left breast pocket. He had a microphone, barely larger than one of the buttons of his blazer, fastened to his lapel. On the wall behind him hung a gold-fringed scarlet banner bearing the same golden triangle as the blazer.

Though shaved and scrubbed, the Barry on display today reminded Dr. Rosen of the wild man who had so discomfited him in the Chicago hotel room. In pace, his speech approached that of an auctioneer; in volume, that of a barrage of fireworks. His jerky hand gestures rarely dovetailed with his words. His frequent sniffling, along with the curious tic he had of rubbing the back of his right index finger against the underside of his nose, led Dr. Rosen to suspect that he had prepared for his talk by indulging in the same illicit pastime that he had in Chicago.

"You see that symbol?" Barry asked the audience while pointing at the banner. "That's the Greek letter delta. Why is that our logo? Why do we call this program Delta? In math, delta symbolizes change. Now maybe you're thinking, 'Barry, I didn't come here for an algebra lesson. What does that Greek letter have to do with me?' The answer is everything. Isn't that why we're all here today? If your lives were perfect, would you be here? No. You may be doing OK, but you want more out of life than OK. More money. More house. A bigger and better car. More fun. And let's be honest—more sex."

The audience tittered.

"Yeah, you know what I'm talkin' about."

He pointed again at the banner.

"Now what else can you tell me about that delta up there? Anyone?"

From the audience came head shakes, puzzled looks, and silence.

"Maybe you haven't had your morning coffee yet. Me, I don't need coffee. I got something better. Something in here. Life!"

He pounded his chest.

"Come on. It's obvious. What color is the delta?"

"Gold," said two or three voices simultaneously.

"That's right. Gold. And gold is what I want to talk to you about today. Your gold. The gold you have within you, in every one of you. Your happiness is already within you. Your success is already within you.

"But all that gold, all the gold in the world, won't make you rich if you can't get to it. And how do you get to it? You work. That's how. You work your ass off for it. You don't get to be a success like me by picking little nuggets off the surface. No, you got to dig into that rock. You got to mine that gold."

Stepping out from behind the lectern, he draped his blazer over a nearby chair, undid his tie, opened his collar button, and rolled up the sleeves of his sweat-darkened white shirt. He spit—or pantomimed spitting—into his hands, rubbed them together, lifted an invisible pick high over his shoulder, and swung it down viciously. He swung it a second time and a third, paused to run his forearm over his brow, and then swung it again.

Tossing aside the imaginary pick, he cried, "You may have to break your back to get to that gold, but when you do—oh, boy!—you'll know it was worth the effort and then some."

The audience applauded, Dr. Rosen belatedly joining in when he saw Barry looking his way.

Mining gold from the ground, Barry continued, required tools, such as a pick. Mining the gold within required less tangible, but no less important, mental and emotional tools, self-knowledge foremost among them.

"People tell us stories about ourselves, and we believe them. And so often those stories are wrong. And that's where our lives go wrong. What you're going to learn here is how to write your own stories. But before you can do that, you have to put in the work. You have to do that mining I was talking about. You have to dig down and uncover your truth. Notice I didn't say *the truth*. I said *your truth*. Your truth is the only one that matters. And it's all in here."

He held his index finger up against his right temple.

Rarely pausing for breath, Barry spoke for two-and-a-half hours before allowing the audience a ten-minute break. As the attendees filed out of the auditorium, they were met at the doors by young men in scarlet blazers identical to Barry's who handed out fliers and tried to entice them into signing up for additional seminars.

The presentation resumed with the two audience members whom Dr. Rosen had thought he had recognized earlier joining Barry onstage. They too had put on scarlet blazers. Dr. Rosen remembered them now: A husband-and-wife team, they had recorded video endorsements for Barry's website.

Today they had come to offer testimonials for Delta and some advice on how to get *more* out of life. The wife, a stocky blond woman, heavily made up, adorned with an abundance of bracelets and rings and golden triangles hanging from her earlobes, spoke of emotional intelligence as the key to success, citing a variety of celebrities and billionaires, including President Dreck, as examples. The husband, a silver-haired man whose leathery skin suggested that he had spent too much time in a tanning spa, expounded on how to generate passive income, which he touted as the secret to accumulating wealth. Dr. Rosen found that topic of far greater interest than emotional intelligence, but as he listened, he felt a gnawing resentment. His penury would not allow him to deploy the strategies touted by the speaker.

After Barry wrapped up the presentation, the audience gave him and the other speakers a standing ovation. Outside the lecture hall, one of the importuning red-blazered recruiters accosted Dr. Rosen and urged him to take advantage of an incredible limited-time offer for an advanced three-day Delta seminar.

"I'm not even in the program," Dr. Rosen said. "I'm here as a guest of Barry."

His demurral did not deter the recruiter, who relented only when Barry emerged from the lecture hall. Draping his arm over Dr. Rosen's shoulders, he said, "Let's go get some lunch. My treat. I'm starved."

They drove out to Port Jefferson and dined at a nautical-themed harbor-side seafood restaurant. From the paneled walls hung life preservers, ships wheels, harpoons, and painted wooden swordfish. While Barry talked up his new venture, Dr. Rosen, sipping a glass of pinot grigio and gazing out at the boats at anchor bobbing atop the water on this mild early spring afternoon, paid him but intermittent attention.

"It's a franchise operation. The parent company is called Multiform. They provide the blazers, the banners, even a curriculum, though I kind of like to do my own thing. Anyway, this half-day thing is just the hook. You get people in, and then you pitch them on a three-day seminar. I've been to one of them. A lot of what goes on there takes place in small-group breakout sessions. It gets pretty intense, pretty confrontational."

Recalling his sessions in Catherine Connolly's group, Dr. Rosen replied, "Yeah, I've had enough of that sort of thing for one lifetime."

"A lot of people think that before they give it a try. Then they're like—wow!"

"I'm broke, Barry. Whatever the seminar costs, I can't afford it."

"It doesn't have to cost you anything. Here's the deal. The way you make money in this Delta business is to put butts in the seats. For each person I get to attend a seminar, Delta-Multiform gives me 33 percent of the tuition. To rent a hall for three days and make real money, I'd need an audience two or three times the size of today's. If you can get to sixty-five, seventy, seventy-five per seminar—a critical mass, they call it—that's when it really starts to pay. Then you get peer pressure working for you. You push the suckers to recruit their friends and family. It's multilevel marketing, basically. That's where you come in. I need some help to get there. I'm too busy putting everything together to spend enough time recruiting. Those schmucks I got working for me now—college seniors, recent grads, guys who've never had a real job—they're just about useless. Sometimes, they don't even show up."

"So what would I be doing?"

"Making calls. Getting people to book sessions, so I start to break even at least. Then doing some selling at the sessions."

Dr. Rosen finished his wine and poured himself another glass.

"Cold calls? I don't know about that."

"You can be very persuasive. And you have a damn good product to sell here."

"Do I get paid for this?"

"You'll be a featured speaker. You got a story to tell that a lot of people are gonna want to hear. You can get a book out of it too. A bestseller. Americans are suckers for redemption stories."

"I don't know, Barry. It sounds good, but I can't work for free. The way things are going, I'll be out on the street before long."

"All right. All right. Five percent commission for every recruit you bring me for the three-day seminar."

"So my share would be what? Twenty-five dollars a head? That's not worth my time. Make it 25 percent of your share, and then I'll think about it."

"Seven-and-a-half."

"Twenty."

"Eight."

"Fifteen."

"Nine."

"Ten. I'm not going below that."

"Hmm."

Frowning, Barry took out his phone and brought up the calculator app. Affording Dr. Rosen a partial view of the screen, he performed, or skillfully pantomimed the performance of, a series of complex calculations.

"Deal," he said, extending his hand. "Ten percent."

Dr. Rosen hesitated.

"I don't know. That's not a lot of money for all that calling. I'll be lucky if I get one bite for every hundred calls."

"Best I can do, bro," Barry replied, his arm still extended across the table. "Fifty is better than nothing."

Grudgingly, Dr. Rosen shook his hand.

CHAPTER 38

Though Dr. Rosen could not afford to quit his telemarketing job, he reduced his hours and set to work in his spare time recruiting customers for Barry's next seminar. The cold calling proved as frustrating as he had anticipated. In desperation, he turned once more to family.

Jeffrey was again sitting in his living room drinking Chianti, contemplating *The Drowning Dog*, and conversing with his late wife when his brother called. He waited until the fourth ring to answer, seconds before the call would have gone to voicemail. After exchanging hellos, neither brother could think of anything to say for nearly half a minute.

"So, how have you been?" Jeffrey asked at last. "You're feeling, uh, OK now?"

"Fine. Good. I've gotten some consulting work. The money is pretty good. Not like what I was getting, but I can't complain."

"That's good."

"I'm working for an organization called Delta-Multiform. It's a continuing life-affirmation project."

"A what?"

Dr. Rosen launched into his pitch.

"For many people, these seminars are a life-changing experience. You should see the testimonials on the website. Marriages saved. Friendships repaired. Family members who haven't spoken in decades reconciling during a seminar. People making career changes or going into business for themselves. Trust me. This is the real deal."

"So this is why you called me?"

Jeffrey's thumb hovered over the "End" button on the telephone keypad.

"I'm calling you because I want to repair our relationship, and I think this is the way to do it. It's very important to me."

"Since when? And how much would one of these seminars cost me?"

"I'm talking about changing your life and repairing our relationship, and you're talking about money."

"With you, it always comes down to money. How much do you get for recruiting me?"

"That's not who I am now. I'm a changed person. I'm offering you help and hope, and frankly, you need it. Think about it. Your whole life has gone down the toilet. Your career is shot. You drink too much. You're chronically depressed. I'm telling you I know a way out of all that."

"Right. What did you say the name of this outfit was?"

"Delta-Multiform."

"Like glioblastoma multiforme? Sounds like a scam to me. The only thing I can't tell is whether you're one of the scammers or one of the marks."

"You think you're better than me just because I made one mistake in my life? You've never done anything wrong, ever?"

"Nothing actionable under the US Code, so far as I know. But it's not your felonies that I hold against you."

"What then?"

"It's that you are what you are and what you always will be."

"Yeah, well, I've accomplished a lot more than you have. I've made more money, had more women, been on TV."

"Good for you."

"What have you done with your life that's so great? Loser!"

Dr. Rosen decided to try his luck with Sheila in person. As often happened, he found her asleep in her wheelchair with the television turned to the news. President Dreck, speaking at a rally in Butler, Pennsylvania, was exhorting his followers to arm themselves and join Dreck's Army, a force of citizen-soldiers dedicated to wresting back control of America's cities from the lawless mobs rampaging therein. Dr. Rosen, who in his preoccupation with his own problems had largely tuned out the news, turned off the television.

"Mom?" he called and tapped her on the shoulder.

She blinked several times, as if uncertain as to whether to trust her eyes, then gave him a warm smile. She had lost still more weight since he had seen her last. Her blouse hung upon her like a shroud. Her lips and fingertips had a bluish cast, and when he took her hand, it chilled him. Nevertheless, she fussed over him. Was he still able to work as a doctor? Was he eating and sleeping all right? Had he spoken to Jeffrey? Was Nathan all right?

No, he replied, he could no longer work as a doctor, having had to surrender his license. Otherwise, he was doing very well. He had gone to work for an organization called Delta-Multiform and was happy in the job and well remunerated. As he embarked upon his pitch, however, he saw her smile fade and her eyes grow distant. A faint look of disgust appeared on her face.

"You want me to go to one of those things? How would I even get there?"

"I'll drive you."

"And it's three full days of lectures?"

"And small-group breakout sessions."

"I can't sit in my wheelchair all day long for that."

"Isn't that what you do here, sit all day in your room?"

"No, I don't. And what would I do when I need to use the bathroom?"

"Can't you think about something other than shit for once? Like repairing our relationship? Isn't that important to you?"

"No, I can't. When you need someone's help to use the toilet, that's what you think about. All the time. Now leave me alone. I'm tired."

She closed her eyes. Her mouth fell open, and she immediately began to snore.

Leaving the room, he slammed the door shut behind him.

Even while he continued to labor, with little reward, at recruiting for Barry, Dr. Rosen began to develop his own motivational speech, building on the story he had sketched out during the lifeline exercise in Catherine Connolly's therapy group for felons. The talk would trace the arc, or arcs, of his life: the rise from a difficult childhood to prominence as a doctor and television star, the shattering fall occasioned by his arrest, and the comeback from the depths of despair and disgrace. His story would be part cautionary tale, a warning against the dangers of hubris and willful blindness, but also a paean to the values of persistence and resilience that had enabled him to rise again despite the loss of his livelihood and the stigma of a felony conviction. Over drinks with Barry, he spoke of his vision.

"Good. You're on the right track. Just throw in a little of the two Fs—faith and family—and you've got it. People will lap it right up."

Estranged from his son and lacking both a present love interest and the slightest inclination toward religious belief of any sort, notwithstanding the tale he had told Catherine Connolly at their last appointment, Dr. Rosen cast around for ideas. Of the three, he needed Nathan the most, for in him resided the premise of an irresistible narrative: that of a lost man guided toward redemption by the love he and his son shared. The plan had one drawback: He had not spoken to Nathan since kicking him out of the CRV in the South Bronx. To avoid potential embarrassment, a rapprochement would be needed. He would have to think on how to approach that.

His work on his redemption fable progressed much more surely than did his recruiting efforts, and with Barry's encouragement, he began to contemplate a book. Five bulleted items in an outline seemed to grow effortlessly into five chapters, the last describing his appearance in Chicago. The manuscript bore the working title *Starting Over: How to Overcome Adversity and Live the Life You Want.* As in life, though, so went his literary endeavor; after Chicago, he found himself stymied. His unwillingness to account himself guilty of anything more than poor judgment, along with his fear of placing himself in further legal jeopardy, led him to elide much of what had occurred between his Chicago appearance and the present day, save for a brief description of the arrest itself; nor could he yet envision, beyond some vague contours, the final third of his story—that of the comeback that had barely begun.

For a while, he diverted himself by searching for graphics on the internet that he might employ when designing the cover for *Starting Over,* and then he had Kenny develop several mockups. To the drrobert.co bio page, where Kenny had listed the doctor's current occupations as ENTRAPENOUR, CONSULTITANT, and LIFECOACH, Dr. Rosen added BEST-SELLING AUTHOR. He also had Kenny add a new BOOKS page, which featured one of the cover mockups, and advised the public that the anticipated bestseller would be "coming soon."

From time to time, Dr. Rosen would practice his speaking, drawing on material from the manuscript and elsewhere. Kenny served as both audience and videographer.

"You got it, man," Kenny would say. "Take it from me. I know a thing or two about performing. You're a natural in front of a camera. You're gonna be a rock star."

While his enthusiasm gave Dr. Rosen's confidence a needed boost, Kenny's ineptitude in handling the camera and the erratic lighting in the apartment militated against posting the videos on the drrobert website.

So, too, did Andrew's caution.

"If I were you," said the lawyer, "I'd take down that website altogether until after the sentencing hearing. At a minimum, the white coat videos need to go. I'd change the domain name too."

"Why?"

"Have you read your license surrender agreement? 'Licensee shall refrain from,' blah de blah de blah, 'representing that Licensee is eligible to practice medicine.' You're pushing right up against the line there."

On the phone, Dr. Rosen promised to heed the advice, but he sought out a second opinion—Barry's—and found it more to his liking.

"Leave them up, bro. You think the board has nothing better to do than monitor your website? You need to keep your name out there."

The videos stayed up, and the domain name remained unchanged.

One night, after a bout of serious drinking, he and Kenny set out, in the faltering light of the living room, to make a video on the value of persistence. Kenny hit upon the idea of filming Dr. Rosen in front of the poster above the sofa that showed the grinning President Dreck giving the camera a double thumbs-up while standing amid a group of shell-shocked hurricane survivors.

"I don't know," said Dr. Rosen. "I don't want to make a political statement. I'm trying to reach as wide an audience as possible."

"He has like 80 million followers on Twitter, man. This could go viral."

"Ah, why not?" replied Dr. Rosen, who did not feel like arguing and anticipated that the recording session would result in yet another mess of a video that no one would ever see.

Moving the sofa out of the picture took much effort, necessitating a rest and another couple of beers for both Kenny and Dr. Rosen before they started recording.

Unsteady on his feet and unable to sync his hand gestures with his words, Dr. Rosen quickly aborted his first two attempts, despite Kenny's encouragement to keep going.

"This time just do it, man. Do the whole talk from beginning to end. Keep going, no matter what comes out. We can always edit it later. Ready? Good. One, two, three, go!"

Dr. Rosen took a deep breath and began, loudly enough so the sounds of sex in the room above barely registered.

"Hello, I'm Dr. Robert Rosen, and I'm here today to talk about persistence. Persistence is very important if you want to succeed in having success in life. You could have all the talent in the world, but without, uh, without resilience, you'll never get ahead. And when things don't go well, because they don't always. Even for me they haven't. In fact, I've been through hell. And that's when you really need resilience. Take it from me. I know what I'm talking about. Persistence.

"I was on top of the world. I had a thriving practice. I had a substance abuse clinic on-site, a partnership in another clinic for treatment of chronic pain. I had several TV appearances under my belt. I did a talk on addiction on the *Windy City A.M.* show in Chicago, third-largest media market in the country. I was on my way to the top.

"But when you have success, people get envious. Envy. There's nothing more destructive. That's why you have to let go. And that's what I'm here to talk about today. Letting go.

"I had this patient. Her name was . . . Well, for legal reasons, I won't say her name. Ah, the hell with that. Her name was Boadecia Wilde. Very disturbed woman. Borderline personality disorder. Probably an eating disorder too. All kinds of comorbid shit. A total freak. Well, she had a huge crush on me. Not only didn't I have the same feelings about her, but messing around with female patients—uh uh. You don't do that. Well, borderlines can't handle rejection. You know, like in that movie *Fatal Attraction*, where Glenn Close boils the family rabbit? That's what I'm talking about. Textbook borderline.

"Now I was saying . . . I was saying . . . This patient—like I said, she can't handle rejection. And she's really vindictive. So what she does is she goes running to the FBI and makes up this wild story about me, saying I've been selling her oxyco-done scripts for cash. Total fabrication."

"A rat," muttered Kenny from behind the camera.

"She was the one who was in trouble for dealing, and she was looking to get off, so she thought she could kill two birds with one stone and turn me in. Totally unscrupulous.

"Enter Agent W.E. Friggin' Hardin and his crew. I don't know why they ever would have believed anything the rat told them. Maybe they have an arrest quota or something. Anyway, Agent W.E. Friggin' Hardin sends these two undercover rats around to my office."

"Dirty cops!" cried Kenny. "Scum!"

In Kenny, a fervent belief in law 'n' order in the abstract and its forceful application against certain populations coex-isted with a visceral loathing of actual law enforcement per-sonnel, likely stemming from his own unpleasant encounters with them.

"And get this. One of the dirty cops called herself Carol Burnett. I should have figured something was up. I used to watch *Carol Burnett* reruns when I was a kid. I'll never be able to watch her show again. Anyway, these dirty cops come around, and they keep offering me more and more money if I'd sell them oxy prescriptions. And I tell them I don't pre-scribe pain meds for anyone who comes in off the street. I need to be able to make a legitimate diagnosis. I need a refer-ral. I need X-rays. I need MRI results. They kept on coming back, trying to wear me down, and I kept telling them to get lost. Then they bring me some X-rays. They were probably phony, now that I think about it. But I had no way to know that. What the films showed was consistent with the kind of pain they said they were having. So I wrote out a couple of prescriptions for them, even though I had a bad feeling about it. Entirely justifiable based on what I knew, or thought I knew. And then one day at 6 a.m., the FBI comes around and knocks my door off the hinges. And there went my freedom, my livelihood, my reputation, everything I worked so hard to build over so many years."

"Bastards! They're the ones who belong in jail!"

In the sober light of the following morning, Dr. Rosen told Kenny to erase the video. Unbeknownst to him, however, Kenny had already posted it to drrobert.co under the title "DR. ROBERT ROSEN FRAMED BY FBI."

CHAPTER 39

Most of the minuscule number of people who would view the video happened upon it by chance—but not Michael Stonecypher, the president's bastard son. Obsession led him to it. Like Dr. Rosen, Stonecypher harbored a grudge against the FBI, one that compelled him to scour the internet at all hours of the day and night for evidence of the bureau's real and imagined malfeasance. A few years earlier, he had pleaded guilty to trafficking in cocaine after making the mistake of doing business with undercover agents working under the supervision of Special Agent Hardin. Agreeing to a guilty plea, he had also drawn Judge Pound, who had sentenced him to five years of probation.

Despite the private resentments he may have harbored toward the extended Dreck clan, in public, aside from that one unfortunate incident outside Maxwell's that Dr. Rosen had witnessed, Stonecypher directed his vitriol at the FBI. He could do so without consequences because the president, who had had numerous associates investigated by the FBI, shared his rage at the bureau. The more loyal of those presidential cronies had reaped their rewards in the form of pardons, commutations, or dropped charges. Having kept silent about his origins and endured the humiliation of his bastardy without embarrassing the Drecks, Michael Stonecypher felt entitled to similar consideration. He hoped to have his name cleared retroactively.

Dr. Rosen's video screed thus caught his attention when he came upon the link while searching YouTube at 2:59 a.m. one random Tuesday. He had a foggy memory of having met the ex-doctor once, though he could not recall when or where. Inspired by what he saw, he made a video of his own, a much more polished production, recorded on a set made up to look like an executive's office, though it featured the same poster of Dreck and the hurricane survivors that Kenny had used as a backdrop when filming Dr. Rosen. In his video, Stonecypher aired many of the same grievances as Dr. Rosen had, adding in some dark suggestions of political bias on the part of Agent Hardin and the undercover agents who had arrested him.

"I am a political prisoner," he proclaimed, despite the probationary sentence that Judge Pound had given him.

Aside from that one rhetorical flourish, he employed more judicious language than Dr. Rosen had, while also tempering the volume and avoiding the jerky hand gestures that so distracted the viewer from Dr. Rosen's message. Stonecypher's video went viral when the president, ever in search of social media affirmation and ever careless about whom he retweeted, sent it out to his tens of millions of followers.

At once, the rumors about Michael Stonecypher's parentage that had circulated during the last campaign and faded from public memory after President Dreck's inauguration surfaced anew. Day after day, the president's press secretary attempted to quash them, first refusing to dignify them with a comment, then attacking the media and the opposition party for spreading the story, and finally denouncing Michael Stonecypher himself as a liar and opportunist when he coyly refused either to confirm or deny the rumors.

The uproar caused by his own blunder drove the president to greater than usual distraction. One gray Washington afternoon, he summoned Attorney General William Stuckart and Acting FBI Director Tom Hagen to the Oval Office.

Since his last meeting with Dreck in the Oval Office, Attorney General Stuckart observed, the president had been busy in his fashion. He had had the walls papered over in faux gold leaf. On the small table to the right of the Resolute Desk, a new marble bust of the president—an uncanny likeness with jutting jaw and pursed lips—had replaced the one of Martin Luther King Jr. that had stood there throughout his predecessor's administration. At the opposite end of the room, above the fireplace, where once had hung a painting of Franklin Delano Roosevelt, the official portrait of President Dreck now held pride of place. A reproduction of that image—the very one that Agent Hardin found so oppressive lurking over his shoulder—hung in the offices of innumerable federal bureaucrats.

Glowering behind the Resolute Desk, President Dreck looked like a rhino poised to charge. Whether due to his ire or a botched makeup application, his complexion had taken on the hue of a raw steak. His voice was that of an angry elephant.

"How the hell did this happen? I want to know who's responsible."

Attorney General Stuckart, a rotund man with a helmet of black-and-gray hair, narrow, devious-looking eyes, and the jowls of a mastiff, was an old Washington hand. His reputation as a wise counselor, which had enabled him to ingratiate himself to three presidents and outstrip legions of other government lawyers to attain, finally, primacy among them, he owed primarily to his parsimoniousness of speech. Thus, when the president inquired as to the origins of the scandal, Stuckart refrained from giving voice to the first answer that came to mind ("It all started, you dolt, when you knocked up one of your secretaries thirty-four years ago.") or even the second ("Then you went and blasted out a video to your 80 million slack-jawed followers without noticing that what you were retweeting came from your own idiot bastard son, you nincompoop."). Instead, he replied, in the most judicious tone he could muster, "Well, sir, it began with an arrest by the FBI that, if I may say so, was rather weakly predicated."

The president glared at Acting Director Hagen, a fair-haired, square-jawed man who boasted, in addition to his leading man looks, the height and musculature of an NBA power forward. Despite his stature, he looked small relative to the president, as did all visitors who sat on the opposite side of the Resolute Desk from the president. The chairs put out for the help stood several inches lower than the one in which the president sat.

"That happened under the previous administration, of course," the attorney general hastened to add. "They were the ones that brought the case against Stonecypher. I have no doubt that Director Hagen would have shown better judgment."

"Bastards! It wasn't enough that they spied on my campaign. They were going after my family too."

The attorney general did not see fit to mention that the arrest had occurred well before the president had declared his candidacy or that Dreck, apropos of bastards, had never acknowledged Stonecypher as family.

"I want that conviction thrown out."

"Yes, sir," replied the attorney general.

Open-mouthed, Hagan gaped at Stuckart.

"But . . . But . . . Undo a guilty plea retroactively? How in the world . . .? You can't."

"Listen, and listen good," replied the president of the United States. "I don't know how you're used to doing things, but you're working for me now. And when you work for me, and I tell you to do something, you do it. Got it?"

"Well, sir, it's really more the attorney general's call. At the FBI, we're just the enforcement people."

"If the president wants it done," said Stuckart piously, "it will be done. Nobody in the Executive Branch may question the president." He thought, but did not say aloud, "Even if he's as crazy as a shithouse rat."

"And I want some heads to roll. I want everyone connected with the case out on the street. Yesterday. Anyone involved with the arrest. Anyone involved with the prosecution. It's past time to weed out these holdovers. They're destroying my presidency."

"Sir, if I may," ventured Director Hagen, "with all due respect, I think there are a couple of aspects to consider. Politics and polling and the like are certainly outside of my bailiwick, but I can't help but wonder whether expending that kind of political capital on someone like Stonecypher is worth it. The whole business will probably be forgotten in a few days. Secondly, there's a question of morale at FBI New York and the ripple effect elsewhere that such a move would have throughout the bureau. The branch we're talking about deals strictly with drug-related crime, not any of that . . ." Hagen groped for a tactful way to refer to the money laundering, tax fraud, and racketeering offenses for which FBI New York had investigated a half-dozen or so of the president's business and legal associates. "That other stuff."

The president slammed his fist on the desk. Hagen's 6-foot, 8-inch frame seemed to contract to half its size.

"When I nominated you, I said I expected one thing from you. One thing. Do you remember what that one thing was?"

"Yes, sir. You said you expected loyalty, sir."

"Correct. Can I count on you, Hagen?"

"I'll do my best, sir."

"That's not good enough!" the president roared, his face now maroon. "I want these losers the hell out of there."

"Yes, sir. I'll take care of it right away."

"Good. Now, get on it. Get out of here. You're dismissed."

"Yes, sir. Thank you, sir."

The president cackled as the acting director slunk out of the room.

"What a pussy. I should have had him go get me a Diet Coke. I gotta think of a good nickname for him. Teeny Tiny Tom. Little Tommy Boy. Tom Thumb. Or something like that.

"What do you think, Tubs? Did I do right in picking him?"

"He's exactly what you want in an FBI director, Mr. President," said the poker-faced attorney general of the protégé whose appointment he had engineered.

His tone gave away no more than his expression. To express his resentment at the humiliating moniker the president had pinned on him would jeopardize his position. To share a complicit laugh with President Dreck at Hagen's expense, however, would mean compromising his dignity—the very quality that in his mind, if not the president's, set him apart from the Hagens and all the other toadies allowed or denied access to the Oval Office according to presidential whim. He regretted that he could not show his independence more overtly. Someday, though, he would get his own back. He would write a book.

"Yeah, I think I made a good choice. Nobody ever heard of this clown before I picked him. The media said, 'Tom who?' They won't be saying that when I turn him loose on them. It's about time for the law enforcers to do some enforcing."

Craving a Diet Coke, the president summoned the butler on the intercom.

The consequences of having performed his job in accordance with the law and Department of Justice policy years earlier and thereby arousing the retroactive wrath of the sitting president fell swiftly and heavily upon FBI Special Agent W.E. Hardin. Within a week, by direct order of Director Hagen, the FBI had placed him on administrative leave. The notice he received alluded vaguely to certain "irregularities" in some of his cases. While Hardin sat at home worrying over how he would pay his mortgage if fired, a server brought him a subpoena from the Senate Judiciary Committee. The majority, ever eager to do the president's bidding, had decided to stage a hearing on alleged political bias within the FBI.

Presiding over the hearing was the committee chairman, Senator Roy Smegley, a long-serving, ill-tempered, reactionary septuagenarian. Dubbed by a waggish colleague from New York "The Golem of Georgia," Smegley had a flat face and an outsized bald head that, absent a visible neck, merged into a nearly spherical torso. Two impossibly short, thick legs supported the whole assembly.

Staring into the C-SPAN camera, Smegley gaveled the hearing to order and then proceeded to deliver a ten-minute philippic against the previous FBI director, whom he accused of undermining the president out of rank political bias. There existed no greater danger to the republic, he warned gravely, than an out-of-control FBI seeking to undo the will of the people.

Calling Agent Hardin as his first witness, Smegley proceeded to give him a thorough grilling.

"You talk politics much in your office, Agent Haw-dun?"

"No, sir. It's a subject we have always avoided. Intentionally. I couldn't tell you which party most of my colleagues belong to."

"Would you say, though, that there are people you work with, or work under you, who don't like the pres'dent? People who might want to do something to hurt him politically? Prosecute someone close to him, for example, for no very good reason?"

"No, sir, I would not. I don't know of any such people or any such prosecution."

"Well, I have to say I find that hard to believe, when you consider some of what's been goin' on in the New York headquarters."

"If you're referring to the Stonecypher case . . ."

Senator Smegley interrupted him sharply: "Do you dislike the pres'dent, Haw-dun?"

"No, senator. I don't know him. I've never met him in person."

"But you must have some opinions about him. About the job he's doin'. What do you think of it, Haw-dun?"

"My political opinions are not relevant to the work I do. Nor are those of my colleagues."

"I think there's a lot of folks watchin' at home," replied the senator, a Harvard Law graduate, "who wouldn't agree. They're angry. They want some answers. When you have a cabal of people in the New York headquarters, people with New York values, who take it upon themselves to bring down a sitting pres'dent—well, that's a real big problem."

"That would be—if such a cabal existed. And I'm not sure what you mean by 'New York values.' I'm from Ohio."

"Let's be serious here, Haw-dun. We both know what's what."

Agent Hardin, feeling his own gorge rising, struggled to restrain himself.

"I don't know what's what. I'm on administrative leave, and I still don't know why. I've heard rumors, but nobody has told me anything officially. I suspect it has something to do with the Stonecypher . . ."

"You despise Pres'dent Dreck, don't cha?"

Senator Smegley's display of righteous anger met with general approval from the C-SPAN audience and outright joy from the occupant of a Moscow flat, in the living room of which a photograph of an elegant couple riding in a carriage in Central Park occupied pride of place. There Alexey Ivanovich Golovorez, at the urging of Michael Stonecypher, who hoped to recruit him as an investor, was streaming the proceedings on his laptop. By the time Hardin had concluded his testimony, Golovorez had satisfied himself that a decapitated FBI would no longer prove a hindrance to conducting business in New York. To that extent, at least, the word of the otherwise unreliable Stonecypher had proved good. Golovorez gazed lovingly at the picture of the couple in the carriage in Central Park.

The occupant of the residence at 1600 Pennsylvania Avenue, NW, Washington, DC, also liked what he saw on C-SPAN. If ever Stuckart were to prove insufficiently loyal, he thought, Roy Smegley might fill the bill very nicely as attorney general. With the hearing still in progress, President Dreck sent out a tweet to his legions of followers accusing Agent Hardin of treason.

The phone began ringing at chez Hardin even before the FBI man's return. "Traitor!" one caller roared, echoing the president. "Enemy of the people! Socialist scum! Child molester!" A barrage of emails and text messages followed. Littered with RANdom CAPitaLIZation and mizPellings, many threatened death and dismemberment. "Your good for nothing but TARGET practice!!!" one correspondent wrote. "NO ON 2ND THOUGHT SHOOTINGS TO GOOD FOR U U should be DRAW and QUARTER!" Another extended wishes for something other than a happy and healthy future: "May YOU and YOUR wife and YOUR freak inbred children die of some horrible disease." Someone hacked Agent Hardin's daughters' Facebook pages, filling their timelines with pornographic pictures and videos. Then one day, Acting Director Hagen and Attorney General Stuckart appeared on television to give a press conference. Said Hagen: "It's no secret that there were some bad actors in the New York office. They're gone now. We've weeded them out. What happened there will not happen again." Attorney General Stuckart added, "I don't think treason is too strong a word."

That same day, Agent Hardin tendered his resignation to the FBI.

CHAPTER 40

One evening, a week or so later, Andrew Le Bâtard called Dr. Rosen with "big fucking news."

"The FBI's ready to close out your case. They're not going to use you as an informant. You won't have to worry about any Russians bashing your skull in."

Dr. Rosen pumped his fist like a tennis player who had just aced his opponent, but new worries soon eclipsed his euphoria. His experiences over the months since his arrest had taught him that a man in his legal position who dared imagine that he had served an ace had better duck nonetheless because the ball was certain to come back at his head at double the speed.

"Why did they decide not to use me? And where does that leave me as far as my sentencing goes?"

"To take your questions in reverse order. One: In very good shape, much better than you would be if you were poor and Black."

"I am poor."

"With the caveat that that's as long as Pound doesn't croak before the hearing, and we get a judge who actually cares about justice rather than LAW AND ORDER."

"Spare me the preaching, all right? The last thing I need is a holier-than-thou lawyer. I already had one of those, and he fucked me over good."

"Holier-than-thou? Me? Ha! I'm billing you for this call, sucker. Ka-ching!"

"Very funny."

"Anyway, what matters to the government, or what's left of it in Year 2 of the Reign of Dreck, is that you were willing to cooperate with the FBI. It's not your fault that everything went to shit with them. We should be getting a date for a hearing in the next week or two. Now, what you need to do is collect some written testimonials to show Judge Pound. As many as you can get. From family, friends, colleagues, the mailman, anyone you can think of to whom you didn't sell oxycodone. We want to convince him that you've learned your lesson and are a changed man, that there's nothing to be gained by locking you up, that you can be an asset to the community, blah, blah, blah.

"No problem there. I can get dozens."

"As for your first question, what happened was a big purge at FBI New York, on orders from the White House, no doubt. Like the end of *The Godfather*. Hardin was forced out. Same for his supervisor. Both of the undercovers who busted you quit. A bunch of the US attorneys over at SDNY are gone, too. Janel Moore is out. I hear they were going to demote her and ship her off to Oklahoma City. She quit instead. I can't say I blame her. Oklahoma City. Jeez!"

"Good. That's what they deserve."

"No, they don't. They're getting screwed over."

"Whose side are you on?"

"I think I've made that pretty clear whenever we've met with them. That doesn't mean I have to ignore what I see and hear and suspend my ability to reason. Only when I'm in court representing you do I have to do that."

His rising anger would have led Dr. Rosen to hang up on his attorney had he not had another question for him: "What do you know about Michael Stonecypher?"

"Ah, that nutcase. Funny you should ask about him. You might say he was the spark that started the fire at the FBI and SDNY. Why?"

"I met him once, a while back. He was supposed to have some business proposition for me then, but he was drunk, and nothing came of it. He must have just remembered me for some reason because he sent me this weird email the other day. Wanted to know if I'd be interested in working for him. Something to do with so-called male health and enhancement products. He was pretty vague about what he wanted me to do. He said he had White House connections. I don't know what to make of the email or him. Is this business for real? Is he a crackpot, a con man? Is he really the president's illegitimate son, as I've heard?"

"He's all of those and a felon too. Convicted of cocaine trafficking. You're not supposed to associate with felons. Steer clear. Don't answer the email."

Though Dr. Rosen resolved to follow his lawyer's advice, his curiosity led him to search the internet for what he could find on Michael Stonecypher. The search led him to the website of an enterprise called King Cobra Men's Health Products, which touted supplements with names such as Black Rhino, White Rhino, King Cobra, Texas Longhorn, and Tusk, all of them manufactured using "natural" ingredients that Dr. Rosen had never heard of and suspected did not exist in nature. The site's "About Us" page featured a photograph, taken on Dreck Plaza, of CEO Michael Stonecypher, flanked by COO Sergei Zhukov and CFO Alexey Golovorez, all three standing with their legs slightly spread and their arms folded across their chests. With his forward-leaning posture, tight-fitting dark blue suit, long red tie, jutting chin, and protruding lips, Stonecypher looked every inch his father's son. The Russians appeared much more dapper in their charcoal suits and burgundy ties. Zhukov glowered at the camera. In Golovorez's crooked half-smile, Dr. Rosen saw both archness and a threat.

A flame erupted in Dr. Rosen's esophagus.

CHAPTER 41

He deleted the email from Stonecypher, along with another that appeared in his inbox two days later. When Stonecypher sent him a text, he smashed his phone with a hammer and went out and purchased a new burner phone with a different number. Searching his own name on the internet, he found, to his relief, no address more recent than that of the Manhattan co-op listed anywhere.

Nonetheless, in the middle of the following week, after deciding to call four hours of fruitless toil as Officer Charlie Johnson a day, a frustrated and irritable Dr. Rosen came home to find the COO of King Cobra Men's Health Products, Alexey Golovorez, sprawled across the sofa in Kenny's living room. Since Dr. Rosen had last seen him, the Russian had added some bulk to his chest, shoulders, arms, and neck. He had, as well, acquired several new tattoos: snakes on each bicep, a scythe on one side of his neck, and a death's head on the other. On his right forearm, however, there remained but one adornment: the image of the dagger with the red tip. He smiled broadly, as though greeting a friend he had not seen in a long while.

"Dr. Robert," he said, rising and extending his hand. "Is so good to see you again."

Dr. Rosen, who had lost command of his limbs, did not reciprocate.

"You are not glad to see me?"

"When . . .? How . . .? Why . . .? What are you doing here?"

"Well, is like this. All through cold, dark Moscow winter, I am missing New York. One day Dr. Zhukov and I get tempting business offer from your insane president's moron bastard son, Mr. Michael Stonecypher. But what can we do from Moscow? We can't give idiot Stonecypher our money and leave him to run business into ground. But then we get lucky break. I am following American news every day, and I see your madman President Dreck gets rid of everyone in FBI in New York. I say to Dr. Zhukov, 'Sergei Mikhailovich, thanks to insane criminal President Dreck, is now safe for us to go back to New York and pursue American dream.' Dr. Zhukov agrees. So here we are."

"How did you find my address?"

"Is not hard. I just call up old friend Barry Boucek."

"That figures."

Golovorez sighed.

"Was such long, cold, sad winter. Every day I am looking at picture on wall of my living room of elegant couple in Central Park and wishing I am back in New York."

"My picture. And that's my Rolex you're still wearing."

"As I tell you before, is better these things are with someone who appreciates them instead of crass poseur who cares only about price. Why you are not in Manhattan anymore?"

"Because this dump is all I can afford now. I lost my medical license, thanks to you and Zhukov and the FBI."

Surveying the apartment, Golovorez replied, "Yes, I see you have come down in world. Is pity."

"I don't think you'll find anything worth stealing here."

"True. Is nothing of beauty here. Everything is Dreck. I see you have become big slave worshiper of your president."

"The posters are my roommate's. I don't have strong feelings about Dreck one way or the other."

"He is mad fool but good for business. On subject of which I have come to speak to you as representative of Mr. Stonecypher. Why you don't answer his emails?"

"I'm broke. I don't have any money to invest in whatever scam you guys are running."

Golovorez looked offended.

"Scam? Is legitimate American business. Is called King Cobra Men's Health Products. Is for sale of supplements to restore health and vigor and hair to middle-aged men and to make *khui* bigger and harder so they have many young women and can fuck all night like they imagine they used to do."

"Yeah, well, it sounds like a scam to me. There is no drug that can make you bigger."

"But customers don't know that. Anyway, business works like this. Materials for supplements we get from India. Some products we sell here, some in China. Mr. Stonecypher wants real American doctor in white coat representing company to show Chinese partners business is real and makes profit. I tell him I know perfect doctor for such respectable enterprise as this: old friend Dr. Robert."

"As I said, I'm not a doctor anymore, so I can't help you. I also don't speak a word of Chinese."

"Is no matter. Chinese partners speak the English well. Dr. Zhukov not so well. Is why we need you. Most of time, you will just be on Zoom screen wearing white coat, looking serious like American TV doctor. Sometimes the Chinese ask questions. Then you make up something that sounds like doctor talk, very full of the science words, to confuse them. They will not know you are disgraced criminal ex-doctor who sold oxycodone prescriptions to addicts for cash. Google is much censored there."

"Right. Well, I can't. For one thing, you're right. As far as the law is concerned, I am a criminal now, just like you."

"I beg pardon, Dr. Robert. FBI has not arrested me. I am not convicted felon like you but law-abiding US resident with Green Card."

"Law abiding meaning that you haven't got caught yet. I have my sentencing hearing coming up. The last thing I need is to get involved with another illegal business. Secondly, I'm not allowed to represent myself in any capacity as a practicing physician. That was one of the conditions of my license surrender agreement."

"Is no worries. In first place, I do my research, and I find out in American supplement business, everything is legal. No prescriptions, no regulations. Anyone can sell anything. In second place, even if something we do is not perfectly legal, is no problem. Michael Stonecypher is moron, but he has protection. Tonight he goes on Sean Hannity show to deny scurrilous rumors of parentage by president circulated by fake news media. Tomorrow, Tucker Carlson. As long as he plays part right, Justice Department will not bother him. In third place, Department of Health of New York State is not caring about you anymore. Every day they are busy taking away license from other crooked doctors who sell much more opioid prescriptions for big cash. They don't check up on small-potatoes crooked doctor whose license they already took away."

"That may be. But I hope to get my license back one day, so I really need to stay out of trouble."

"Everybody has trouble. Is one thing in life you can't avoid."

"There are some kinds that you can."

Golovorez, stepping nearer, reached into his suit jacket and produced a folded document and a pen.

"Maybe some kinds you can avoid before you decide to sell oxycodone, but now not so much. I told partners, Mr. Stonecypher and Dr. Zhukov, I would bring back answer from you today. Surely you would not wish to disappoint. Especially Dr. Zhukov. He is such irritable man when he is disappointed."

As he remembered the gut punch that Golovorez had dealt him in the Upper West Side apartment, Dr. Rosen felt his legs wobble beneath him. Sinking into the sole armchair in the room, he took the document Golovorez thrust at him, but he could not read it. The print was moving, undulating across the page.

"Sign where yellow stickers are, please."

Dr. Rosen did as Golovorez ordered. Signing the document seemed the quickest way to get rid of the Russian, if only for the moment, and whether he did so or not made not a whit of difference in practical terms. Golovorez and Zhukov enforced their agreements, whether oral, written, or existing only in the imagination of one of the putative parties, with their fists or worse rather than through the courts. As long as they had a use for him, Dr. Rosen would remain subject to the terms of their contract, even without his signature on a piece of paper. Perhaps, he mused, a life inside a Club Fed prison offered greater freedom than did a life of fear and penury on the outside.

"Excellent. You will not regret. You will get rich. Stonecypher is idiot, but he is just figurehead. Dr. Zhukov and I run business."

"I'll get rich, huh? Just like I did with the pain center."

When the door closed behind Golovorez, Dr. Rosen's body went limp. Once again, he felt his chest ignite.

CHAPTER 42

With the aid of time, antacid tablets, and a self-administered Delta pep talk, Dr. Rosen roused himself from his funk. With all that had gone wrong, he told himself, he remained, at least for the present, a free man, one who still had hopes and possibilities and the talent and drive to bring them to fruition. With any luck, Stonecypher's ineptitude would cause the supplement business to fizzle, leaving Golovorez and Zhukov with no further use for Dr. Rosen. Maybe, too, he thought, recalling his success in Chicago, he could make his work for Delta pay, maneuver his way around Barry, and rise to a more satisfying and remunerative position in the organization. If chop shop proprietor Barry Boucek could do it, why not someone with his credentials?

For that to happen, though, he had to stay out of prison. As instructed by his attorney, Dr. Rosen set about collecting testimonials that might move Judge Pound in the direction of leniency. Kenny wrote one for him that same night. Regrettably, it was so garbled, so riddled with errors of grammar, syntax, and punctuation that Dr. Rosen had to rewrite most of it. The next day Dr. Rosen emailed Barry. Some fifteen minutes later, Barry sent him back a scanned, signed PDF, chock full of <u>ALL-CAPS SUPERLATIVES!!!!</u> The ever-accommodating Catherine Connolly attested that Dr. Rosen had expressed sincere remorse for his crimes and taken full responsibility and that she felt as confident in his rehabilitation as that of anyone she had treated in her nearly three decades of practice.

Once he had secured those first few letters, however, the harvest grew leaner. He emailed Jerry Karpinski, his old acquaintance from Catherine Connolly's therapy group and one-time employer, but he got no response. Concluding that the owner of a fraudulent telemarketing enterprise might not make an optimal character witness anyway, Dr. Rosen did not try Jerry again. One of the few former colleagues with whom Dr. Rosen remained in touch sent him a letter so neutral in tone and sparing in content that he deleted the document without even acknowledging its receipt. He left four messages for Jeffrey before his brother called back. When, after few minutes of halting conversation, Dr. Rosen relayed his "ask," Jeffrey replied, "I can't do that."

"Why not? All I'm asking for is a letter. It won't cost you anything."

"If I were to write a letter attesting to your good character, I would be lying to the court."

"Screw you!"

The next day Dr. Rosen barged into Sheila's room bearing a testimonial letter that he had written himself.

"Mom, I need help. I'm desperate. All you need to do is sign this."

"Go away," she said. "You've tried to pull this on me before."

"This isn't a power of attorney or anything like that. It's just a letter to the judge. For my sentencing hearing. That's all I'm asking. It's not enough that you let Jeffrey steal what was rightfully mine. Do you want me to go to jail too?"

"It would be nice if, just once, you would come around when you didn't want something."

"What are you talking about? I've been visiting you all the time since I moved back to Long Island. I was here just last week."

"Last week?"

"Don't you remember?"

Her rheumy eyes turned toward the wedding picture.

"I've become very forgetful. Or maybe I just imagined that you weren't here last week. I remember when you were in high school and you broke into that model house and trashed it. You and those two hoodlums you used to hang around with. The twins. What were their names? Your father said to me, 'Sheila, who is that kid? Is he really my son?' I said, 'I swear he's not a bastard by birth.' Give me the paper. I'll sign it. And then go. And don't ever come back."

When she had signed, he snatched the letter from her tray and ran off without another word. As she watched him go, her head sank onto her chest, and her body seemed to shrivel.

Nathan answered his father's first phone call with an obscene two-word imperative and then hung up. Dr. Rosen tried again.

"Why don't you ask the Russian goon who almost broke my arm? Or the other Russian goon who pointed a gun at me?"

"That was ages ago. I'm not mixed up with people like that anymore. I'm a different person now."

"I saw that when you kicked me out of the car in the South Bronx. Don't call me again. Ever. You've never been a father to me."

Briefly he considered asking Tamika, but the memory of her spitting in his face rekindled his heartburn.

Pam Tucci, he thought, would likely prove more amenable. The merest hint of affection would do the trick—but could he manage even that? His involvement with her had been born of a desperation of which he was now ashamed. To think of her was to relive that cold, windy morning at Sunken Meadow when he sat on the rocks wondering who in the world would miss him if he vanished into the murky waters of the sound.

He made no further efforts that day. Perhaps, he told himself, the letters he already had would suffice. A notice from the court that arrived the following morning, however, which informed him of his sentencing date, spurred him to redouble his efforts. Having already drafted all of his mother's letter and much of Kenny's, Dr. Rosen realized that he could generate his own testimonials more quickly and easily than he could cajole or bully others into supplying them. He could enlist the aid of Pam and Tamika without taking the trouble of asking them. In short order, he produced a letter from his erstwhile landlords holding him up as a model tenant who always paid his rent on time and took better care of the apartment than they did themselves. Writing as Tamika, he lauded himself as a great boss who had treated his employee "just like family." Next came a letter from an eminent former colleague named Sergei Zhukov, followed by heartfelt recommendations from patients named Ben Oster, Ben Resor, Ben Roter, Rose Torre, Orest Orr, and Terri Roos. All the fake letters he signed with eyes closed or with his left hand so as to vary the signatures.

As the hearing drew closer, nightmares vexed his sleep. The most harrowing of them, which terrorized him for three nights running, found him on an airplane that, after an inordinately slow takeoff roll, struggled to gain altitude. Flying at tree top level, the plane banked sharply to the right, the tip of its wing tearing the roof off a house. Then Dr. Rosen saw a great expanse of turbulent water just beneath his window. As the other passengers screamed, prayed, or called their loved ones to bid them goodbye, he tried every number on his contact list, hoping he could summon someone—anyone—to come rescue him. Every call he made went directly to voicemail. When the plane hit the water, the impact dislodged Dr. Rosen from his seat and sent him hurtling forward through the cabin—until he awoke with the word *no* frozen on his lips.

On other nights, he barely slept at all. He sweated, shivered, and tossed about, tormented by the fiercest heartburn he had experienced since his visit to the emergency room. One night he felt a fluttering in his chest and then a constriction, as if a snake had him in its coils. Was this the real thing, he wondered, the BIG ONE? It was not. The episode proved fleeting, but it left him profoundly shaken. Perhaps, he reflected, his eyes tearing up, he had taken too little heed of the terrors of his economy-class patients, whose mewling had evoked in him only contempt. As he had while stretched out on the gurney in the emergency room, he remembered his last session with the dying Herb Wasserman. The recollection pained him, but for that anguish, Delta had a quick cure: an entire module on self-forgiveness, one that taught that intentions mattered at least as much as actions. Dr. Rosen had taken the lesson to heart. But for the stress placed on him by the Agnellos and their lawsuit, he told himself, he would have had a much better result with Mr. Wasserman and with others as well. If he could avoid prison and get his license back, he would give all his future patients his full measure of time and attention. Further, he would change his entire life for the better: eat a healthier diet, exercise regularly, even try to forgive and, if possible, reconcile with Nathan, Jeffrey, and his mother. True, they had wronged him, but they were all the family he had left, and family, as he had often said to Catherine Connolly, was everything.

One morning following an especially wretched night, he booked an appointment with her, vowing that he would speak honestly for once. Even an idiot like Catherine Connolly, he reasoned, might have something of value to impart to him at such a time. He soon began to have his doubts about that proposition though, and the day before the appointment, he cancelled.

Alone and desperate for fellowship on a Friday night, he attended services at a nearby synagogue, something he had not done since his bar mitzvah decades before. The temple, dim and chilly inside and less than half-full, felt like a mausoleum. Most of the worshippers were many years older than he, and walkers, quad canes, and wheelchairs abounded. Having forgotten all the Hebrew he had once known, he found the service unintelligible and tedious, and he walked out in the middle.

In the light of day, he sometimes thought his night terrors exaggerated and even contemptible. He felt fortunate to have work that kept him sufficiently occupied to distract him from his nocturnal worries and ruminations.

Still laboring half-time as Officer or, sometimes, Technical Specialist Charlie Johnson of the police, Microsoft, the IRS, or Amazon to separate frightened shut-ins from their money, he devoted the remainder of his working days to recruiting for Barry. In that endeavor, he attained some hard-won success. A three-day seminar in Paramus, New Jersey, drew thirty-one participants, enough to earn a small profit—for Barry. The realization dawned on Robert that he and the other recruiters made up the base of a pyramid with Barry comfortably perched at the top. He reproached himself for his failure to anticipate that the helping hand Barry offered him would turn out to be a slippery one.

In Langhorne, Pennsylvania, where he and the other recruiters reeled in thirty-four lost souls, Dr. Rosen had his first chance to rise above the base. Employing the lifeline exercise and others he had learned from Catherine Connolly, he led a successful breakout group.

In Lancaster, he gave his first lecture, which he titled "Persistence"—the ostensible subject of the video that had caught Michael Stonecypher's attention. Barry's coaching resulted in a more polished delivery this time. In content, however, the speech ran aground on the same shoal that it had in that earlier iteration. Dr. Rosen spent much of it lamenting the suffering inflicted on him by a devious and vindictive informant and a coterie of treacherous FBI agents. Seeing the audience disengaging, he cut the talk short, all but omitting any discussion of persistence. His efforts earned him tepid applause.

"It's all right, bro," Barry told him afterward. "It's been a while for you. You need to shake the rust off. Next time will be better. There's just one thing you need to do different. People don't want to hear you bitching about how the FBI screwed you over. The way to get the audience on your side is to make them think that you're sorry and you've learned your lesson."

The next talk, in Dover, Delaware, did prove somewhat more successful. He followed Barry's advice but overplayed his part, dissolving into tears as he described his arrest and its aftermath, and speaking for nearly twice his allotted time. Still, he induced a few tears from the women in the audience and received a warm ovation when he finished. The next day one of the female attendees sent him a nude selfie.

After a talk in Metropark, New Jersey, he slept with one of the attendees. His boasting about the episode led to a brief falling out with Barry.

"You don't shit where you eat," Barry warned him. "What were you thinking? We have a good thing going here. That's just the way to screw it up."

"A good thing for you, maybe. I'm sure as hell not getting rich. I may as well get something for all the work I do. Oh, and thanks for giving my address to Golovorez, asshole."

"What was I supposed to do, bro? You don't say no to Golovorez."

That much, Dr. Rosen had to admit, was true. He decided not to see the woman again, and he reconciled with Barry in time for a presentation in Hartford, Connecticut, to a middle management team at an insurance company, the CEO of which was a major investor in, and something of an evangelist for, Delta-Multiform. There Dr. Rosen gave his most successful talk yet, which he dedicated to resilience, purging from his notes beforehand all references to persistence so he would not inadvertently substitute the latter term for the former. He conceded that his own "mistakes" and "bad judgment" had caused many of his hardships, and he even praised the FBI for the professionalism and civility of the agents who questioned him after the arrest. He had but one criticism: "True, they didn't have to come armed to the teeth and break down my door at 6 in the morning, but that's just the way they do things.

"And on that subject, I have to give President Dreck some credit," he added, evoking surprised looks and murmurs from some of the middle managers. "True, there's a lot of things he does that I don't agree with. And, granted, he can be pretty obnoxious at times."

Some in the audience tittered knowingly.

"But I think he really cares about civil liberties. He really is trying to keep the FBI and the police from getting out of hand. And that's a good thing, whatever else you may think of him otherwise.

"Anyway, to get back on point, it's a long way down from doctor to felon. Believe me. I lost my livelihood, for one thing. I've gone from being very well off to one step from homelessness. But what hurts the most is not being able to practice anymore. Being a doctor has been a big part of my identity. Helping people is one of my core values.

"But I've learned an important lesson. It would have been the easiest thing in the world for me to just lie down and die. But that's not in my makeup. That's not who I am. Instead, I said to myself, 'All right. I've been dealt a lousy hand, but it's the only hand I have to play, so I'd better play it.' I put my pride aside. To keep a roof over my head, I took whatever job came along. Imagine going from being a doctor to a telemarketer. But I did it, and I didn't complain, and here I am today. And you know why I'm here today and not out on the street begging? One word: resilience. Resilience is the key."

When he concluded, the middle managers stood and cheered, and Dr. Rosen felt a jubilation that he had not known since Chicago.

"You're on your way, bro," said Barry. "The sky's the limit. You're a star. I liked the bit about President Dreck. You should keep that."

"The assholes ate it right up, didn't they? Five more minutes, and I could have had them attending Dreck rallies, and I bet there wasn't one Republican among them. It's because they're weak. You can get a weak person to do anything."

Though still disdaining Kenny's conspiratorial worldview, Dr. Rosen nevertheless had seen his own opinion of President Dreck bend slowly toward that of his roommate. More and more, he had come to admire the man who, by mere force of will, had remade the world around him, crushing allies and enemies alike, making unctuous sycophants of the former and squealing eunuchs of the latter. Dr. Rosen wished he had such power.

The high that lingered all the way home from Hartford dissipated as soon as he returned to the apartment. He found Kenny in the living room working on a guitar solo for his new song, "I Got My Laser Eye on You."

"I think I got it, man. Would you go get the camcorder? I want to get this on video before I forget it."

Two hours later, Kenny was still trying to reproduce his musical miracle, while Dr. Rosen struggled to suppress a very powerful impulse to brain him with the camcorder. Dr. Rosen vowed that the day after the sentencing hearing, when he would have the bulk of his legal expenses behind him, he would begin searching in earnest for a new place to live.

The thumping, moans, and grunts coming from upstairs kept Dr. Rosen awake for much of the night. At around 4 a.m., he turned on his computer and deleted from his website the video he had recorded with Kenny in the apartment while drunk. The Hartford video would soon go up in its place, for whatever it was worth. He had become Barry's best recruiter and star speaker but still had to labor as a telemarketer one or two days a week and, for the time being at least, could not afford to leave Kenny and the shithole apartment behind. Its core values of honesty, compassion, communication, and helping others notwithstanding, at Delta-Multiform, as everywhere else, one was either at the top of the pyramid or nowhere.

CHAPTER 43

Jeffrey arrived in New York on a Thursday night. On Friday morning, Sheila asked him to drive her to the beach at Sunken Meadow.

The task of transferring his mother from her wheelchair into his Prius involved numerous steps, each presenting its own set of complexities. First: wheel her up as closely as he could to the passenger-side door. Second: lock the wheels of the wheelchair and remove its footrest and armrest. Third: place his leg between hers, swing his arm around behind her, and grab hold of her sweatpants from the rear, while she gripped his shoulder with her good hand. Fourth: lift her up, and then pivot her 90 degrees so her back faced the car. Fifth: slowly maneuver her inside and onto the seat, taking care that she did not bump her head against the roof. Sixth: turn her legs 90 degrees back the other way so she faced frontward. Seventh: pull and push her torso up to as comfortable a position for her as possible, and then buckle her seatbelt. Extracting her from the car entailed performing the same ritual in reverse. He would think, sometimes, of the Roethke poem about the boy grimly hanging on while his drunken father whirls him around the kitchen.

Though much slower and less kinetic than Roethke's fraught father-son waltz, Jeffrey and Sheila's also had its hazards. Once they had danced mostly in sync: As he pulled, she would push herself up from the wheelchair with her good leg. Over time, she had become weaker, less able to bear her own weight, more of it falling on Jeffrey. The waltz had become almost impossible to perform.

That morning, with the pavement of the North Shore Nursing & Rehab parking lot still slick from the downpour that had delayed him the night before, he lost his footing and stumbled while executing the transfer. Slipping from his grasp, she became wedged between the seat and the dashboard.

"Are you trying to kill me?"

Apologizing all the while, he pulled her up from the crevice in which she had become lodged, lifted her onto the seat, pivoted her body, and fastened her seatbelt.

Gray skies notwithstanding, a mild spring day seemed in store when the two set off from North Shore. By the time they reached Sunken Meadow, however, the clouds had darkened, and a chilling mist suffused the air. The boardwalk was nearly empty of people, and the beach entirely so but for an elderly man in a yellow rain slicker, who was sweeping the wet sand near the water with a metal detector.

Starting from the pavilion, Jeffrey wheeled his mother toward the west end of the boardwalk. They had not gone far when he saw that she was shivering.

"Are you cold, Mom? Do you want to go back to the car?"

He hoped that she would, for he, too, felt a chill—one that would plague him for the rest of the weekend.

"No, I'm fine. Keep going."

He asked again a few minutes later and elicited the same reply. A mere 20 feet or so farther on, however, she said, "Turn around. I want to go back now."

The rain began to fall harder, and by the time they reached the car, both were soaked to the skin.

Back at North Shore, she told him, "Tomorrow I'd like you to take me to see the house. I haven't since . . . that night."

Had she ever uttered the word *stroke* since that life-upending catastrophe? He could not recall her doing so.

"Your brother may be here too, this weekend. I asked him to come. He said he would, but he probably won't. Just the other day I told him that I never wanted to see him again. But if he does come, I hope . . . Ah, what's the point. Just try to be civil. I expect more from you than I do from him, but I suppose that's the most I can ask."

"I will, Mom."

"He tells me he visits me all the time, and I forget that he came. It's like that film with Charles Boyer and Ingrid Berg- man."

"Mom, I think you should . . ." Jeffrey began, but he stopped midsentence.

"You think I should what?"

"Nothing."

"Tell the staff not to let him in anymore?"

"Yes."

"I'm not going to do that.

"I didn't think you would."

"He's my son, just as much as you are, even if he is a . . . Ah."

Because Dr. Rosen had not indicated when he might visit, Sheila insisted that Jeffrey wait with her in her room the next morning before driving to the house. At 11:30, when Dr. Rosen had yet to show, they departed.

When he pulled the Prius up to the curb, Jeffrey wondered for a moment whether he had come to the right place. He barely recognized the house he had parked in front of as the one in which he had grown up. The new owner had replaced the garage doors, the front door, the gutters and downspouts, and all the windows visible from the street. The cedar shingles in front had come down; a mustard-colored vinyl siding now covered the façade. In the driveway sat a black BMW.

"That siding is hideous," Sheila said. "Why did they take down the cedar?"

Her voice was laden with reproach. He suspected that even the more salutary alterations did not sit well with her. She had come here to see the house as it was.

"The yellow is hideous," Jeffrey agreed.

"Money doesn't buy taste. I wish we could have kept the house in the family."

"I wish we could have too, but it wasn't possible. The nursing home had to be paid."

"I've seen enough. I want to go back to my room now. I hope we haven't missed Robbie."

Dr. Rosen had not shown up while they were out, nor did he after their return to the nursing home. Sheila fell into a deep funk and spoke little the rest of the day.

The next morning—the third successive one of leaden skies and mist—Jeffrey drove her to the cemetery where Sheldon Rosen lay buried. The gravesite lay some distance from the road, at the far end of a gravel path clearly not designed with wheelchairs in mind. With Jeffrey pausing frequently to give Sheila a rest from the jostling, the trek took fifteen minutes.

A modest gray footstone with a slanted top marked the grave. It lay at the periphery of the Weinberg Family Plot, an ample stretch of ground named, presumably, for the family that had founded the burial society. The deceased Weinbergs boasted much more elaborate markers than did Sheldon Rosen.

While Sheila stared in silence at the gravestone, Jeffrey placed a pebble on the top and softly read an English transliteration of the Kaddish. Then he stepped back from the grave.

As she had countless times, Sheila Rosen was puzzling over something Sheldon had said to her one fine spring afternoon in the garden at Ocean View Nursing Home, where with nary a chance to view the ocean, he endured his final weeks. Eleven years, seven months, and sixteen more days have passed since that one—his last among the living—yet for her, it has never ended. It exists simultaneously with all her other days, leaching into them, and now, at Sheldon's graveside, it has come round again, and she must relive what she lived then.

Flanked by dogwoods in full pink flower, Sheila and Sheldon Rosen sit beside one another, she on a wooden bench, he in his wheelchair. They like that spot because it looks out on a small pond where plump goldfish swim. The April sky is cloudless, an indigo dome; the soft breeze bears the scent of dianthus. A blue jay in a sycamore tree behind the bench makes a creaking sound, like that of a hinge in need of oil. A second jay, perched atop a tall birch in the farthest corner of the garden, answers in kind. In the occasional pauses between the call and response, they hear the rat-tat-tat of a woodpecker drilling into a tree trunk with its beak. A cardinal alights for just an instant upon the log fence behind Sheila's back, emits three long tweets and six short ones, and then takes off again, vanishing into the foliage of a sugar maple.

The Sheila at the graveside pities the Sheila in the garden. The latter has no inkling that within twelve hours, she will be asked for and give her consent to disconnect her husband from the respirator that has kept his heart and lungs working long after any hope that he will ever awaken again has vanished.

"Is he doing the . . . the beds?" Sheldon asks her.

"Who?"

"You know. The lawn guy. Is he doing the . . . weeding the azalea beds?"

"Vito? Yes, of course."

Sheldon looks doubtful.

"You have to check up on him. Just because he tells you he's going to do something doesn't mean he will. It only means he'll bill you for it. I could do a better job myself, even in my condition. Maybe I'll fire him when I get back home."

"He's taking care of it. There's no need to worry about that now. I don't want to see you get agitated."

"When will I be leaving here anyway?"

"Soon. Soon. As soon as the doctor says you're ready."

In his eyes, she sees suspicion. He may forget the name of the man who has tended their lawn for the past twenty-three years or recount with eerily perfect recall a conversation he had just the day before yesterday with his sister who died seventeen years ago, but after more than five decades of marriage, Sheila cannot deceive him. In the garden then and at the graveside now—for in the interval she has come to understand just how fluid the boundaries between past and present can be—her remorse feels like a stab to the heart.

For a long time, the two of them gaze in silence at the gold-fish, and then at last Sheldon speaks: "I'm sorry. It was stupid of me to get so upset about something like that. Let's not let it spoil the rest of the evening."

"Evening?" she asks, frightened. "What evening? What are you sorry about?"

"The drink."

"What drink?"

Closing his eyes, he grimaces.

She grips his hand.

"Sheldon, are you in pain? Is it your chest?"

"No. No, I'm fine."

"You're not fine. What's wrong?"

Sheldon shakes his head. In his eyes, she sees a sadness far deeper than that maddeningly taciturn man can ever express.

Does he utter another word after that "fine"? Tell her good-bye when she leaves the nursing home and promises to return the next day? She remembers only silence.

Her mistake, she realizes, lay in not listening to that silence, for now she does hear: the sound of a cocktail glass breaking against concrete—a compressed thunderclap that reverberates still. She knows now what caused Sheldon such anguish on that last afternoon of his life in the garden at Ocean View. Perhaps she has known all along or would have if she had not resisted knowing.

She is with him again, a thousand miles and more than half a century away. They make a handsome couple, she and Sheldon, sitting at a round wrought iron table on a hotel patio ringed with varicolored paper lanterns. A slender, delicate brunette with her hair cut short and sculpted into a swirl on the right side, she has a heart-shaped face, luminous eyes, and a ready and slightly mischievous smile. Sheldon, with his angular face, prominent nose, and brown eyes that look warily out at the world, has a much more serious aspect. While she wears a green-and-white summer dress with a leaf pattern, he sweats in his dark blue wool suit on this muggy Florida night. Though they can hear the rumbling of the surf in the distance, no cooling breeze comes their way. His Brylcreemed hair, as black and glossy as patent leather, rises above his forehead. Sheldon and Sheila sip gingerly from cocktail glasses with paper umbrellas, avoiding each other's gaze. Unlike the other guests, they do not laugh at the lewd jokes of the comedian holding court in the center of the patio. Owing to nerves and inexperience, they fumbled in the bedroom, consummating the marriage only on the second night of their honeymoon, and that just barely. On this, the fourth night, they struggle even to make conversation. The terrible question hangs over both of them: Could they have made the mistake of their lives?

Sheldon tugs at the knot of his tie, smooths his hair back, wipes the sweat from his face with his handkerchief, then starts on the tie again. Holding the stem of his glass between his thumb and his middle and index fingers, he rotates it back and forth, back and forth, until he loses his grip. The glass falls, the freezing cocktail spilling in his lap. Sheila giggles nervously.

"Do you think that's funny?" Sheldon roars. "Do you think that's funny?"

Around the patio, heads turn in their direction. Stunned, Sheila leaves the table and hurries across the patio back to their room. There she locks the door and, sobbing, throws herself face down onto the bed. During the night, she awakens and hears a stirring and a murmuring. In a corner near the door, Sheldon sleeps in an armchair. She wonders whether to wake him and tell him to come to bed, but some unknown force, far greater than Earth's gravity, will not let her rise.

She wishes now that she could tell Sheldon that she forgave him long ago, not only for that display of temper but for all the recriminations and misunderstandings that followed, and that she feels grateful for every minute of their fifty-two years together, the best ones and the worst.

"I'll see you soon, Sheldon," she says aloud.

A voice from behind startles her: "Not so fast, Mom. I think you'll be around for quite a while yet."

"I wasn't talking to you," she replies, as if addressing an eavesdropper.

"I wasn't talking to you."

Perhaps, Jeffrey reflected later, Sheila, like him, preferred the company of a deceased spouse to that of the living. The visit to the cemetery had left him feeling uneasy. Though he had intended to drive home to Maryland that Sunday and had already checked out of his motel room, he decided to stay for at least one more day.

Awakening at 2:30 a.m. from a turbulent sleep, Jeffrey gazed out the window of his room in the Turnpike Inn. The strip mall on the opposite side of Route 25 contained a 7-Eleven, the Stadium 300 Sports Bar, and DIVA NAILS—OPEN 24 HOURS.

Why, he demanded of Lori, did such a thing as a twenty-four-hour nail spa exist? He waited expectantly for one of her usual tart replies. It did not come. When had she last answered him? Two weeks ago? Three? Had she fallen silent for good? He felt again the chill that had first gripped him at the beach.

Shortly before 8 a.m., the chirping of his phone awakened him from a fitful sleep.

"Mr. Rosen?" said a male voice that Jeffrey did not recognize. "I'm calling about Sheila Rosen. I'm sorry to tell you that she expired during the night."

The word *expired* threw him. It did not fit; therefore, it could not possibly mean what he feared. Could it?

"What do you mean *expired*? Expired like a container of milk? How does a person expire? I want to know what happened."

"I'm sorry," the man repeated. "Let me see if her nurse is available."

"We haven't moved her yet," said the nurse to whom he had spoken on the phone. "She's still in the room, if you'd like to say goodbye. As I said, it happened in her sleep. It was peaceful. She didn't suffer at all."

Though Jeffrey wondered how the nurse could possibly know, to express any doubt would have amounted to calling her a liar. Instead, he thanked her and the other nurses and aides on duty for their condolences and declined the social worker's invitation to talk in her office.

He did not say goodbye to Sheila, for he had arrived far too late. The figure lying on the bed, inert and as stiff as a mannequin, did not at all resemble his mother. Its mouth was agape, its eyes wide, its complexion an indeterminate shade between beige and white—not so much a color as an absence of color. Lori, though positioned differently—head tilted to the right, mouth half-open—had undergone the same transformation almost the moment her breath left her. Jeffrey gathered up Sheila's belongings as quickly has he could and then hurried out of the building.

CHAPTER 44

In a lecture hall on the Princeton University campus, Dr. Rosen was exhorting seventy-one captivated attendees to live their best lives. Having refined his fall-and-redemption narrative to the point at which Barry declared it "perfect," he had developed a new acronym to structure his closing exhortation.

"REACH!" he cried, raising his arms high. "R is for Readiness. Be aware. Be alert. Always be ready to spot an opportunity. E. Educate. Whatever your field is—investing, real estate, sales—the way to get ahead is to know more than the other guy or gal. Know everything there is to know about it. Because that E gives you another E—an edge over the competition. A is for Act. Once you've seen your opportunity and learned what you need to know, then comes the time to act. Seize that chance. Don't wait because it may never come again. C is for Challenge. Always keep pushing yourself. Don't ever be satisfied. Don't ever rest on your laurels. Because somebody's always gaining on you. Finally, H. H is for Hold. Hold onto your dream. There will always be setbacks on the road to success. Things will go wrong. But the worst thing you can do is give up. Successful people are tenacious. When they're knocked down, they get right back up, dust themselves off, and start punching again. Walt Disney started out as a newspaper reporter. His editor told him he lacked imagination and fired him. Thomas Edison's teachers told him he was too stupid to learn anything. Can you imagine if Disney had listened to that editor and Edison had believed those teachers? Only you know what you can do. Never let anybody tell you that you can't be anything you want to be or do anything you want to do."

The standing ovation his talk won him far eclipsed in duration and volume the one he had received in Hartford.

Afterwards, he found to his surprise that Jeffrey had left him two voicemail messages, but he felt no urgency about calling back. Still on a high, he accompanied Barry and several of the attendees to a nearby student hangout for happy hour. While Barry was in the restroom, Dr. Rosen obtained the cellphone numbers of two women in the group. He and Barry then continued the celebration in Manhattan, enjoying a steak dinner and martinis at the same restaurant in which they had dined with Tamika nearly a year before after returning from the triumphant appearance in Chicago.

"Hey, what ever happened to that cute little Black girl you had with you then? What was her name?"

"Tamika."

Dr. Rosen's mood darkened.

"I got rid of the bitch. She was no good. A lousy employee, a gold digger, a drug dealer, and a blackmailer too. I never would have gotten involved in that whole oxy mess if it weren't for her. I never would have got arrested and lost my license. She was the worst mistake of my life."

After four martinis, he half-believed the calumnies he spouted.

"Why'd you have to remind me of her anyway?"

"Forget it, bro. Have another martini."

Though Dr. Rosen did have another martini, he could not forget all the indignities he had suffered over the past year and all the ways that Barry and so many others had wronged him. Who or what had ordered the world such that Dr. Rosen, the victim, had hanging over his neck a sentencing hearing and possible prison time, while his exploiter, Barry, could drink and dine without a care? Without waiting for the waitress to bring the bill, he rose and said in a surly tone, "I've got to go.

It's late, and I'm tired, and I still have an hour's train ride back to Long Island."

When Dr. Rosen checked his call log the next morning, after first consuming a Bloody Mary to ease his hangover, he saw Jeffrey's number listed several times. He called his brother back.

Jeffrey relayed his news tersely: "Mom died yesterday."

"What? When?"

"Yesterday morning."

"And you waited twenty-four hours to tell me?"

"I called you a bunch of times yesterday."

"What was the cause?"

"It happened in her sleep. She stopped breathing."

"Just like that? I bet they told you it was quick, too, and peaceful. I want to know what happened, and I'm going to find out."

With any other interlocutor, Jeffrey might well have given voice to his own doubts. To his brother, he said, "What difference does it make to you how she died? All you care about is that she did it without giving you power of attorney."

"How long was she laying there dying while nobody did anything for her? Did they try to resuscitate her?"

"She had a DNR order."

"Whose idea was that?"

"Hers."

"So you say. Why should I believe you?"

"I don't give a damn whether you believe me or not. The funeral is on Friday. If you do plan on attending, try to behave. I'd like to lay her to rest with the dignity she deserves."

"This is what comes of leaving things to you. If she had given me power of attorney, she'd still be alive now. I'd have found a better place for her. I'd have known how to manage her money too. I would have made sure the nursing home didn't get any of it. Did she have a will?"

"Ah, now we're getting to what really matters."

"I better be in it. If not, I'll know why, and you can look forward to spending a lot of time in court."

"Not as much as you. Goodbye."

CHAPTER 45

Having outlived most everyone she knew, Sheila had just a handful of mourners at her funeral. Jeffrey came alone, while Dr. Rosen brought Barry, Kenny, and Nathan with him. Leon and Carol Brownstein, septuagenarian cousins from New Jersey whom neither of Sheila's sons had seen since Sheldon Rosen's funeral some dozen years before, also made the trip.

Barry had never met Sheila, and Dr. Rosen, whose already growing resentment toward him had spiked since the Princeton gig, had not intended to bring him. The night before the funeral, however, when Dr. Rosen found himself at a loss in trying to compose a eulogy, he turned to his employer and coach "as a friend" for help. Barry's presence was the price of that appeal to friendship.

In that same spirit of transactional friendship, he had asked the volatile Kenny to come along, hoping he would pass on the invitation. Because the paltry income Dr. Rosen earned through his gigs with Barry and his efforts on behalf of the crooked telemarketing firm mostly went to cover his legal expenses, he still could not realize his fervent desires to find better lodgings and banish Kenny from his life. For Kenny, by contrast, Dr. Rosen had become no mere roommate but a confidant, a creative collaborator, and a role model. In Kenny's cosmos, he now ranked second only to President Dreck. The odds that snubbing Kenny might transform him into a homicidal maniac were less than even, Dr. Rosen calculated, but not low enough to take the chance. The effort required to refrain from commenting on Kenny's funeral attire tested the limits of his self-control. For the occasion, Kenny had chosen to complement the DRECK FOR AMERICA!© cap that he always wore with a red, white, and blue football jersey that had the name DRECK printed across the back above a large number 1, the latter intended, presumably, to indicate the stature of the present occupant of the White House relative to all those who had preceded him, living or dead.

Nathan's attendance at the funeral came about as a result of calculations on both sides. Dr. Rosen wanted to have his son at the sentencing hearing; therefore, he needed to effect a truce with him. Nathan, whose anger at his father had not abated since the incident in the Bronx, regretted having seen so little of his grandmother in recent years, and in the end, his desire to pay his respects proved stronger than his rage. Also, the risk-benefit calculus worked out favorably: In taking the train to Long Island, he would have to rely on his dad only for the short trip from the station to the cemetery and back.

While waiting for the rabbi in the administration building before the service, Jeffrey chatted briefly with the Brownsteins, who expressed sorrow that their own health challenges had kept them from visiting Sheila at North Shore as often as they had wished. Leon Brownstein relied on a quad cane to keep his balance, his hands trembled, and he smacked his lips together incessantly.

"Your calls and visits meant a lot to her," Jeffrey told them. "And I'm very glad that you were able to come today."

As Dr. Rosen huddled with Barry and Kenny, Nathan wandered over to the other group and introduced himself to the Brownsteins, who had last seen him when he was a boy. He told them of his plans to return to NYU in the fall, adding that while he had yet to choose a major, he was considering, among others, a pre-med or pre-law curriculum.

"That's wonderful," said Carol Brownstein.

Dr. Rosen, his heartburn flaring, glowered at his son.

The afternoon had the feel of midsummer, with the sun hanging directly overhead in a gauzy sky. At the graveside, the rabbi called upon Jeffrey to deliver the first eulogy.

Jeffrey began by citing a line from *King Lear*—"Ripeness is all."—a fitting tribute, he said, given Sheila's lifelong love of literature and theatre. Building on the theme, he lauded Sheila for having lived a rich, full life, one that had attained an ideal ripeness. As wife, mother, and later, caregiver, she was the force that held the family together—and much more. Jeffrey spoke of the strength and tenacity that had enabled her not merely to survive for a decade after a catastrophic stroke but to experience joy and spread it to those she loved. He talked, too, of her intelligence, her fondness for opera, her keen interest in politics, and her quick and sometimes caustic wit, which, he confessed, she had directed at him many times.

"Usually when I deserved it."

The remark earned a chuckle from the rabbi, a light-haired, clean-shaven man in his early or mid-thirties, and knowing smiles from the Brownsteins.

Dr. Rosen talked of how, above all, Sheila had taught him resilience—the quality that had enabled him to cope with all that life had thrown at him and emerge stronger than ever.

"From her I learned never to give up and always to believe in myself."

When he finished, Barry embraced him and said, too loudly, "That was beautiful, bro. You crushed it."

The Brownsteins exchanged disapproving looks.

"*Al mekomah tavo veshalom,*" intoned the rabbi.

He reached for the spade embedded in the pile of earth beside the grave.

"Why," he asked, "do we conclude the ceremony with the mourners shoveling earth into the grave? It signifies that painful as our loss may be, we accept it. We accept the finality of death." Handing Jeffrey the spade, he added, "As the elder son, Jeffrey will begin."

The clod of earth that Jeffrey dropped into the grave struck the coffin with a hollow thud—a sound that nobody beyond the confines of the Weinberg family plot would hear, but that, for an instant, stopped the hearts and froze the blood of all who did. It was the terminal punctuation of a life. Jeffrey felt the sound in his chest, like a blow. He handed the spade back to the rabbi.

Dr. Rosen took his turn next. He, too, dropped a clod of earth into the grave—and then another and another and another. Four times that terrible sound was heard before the rabbi reached for the spade. Dr. Rosen, ignoring or failing to notice the rabbi's outstretched arm, slammed the spade into the pile of earth from whence it had come with sufficient force to bury the blade.

Then, for the first and only time that day, Dr. Rosen and his brother looked each other's way. In Jeffrey's eyes, Dr. Rosen saw an incomprehension that he took for weakness. He regretted only that he had yielded the spade too soon. Jeffrey, who had long ago come to view his estrangement from his younger sibling as an immutable fact, nevertheless felt a profound sadness. He had good reason to doubt that he would ever see him again. Memory would fade until all that remained of Rob would be those eyes as they appeared today at the graveside—roiling whirlpools of contempt, triumph, and rage.

As soon as the service ended, Dr. Rosen, Barry, and Nathan drove off in the CRV, the latter in the back seat. No sooner had they passed through the cemetery gates than Dr. Rosen turned on his son: "I hope you enjoyed talking to my crook of a brother. Did he tell you about how he stole your grandma's money? About how he turned her against me?"

"We talked about a subject that wouldn't interest you. He asked me how I've been."

"Meanwhile, you ignored your father in front of the rabbi and the cousins. You embarrassed me. You've always been an embarrassment."

"I'm an embarrassment? Speaking of crooks, when's your sentencing? I'm looking forward to that. Maybe I will write a letter to the court. Only you might not like it too much."

Dr. Rosen cut the steering wheel sharply to the right and pulled the CRV up to the curb.

"Get out of the car! Now!"

This time Nathan exited the car laughing.

Jeffrey, meanwhile, went to lunch with the Brownsteins at an Italian restaurant near the cemetery. The three shared some anodyne reminiscences of Sheila.

"I was so sorry to hear about Lori," said Carol, touching Jeffrey's arm. "I remember she was at Sheldon's funeral. We spoke afterwards. She was such a lovely person."

"She was, and I was very lucky to have her."

Inevitably, the conversation turned toward his brother. The Brownsteins had heard about the doctor's legal troubles from Sheila.

"It has been tough for him," said Jeffrey, who preferred to avoid any discussion of his own and Sheila's vexed relationships with Rob. "I guess he's holding up all right though. Or so he tells me."

"Who were those other two men with him?" Carol asked.

"I don't know them. I had never seen either of them before today. I don't think Mom would have appreciated the Dreck cap and jersey."

"That dirty little man. She would have been appalled. And then Robbie with all the shoveling. I've never seen anyone do that before. I thought he was going to bury her all by himself."

"And me with her," Jeffrey thought, recalling the way his brother had looked at him. Aloud he said only, "It was odd."

Outside the restaurant, Carol hugged Jeffrey tightly, and Leon offered him one trembling hand to shake and patted him on the shoulder with the other.

"It's so sad that we only see you at funerals," said Leon. "We're not able to travel as much as we would like anymore, but you should come visit us sometime."

"I'd love to. Next time I plan to be up this way, I'll let you know. I promise."

He did not know when, or if, he would make the trip again.

CHAPTER 46

A week before the sentencing hearing, Dr. Rosen, laboring over the plea for mercy he would deliver in court, sought Barry's help, as he had when composing Sheila's eulogy. Barry not only insisted on accompanying him to the hearing but, to lend additional support, invited the Cavalear twins, Chevy and Nova, two Delta-Multiform seminar leaders gifted with the ability to cry on cue. Though they had never met Dr. Rosen, they also provided written testimonials to add to his pile of actual and fictitious ones. As much as he would have liked to, Dr. Rosen could not avoid inviting his roommate, who had, after all, conducted himself with appropriate decorum at the funeral. There did remain the vexing question of what Kenny would wear for this occasion. He did not own a suit, and his wardrobe increasingly consisted of DRECK FOR AMERICA!© licensed apparel, which he ordered regularly online, though he could ill afford the inflated prices. Dr. Rosen, fearing that his roommate would show up in court dressed as a human Dreck billboard, offered to lend Kenny one of his own suits. A less credulous person might have taken offense, but Dr. Rosen's insistence that the bailiff would evict from the court-room anyone not properly attired proved sufficient to per-suade Kenny to don the suit, though it hung on him like a sack.

Nathan, on the other hand, refused his father's repeated entreaties to attend the hearing.

"I hope you spend the rest of your life in prison," he said.

Dr. Rosen slept little the night before his court date, plagued again by the airplane nightmare, this time with a new and mortifying twist. As the aircraft careened over the water, tossing bodies, luggage, and food carts every which way, someone finally answered his desperate phone call. To his surprise and consternation though, the phlegmy voice on the other end, which sounded vaguely familiar, was not that of his mother, whose number he had called, but of a man.

"Yes, I'd like to speak to Sheila Rosen, please."

"'Fraid not, doc. Your mother says she doesn't want to talk to you. She said she's sorry she ever had you, and she hopes the judge throws the book at you."

"What? Excuse me? She told you to say this?"

"What do you expect? You embarrassed her at her own funeral. The people you brought with you. My God! That nasty little man with the Dreck this and Dreck that on all his clothes. And that other one—the loudmouth. Who brings such people to his mother's funeral? And then the four shovelfuls of dirt. Because they weren't burying her quickly enough to suit you? And would it have killed you to be civil to your brother? What kind of a son acts that way?"

"Excuse me? Were you there? Who the hell are you anyway?"

"Herb Wasserman. Remember me? One of those economy-class patients you wouldn't give the time of day, even when I was dying. The funny thing is, I got better treatment from the airlines. I used to fly business class as often as not. But as soon as I got sick, you put me down in economy. No time to waste on the dying, is that it? Ha! It looks like the shoe's on the other foot now, isn't it? Too bad though. You can't expect much help from the dead. Besides, if there is still any justice where you are, that judge will throw the book at you."

"That's enough! Will you please put my mother on the phone?"

"Why don't you leave the poor woman alone already? You caused her enough grief when she was alive."

The phone went silent, and Dr. Rosen, thrown from his seat, went flying once more through the cabin of the ill-fated aircraft.

The brilliant sun that rose over the city on the morning of the hearing did nothing to improve Dr. Rosen's mood, and his apprehensions only grew when he entered the courtroom with his entourage and spied some very unwelcome faces in the gallery. The scowling Nick Agnello, wearing his usual ill-fitting green suit, had perched himself in the first row, separated from the defense table only by a wooden railing. Former Special Agent W.E. Hardin, now unemployed, sat at the rear of the courtroom on the left side. Most worrisome of all, in the back row on the far right sat Alexey Golovorez, dressed in the same natty charcoal suit he had donned for the photograph on Dreck Plaza. One of the henchmen who had made off with Dr. Rosen's sofa slouched beside him. Dr. Rosen felt a surge of nausea when he saw Golovorez waving at him. Barry, equally discomposed by the Russian's presence, scrunched himself up in his seat so as to become as close to invisible as he could.

"I needed him here like a hole in my head."

Dr. Rosen did not realize he had spoken aloud until Andrew Le Bâtard answered, "You mean the thug over there waving and grinning at you? A business associate of yours?"

"What? No. I don't even know the guy."

"He sure seems to know you. That's the problem with committing crimes; you get mixed up with other criminals. It's a dangerous way of life. Anyway, there's nothing you or I can do about him. The court's open to the public, and he has a right to be here, along with Agnello and poor Hardin back there who's likely to have whatever embers of faith in humanity and justice remain alive in him snuffed out once and for all today. Forget about them all. You have one job today: to fake it. To fake humility, fake remorse, and convince that idiot of a judge that you're something other than the irredeemable sociopath I know you to be."

"You know, I'm fucking tired of your abuse. After today, I'm done with you."

Surprisingly, Andrew managed to modulate the volume of his reply, if not the content, in a manner suited to the venue: "Same here. There are lots of fucking lawyers out there who will take your fucking money and tell you whatever the fuck you want to hear. When you commit your next boatload of felonies—and I know you will, unless Agnello or somebody else you've fucked over kills you first—you can go hire one of them."

Judge Pound shuffled into the courtroom and took his place behind the bench. Once the preliminaries were out of the way, Andrew Le Bâtard commenced his argument for a noncustodial sentence. He spoke first of Dr. Rosen's cooperation with the FBI and the prosecutors.

"Dr. Rosen clearly upheld his end of the bargain. He met with FBI agents repeatedly and worked with them willingly, as the government has acknowledged. It's true he was not utilized fully, but that was due to factors beyond his control."

Next he spoke of the losses the defrocked doctor had suffered as a result of his lapses in judgment: his reputation, his livelihood, his identity as a physician. Following his arrest and the loss of his medical license, he had struggled to find work and an affordable place to live. Once well off, he had become financially insolvent. To illustrate those losses, Andrew offered as exhibits the *New York Post* story with the "HIPPO-CRATIC OAF" headline, as well as other media accounts of Dr. Rosen's arrest. In the back, the Russians snickered, and even the stoic Hardin cracked a smile.

Andrew continued. "With all that he has lost professionally, though, by far the most painful consequence of his mistakes has been the fraying of his relationships with the people he loves. Sadly, one of those relationships was the one he had with his mother, Sheila Rosen. Her recent death, coming when his hopes for a reconciliation had just begun to blossom, dealt him a devastating blow."

The last of the three prongs of Andrew's argument listed the steps Dr. Rosen had taken to rehabilitate himself and recover his good name.

"He has complied fully with the treatment prescribed by the court, attending individual and group therapy sessions conducted by Catherine Connolly, and as she attests in her letter to the court, he has accepted full responsibility for his actions and shown genuine remorse. I think, Your Honor, that you can see the difference the treatment has made, as evidenced by his appearance and demeanor today, as compared with the first time he came before you. And you will hear the difference, as well, when he speaks.

"Further, while Dr. Rosen no longer has the prestige or income he did as a physician, his work ethic remains as strong as ever. He has taken various jobs to keep body and soul together. Recently, in collaboration with his coach and mentor Barry Bullard, who is here in the courtroom today, he has given motivational speeches at a number of venues, including Princeton University. These talks have not only provided him with some much-needed income but something far more important. For the first time since he lost his license to practice medicine, he is helping people again—an endeavor to which he has devoted his entire adult life. There are several people here in the gallery today, seated behind me, who have attended his talks and have written letters attesting to the positive influence Dr. Robert Rosen has had on their lives. I would add, also, that during these presentations, Dr. Rosen has discussed very frankly and in great detail the actions that cost him his livelihood and his reputation and has admitted to his wrongdoing. Sharing his painful experiences has enabled him to connect with his audiences and inspire them to change their lives for the better, just as he is attempting to do with his."

Summing up, the lawyer stated that the punishments Dr. Rosen had suffered already, the professional, financial, and personal losses, constituted a sort of rough justice, obviating the need for a custodial sentence. The disgrace he had endured, as manifested, to cite just one example, in the mocking *New York Post* headline, offered a strong deterrent to other would-be offenders. His willingness to cooperate with the FBI, his acceptance of responsibility, and the steps he had taken on his own and with the court's assistance toward rehabilitation showed that he had been chastened and humbled and genuinely reformed. For all those reasons, he should get only a probationary sentence.

Throughout the presentation, Nick Agnello glared at the lawyer and muttered imprecations. In the rear of the courtroom, former Agent Hardin looked on with a poker face, while Golovorez yawned demonstratively.

The prosecutor stood up. A morbidly thin man with a face so white and smooth that it looked as though it had yet to sprout whiskers, he spoke rapidly and in a whine that hurt the ears. He conceded Andrew Le Bâtard's point that the defendant had shown a willingness to cooperate with the government. While the prosecution did not oppose a noncustodial sentence for Dr. Rosen in principle, he argued that the court, when weighing its decision, should take into account the seriousness of the former doctor's crimes.

Dr. Rosen then rose to speak on his own behalf. In contrast to his previous appearances in the same courtroom, he was clean-cut and well-turned-out, as befit a man on the road to rehabilitation thanks to the wisdom and magnanimity of a perspicacious judge. Speaking clearly but striving for a humble tone, he began with a quick resume of his credentials and accomplishments.

"And then, thanks to my own foolishness, I threw all that away. I abused my position, I violated my Hippocratic Oath, and I caused great pain to people who trusted me and to my own family. Every day I regret what I have done. Every day I think about how I can make amends for the harm I have caused. Today I want to apologize to all those I have hurt."

Not only did he look remorseful; he even squeezed out a tear. The Cavalear twins, seated to Nick Agnello's right, began to weep. Alexey Golovorez dabbed at his eyes with a handkerchief, wiping away mock tears. Barry Bullard looked the part of a proud coach. Even the notoriously impatient Judge Pound listened with rapt attention—a good sign, for attentiveness was the closest approximation to sympathy one could ever hope for from him. Two attendees remained unmoved. Nick Agnello, eyes ablaze, fists clenched, was snorting like a bull. Former Agent Hardin wore a scornful half-smile.

Next Dr. Rosen spoke of his own suffering and loss, of the estrangement from his late mother that his actions had caused, and of the despair and disorientation that followed the compulsory surrender of his medical license.

"My whole identity was bound up in being a doctor. It was all I had done for my whole adult life and all I had ever wanted to do."

The sobbing of the Cavalear twins filled the courtroom. Golovorez clapped softly.

"What bullshit," growled Nick Agnello.

"Who said that?"

Four times Judge Pound banged his gavel against the bench. The crusty lesions on his nose brightened to scarlet as he cast his cold scavenger's eyes out over the courtroom, which had suddenly fallen silent.

"If I hear another sound from the gallery, someone will be spending the night in jail. Is that clear? Please proceed, Dr. Rosen."

"Thank you, Your Honor. I just have one more thing to add, and that is to say how grateful I am that you recognized— and you were the first person who did—the illness that was driving my self-destructive behavior. Because you were concerned enough about me, Your Honor, to order me to seek treatment, I finally got the help I needed. And that may be the one silver lining in all this. I don't think it's an exaggeration, Your Honor, to say that you literally saved my life."

Humbly, Dr. Rosen lowered his head. Chevy and Nova Cavalear wailed, Agnello emitted another snort, former Agent Hardin mouthed the word "wow," and Golovorez loudly blew his nose.

"Thank you, Dr. Rosen," replied Judge Pound. "I don't know that I deserve that much credit, but it appears to me that you are on the right path now, and I'm very pleased to see that."

During the recess that followed, Dr. Rosen and Andrew remained in the courtroom. Disconcertingly, so, too, did Nick Agnello.

"You got this," Andrew whispered. "Probation for sure. And I'm hating myself already."

After deliberating for slightly over a quarter-hour, Judge Pound reappeared to pronounce sentence.

"Taking into account the various factors that have been discussed today—Dr. Rosen's willingness to cooperate, the professional and personal losses he has suffered, his genuine remorse and acceptance of responsibility, and the positive steps he has taken in recent months—I have decided that a variance from the sentencing guidelines is warranted. I have determined that incarceration is neither necessary nor desirable in this case and that justice can best be served by means of a probationary sentence."

The sigh emitted by former FBI Agent Hardin sounded like a tire deflating. Then a crash was heard, as Nick Agnello's fist struck the top of the wooden railing in front of him. The noise sent the Cavalears scampering into the aisle. Dr. Rosen, convinced that Agnello or somebody had shot him, ran his hands over his back, neck, chest, and belly, feeling for wounds. The absence of blood evoked as much puzzlement as relief. Had the shot missed? Had there been a shot at all? He looked over his shoulder. Agnello, flushed and quaking with rage, stood little more than an arm's length behind him, with only the railing between them. But he did not have a gun.

"You call this justice? This is a joke."

Judge Pound, nose lesions aflame, hammered at the bench with his gavel.

"Order! There will be order in my courtroom! Get that man out of here!" he commanded the burly US Marshal seated to the right of his bench.

Already, though, Agnello was on the move, reaching the courtroom door and kicking it open before the marshal had stirred from his chair. The marshal waddled out of the courtroom in a slow-motion pursuit. He soon returned empty-handed and took his seat again.

The court had quieted, but Judge Pound's anger had not abated.

"Obscenity in my courtroom. It used to be unheard of. Now it happens every other day. Where does it end?"

For reasons known only to himself, he turned his wrath upon the young prosecutor.

"Why don't you people prosecute anyone for obscenity anymore? There's all this filth out there, all this pornography. It's in movies, books, television, everywhere. But prosecute someone for it? I can't remember the last obscenity case I had. When are we going to start seeing some obscenity prosecutions again?"

"We'll, uh, look into it, Your Honor," said the bewildered-looking young attorney. He stole a glance at his opposite number as if seeking guidance. Andrew shrugged.

"You'll look into it? Why don't you do something about it? Instead, you waste the taxpayers' money prosecuting decent, productive citizens like Dr. Rosen. That's why this country is going to hell in a hand basket."

The prosecutor dropped back into his chair and gazed blankly at his hands while Judge Pound continued his diatribe. After the judge had finished speaking and retreated to his chambers, Andrew took the opportunity to offer his young counterpart a few words of reassurance: "First go-round with the old vulture? There'll be better days, and better judges. I've learned not to take his abuse personally."

Dr. Rosen stumbled out of the courtroom. Though he had obtained exactly the result for which he had hoped, he felt no relief. He was still shaking from the faux gunshot.

Ducking into a men's room to compose himself, he splashed cold water on his face. When he stood up, he saw in the mirror, looming behind him, the hulking form of Nick Agnello. As Dr. Rosen turned around, the big man grabbed him by the collar and pulled him close. Agnello smelled strongly of Old Spice cologne and, faintly, of underarm sweat. In the eyes of his nemesis, Dr. Rosen saw murder.

"You're good, doc. Real slick. You sure snowed that judge. You think you can get away with anything, don't you? But you still have a bill that's past due. And one way or another, you will pay, believe me. You'll pay in cash, or you'll pay some other way that you'll like even less. Meantime, wherever you are—where you live, where you work, where you hang out— that's where I'll be. You won't be able to take a shit without looking over your shoulder."

The pressure on Dr. Rosen's Adam's apple became unbearable. Had his nemesis squeezed his windpipe for but a few seconds more, the ex-doctor might well have blacked out. Even when Agnello did release him, Dr. Rosen felt his legs faltering. Only by bracing himself against the sink did he remain upright long enough to watch Agnello depart. Then Dr. Rosen dropped to his knees. When, after several minutes, he rose again, he yanked off his tie, opened his collar, and gave his face, and his neck as well, another splash of cold water.

Outside on the portico, he leaned against a column and rubbed the raw skin of his neck. His heart was galloping, skipping beats, squirming in his chest cavity.

"There you are. I was looking all over for you," said Barry, enfolding him in a smothering bear hug. "You were awesome, bro! You had that judge wrapped around your little finger."

The rest of Dr. Rosen's entourage had regathered on the portico. The Cavalear twins, their eyes now dry, hugged Dr. Rosen in tandem, and Kenny gave him the two-thumbs-up gesture for which President Dreck had a trademark pending.

"I'm just glad it's over," said Dr. Rosen.

He looked out over the courthouse steps and the sidewalk below. To his immense relief, he saw neither Agnello nor Golovorez.

"It is all over, bro. You won. You beat the bastards."

"I did, didn't I? I really did. Ha! Suck on that, Mr. Prosecutor. You, too, Agent Hardin. Or should I say former Agent Hardin? Either way, suck on it. I bet he came here today expecting to see me get tossed into prison."

"Yeah, suck on it, Agent Hardin!" Kenny echoed. "Suck on it, FBI! And that Deep State government lawyer—he can suck on it too. The punk."

Neither the prosecutor nor the ex-FBI man heard the insults directed at them. The young attorney had another case to prepare for in the same building but before a different and, he hoped, more sympathetic judge. Former Agent Hardin, meanwhile, having remained in the courtroom after everyone else departed, sat there still, stunned and motionless, as if he had stared into the eyes of Medusa.

"And you!" said Barry, clapping Andrew on the shoulder. "You kicked ass in there too, bro!" More softly, he added, "Just between you and me, there was a time when I could have used a lawyer like you."

Andrew, appearing strangely downcast for someone who had just triumphed in court, replied, "It's amazing how much better I am at playing judges and keeping defendants out of prison than I was as a public defender. It certainly helps to have the right kind of client when you have to go before a gullible, bigoted fool like Pound, who, in a sane world, would never be allowed to wield power over anyone's life."

"You need to lighten up, bro. If this is what you're like when you win, I'd hate to see you when you lose."

On the sidewalk at the bottom of the courthouse steps, the same Fox reporter and camera crew who had ambushed Dr. Rosen after his arrest stood waiting for him again. Now, flush with his triumph, he made a beeline for the camera. Andrew, however, caught up with him and grabbed him by the wrist.

"Let me handle this. I'd hate to have you go on camera and forget you're a changed man. It might work against you when you violate your probation."

Inserting himself between his client and the camera, Andrew said to the reporter, "We're very pleased with today's result. The court recognized that my client has taken full responsibility for his actions, has shown genuine remorse, has worked hard to rehabilitate himself, and has a lot to contribute to society. I think it's fair to say that justice has been served. Thank you."

As the lawyer spoke, a small group consisting of Dr. Rosen's supporters and several onlookers gathered behind him. Some of the latter began to mug for the camera. All around them, briefcase-toting lawyers swarmed past, many barking into cellphones. High heels clattered against the courthouse steps.

No sooner had Andrew stepped away from the microphone than Kenny, looking like a scarecrow in his borrowed suit, thrust himself forward.

"Damn right, this is justice! Dr. Robert Rosen was framed! He did nothing wrong. He had his life turned upside down by blackmailers, lying informants, crooked cops, and pedophiles. It shouldn't happen to anyone, and when President Dreck is through cleaning house at the FBI and the Justice Department, it never will again."

The reporter gave her cameraman a nervous glance.

"Why did you bring this lunatic?" Andrew whispered to Dr. Rosen.

Barry, seeing an opportunity for a few seconds of exposure on the evening news, bulled his way up to the microphone, shouldering Kenny aside.

"I'm Dr. Barry Bullard, Dr. Rosen's business and life coach and partner in Delta-Multiform, a continuing-life affirmation project. I'm here to tell you that I never had any doubt about what would happen in that courtroom today because I know Dr. Rosen. He's a bulldog. He's tough, he's fierce, and he's persistent as hell. He had that judge wrapped around his little finger."

"If you ask me," whispered Andrew, "this life coach of yours is not exactly championship material. You'd do better to sack him."

Irksome as he found the sight of Barry hogging the camera while his lawyer refused to allow him his moment in the sun, Dr. Rosen refused to concede the point.

"Barry's done a lot for me. I wouldn't be where I am if not for him."

"Can't argue with that. But he's certainly not doing you any favors right now. Let's get out of here."

Dr. Rosen, feeling the lawyer's hand pushing against the small of his back, refused to budge.

"No! I'm going to speak. I've been biting my tongue all these months while the government has lied about me and put me through hell. Enough!"

"As your lawyer, I advise you to keep biting."

"Screw you. You're not telling me what to do anymore."

Andrew sighed.

"You want to be on TV that bad? Go ahead. And go find yourself a new attorney while you're at it. I'm done here."

"Fine. I wish I'd had a lawyer willing to fight for me instead of forcing me to take this shitty plea deal. Thanks to you, people will be calling me a felon for the rest of my life."

"That's because you are a felon. And I didn't force you to do anything. I just offered you the best advice I could, given the circumstances. It's kind of hard to win at trial when your client is caught on video committing multiple felonies. Ah, but maybe I should have tried—and got you ten years in prison instead of probation. It would have been malpractice on my part, but maybe it would have been the right thing to do. The public needs protection against people like you."

"You can go to hell. You're a loser. I'm going to file a bar complaint against you."

"Good luck with that, loser."

Turning his back on the lawyer, Dr. Rosen strutted to the microphone.

"Dr. Rosen, how do you feel?" asked the reporter.

Beaming, he gave her a double-barreled thumbs-up worthy of the man attempting to trademark the gesture. The impromptu assemblage, Dr. Rosen saw, had grown. Upwards of two dozen people now hovered around the Fox news crew. Andrew Le Bâtard was no longer among them.

"I feel great! Couldn't be better. Totally vindicated. Today is a new beginning for me. Today I got my life back. And now, the first thing I'm going to do is apply to get my medical license reinstated so I can practice again. And then I'm going to get my conviction overturned and clear my name. These charges against me never should have been brought. The FBI sent undercover agents to entrap me. Then they broke down my door and threw me in jail. The prosecutors lied about me. They took away my livelihood and made me a pariah. Nobody should have to go through what I did."

As he raged on, some in the crowd began to murmur, to shuffle their feet. A few drifted away. Their indifference further infuriated him. His voice grew louder, his invective more inflammatory. His eyes stung as they filled with tears.

"The FBI, the government, the Deep State—they persecuted me. They put me through hell. I will never forget, and I will never forgive. I will sue everyone involved in this travesty."

A mocking "bravo," followed by three loud, slow, solitary claps, cut his jeremiad short. To his horror, he saw Alexey Golovorez approaching. The Russian, having left his suit jacket, tie, and dress shirt in the care of his henchman, now sported a black T-shirt with a gold cobra on the front. The cobra's head rose at a 90-degree angle above its coiled body, and its forked tongue extended farther than any found in nature. Beneath the animal's coils, gold block letters spelled out KING COBRA MEN'S HEALTH PRODUCTS and underneath it, the URL www.kingcobramanstore.com. In the dazzling sunlight, the red tip of Golovorez's dagger tattoo glowed like a flame.

Hooking his right arm over the shoulders of the newly minted probationer and pushing against him with his hip, Golovorez deftly maneuvered Dr. Rosen away from the microphone. "Dr. Robert is man with big heart. Too big heart. He wants to help people who suffer great pain, so he sells them pain medicine for cash. Where I come from is not crime. But here everything is. I say is wrong when American federal police arrest Dr. Robert and Department of Health of New York State takes his medical license away. But today is great wrong made right by wise American Judge Pound. Today shows beauty of America's system of equal justice. Like motto on court building says: True administration of justice is firm pillow of good government.

"And now that he is free man, Dr. Robert is ready for bright future as marketing, communications, and branding specialist with King Cobra Men's Health Products, LLC."

As Dr. Rosen tried to sidestep away, Golovorez's arm, steely as a high-tension cable, tightened around his neck.

"At King Cobra Men's Health Products, which is at URL www.kingcobramanstore.com," Golovorez continued, his left hand patting the cobra emblem on his shirt, "we have big heart, like Dr. Robert. We help men of middle age who suffer from low energy and limp *khui*. Men like Dr. Robert, who is not only employee but also satisfied customer. Since he takes our new Texas Longhorn supplement product with five active ingredients for male virility, he has become new man."

The slap on the back Golovorez gave him may have appeared comradely to the onlookers, but it stung. Amid the assemblage, a tittering was heard. The laughter spread, even infecting the camera crew. The reporter, her face flushed, bit her lip.

While Golovorez, having concluded his pitch, passed out business cards and King Cobra pens and key chains, Dr. Rosen slipped away. Quickening his pace, he began to run, zigzagging up the street against the tide of lawyers and litigants surging toward the courthouse.

Acknowledgments

Many people contributed to bringing this book into the world, and to all of them I owe a debt of gratitude. The list below is by no means exhaustive.

I would, first of all, like to thank Bill Burleson, publisher of Flexible Press, for believing in *A Very Innocent Man*, improving it through judicious editing and suggestions for revision, and designing a cover that encapsulates the narrative in a single striking image.

Thanks are due also to Vicki Adang for her meticulous copyediting and proofreading, and to the other contributors on the Flexible Press team, including Michael Ronn, Edward Sheehy, Vincent Wyckoff, and Ross Phernetton.

Many thanks to Jerry Mikorenda, Kathy Fish, Caitlin Horrocks, and Brian Duren for the time and care they took in reading the novel and writing their very kind blurbs.

Much appreciation goes to Jim Murphy and T.J. Beitelman, whose insightful commentary on early drafts of the novel proved vital to its subsequent development.

For offering me the benefits of their expertise in the fields of law and medicine, which figure so prominently in *A Very Innocent Man*, I am grateful to Jeremy Silverfine and Drs. Rachel Land and Alexandra Belfar. The blame for any errors in description lies with me alone.

To the editors of *The Write Launch, The Ekphrastic Review*, and *The Loch Raven Review*: thank you for publishing, respectively, an excerpt of one chapter and short stories adapted from two others.

Last, but certainly not least, to my wife, Kathleen, always my first and best reader—and, in the case of *A Very Innocent Man*, re-reader many times over: thank you for the love, patience, support, and encouragement, but for which *A Very Innocent Man* would have languished on my computer as an abandoned, half-finished Word file.

About Edward Belfar

Edward Belfar's collection of short stories, *Wanderers*, was published by Stephen F. Austin State University Press in 2012. One of the stories in the collection was chosen as the winning entry in the Sports Literature Association 2008 fiction competition, while another was nominated for a Pushcart Prize. His fiction and essays have appeared in numerous literary journals, including *Shenandoah*, *The Baltimore Review*, *Potpourri*, *Confrontation*, *Natural Bridge*, *Schuylkill Valley Journal*, and *Tampa Review*. As a reader for *The Plentitudes*, he reviews both fiction and nonfiction submissions. He earned his BA in history and MA in creative writing at the State University of New York at Stony Brook and his PhD in literature at Temple University. He lives with his wife in Maryland, where he works as a writer and editor, and can be reached through his website at www.edward-belfar.com.

Made in the USA
Middletown, DE
12 May 2023

29859095R00179